Love, Inc.

Love, Inc.

Yvonne Collins & Sandy Rideout

HYPERION
New York

Acknowledgments

Thanks to the team behind *Love, Inc.*,
especially Jennifer Besser, Arianne Lewin,
Jenny Bent, and Alyssa Eisner Henkin.

A very special thanks to "Real Zahra,"
our cultural attaché, who let us borrow her name
and answered all our questions—including the really
stupid ones—with humor and grace.

All rights reserved. Published by Hyperion, an imprint of Disney Book Group. No part of this book may be reproduced or transmitted in any form or by any means, electronic or mechanical, including photocopying, recording, or by any information storage and retrieval system, without written permission from the publisher. For information address Hyperion, 114 Fifth Avenue, New York, New York 10011-5690.

First Edition
1 3 5 7 9 10 8 6 4 2

G475-5664-5-10288

Printed in the United States of America

Designed by Tanya Ross-Hughes

Library of Congress Cataloging-in-Publication Data on file.
ISBN 978-1-4231-3115-1

Reinforced binding

Visit www.hyperionteens.com

SUSTAINABLE FORESTRY INITIATIVE

Certified Fiber Sourcing

www.sfiprogram.org

THIS LABEL APPLIES TO TEXT STOCK

*To Dave, for his unflagging enthusiasm
and support for "Mercury Ink."*

chapter 1

Señora Mendoza keeps a hand on the doorknob and her eyes on the clock. At precisely three minutes past nine she closes the door with a firm click. "Summer's over, people. Time to get to work." She crosses the room on her toes, like a ballroom dancer, and repeats her point in Spanish. *"Hora de trabajar."*

I can tell by the way she rolls her R's that she learned Spanish at home as a kid. I'd respect her more if she'd learned the hard way, like us, or taught German. But I'm looking for flaws. I expect to hate everything here, from the teachers to the cafeteria fries. It smells worse than my old school, too—like perfume mixed with sweat and chalk dust.

The door opens again and a guy with unruly brown hair blocks the entrance. Even without the football jersey, you'd know he's a jock from the build and the confident smile. I suppose he's good-looking, if you're into big guys with small heads. Some girls must be, because I can hear giggles behind me.

"Sorry, Ms. Mendoza," the guy says.

"Fletcher," she says, *"aquí, se habla español."*

"Disculpe el retraso, Señora." The words slip easily off

Fletcher's tongue. He's used to apologizing for being late.

A girl steps out from behind Fletcher and repeats, *"Disculpe el retraso."* She's all sharp edges, but somehow still pretty. Great hair makes up for anything.

Señora Mendoza rolls her eyes at the girl's pronunciation. *"Siéntese,* Hollis. *Mañana, llegue a tiempo."*

"Excuse me?" Hollis asks. Her highlights shimmer as she tilts her head.

"I said, be on time tomorrow." The teacher points to the empty seat to my right.

Hollis lifts her right hand, which is clasped in Fletcher's left. "We always sit together."

Señora Mendoza points to the empty desk on my left. "Let me introduce you to Zahra MacDuff. She'll be sitting between the two of you this year."

"But, Señora—" Hollis tries again.

The teacher cuts her off with a stamp of a high heel. *"Siéntese. Por favor."*

Fletcher releases Hollis's hand and they walk down the rows on either side of me. Dumping his backpack on the floor with a thud, Fletcher slides into his seat and turns to stare at me with eyes the color of a stagnant pond. Meanwhile, Hollis stands over me for a moment, hoping I'll volunteer my seat.

I knew starting tenth grade at Austin High would be tough. Hollis and Fletcher seem to rank pretty high in the sophomore chain of command, and the way I react now could make or break my year.

Still, I got to class fifteen minutes early to stake my claim on exactly the right desk—second row in from the window, five rows from the front. I assumed (wrongly, as it turns out) that this was the perfect place to be overlooked. If I give it up now, will it say I'm a loser who's desperate to please? Or will it say I'm a team player?

I stare down at Hollis's flip-flops as I ponder. Her toenails are polished a deep metallic blue embellished with tiny daisies. She has rings on four toes.

Finally I look up. "Take—"

"—the empty seat, Hollis," Señora interrupts. "Now."

Hollis's flip-flops turn and she drops her purse, her backpack, and another bag to the floor, each landing a little closer to my feet. Finally she settles into her seat and crosses her legs. Five little daisies bob into my sight line to remind me I'm in trouble. Fletcher's swampy eyes are still boring into me from the other side.

Obviously, indecision was the wrong decision. I should have gotten my butt out of this seat and laid a red carpet for Hollis. I'm always a beat late. It's the story of my life.

I let my hair fall forward, grateful for the cover of the mass of red curls that polite people call auburn. I wish I could go back to my old school. Mom would be glad to have me at home, but I've vowed not to return while my grandparents are there.

When they flew in from Pakistan last spring, I had no idea their visit would push my family over the edge. Mom had barely spoken to them since they'd disowned her for marrying a Scottish-American instead of what my sister and I secretly call an MOT—a Member of the Tribe. My parents' marriage may not have been solid, but it was holding together until my grandparents put down roots in my bedroom. Mom talked less and less and Dad worked more and more, until July, when Dad finally realized he wasn't wanted and moved out. I went with him, partly to make a grand statement, and partly to divide and conquer. My sister, Saliyah, is working the reunion angle at Mom's end.

At first I thought living downtown was kind of cool, and I went back to Anderson Mill a lot over the summer to visit my best friends, Shanna and Morgan. Now that I'm in school and working part-time, I won't be able to tackle the one-and-a-half-hour bus ride as often. I feel homesick and friend-sick. Too bad grand statements don't come with back doors.

Señora Mendoza turns to the board. "Let's start by reviewing some verbs you learned last year. Suggestions?"

I start conjugating in my notebook:

I hate it here.

You hate it here.

She hates it here.

He hates it here.

We hate it here.

They hate it here.

It's unanimous. But that doesn't change the fact that I'm stuck between a jock and a hard face for another forty-two minutes.

Luckily, I'm easily distracted.

The classroom recedes as I drift to the set of my imaginary cooking show, *The Sweet Tooth.* Normally, I come here to escape my worries, but today I have something exciting on the agenda. Since Dad is out of town till late, I've decided to invite Rico over. Tonight will be the very first time I've ever . . .

4

"*Really? Your first time?*" Oliver James, celebrity chef and a frequent guest on my show feigns surprise. *He leans against the granite counter and crosses his arms.* "*You seem so . . . experienced.*"

"*Thanks—I think.*" *Oliver gets away with murder because of his impish smile and English accent.* "*This is definitely a first, and Rico is special.*"

"*Cracking, is he?*"

I nod. "*He's just . . . perfect. So I need tonight to be perfect, too. That's why I called you.*"

"*Brilliant,*" Oliver says. "*But are you sure you're ready for this, pet?*"

Rico and I have been seeing each other for exactly nine weeks, although it seems longer. He's not only incredibly hot; he's sweet and thoughtful, too. I've never felt this way about a guy before, and I want to take it to the next level.

"*Yeah,*" I say, "*I'm ready. But I'm a bit nervous.*"

"*Don't worry; no one knows her way around a kitchen better than you do.*" *He walks over to the chalkboard I use to share the day's food plan with my viewers and writes:* GET NAKED MENU.

"*Oliver! I'm cooking for Rico, that's all.*"

He turns and cocks an eyebrow. "*I thought you wanted a little rumpy bumpy. I'm setting the stage.*"

The older ladies in the audience murmur disapprovingly. I'm the youngest girl in the country to have her own cooking show, and as much as they adore Oliver, they don't want him leading me down the wrong path.

"*This is about love, not sex,*" I say. "*All I want to do is talk to Rico about our relationship.*"

There's a relieved sigh from the audience, but Oliver looks horrified. "Flippin' heck. You're too young to be playing Happy Families."

"I'm not pretending we're married," I say, striking through Oliver's words and writing ROMANTIC DINNER À DEUX. "But I want to tell him how I feel and find out if he feels the same way."

"Bollocks," Oliver says. "Let him tell you how he feels when he's ready."

"But I'm ready now, and I communicate best through my cooking."

On the board, I sketch out my dinner menu: oysters on the half shell, steak au poivre, baked potatoes, and chocolate volcano cake.

"You're off your trolley," Oliver says, mussing his permanently mussed hair. "Mollusks are about as useful as a chocolate teapot in the romance department, and steak is too heavy. The point is to throw something casual together. If it looks like you've been fannying around for hours, he'll run for the hills. It's like asking for a commitment."

I lean against the stainless steel refrigerator. "You're underestimating Rico. Besides, I just want him to say I'm his girlfriend."

"Then trust me on this: Make it easy-peasy. No oysters, no candles, no rose petals, no frills." On the board he writes PENNE ALLA ARRABBIATA AND STRAWBERRIES.

"But dessert's my specialty," I whine.

"You don't need the aggro." Oliver lifts the lid off a pot of simmering sauce and fills the air with the aroma of tomato, herbs, and garlic. "Pump up the heat with this, and Romeo will be on his knees under your balcony. And you, unlike Juliet, may live happily ever after."

"So you're saying I should deny every romantic impulse I have?"

"Correct. Do exactly the opposite of what you want to do. Hear me?"

Oliver's hand drops onto my shoulder and squeezes. Hard.

Only it can't be Oliver's hand, because he doesn't have long nails like daggers.

Señora Mendoza does. I see them as she picks up my notebook and reads aloud to the class: "'Get Naked Menu: pasta arrabbiata and strawberries. Or . . . Romantic Dinner à Deux: oysters on the half shell, steak au poivre with baked potatoes, and chocolate volcano cake.'"

She rolls every *R* suggestively, making it sound far worse than it actually is. Hollis is laughing so hard her toes are clenched to keep her flip-flops on.

Señora Mendoza drops the notebook onto my desk. "I recommend keeping your clothes on, especially near a hot stove. In the meantime, Zahra, conjugate *to listen. En español, por favor.*"

I do it, noticing that my voice sounds like it belongs to someone else—someone who knows she's committed social suicide. Then I let my hair swallow me whole until the bell rings twenty-nine minutes later.

Hollis is smiling when I emerge, happy that I've saved her the trouble of kicking me to the bottom of the school food chain.

Fletcher is smiling too, but he seems intrigued. "Go with the steak," he says, in a faux whisper. "But getting naked wouldn't hurt, either."

Hollis stands and pushes past me, hitting my head with her bags—one, two, three. She pulls Fletcher to his feet, and he gives me a thumbs-up as they leave.

Austin High, I've arrived.

·· ♥ ··

Cooking at Mom's is a combat sport. There are too many people with too many opinions sticking their spoons where they don't belong. Cooking at Dad's, on the other hand, is virtually impossible. The apartment's kitchenette was designed for reheating frozen food, not making romantic dinners. Even if there was more room, Dad has refused to buy me a set of basic kitchen equipment. He actually suggested I carry my blender back and forth from Mom's on the two-bus commute. You'd think he'd be more supportive, knowing my goal is to become a celebrity pastry chef.

Luckily, my twelve-year-old sister, Saliyah, is easily bribed. In exchange for her getting Mom and my grandparents out of the house for three hours, I promised to do all her homework for a week. Three hours is plenty of time to make the arrabbiata sauce, dip the strawberries in chocolate (still easy-peasy), and be on my way.

The stresses of the day fade as I set out my magical glass mixing bowls, a complete rainbow of colors nested one inside the other. The violet bowl is my favorite, although it's too small to hold more than the chilies that will hopefully turn this tomato sauce into a truth serum. The bowls aren't really magic, but I've had more successes than failures with them. I had cooked Sunday dinner for years, until my parents ruined the tradition by breaking the news about their split over dessert.

Now I've sworn off cooking for family, with the exception of Saliyah.

I start by opening the windows, turning on a fan, and flash frying the pancetta. Then I chop the onions and get to work on the tomatoes. By the time six of my seven bowls are full, I'm so calm that I actually believe I can pull this dinner off without triggering the Cookie Curse that has caused every guy I've baked for to dump me.

It all started with Sam Hoffler, my sixth-grade boyfriend, who walked me home from school for two solid weeks before finally kissing me. Back then, I thought a kiss really meant something, so I decided to show Sam how I felt by doing what came naturally: baking cookies. "The Sam" was delicious—a basic sugar cookie with chocolate rosebuds. But the cookies were barely cool before Sam started walking home with a girl who brought grocery store brownies to school bake sales.

In seventh grade I created "The Tyrell" for Tyrell Travers. We met at swimming lessons, and he rode his bike back and forth in front of our house until Dad threatened to line the road with tacks. Once Tyrell got the nerve to come to the door, I gave in and baked. The white chocolate Hershey's Kisses on the dark chocolate cookies must have spooked him, because he dumped me the next day.

In eighth grade I created "The Logan," with ground almonds and a raspberry center. Logan Duprey and I had been together nearly four weeks, but he hadn't bothered to mention his nut allergy. He survived; the relationship didn't.

In ninth grade I created "The Jonah" for Jonah Coen, who was *so* cute, but in retrospect, *so* selfish. I couldn't see it at the time, though, and when Valentine's Day rolled around, I rolled into the kitchen. "The Jonah" was the finest of my boyfriend line: shortbread laced with Skor bars. I carried a tub of them over to his place for a romantic movie night, not realizing Jonah had also invited six of his buddies for a zombie-fest. The guys ate all the cookies and teased Jonah so much about being "whipped" that the breakup text he sent two days later wasn't a big surprise.

Oliver was right. I can't risk baking today, although if anyone could survive the Cookie Curse, it would be Rico. He's not afraid of romantic gestures. The day after Dad and I moved, Rico showed up at the Recipe Box, the cookbook store where I work, with a triple ice cream sundae. We sat on the curb after my shift and ate it together as the sun went down.

I've finally hit the boyfriend jackpot, and I sense my timing for the big meal is just right. After cooking my way into Rico's heart tonight, I'll tell him exactly how I feel.

If he hasn't told me first.

He'd *better* tell me first. I've just spent half an hour peeling and seeding fresh tomatoes when I could have opened a can.

He'll tell me first. Rico obviously feels the same way I do. When we're together, he acts like I'm the most important person in his world.

I can't let doubts get to me now. Just because my parents' marriage collapsed doesn't mean the same thing will happen to me. I realize how important romance is to a relationship. If Mom and Dad had made more of an effort in that department, our family might not be in ruins today.

The sauce is almost done when I hear the car in the driveway. There's the bang of a car door and the sound of running footsteps on the stairs. Saliyah turns the key in the lock and bursts into the kitchen, her long dark hair disheveled. "Sorry," she puffs, "I couldn't stall them anymore. But I knocked over a flowerpot on the way in to keep them busy for a few more minutes."

I crumple the recipe and toss it into the trash can. "You're doing your own math homework," I say, shoving things into the cupboard.

Mom comes in two minutes later, and her face lights up. "Zahra, you're cooking!"

I resist the urge to say, "Not for you." I can't afford to raise any suspicions. So I give her a kiss on the cheek and say, "Just making pasta sauce."

Her smile fades as she takes in the tomato juice splattered from one end of the counter to the other. "It looks like a crime scene."

Mom tries to keep the kitchen sterile enough for surgery at all times—great if your appendix detonates, not so great if you like to get creative with food.

Sniffing like a hound, she says, "Do I smell . . . *bacon?*"

"No." I stare into the pot until her dark eyes force the truth out of me. "Pancetta."

"Zahra!"

"It was only two ounces."

"The quantity is hardly the point. It's pork."

"Dad used to cook bacon sometimes."

She shakes her head. "It's different now."

That's for sure. Now all my parents think about is themselves. Mom's obsessed with her parents and her culture crisis, and Dad's become a workaholic. I'm basically raising myself.

"Eating pork is forbidden for Muslims, you know that," Mom continues. "Your grandparents would see it as breaking faith with God."

"But *they* won't be eating it," I say.

Relief and disappointment flood Mom's face. "So you're not cooking for us?"

What part of "never again" didn't she understand? "Mom, I wouldn't serve Nani and Nana pork." I'm cursed enough without bringing the wrath of God into it.

Reaching for her trusty bottle of bleach, Mom prepares to purify. "Saliyah. Keep your grandparents busy in the garden till I can clean up. Tip over another begonia if you have to."

My sister turns from the fridge. There's a ring of chocolate around her mouth and two strawberries husks in the palm of her hand. Grinning at me, she grabs another strawberry and heads for the door.

Mom lights a homemade vanilla-and-bergamot candle to mask the scent of sin. Then she pulls on industrial rubber gloves and rinses pots and cutlery before stacking them in the dishwasher.

An expert in forensic cookery, she opens cupboards one by one to take inventory, wiping each item I touched. She checks the fridge, the recycling bin, and the garbage pail before announcing her conclusion. "You're cooking dinner for Rico."

"I'm cooking for Dad." It's not a total lie. He'll get the leftovers.

She crosses her arms, rubber gloves and all. "You used hot pepper flakes and chilies. But you hate spicy food, and so does your father."

"Dad's changed since you kicked him out." Again, not a

total lie. "Now he brings home curry a lot. I guess it reminds him of home."

"I did not kick him out," she says. "It takes two people to make or break a marriage."

"Fine. I'm just saying he's lonely." I taste the tomato sauce and make a show of putting the spoon back into the pot.

Mom shudders. "Use a fresh spoon."

"The germs will boil off," I say. "It needs more basil."

Naturally, Mom's already put the basil away and washed the cutting board. I take them out again.

"I thought your dad was in Chicago," she says.

Saliyah must be the weak link. My parents avoid communicating directly if they can, and I'm counting on that today. If Mom decides to confirm Dad's plans, I'll be setting another place for dinner.

"He'll be home early," I say. Early tomorrow, since his plane lands close to midnight. "And he wants to meet Rico."

True again, although I've worked hard to keep that from happening. Dad dislikes any guy I bring home until they're history, at which point he starts talking about how great the guy is.

"I'm surprised you're subjecting that boy to your father already," Mom says.

I stay focused on my priorities, specifically getting home in time to straighten my hair. "You've met Rico, so now Dad wants to."

"Bumping into you two making out in the Arboretum Mall parking lot hardly constitutes a meeting."

"It was just a kiss good-bye."

"Tonsils included," she says, putting the basil back in the

fridge. "This Rico . . . is he treating you well?"

"Mom." I test the sauce again and decide it needs another pinch of pepper. I might not like heat, but Rico loves it, and the dinner's for him. "Rico's a really nice guy."

She's scrubbing the cutting board hard enough to break a normal woman's fingers. "You said he doesn't always return your calls."

Mom and I haven't had one of our heart-to-hearts over chai tea since the day Dad and I moved out, yet she still manages to collect and catalogue information to use against me. She has too much time on her hands. I wish she'd get a job or something. "Rico's a busy guy. He has a lot of interests."

"You're sure?"

There's only one way to get her off my case. Turning away from the stove, I let tomato sauce drip off the spoon in a wide arc onto her clean counter and the floor. "Yes, Mom, I'm sure my boyfriend is a nice guy."

Happily, her need to sterilize outweighs her desire to follow up on the B-word. Because it's not exactly official.

Yet.

·· ♥ ··

The evening is going exactly as planned. The pasta is delicious. Rico is saying all the right things. I am saying all the right things. Even my hair cooperated. Rico pushed it aside to kiss my neck earlier, and it didn't snag his hand like a Venus flytrap.

I worked hard to keep things completely casual. It was Rico who arrived with the single red rose that's now standing on the table in a water glass, since we don't have a vase. It was Rico who dimmed the lights as we sat down. And it was Rico who lit the only candle I had on hand—a fat, wax Santa Claus that Mom nearly sent the way of pork. Oliver James might not approve, but no one is running for the hills. The boyfriend-killing Cookie Curse appears to have been broken.

The conversation flows easily, about music and art and places we want to see someday. For once I manage not to rant about my parents and ask about his instead.

"Just the usual," he says, helping himself to more pasta. There's plenty left because it burned the skin off my tongue. "Dad's got a big court case and Mom's still teaching yoga. But let's talk about you."

Rico's phone buzzes again, for maybe the fifteenth time, and although he ignores it, I start to feel a bit insecure.

"Did you want to get that?" I fully expect him to say no, but he pulls the phone out of his pocket, checks his texts, and grins. "What's so funny?" I ask.

"Nothing," he says. "Just a friend goofing around."

His grin worries me. It's the same one he gives me when I tease him about his cowlick. That grin is supposed to be just for me. "Which friend?"

"Pete," he says, without a second's hesitation. "The guys are checking out a band tonight and want to know if I'll meet them there."

"You made plans for later?" I try not to sound hurt, but I can't help it. I slaved to make this night special, and Rico cutting out early was not on the agenda.

"Of course not," he says, tapping at his phone. "I'm telling Pete to stop bugging me." He drops the phone in his pocket and reaches for my hand. I try to pull it away, but he quickly links his fingers through mine. "Did I mention that you're the best cook I've ever met?"

It might be a line, but it's one I like hearing. "You did mention that."

He leans forward and gazes at me with eyes that look black in the dim light, but are really the most beautiful blue. "You're going to be a famous chef someday," he says, with a dazzling smile. "But tell me this: if you plan on calling your show *The Sweet Tooth*, how come you've never baked for me?"

I lean forward in my seat, too. "Who says I haven't?"

"Oh, right." He runs his fingers lightly along my forearm until my skin tingles. "We haven't gotten to dessert."

Thank God I ignored the dissenting voice in my head and followed my instincts. There's a tub of cookies sitting on the kitchen counter now—peanut butter with dark chocolate chunks. I managed to whip them up because Rico was nearly an hour late for dinner.

I think about getting them, but I don't want to spoil the moment. He's gazing and I'm gazing, and though it's intense, I could definitely get used to it.

"You have the most beautiful eyes," he says. "And you're so talented."

Okay, he's really laying it on thick now. He must feel bad about Pete's calls.

"You are," he insists, reading my expression. "I admire your commitment."

That's nice, but I was hoping he'd talk about another kind of commitment.

"I have something for you." He reaches into the pocket of his coat draped over the back of his chair. "A hostess gift."

I tear off the tissue and try not to look disappointed when I find a pot holder inside. A romance vacuum has opened under the table.

"Turn it over," Rico says, grinning.

On the flip side is an adorable, long-lashed cartoon character in the shape of a molar. She's wearing a pink gingham apron with a matching bow in her curly red hair, and holding a cupcake. Underneath are the words *The Sweet Tooth*.

"I figured you'd need a logo," he says. "So I designed it and had it printed."

I was wrong—this is the most romantic gift ever, because it says he believes in me. It's a grand statement. Today a pot holder, tomorrow a diamond. I can imagine us sitting this way when Rico's hair is silvery in the candlelight. Hopefully, I'll still be surprising him with my cooking. That never gets old.

"You like?" Rico prompts me.

I snap out of my trance and reach across the table for his hand. "I *love*."

"Good," Rico says. "Because there's something I want to tell you."

This is it! Our big moment. My heart is racing but I try to sound cool. "Yes?"

He leans so far forward that all I can see are teeth and eyes. "Zahra, I—"

The phone cuts him off. Mine, not his. It's probably Mom, and if I don't pick up, she'll call the cops. Or Dad's cell. Either way, I'll be dead.

"Hold that thought," I say, reaching for the phone. Rico does better than that. He continues to hold my hand as I say, "Oh, hi, Dad." Brightly. Casually. "Where are you? Oh. You caught an earlier flight." Rico lets go of my hand. "No, nothing's wrong. I have leftovers for you. See you soon."

Rico is already slipping his arms into his jacket when I hang up.

"You don't have to leave," I say. "He's still a half hour away."

Rico's phone buzzes again, and he pulls it out of his pocket. "No worries. I should get going anyway."

I trail after him to the door. "But you were about to tell me something."

"This weekend," he says. "We'll go for a drive and talk." What felt so right now feels so wrong.

"Wait," I say, heading into the kitchen to get the cookies. "At least take these."

"Thanks," he says, leaning down to kiss me.

With Rico's lips on mine, and his hands in my hair, everything starts to feel right again—so right that we're still kissing twenty minutes later when a key turns in the lock. We look up, stunned, as the door opens and light from the hall floods in.

Dad looks stunned, too. His eyes bulge as they drop from my face to Rico's hand, which has migrated to the small of my back, under my T-shirt, then jump to my hand, which is in Rico's back pocket. "Zahra, what is going on here?"

His eyes bounce up and almost pop out of his head as he looks over my shoulder.

I turn quickly to see flames licking across the dining room table.

"My pot holder!" I scream. "Oh, Rico!"

But when I turn back, Rico is gone.

chapter 2

Dad didn't need to wreck his suit jacket. The old blanket on the couch would have done a better job putting out the fire, and maybe saved the table, too. Besides, this whole situation could have been avoided if he'd tested the smoke alarm and let me equip the kitchen properly. All the cooking shows warn you to have a fire extinguisher on hand. Maybe Dad expects me to carry that back and forth from Mom's, too.

Rico feels terrible about what happened. I wish he'd stuck around to help put out the fire, but while Dad and I were panicking, it was Rico who called 911 and waited downstairs until the fire trucks came. I guess he was scared of Dad, and I can't blame him. But Dad didn't say much that night. He just kept checking and rechecking the dining room to make sure the fire was really out.

The ax fell the next day. I expected grounding. I expected withdrawal of e-privileges. I even expected Dad to send me back to Mom's for round-the-clock supervision.

I did not expect to end up in group therapy. Yet that's where I am only three days later, sitting on a folding chair in a church basement with three other girls and two guys. My parents, who took years to decide to split, managed to make this decision overnight so I could enroll in the fall session. They even sat in the same room for ten minutes to break the news that I'll be attending every Thursday after school. Apparently it's not "real therapy," just a support group for teens who have "families in transition." In other words, we're not crazy, we just have crappy parents.

They claimed it's not a punishment for the "Rico incident," but it sure feels like one. I should have told the whole truth and nothing but the truth (and kept an eye on the candle), but is it so wrong to want a little romance in my life? I guess it is, or I wouldn't be plagued by the Cookie Curse. Well, I will never bake for a guy I like again. Lesson learned. No need for group therapy.

My parents could use some counseling themselves. They sat at opposite ends of the couch during the sentencing, and the second they finished, Mom bolted. She accidentally brushed Dad's leg on her way out, and they both flinched. That's messed up.

Well, I'm done with them anyway. I'm not going to waste another second worrying about their happiness when they're so willing to hand over their parental responsibilities to a complete stranger—a stranger who looks more like an avatar than a human being. The guy is tall, thin, and dressed entirely in black. His blond hair is precisely cut, and his blue eyes are so pale they're frosty. I'm pulling up the drawbridge and filling the moat. This guy isn't getting near my brain.

On the bright side, with an avatar in charge, there shouldn't be much hugging. I was worried about that, even before I saw the other people in my group. One of the guys looks ready to blow. His eyes are dark and sinister under the brim of his black baseball cap. It's a warm day, yet he's wearing a worn leather jacket, with his hands buried so deep in the pockets that I can't help wondering about concealed weapons.

The other guy looks stoned. Crossing his scuffed work boots, he checks me out and gives me a lopsided smile. He can't be serious. Even if I didn't have Rico, I'd never hook up with someone from group. The "how we met" story would be too embarrassing.

The avatar claps three times to bring the meeting to order. "Welcome to Transitions," he says, circling behind our folding chairs. "My name is Dieter Schmitt and I'm a licensed therapist. Before we begin, I want to lay out a few ground rules. No electronic devices. No bullying. No whining. No tardiness. No—"

"That's more than a few," one of the girls says, as she digs through a gorgeous red leather bag that I recognize from *In Style* magazine. In fact, her entire outfit looks high-end. I'm sure she'd rather be shopping than stuck here with us.

"No wallowing in self-pity," Dieter continues as if she hasn't spoken. "No wishing you could change the things you can't, or excuses for not changing the things you can."

Rather-Be-Shopping looks up from her bag. "Did I walk into Alcoholics Anonymous by mistake?"

"No snarky asides," Dieter says. "No disrespecting the process." He comes to a stop beside another seat. "And no dogs."

A girl who looks pissed off at the world is twisting a brown leather leash around her fingers. At her feet is a hundred pounds of snoozing Rottweiler.

"Banksy goes wherever I go," Pissed-Off-at-the-World says in a low, raspy voice that suits her offbeat style. She's wearing a frayed velvet skirt with motorcycle boots, and her shiny black hair is cut into a 1920s-style bob. On her cheek is a black beauty mark that may or may not be penciled on.

"Not to school, I'm sure," Dieter says. "And I doubt he'll benefit from therapy."

Banksy stirs in his sleep and bares two rows of very sharp teeth. Pissed Off smirks as I tuck my feet under my chair. Well, she can smirk all she likes. These boots were a guilt gift from Mom, and I don't plan on leaving with fang marks in them.

Holding out his hand for the leash, Dieter stares the girl down with unblinking eyes until she releases it. "Good luck getting him to move," she says.

Dieter gives the leash a single, sharp tug. "Banksy, come." The dog stands immediately and follows Dieter out the door.

"I've tied him up in the shade," Dieter says when he returns. "The tai chi group will keep an eye on him."

He spends a few moments rolling up the sleeves of his shirt. When they're just right, he continues his speech. "Group therapy works, but it also *takes* work. You have to listen to each other and offer your perspective. You have to come to terms with your new family situation and focus on moving on with your own life."

"Moving on," repeats a girl with blond curls and green eyes. Her long legs are crossed in front of her, and she looks so relaxed that I wonder if she's been here before.

Dieter reaches for his clipboard to take attendance. "Evan Garrett?"

Stoned gives a lazy wave with one hand while scratching

his bare knee through a hole in his jeans with the other. His bloodshot eyes are half closed. "Here," he says. "Mostly."

Ignoring the snuffle of laughter, Dieter ticks off Evan's name with a silver pen. "Lauren Archer?"

Rather-Be-Shopping nods. Her hair is shiny and straight, a mockery of my own, which is threatening to take over the room. The basement of this huge old church is so damp that the industrial gray carpet is curling up in the corners, and the framed picture of Noah's ark is swampy with mildew. You'd think the least my parents could do is send me to some upscale therapist with a leather couch. But Dad just couldn't pass up a cheap community program that's way too close to school for my liking. I'm bound to run into people I know— once I actually know people. "Sydney Stark?"

Pissed-Off-at-the-World flashes eerie, topaz eyes at Dieter and grunts an acknowledgment.

"Zahra Ahmed-MacDuff?"

"Here." I aim for casual but it comes out overly cheery. I can't help it. No matter how I really feel, cheery is my default. I have a future in customer service. "But it's just 'MacDuff' now."

"Interesting," Dieter says, making a note on his clipboard.

Great. The session hasn't even started and I'm already noteworthy. My goal in dropping Mom's Pakistani surname was to distance myself and start fresh. Instead it's made me look like I have issues.

Been-Here-Before starts singing: "'Nameless faces, trading places. I can run, but I can't hide in the crowd. . . .'" Her eyes are closed and she's fingering an imaginary guitar.

Ready-to-Blow rolls his eyes and says, "Freak."

"Rude," I say, before Been-Here-Before has time to respond. "There's no need to be mean. It's not like any of us wants to be here." I glance at Dieter. "No offense."

Dieter's thin lips tighten. He probably doesn't want to be here either. Maybe he's paying his dues so he can move on to real therapy. "Zahra's right—" He scans his clipboard and comes up with "Simon. I already told you, no bullying. As for you, Kalista," he says, "save your songwriting for your own time."

"You know it's Kali," she says, proving she *has* been here before. "And I didn't actually write those lyrics."

"Notts County?" I ask. I've learned a few things about indie bands from Rico.

Kali nods and smiles. "Isn't Owen Gaines the cutest?"

"Totally," Evan answers, rolling his eyes.

Dieter stares at Evan until he squirms in his chair. "A couple of last points before we get started. You need to be discreet and respect one another's privacy. What happens in group stays in group. Understood?"

There's a general murmur of agreement on this one.

"The only thing I'll discuss with your parents is your attendance." Dieter gets up to pace again. "Because they're picking up the tab."

"Is this on the test?" Stoned asks.

"No tests and no grades, Evan," Dieter says. "The rewards may not be tangible, but they'll last a lifetime. You are about to discover the healing powers of group therapy."

Simon throws himself back in his chair so hard it almost tips. His hands come out of his pockets. One's holding an iPod, the other a set of keys. "Just kill me now," he says.

Dieter plants shiny black shoes in front of Simon. "No such luck."

"If your 'process' works," Simon says, "how come the Air Guitar Freak is back for seconds?"

"Keep up the personal attacks and you'll be back for seconds as well," Dieter says. "Why not just open up and share?"

We all groan.

"That's right, *share*," Dieter repeats. "You'll be amazed at how much you can help each other when you see past your differences. Every one of you is in a similar situation. Your family has hit the rocks. You hate them. You think they hate you. Maybe you even blame yourselves."

Nope, I still blame my grandparents. If they hadn't come here, Mom and Dad probably would have carried on as they were—which didn't look that bad to me. It was just chilly around the house. I guess their marriage was like an iceberg, with the big scary part hidden beneath the water. At any rate, with my grandparents now trying to de-assimilate Mom, Dad will never win her back. Not that he's trying.

"Tell us about it. Listen. Support. Trust." Dieter claps three times. "Now, who wants to start?"

I was sure Kali would be the first to wave her hand, but she's gone back to swaying to unheard music with her eyes closed.

In the distance, a dog howls.

Sydney stands. "I'm outta here. You're torturing my baby."

Before she can leave, an elderly priest appears in the doorway, holding Banksy's leash. The dog breaks free and runs to Sydney, stumpy tail wagging madly.

"Sorry about the ruckus, Father Casey," Dieter says. "Sydney will leave the dog at home next week."

"Nonsense," Father Casey says, smiling. "Well-behaved dogs are welcome at St. Joe's." Banksy sits quietly at Sydney's feet. "Bring him inside next time, Sydney."

Sydney's bright red lips curl into a smile that transforms her face. "Thank you, Father Casey."

Dieter takes a seat and waits till the priest leaves before saying, "Kali, you know how this works. Could you get the ball rolling?"

"Sure," she says. "My mom just dumped her fourth husband, and *that* is why I'm back."

"Wow!" The word is out of my mouth before I can stop it.

"I know, crazy, right?" Kali says. "I really liked Husband Number Four, and now he's just . . . gone."

"Parents are selfish pigs," Lauren says. She puts her bag down beside her chair, forming a designer barrier between herself and Banksy. "My mom had an affair with her boss, and Dad sent me here because he thought I'd be devastated. But I get that relationships don't always work." She gives Dieter a bright smile. "I'm fine."

Dieter raises an eyebrow. "Sometimes it takes a while for the truth to sink in."

"Oh, I'm not in denial or anything," Lauren says. "I just focus on the good things."

"Like Prada and Gucci?" Sydney asks, looking down at Lauren's bag.

"And Hermès and Coach," Lauren counters. "Retail therapy does help." She inspects Sydney's vintage fashion. "But you have to steer clear of thrift shops."

"What else helps you cope, Lauren?" Dieter intervenes.

"My boyfriend," Lauren says, pushing her hair behind her ears with French-manicured nails. "I can tell Trey anything."

Sydney repeats the last sentence in a singsong voice as she takes a plastic bag out of her backpack and offers Banksy a dog biscuit.

Dieter shoots a pointed look in Sydney's direction. Her kohl-lined eyes are all innocence. "What? I'm agreeing with her." She balls up the empty plastic bag and tosses it into the trash can.

Kali is out of her seat in a flash to pluck the bag out of the trash and wave it under Sydney's nose. "Hello? You can reuse this."

"Reuse this," Syd says, flipping her the bird. I notice her fingernails are chewed down and her left hand is splotched with red and blue paint.

Kali looks to Dieter, but he's momentarily distracted by Simon, who's plugging in his earbuds.

"You should use biodegradable bags anyway," Kali says. "Especially to stoop-and-scoop for your canine Prince Charming."

Dieter confiscates Simon's iPod and shoots Kali a warning glance. "Some people take comfort from animals in times of stress."

"Others just get stoned," Sydney says, trying to shift attention to Evan.

"Or sublimate their grief with anger and sex," Simon says. "Like I do."

Evan almost falls into Lauren's lap, laughing. I'm surprised he has enough brain cells left to know what *sublimate* means.

Kali talks over the guys' laughter. "I agree with Lauren. A

good relationship is the best distraction from family drama. When I see my boyfriend, Rick, the rest of the world just fades away. And then the songs come." She closes her eyes and hums a few stray notes. "It's the ultimate therapy."

Sydney isn't the only one to snort, but hers is the loudest. "I had you pegged at school. You and your friends are too much." She turns to Simon. "It's constant hallway karaoke."

Kali crosses her legs again, and her arms too. "At least I don't roll with thugs."

"Stains and Rambo are my best friends," Sydney says. "Even if we don't sing together."

"You want to be scary by association," Kali says. "Dieter would say you hang with them to avoid making real friends."

"Don't put words in my mouth, Kali," Dieter says, although he seems fine with the direction the conversation is taking. He's even slouched a little in his chair.

"I like hanging with guys because girls overanalyze everything," Sydney says.

I try steering the conversation to safer ground. "Does everyone here go to Austin High? I just started there this week."

They tell me that Evan and Simon go to Travis, the other high school in the area, while Lauren attends a private school in the east end.

Syd confronts Lauren. "You probably come downtown for this so your society friends won't know you're in group."

"Of course I do," Lauren says. "I bet no one here is telling their friends."

Dieter weighs in. "You should all be proud of yourselves for trying to deal with your challenges in a constructive way."

Everyone single one of us laughs.

"I'm not even telling my boyfriend," Kali says. "We're pretty solid, but still."

"You don't want him to think you're a head case," Simon offers.

"Exactly," Kali says.

"I'm not telling my boyfriend either," I say.

"Why not, Zahra?" Dieter asks.

"I don't want to bring Rico down with my problems, that's all," I say. "I'm sure he'd be totally supportive."

"Trey already knows all about my problems, including group," Lauren says. "But we've been together over a year. How did you and Rico meet?"

"We met in a music store near the cookbook shop where I work."

Kali uncrosses her legs and leans forward in her seat. "Is he cute?"

I nod, relaxing a little as I tell the story. "I'm not that into music, but he was so excited about all these new bands, I spent thirty bucks on his favorite CD. Who even buys CDs anymore? Anyway, I hated it, but I went back the next day and sunk another forty into a live bootleg album."

Lauren laughs. "Did you get a decent return on your investment?"

"Yep," I say. "We started talking about an art exhibit, and he invited me to come."

"*You're* into art?" Sydney says, running her eyes over my outfit. Obviously someone who wears regular jeans and sneakers can't be arty.

"I'm into Rico," I say. "If he'd invited me to a monster truck rally, I'd have been into that too."

"Girls," Simon says, in disgust. "You're all frauds."

"It's polite to show interest in other people's passions," I say. "And it goes both ways. Rico backs my dream of becoming a chef."

"It's not hard to show interest in eating," Evan says. His hair's even curlier than mine—a big brown afro.

"He made me a pot holder with my company logo," I say, regretting it immediately as the guys snicker.

"That's very romantic," Lauren says. "It shows he gets what you're all about."

"Sugar and spice and everything nice," Syd says, smirking.

I simply smile because I happen to believe "Everything's Better with a Little Sugar." It's the *Sweet Tooth* motto.

"My boyfriend burned me a killer CD of his favorite songs," Kali says, beaming as she reapplies peachy lip gloss. Her teeth are white and straight.

"That's the oldest move in the book," Simon says. "I have copies of my seduction playlist on standby."

Evan turns to me, and his eyes are finally wide open. "So, did Betty Crocker give it up for the pot holder?"

Dieter claps and says, "Crossing the line. Anyway, we're nearly done for today."

"Thank God," Simon says, heaving himself off his chair. "I was afraid manis and pedis were next."

"Actually, team building exercises are next," Dieter says.

Kali's the first to protest. "We never did exercises last time."

"Your last group didn't need them. I'm assigning you a project to be done in teams." Dieter claps over us as we all start talking. "I pick the teams. And what did I say about whining?"

·· ♥ ··

"Zahra."

Mom doesn't have to say much to get her point across. There's something in her tone that commands attention.

"What?"

She gives me the look. "You know what."

We've just sat down at the table and she wants me to cover my head. Before my grandparents moved in, Mom only cared about that on religious holidays, if then. Now it's every meal, even a regular Friday night dinner like this one.

I understand that wearing a *dupatta*, or scarf, signifies respect to God and all that, and if Nani wants to wear one, fine. But I don't think I should have to wear it, or pretend it means something to me. I'm fifteen. I can make my own decisions. And at the moment, all a scarf symbolizes for me is my family's collapse.

To Saliyah, however, a scarf is dress-up. Today's is mauve and sparkly and looks awful with her baggy tunic, which happens to be the top half of the *salwar kameez* Nani brought me from Pakistan. Why Nani would choose orange for my coloring is beyond me. It's like she *wants* to piss me off.

Mom's scarf is rose chiffon, a sunset surrounding her pretty face. From the neck down she's in her usual Banana Republic shirt and pants.

Nani glowers at me from under her heavily embroidered turquoise scarf. If it weren't for my grandfather's hand over hers, she'd be giving me an earful. That hand serves as a plug.

Without it, Nani pretty much yammers nonstop, and what she says is usually irritating.

With Nana doing his best to restrain Nani, I give in. Yanking the hood from my sweatshirt up over my hair, I say, "There. Everybody happy?"

Nani opens her mouth, but Nana tightens his grip on her hand. Technically I'm observing the rules. My head is covered and he's hungry. He says a quick blessing, takes a hamburger, and passes the platter.

With the gag order lifted, Nani turns to my mom. "Sana, I gave Zahra a lovely dupatta for her birthday."

The scarf in question is loaded with so many rhinestones that it squashes even *my* bushy hair. That was probably the point. Red is an uncommon hair color for East Asians, so it's a constant reminder to her of my dad, or more specifically, of how my mom abandoned her family and customs.

I've already explained to her that red hair is a recessive trait that requires a gene from each parent. It's beginner biology and Nani's not stupid. She just doesn't want to admit that Mom's equally to blame for the mess on my head. The gene must have crept stealthily through generations of Nana's Persian ancestors until it ambushed me.

Saliyah tries to change the subject. "Are you going to bake for me today, Zahra?"

"I'm not in the mood," I say.

My "cheery" default doesn't always work at home, and with all that's happened this week, it may be permanently broken. I didn't want to come for dinner tonight, in case Mom brought up the fire or group therapy, but so far she hasn't.

Actually, I never enjoy dinner here anymore, but Dad

insists I come once a week whether I like it or not. He's afraid Saliyah and I will grow apart. There's no risk of that. My sister drives me crazy, but I love her. We can survive a separation.

Still, these dinners are uncomfortable. This is my home, but I don't live here. Dad's place isn't my home, but it's where I live. In other words, I have two homes and none at all. I'm a nomad in a green hoodie.

Nani mutters something in Urdu. Her English is excellent, so she switches it up if she doesn't want me to know what she's saying.

Saliyah has picked up a fair bit of Urdu, but she doesn't like being caught in the middle, so she answers Nani in English. "Zahra's in boyfriend withdrawal. She hasn't seen Rico since Dad grounded her."

I do hope to see him on Sunday afternoon, if he's free and I can come up with a foolproof alibi.

"You should be thinking about college, not boys," Nana says. He takes a bite of his hamburger and frowns. "American boys only think about themselves."

"Rico is very thoughtful," I tell him. "He just gave me the nicest gift ever."

Mom slides the dish of *achaar*—spicy pickles—toward Nana. She must have made the burgers my way tonight. Usually she laces them with cumin, chili, and turmeric, and tries to pass them off as normal. "He did? You didn't mention a gift."

Of course not. I've revoked her clearance for insider information.

Saliyah whispers to Mom, "He gave her a pot holder when she cooked him dinner."

There's nothing wrong with Nani's hearing. "You invited a boy into your home? *Alone?*"

Nana takes another bite of his hamburger and sighs. Even with the pickles there's not enough flavor. He takes the top bun off and adds ketchup and chutney. "This is what happens when you let them think about boys," he says. "Trouble."

"Abba," Mom says, still calm. *"Woh meri beti hai, mera faisla."*

I've heard this one a few times. It means something in the neighborhood of, "My daughter, my decision."

I glare at my sister as I bite into my burger. Perfect. Just plain old beef. "Why'd you blab?"

Although her hair and eyes are a shade lighter than Mom's, Saliyah looks just like her—without all the worry lines. Mom aged ten years overnight after seeing the size of my grandparents' suitcases, and another ten when the trunks arrived.

"I was only explaining that Rico's a good guy," Saliyah says. "He's not shallow just because he's smokin'."

Feeling the tension in the room rise, I jump in to control the spin. "It was an innocent dinner. And you'll be happy to know that Mom and Dad are punishing me for it by making me go to therapy."

"Therapy?" Nana says. "She's sharing personal problems with a stranger?"

Mom gives him an exasperated look. There's no winning with my grandparents. That's probably why she left Karachi when she was seventeen to accept a chemistry scholarship at the University of Texas. Back then she stood up to her parents. Now, not so much.

Nani notices that Nana is still picking at his burger, and

gets up from the table. She takes a dish of curry she made earlier out of the fridge and heats it in the microwave. When she sits beside him again, he just gives her a little smile. Forty-six years ago they were virtual strangers when their parents arranged their marriage. They met only twice, chaperoned, before the wedding.

It's strange to think I've already spent way more time with Rico and I haven't even met his family or friends. But arranged marriages are proof that you don't have to know every detail about the other person to make a relationship last. It's about chemistry. Some couples are just meant to be.

Nana slides me his curry. "Try this."

He knows I hate curry, but he always offers it up. It's like he thinks his genes will suddenly activate in me, and I'll love it.

"No thanks," I say, picking up my hamburger.

Nana shakes his head. "One day you'll realize there's nothing wrong with a little heat."

"Maybe," I say, watching as Nani passes him the hot sauce. It's quite possible that I'll end up liking spicy food once I'm cooking it for Rico every night. After all, marriage is all about compromise.

chapter 3

I'm at the Recipe Box counting cash when someone says, "Can you help me, miss? I'm looking for a killer recipe to impress my boyfriend with."

I look up to find Kali draped over the counter, wearing a green tank top that matches her eyes. Her curls are twisted into a messy knot that somehow looks elegant. She's one of those people who have style without really trying.

Dieter teamed us up with Sydney to do a scavenger hunt. Using the cryptic clues he e-mailed us, we have to visit various locations around the city and present photos of them in next Thursday's session. Dieter said no tests and no grades, but he's still giving us homework.

René, the coolest boss ever, takes Kali's request in stride. "I've got just the thing: *Desserts to Die For.*"

Kali gravitates to his side of the register. René always has this effect on female customers. He has twinkly brown eyes, salt-and-pepper hair, and at six-foot-three, he really works an apron.

I drag Kali to the gluten-free cookbook section, the only quiet place in the store on a busy Saturday afternoon. "What are you doing here? We're supposed to meet at one thirty at Austin Java."

"Can't you get off early? I checked out the clues, and this is going to take a while."

"I already cut my shift short," I say. "So this is costing me money." With Dad's income spread between two households, my allowance has dried up. Now my work paycheck goes to cover my cell phone bill as well as anything I consider a necessity and Dad doesn't. "That's why I wanted to do it tomorrow."

"But tomorrow's the free Notts County concert," Kali says, as if that trumps all. She was singing their song the other day. I wouldn't be surprised if she's a groupie.

"Why don't you meet Syd early and start solving the clues?" I say. "I have to unpack some boxes before I go."

Kali sets her bag on a shelf. "I'll help you if it'll go faster."

I guess she thinks stocking shelves beats spending time alone with Syd. I'd have to agree. Syd seems prickly, and that dog is just scary.

René lets me off half an hour early, but it doesn't get us any further ahead, because Sydney's a no-show. After waiting an hour I suggest starting without her, but Kali's too steamed. "The whole point is to get to know each other," she says. "Plus, the other team has three people, so they'll win. It's no fair."

True, but I bet Simon and Evan aren't exactly Lauren's dream team.

Kali calls the number Sydney gave us again, and finally her mom picks up. When Kali explains our mission, Mrs. Stark gives us Syd's cell number and tells us where to look for her.

After leaving some blistering voice mails on Syd's cell, we start walking. "She better have a good explanation," Kali says, as we circle the old converted warehouse Mrs. Stark told us about. "And she better be damn good at scavenger hunts."

I spot a small plaque on a door in the shape of a stroller with the initials MW painted on its side. "This must be it," I say. "The Maternity Ward. Although I doubt it has anything to do with babies."

We step through the door and find ourselves in a cavernous space, where light streams through floor-to-ceiling windows. Several artists are lined up in front of the windows, working on canvases set on easels. In one corner, two guys are placing papier-mâché possums on the tiers of a giant cake platter. In another, a couple in nude body suits are painting each other green as a girl wearing a kimono videotapes them.

Until today, I considered myself relatively cool. Dad works in advertising and he tries to stay ahead of the curve. We're always checking out the latest Web sites, magazines, TV programs, and movies. But looking around, I realize I need to expand my horizons.

Kali smiles at my dazed expression. "It's like Andy Warhol's Factory," she says. "You probably need the soul of an artist to truly appreciate it." She inhales deeply, as if there's a secret scent only artists—and air guitar players—can pick up.

I notice a sign on the wall made from hundreds of old fuses and circuit boards: WHERE ART IS BORN.

Ah, the maternity ward.

Kali singles out a guy who is applying beige paint to two enormous latex mounds. His hair is pulled into a long ponytail, exposing a stunning face. "Now that," she says, "is art." She doesn't mean the latex mounds. "Hello," she calls to Adonis. "We're looking for Sydney Stark."

He returns Kali's smile, full force. Rubbing a paint-splattered hand over dark stubble, Adonis says, "I haven't seen her today. Try the old Albany Hotel on Ryder."

"Thanks," Kali says. "I'm Kali Esposito, by the way." She looks around and spies a tire that's been painted a brownish-pink. Half a basketball sticks out from the center, painted the same color. "It's nice that you're recycling. I'm a big fan of eco-friendly art."

I cut the conversation short when I notice the nameplate waiting to be attached to Adonis's piece reads QUADRUPLE D.

Kali hasn't clued in to the fact that Adonis is constructing a giant boob. Having the soul of an artist may help you appreciate a hotbed of creativity, but having a imaginary pal like Oliver James makes it easy-peasy to spot a regular perv.

·· ♥ ··

A woman with tattered clothes, matted hair, and a ring of scabs around her mouth stops us as we get off the bus. "Got a cigarette?"

"Sorry, we don't smoke," I say.

"Wait." Kali opens her bag and pulls out a pack. She hands one to the woman and lights a match.

The woman's eyes widen as she takes a drag. Then she mutters something unintelligible and shuffles off.

"With all your rah-rah tree-hugging, you suck on death sticks?" I ask.

"Carrying them doesn't mean I smoke them."

"So you're helping that poor woman kill herself?"

Kali sniffs. "Are you always this self-righteous?"

"You ragged on Syd about biodegradable bags," I point out. But her words sting. What if I inherited a self-righteousness gene from my grandparents along with the rare, Persian redhair gene?

Outside a dodgy sports bar, we pass a guy covered in so many tattoos it's hard to make out his natural skin color. "Got a cigarette?" he asks, leering at Kali.

"We don't smoke," she says.

I wait until we're out of earshot to ask, "Did we just quit?"

"They're Gauloises," Kali says. "Picasso smoked them. And John Lennon. I've decided to save them."

Surveying the street, I wrinkle my nose and say, "Why would Syd hang around here?"

"My third dad is a real estate agent," Kali says. "This neighborhood is what he calls *transitional.*"

"This neighborhood is what *my* dad calls *dangerous.*"

At the end of the block we find the Albany Hotel. It's boarded up and surrounded by safety fencing.

"Maybe there's another Albany Hotel?" Kali says, her confidence waning. "The sign says 'No Trespassing.'"

I slip through a gap in the fence. "Maybe you need the soul of an adventurer to ignore it."

She grins and follows me. "Touché."

Up ahead a dog barks. Banksy?

Picking our way through refuse, we circle the building. At the back, Syd is standing on scaffolding two stories high. She's so focused on spraying paint on the wall that she doesn't notice us. There's a bucket of spray cans at her feet, along with some large sheets of plastic that appear to be stencils. Banksy is lying on the ground under the scaffolding, chewing a bone.

I put a finger to my lips so we can creep a bit closer without being detected. Now we can see that several of the boarded-up windows have been painted to show scenes from the hotel's former glory. In one, a porter accepts a tip from a businessman. In the next, a man and a woman make out. In the third, an older couple bends over a desk to examine a map. The images are bright and full of life.

In contrast, the scene Syd works on now is dark. It shows a young couple arguing. The woman throws a suitcase at the man, and below the window a painted pair of jeans falls to the ground.

Syd bends to switch paint cans, and I see that she's drawn a stylized ax on the windowsill that slices through a heart dripping with blood. Beside the heart, large graffiti letters scream LOVE DESTROYZ.

A crunch breaks the silence as Kali steps on an empty beer can. Syd spins around and Banksy jumps up, poised to attack on Syd's signal.

"Sorry for sneaking up on you," Kali calls up to Syd.

Syd's posture is as hostile as Banksy's. "You're trespassing on private property."

"Says the person defacing private property," Kali replies.

I try to defuse the situation. "This work is amazing. Is it all yours?"

"You think I'd tag someone else's work?"

"No, it's just it's so good—"

"That you don't believe someone like me could have done it?"

"That it looks like a professional did it," I say. "Look, could we start over? You were supposed to meet us at Austin Java two hours ago."

Syd signals Banksy to stand down. "What for?"

"Do the words 'scavenger hunt' ring any bells?" Kali asks.

Gathering her supplies, Syd lowers the bucket to the ground on a rope, before climbing down and starting to fill her backpack. "I don't do extracurricular."

"I have to," Kali says. "Dieter will squeal if we don't, and my mom's already got me on a short leash."

"Tell me about it," I say. "My dad joked about hooking me up to a tracking device." If he had his way, I wouldn't see Rico again until we were old enough to cash pension checks. And he'd have confiscated my phone except I pay the bill myself. Not that the phone has done me much good. I've only spoken to Rico once in the four days since the fire. But he has texted a few times, and today he waved as he walked past the store while tapping his watch to indicate that he was late for work.

"Why should I care about your problems?" Syd asks, still bent over her bag.

"Because your mom said a scavenger hunt sounds like fun," Kali says.

Syd stops packing. "You spoke to my mom?"

"Sure. I was worried when you didn't show." Kali pulls a camera out of her bag. "I promised to send her some pictures of our project today." She aims the camera at one of Syd's murals. "And I bet your mom would love to see this."

Syd rests paint-stained hands on her hips. "Blackmail won't work. My mom knows about my art."

"But does she know the city is your canvas?" I ask.

Glancing from me to Kali, Syd weighs her options. In the

distance, a car door slams. Syd snaps into action, hastily hooking up Banksy and heaving her backpack over her shoulders. "Come on," she says, breaking into a run. "The security guards have been trying to catch me for weeks."

Kali and I can barely keep up, but when the guard rounds the corner and shouts after us, we find a faster gear and scramble through the gap in the fence on Syd's heels.

·· ♥ ··

"Take the picture," Syd says.

"Of what?" Kali asks, confused.

Syd points over her head. "Number three on the list: 'Show me a sign that Pecan Street no longer exists.'"

The sign overhead reads 6TH STREET.

"I don't get it," Kali says.

Sighing, Syd passes Banksy's leash to me, takes the camera from Kali, and snaps the photo. I keep my eye on the dog, who sits quietly at my feet with his tongue hanging out.

"Where does the Pecan Street Arts Festival take place every year?" Syd asks.

"On Sixth Street," Kali says. "Oh . . . right!"

"All the streets around here were named after trees until the city numbered them," Syd says. "I've solved the first three clues, so obviously I'm the brains behind this operation. Good thing you forced me to participate."

"I want the two hours of my life back that it took to track you down," Kali says, watching the guy juggling three torches outside Esther's Follies. "Who'd want to juggle fire in ninety-degree heat?" she asks, plucking a damp curl off her neck and pinning it back up. "That's stupid."

"What's stupid is spending the day walking all over the city with you two, when I could be sitting in Dad's air-conditioned loft," Syd says. There's a sheen of perspiration on her face, and I notice the beauty spot isn't running. It's real. "If you stop your yapping and let me concentrate, I can nail this entire list in an hour," she continues. "Number four: 'Find a stone-faced woman who's made it to the top of our government.'"

"It's the Goddess of Liberty," I say. "You know, the statue that sits on the top of the Texas State Capitol."

"There's a new genius in town," Kali says, reapplying her lip gloss. "But before we hike up to the capitol, let's check out the rest of the clues to make sure we don't backtrack."

"That's actually a good idea," Syd says.

"Don't sound so surprised," Kali says. "I'm not just an awesome musician with a pretty face."

"If you developed some confidence, you'd be perfect." Syd looks at me and nearly smiles.

"Number five," Kali says. "'This last surviving council member has lost a few limbs over the years.'"

"That's the Treaty Oak on Baylor," I say. "It's the last of the Council Oaks, where the Native American tribes used to meet."

Syd snatches the list out of Kali's hand, determined to get the next one. "'Find a father of Texas that can't eat, sleep, move, or think.'"

"Stephen F. Austin," I call out. I'm on a roll now.

"As in our high school?" Kali asks.

"As in the man our high school is named after, not to mention the city. We'll take a picture of his statue in the Texas State Cemetery."

"Right after we grab a couple of cold sodas," Kali says.

Syd shakes her head. "We're not taking a break until we've covered half the list."

Heading west along 7th Street, I manage to solve another clue.

"Are you some kind of history nerd?" Syd asks suspiciously.

I shake my head. "I remember this stuff from class trips."

"Class trips?" Syd says. "Aren't those optional?"

"I love them," Kali says. "And I learn a lot. For example, I learned that Jorge Vega is an excellent kisser when we visited the State Cemetery."

A guy in a cowboy hat turns and smirks as he overhears Kali's comment. "Giddy up," he says, tipping his Stetson in her direction.

"Ew," Kali says. "Cowboys think they can excuse anything with a tip of the hat."

"Can we please focus?" Syd asks.

Ten minutes later, we're standing at the sandstone wall that marks the entrance to the cemetery.

"I can't believe you made out with a guy here," I say to Kali as the two of us head inside. Since dogs aren't allowed in the cemetery, Syd and Banksy stay behind in the parking lot. Passing row upon row of plain white tombstones, we make our way to the shady hill where Stephen Austin is buried.

Kali grins mischievously as I photograph her pointing to the statue of the father of Texas. "I kissed Jacob Rosen at the capitol and Bryan Leslie at the Treaty Oak. That's when Bryan asked me to sixth grade prom—a pivotal moment in *my* history."

When we get back to the parking lot, Syd is waving goodbye to a minibus packed with senior citizens. In her other hand is a can of cold soda that's beaded with moisture. Beside her, Banksy drinks water from an IHOP coffee cup.

"Are you going to share that with us?" Kali asks, eyeing the soda.

Syd snorts. "Not likely. Who knows where your mouths have been?"

"Fine, then we're stopping at the next store," I say, watching Syd chug the contents of the can. She wipes her mouth with her hand and burps.

"Unbelievable," Kali says.

As we head north, I read a riddle aloud: "'What contains twenty-eight stories and is surrounded by brilliance?'"

"I know this one!" Kali exclaims. "The UT Tower. Had my first French kiss there."

"You've gone out with college guys?" I ask, impressed.

"No, just a high school guy who lived in the area," Kali says. "But maybe I'll meet a college guy today."

"Wouldn't Rick the Ultimate Therapy Boyfriend have a problem with that?" Syd asks.

"There's nothing wrong with having a few numbers on your speed dial. No guy lasts forever, right?"

"You can't think that way," I say. "Or you'll jinx it. I want Rico to be my Forever Guy."

"I'm just being realistic," Kali says, shrugging. "Look at my family history."

"I still believe in forever," I say.

"Maybe that's the difference between one family breakup and three," Kali says, walking ahead of us.

"Forever's tough," Syd offers. "Even a year is hard work."

Kali turns around. "You didn't say you had a boyfriend."

"That's right, I didn't." Syd looks as if she regrets mentioning it now.

"What's his name? How old is he? How long have you been together?" Kali can't contain her curiosity. Like me, she probably finds it hard to imagine gruff Syd being in love. But Syd's had plenty of guys checking her out today—not as many as Kali, but probably more than me. Although Syd's more striking than pretty, she's unique, and as Mom always says, unique works in Austin.

Syd ignores Kali's questions, and the silence continues until we're winding our way along a red path through the white buildings of the University of Texas campus. All around us, students are lounging on the lawn or in the shade, reading textbooks or snoozing with their heads resting on their backpacks.

"Can we sit for a second?" Kali asks. "I think I'm going to faint."

"For a second," Syd says, reluctantly sinking to the grass near Littlefield Fountain. I stare at the bronze horses rearing in a steady spray of water, and feel a bit cooler.

Kali starts in on Syd again. "So your boyfriend . . . does he go to Austin High? Or did you meet him at the Maternity Ward?"

"Do you even know the meaning of personal boundaries?" Syd asks.

"Excuse me for taking an interest in your life," Kali says, plucking possible four-leaf clovers from the grass beside her. "Anyway, I can't help it. I love hearing about successful relationships."

"Me too," I say. "It makes me feel like anything is possible."

"Who said anything about success?" Syd says.

Kali switches on a dime. "What happened? When did you break up? Did you end it or did he? Is that why your graffiti is so dark?"

"Kali," I say. "Give her a chance."

As I feared, the barrage shuts Syd down. "It's complicated," is all she says, before focusing on the list of clues again. After a few seconds, she adds, "The Lone Star."

"Oh yeah," Kali says, following Syd's gaze to a guy sitting alone under a tree, strumming his guitar. "They're definitely the sexiest. All the mystery, wrapped up in—"

"Question seven," Syd says. "'Find a heavenly body that marks a gateway to our state's past.' That's gotta be the Lone Star sculpture at the Bob Bullock Museum."

"Right," Kali says. "So, how heavenly was your boyfriend's body?"

.. ♥ ..

"Dieter is a cruel man," Kali says, lagging behind as we make our way toward Zilker Metropolitan Park and the Umlauf Sculpture Garden, site of the final clue. "He could have warned us not to wear heels."

Syd and I are holding up better than Kali, but we're all pretty beat. Despite Syd's laughable early prediction, it's taken us four and a half hours to solve the clues and take the photos. The sun is low in the sky and we're almost back to where we started the hunt. In fact, we've covered every inch of downtown Austin, and despite our efforts to plan ahead, we've covered some parts of it twice.

"Dieter's not stupid," Syd says. "I don't have the energy to hate you guys anymore."

Kali holds out her arms for a hug. "I knew I'd grow on you."

"Back off, Sweaty Betty," Syd says. But she digs a granola bar out of her bag, breaks it in three, and shares it. We crunch in silence as we walk the home stretch.

There's more to these two than I expected. Kali's a quirky free spirit, but she's also bubbly, adventurous, and fun. Syd bubbles in a different way—like a volcano—but she's not quite as intimidating as she seemed. She's pissed off at her parents, like we all are, and probably her boyfriend, too. Some day she may feel like talking about it. I, for one, won't pressure her.

"I thought we'd have to admit defeat on the Tom Miller Dam," Syd says. "Nice one, Kali."

The second to last cryptic clue read: "I'm over seventy, named for a mayor, and known for my power and control."

"Again, I'll ignore the wonder in your voice," Kali says, finding the strength to reapply her lip gloss yet again. "Air guitar and airhead are separate concepts, you know. And tree hugging requires some knowledge of man and the environment."

"Point taken," Syd says.

But Kali is just warming up. "I care about the earth, so flood *control* and hydroelectric *power* are two things I happen to know a bit about. Hydroelectricity is renewable energy. It produces far fewer greenhouse gases than fossil fuels."

"You might consider producing less hot air yourself," Syd says. "To help your immediate environment."

Instead, Kali starts singing. "Hydropower, help save the nation. Spare us from greenhouse radiation."

A woman with a stroller gives Kali a suspicious look and crosses the street. Far from being embarrassed, Kali calls after her, "You can't run away from global warming!"

"She had to ruin the moment," Syd says, shaking her head wearily.

"I don't think she can help herself," I say.

Kali breaks into rap as we enter the sculpture garden: "Atmosphere containing gases, generated by the masses . . ."

"Don't worry," Syd says to an old woman nearby. "She's doing her part to Keep Austin Weird."

The unofficial city slogan fits Kali, and the old lady smiles.

"And this weirdo just nailed it for our team," Kali proclaims.

The old lady offers to take a picture of the three us in front of the sculpture garden sign. "Bunch up!" she says, when we're in position. "I can't get you all in the frame."

Since I'm standing in the middle, Kali and Syd move a little closer, and Banksy sits on my foot.

"Closer," the old lady says. "You're friends, aren't you?"

"Not exactly," Kali whispers.

"Shut up and get this over with," Syd says under her breath.

Now our shoulders are almost touching, and I'm hoping the woman doesn't ask us to put our arms around each other. The day could end in fisticuffs.

Fortunately, the lady has another idea. "Let's see the three wise monkeys," she says.

Kali immediately puts her hands over her ears, I put mine over my eyes, and Syd puts hers over her mouth.

"Perfect!" the woman says, snapping off a couple of shots.

"Better three wise monkeys than the Three Stooges," Kali says, pointing to another trio approaching.

Even from a distance, it's obvious that Lauren is the worse for wear. She's dragging her handbag by a single broken strap, and her hair is stringy and lank. Her clothes are clinging to her.

"Maybe she threw herself in the UT fountain to cool off," Kali says.

Our opposition is in such a heated argument that they don't even notice us. Lauren turns and hits Simon with her bag.

"Should we help her?" I ask.

Evan kneels in front of Lauren, begging for mercy.

We look at each other and say, "Nah." Then we burst into laughter and collapse onto a bench together.

"Much better," the old lady says, snapping another picture. "Now you look like friends."

That's probably a stretch, but it will be nice not to have to sit alone at lunch on Monday.

chapter 4

Weaving through the packed cafeteria, I try to ignore the warning stares of people who don't want the new kid at their table. Instead, I scan for Kali's blond curls or Syd's black bob.

In the end, it's Kali's voice I hear. "Reduce your carbon footprint," she calls, above the lunchtime din. "Sign the petition for cafeteria watercoolers and student discounts on reusable bottles."

I follow the voice past a long table filled with football players, where I get stalled in traffic.

"You are *not* joining the jazz band," one of the guys says. I look down to see Fletcher Longland laying down the law for Hollis Messina.

"Why not?" Hollis says. "Singing is the only thing I'm good at."

Fletcher sighs. "Do I really have to explain this to you? Bands are for geeks."

"But Mr. Jamieson asked me." She strokes his arm. "Please, Fletch?"

Why is it even a question? Fletcher's her boyfriend, not her dad.

Fletcher shakes his tiny head. "Forget it."

But Hollis persists. "Is this about Bronco Garcia?"

"*Quiet,*" Fletcher says, suddenly fierce. "And no."

"Because he knows I wouldn't be interested even if you and I weren't together."

"What kind of guy plays the clarinet?" Fletcher asks. "He's obviously on the wrong team anyway."

"Yeah, I think he's gay, too," Hollis says, taking the path of least resistance. "He likes show tunes."

"What did I tell you?" Fletcher turns to share this news with his teammates.

I stare down at Hollis, knowing Bronco could be in for a world of hurt because she's afraid to stand up to her swamp-eyed boyfriend.

"What do you want?" she says, noticing me at last.

"Nothing, I was—" I glance around and see the crowd has thinned. It looks like I've been deliberately eavesdropping.

"Spying?" Fletcher asks. Without waiting for an answer, he continues. "So, did the steak get you laid or what?"

I try to move on, but my feet are frozen to the dirty linoleum. Meanwhile, Fletcher fills the team in on my dinner plans. Some of the guys openly check me out, laughing when I clutch my bag to my chest.

"Most girls don't have to go to that kind of trouble," Hollis says, slipping her arm through Fletcher's.

"But I never say no to a steak," Fletcher says, smiling suggestively.

Finally my brain connects to my feet, and I start moving again. Kali has stopped shouting, but I see her ahead of me, going from table to table with her petition. She passes Syd, who's sitting at a table with two guys I assume are Stains and

Rambo. One guy is big, sloppy, and unshaven. The other is short, skinny, and pale, yet somehow more menacing than the bigger guy. Syd sees Kali and drops her eyes to her fries.

Kali stops at the table beside Syd's and asks people to sign her petition. She's either ignoring Syd, too, or completely oblivious. Either way, I decide not to risk more embarrassment today.

Instead, I find an empty table, pull out my laptop, and start complaining about my life in an e-mail to Shanna and Morgan. While I eat my sandwich, I write about having to take over most of the housework since Dad shrunk two of my favorite T-shirts in the laundry, then dropped my new cookbook into a pot of stew he was making. I move on to describe the high-lights of my first group session.

That's when a cloud of cheap perfume blocks my windpipe. "What's Transitions?" Hollis asks, reading over my shoulder.

"Nothing," I say, slamming the screen shut. Her features look pointier from below. I was wrong about great hair fixing everything.

"So, the invasion of privacy only goes one way, spy?"

"I didn't mean to eavesdrop," I say. "But since you brought it up, you *should* join the jazz band if you want to. You don't need Fletcher's permission."

She stares down at me. "You're trying to break us up, aren't you?"

"What? How could you even think that?" Surely my disgust for Fletcher shows?

Three of Hollis's friends gather behind her. "Zahra, here, is into Fletch," Hollis tells them.

A dark-haired girl with a ruby nose stud that looks like a

drop of blood laughs. "She doesn't stand a chance."

"What's Transitions?" Hollis asks more forcefully, drawing strength from her crew.

"It's a community group," I say. "Where I volunteer."

Ruby Stud shakes her head. "She's lying. I've heard of Transitions. My cousin's ex-boyfriend had to go when his parents split up. It's group therapy."

"That explains so much," Hollis says, grinning. "Remember I told you about the weirdo from Spanish class and her fantasy menus? Well, this is her."

I try to remember what I've heard about handling bullies, but theory isn't much use when you're in the moment.

"So tell us, spy," Hollis says, "do you talk about your fantasies in group?"

"She does." Kali is standing to my right, petition in hand. "We all do. It gets pretty steamy, actually. I wish I could say more, but what happens in group stays in group. Right, Z?"

"Right," I say.

"So the Jolly Green Flake's back in therapy, too," Hollis says, savoring the news. "I heard about your first trip from Fletcher's friend, Ace. But I'm not too surprised that you're double-crazy. Poor thing."

I'm sure Kali's considered eccentric, with her eco-causes and spontaneous singing, but she's also very pretty from any angle, a fact that can't be lost on Hollis.

"Thanks for caring," Kali says. "Sign my petition?"

Ruby Stud pushes the clipboard aside. "What happened this time, Flake? Another daddy take off?"

"None of your business," I say, since Kali doesn't have a comeback.

Hollis ignores me. "And what happens the *third* time you go nuts? The psych ward?"

"Push us over the edge and you'll find out," a raspy voice says. Syd looks old-school punk today, in combat boots, a blue kilt, leather cuffs, and an oversized T-shirt.

Hollis takes a step backward. Obviously Kali was wrong about Syd needing Stains and Rambo to scare people. She does just fine on her own.

"I've been meaning to talk to you, Hollis," Syd continues. "I've got a problem with your pinhead boyfriend making out with Juanita Lopes next to my locker. Their slobber creates a health hazard. Could you have a word with him?"

"You're lying, you . . . psycho," Hollis says.

"Is that the best you can do?" Syd asks, taking a step closer. "And you must know I'm not lying."

Syd looks from Kali to me. "This strikes me as a teachable moment." She turns back to the bullies. "Listen up, Hollis, and loser friends of Hollis. Dealing with problems in a constructive way doesn't mean we're nuts, it means we're mature. Sticking with a boyfriend who treats you like crap? *That's* nuts."

Hollis's hair seems to have lost its luster. "I—"

"Don't," Syd interrupts. "Anything you say will only make us pity you more. Run back to Fletcher and see if there's any slobber left for you."

Hollis and crew turn to go, firing every synonym for "crazy" they can think of over their shoulders.

When the coast is clear, Kali and Syd drop into the seats beside me.

"You handled that so well," Kali tells Syd. Her face is flushed and her green eyes sparkle with excitement.

"I'll ignore the wonder in your voice," Syd says. "I'm not just an awesome artist with a bad attitude, you know."

We laugh, and it goes a long way toward taking the sting out of what just happened—at least for me.

"Thanks, guys," I say, pulling out some chocolate short-bread cookies I baked in the hopes of having lunch with them today. I'm pretty sure girls are immune to the Cookie Curse.

Syd takes one and pops the whole thing in her mouth. "I've been dying to give Hollis Messina a reality check," she mumbles. "Thanks for giving me an excuse."

"I went out with one of Fletcher's friends a couple of times last year," Kali says. "I mentioned my mom's exes and my first trip to Transitions—obviously a huge mistake."

"Not as big a mistake as going out with Fletcher himself," Syd says. "Everyone knows he plays around on Hollis. She must have heard the rumors."

"Why does she put up with it?" I ask. "She seems so tough."

"Hollis is a marshmallow wrapped in barbed wire," Kali says. "She cuts everyone to make up for a serious lack of self-esteem." She grins at my expression. "You learn a few things at group."

"I guess Hollis hopes he'll change for her," I say. I can understand that. Fabulous as Rico is, there are things I'd change about him. For starters, I'd like to hear from him more often. And I'd love to set up dates in advance instead of on the fly, so I'd have something to look forward to. But I guess that's what happens when you're lucky enough to hook up with a busy, popular guy.

"Fool for love . . ." Kali's fingers move into air guitar

position. "'Nothing but a fo-oo-well . . .'"

"Don't do it," Syd says. "Do *not* sing, you psycho."

Laughing again, I open my laptop to show Syd and Kali the map I've made for Dieter with our scavenger hunt photos. Although I'm far from arty, Dad's a graphic designer and is always happy to teach me the latest technology.

They love it, and we spend the rest of the lunch period reliving the high points of the scavenger hunt. By the time the bell rings, the cookies have disappeared, along with my anxiety.

I'm glad the map turned out so well. I've never been much of a navigator and it's good to have some help finding my way.

· · ♥ · ·

"You missed our turn," I shout to Rico over the noise of the engine and the rattling of windows and loose sun visors.

"There's less traffic on this street," he says, pressing harder on the accelerator.

We're already going ten miles over the speed limit, but I know better than to worry out loud about old brakes, balding tires, or hidden state troopers. When you're riding in Miss Daisy, you keep your eyes open and your mouth shut.

Miss Daisy is a 1986 Shelby Charger, custom-painted powder blue with white racing stripes. She's the number one girl in Rico's life, and it didn't take me long to figure out that anyone else would come second at best.

When it comes to "Miz D," as the vanity plate reads, there's an unwritten code of conduct. Doors are not slammed, seats are not adjusted, buttons are not touched, and food and drink are not permitted. Anyone privileged enough to enter Miss

Daisy is informed once and at length about the history of the Shelby Charger and is thereafter tested on a regular basis.

It's a lot of pressure for someone who generally judges a car solely by its color.

Rico squeals around another corner, and I brace myself on the dashboard. He looks at me sideways, and I know he's wondering if my hand is clean. I tuck it under my leg and brace myself with my elbow instead. I don't want Rico to regret picking me up from work tonight.

Spontaneous as always, he showed up just as my shift ended with a box full of *Sweet Tooth* gear—dish towels, a mug, even a key chain. René was impressed, although I sense he's not big on Rico. That's probably because Miss Daisy left a wicked oil patch in front of the Recipe Box. I think of Rico every time I see it.

I think about him all the time anyway, even more since Sunday, when he suggested a bike ride around town with a picnic in Zilker Park. I didn't mention that I'd been there only the day before with Syd and Kali, since group is still my dirty little secret. I just enjoyed lying on the sun-warmed grass beside Rico, watching the colorful kites soar overhead. The food he picked up at my favorite bakery was delicious. All in all, it was the perfect antidote to my ill-fated dinner.

Whatever he'd planned to say to me never came up, and I decided to leave well enough alone. Just the same, I can't help asking him now if we can stop for coffee and hang out a little longer.

Rico shakes his head. "Can't tonight. Promised to help Pete install new speakers in his car. Which reminds me, do you notice anything different about Daisy?" He doesn't wait for my answer. "New shock absorbers. I can change the size of the constriction valve to stiffen up the suspension."

"Cool," I say, as if his words made sense. "Did you do it yourself?"

"Of course," he says. "No one else touches Miss Daisy unless it's life or death. Besides, I had to fill my lonely Saturday afternoon. My girl was too busy to see me."

Rico describes the installation in detail, using terms like "velocity-sensitive," and "hydraulic damping" that would normally send me rushing into my fantasy TV show to develop a new recipe. But as we weave through the twinkling lights of Austin's evening traffic, I stay in the moment, smiling over the two words purring in my ears:

My Girl.

·· ♥ ··

"I'm so jealous," Kali whispers, as Lauren rattles on about her boyfriend, Trey. "Do you know how rare that is?"

Syd has removed her jacket to reveal a vintage *London Calling* T-shirt. I actually know a lot about '80s bands like the Clash because Dad is a big fan. At least, he used to be. Since we moved, he only listens to jazz. He must think that's a cool, single dad thing to do.

"Yup," Syd says, pulling a collapsible bowl from her knapsack and filling it with water for Banksy. Dieter didn't look thrilled about the dog's return, but Father Casey's word must be the law at St. Joe's. "Eric found it for me on eBay."

"Is Eric your boyfriend?" Kali asks. "Mr. Complicated?"

"Hey," Simon says. "Rude dudes. Lauren's talking about Trevor. Can you keep it down?"

Kali, Syd, and I smother a laugh. "For the record, her boy-friend's name is Trey," I say.

"Since when do you care about the Shopaholic's love life?" Syd asks.

"Nothing wrong with a little shopping," Evan joins in. "A trip to the mall can cure what ails you."

Kali stares at him. "You really are stoned."

Dieter claps three times. "Let's stay focused." He looks more human today in a golf shirt and jeans, although the jeans have been ironed and the fluorescent lights reflect off his polished loafers. "Lauren was telling us how hard it was to bump into her mom and her new boyfriend over the weekend."

"It's fine," Lauren says. "Because Trey was with me. I don't know what I'd do without him."

I expect Syd to mock this, but she's staring down at her T-shirt, absentmindedly tracing the lettering. Evan is so riveted by this that when Syd finally looks up, she says, "Eyes off. Or lose them."

Dieter claps again. "Let's wrap up for today." He opens his briefcase and pulls out the tourist map of Austin I made, along with a sparkly, fuchsia scrapbook. No mystery about who put together the presentation for the opposing team.

Holding one in each hand, Dieter says, "And the winner of the Transitions Fall Session Scavenger Hunt is . . . everyone."

"It was a tie?" Kali asks. She reaches for the scrapbook and flips through it. "What the hell?"

She passes the scrapbook to Syd and me to check out. The only photo that corresponds to the scavenger hunt is one of Simon pushing Lauren into the fountain at UT. Most of the other pictures are of Simon and Evan posing with salesgirls in high-end stores. The final shot features Lauren standing in front of the Barton Creek Mall sign, flanked by Simon and Evan, who are loaded down with shopping bags.

"What happened?" I ask, trying not to jump to conclusions.

"These jokers wouldn't take the scavenger hunt seriously, that's what happened," Lauren says. "Two hours of their screwing around—and wet clothes—and I'd had it. So I went to the mall, and I couldn't shake them."

The guys joined her in the shops when they realized Lauren was the ticket to hitting on pretty salesgirls. Judging by the photos, they grabbed dinner together and closed out the mall.

"Simon has a good eye for a bargain," Lauren says, looking sheepish.

"Dieter, they blew off the exercise," Syd says. "Our team solved every single riddle and we've got the pictures to prove it. We won, fair and square."

"Yeah," I say. "We kicked ass. You can't declare all of us winners."

"In life there are winners and losers, and the losers have to learn to accept it," Kali says. "Isn't that the lesson here?"

Dieter shakes his head. "You spent time together. You got to know each other. You're standing up for each other now. Therefore, you're all winners." He starts packing up. "End of lesson."

·· ♥ ··

"We were robbed," Kali says, leading Syd and me through the basement corridor into the kitchen of St. Joe's. "Instead of running around and wracking our brains over those stupid clues, we could have spent the day shopping, too."

"Except that we wouldn't have," I say, hopping up onto the counter to watch Kali open cupboards and drawers to collect Styrofoam cups and plastic cutlery. "We had to blackmail Syd as it was."

"I admired your ingenuity," Syd says, refilling her water bottle for Banksy. "But right now I'm wondering about Kali's morals—stealing from a church?"

"I'll replace these with eco-friendly alternatives," Kali says. "I think God and Father Casey would approve."

She hands a box to each of us and picks up a third. "Let's get out of here."

"Isn't this stuff going to end up in a landfill anyway?" I ask, as we climb the stairs and take the main hallway toward the exit.

"Nope, because we're taking it to the Maternity Ward. That gorgeous guy we met uses reclaimed objects for his art."

Syd shakes her head. "He only does giant boob jobs, and I'm not sure there's a big market for them."

Kali isn't listening, because she's peeking into Father Casey's office. "Check it out," she whispers.

Father Casey is sitting in an old leather club chair across from Dieter, who's slouched in a matching chair, one leg slung over the arm. Dieter is gesticulating wildly as he tells a story that includes a fall into a fountain and a giant splash. They're still laughing as we continue on down the hall.

"So the hard-ass routine is a front," Kali says as we clear the church grounds and head up the street to the bus stop. "He's probably writing a book about us."

Syd doesn't comment, because she's dropped behind us

to stare into an electronics store.

Kali and I stop and look back. "What's wrong?"

"I see someone I know," Syd says. "In line at the register."

"Mr. Complicated?" Kali asks, reading Syd's expression. "Should we wait for him?"

Syd shakes her head and joins us. "No. Let's go."

As we pass the store's parking lot, I'm the one who stops. "Hey, that's my boyfriend's car."

Kali glances down at the plates and looks at me strangely. "But that's *my* boyfriend's car."

Syd looks from me to Kali and back to the car. Her voice is raspier than ever when she says, "Miss Daisy."

"What's going on?" Kali asks, clutching her box of contraband kitchen supplies so tight that it collapses and Styrofoam cups spill into the street. "I don't get it."

Syd grabs each of us by the arm and pulls us behind a pickup truck. "Give it a minute. You will."

"But—" Kali starts.

"Get down," Syd says, setting her box on the ground and crouching.

Rico comes around the corner, wearing faded jeans and an old cowboy hat. He's whistling a tune I don't recognize.

"It's Rico," I say.

"It's Rick," Kali says.

"It's Eric," Syd finishes.

Unaware that three sets of eyes are peering at him over the bed of the truck, Eric unlocks the driver's door, rolls down the windows, and tosses a bag and his hat onto the passenger seat. Then he unties his sneakers and takes them off before sliding behind the wheel.

When he pulls out of the lot, still whistling, we crumple to the pavement.

.. ♥ ..

Kali jumps up and kicks the tire of the pickup truck. "Rat bastard!"

I'm still trying to digest the news. The Rico I know would never do something like this. The Rico I know is loyal and loving and sweet.

The Rico I know doesn't exist.

What seemed like the truest, best thing in my life was a terrible lie.

We stand beside the truck as Syd scrolls through a dozen pictures on her cell phone. Most of them are of her with Rico, posing cheek to cheek. There's even a picture of them with two people who appear to be Rico's parents.

Kali gropes in her bag for a CD. On the cover is a photo of Rico standing behind her with his arms wrapped around her waist, and his chin resting on her head.

As it turns out, Rico has three identities and no conscience.

"I think I'm going to faint," I say.

Kali pushes me down and puts my head between my knees. "Breathe," she says. "It's just a guy."

Tears sting my eyes as I think about Rico driving off in Miss Daisy, completely oblivious to the devastation he's left in his wake. My sweet, considerate boyfriend managed to keep not one, but *two* other girlfriends without raising any red flags.

I wasn't even important enough for him to tell me his real name. Because if Syd knows his family, Eric has to be his real name.

Only an expert cheat could be that good. And only a desperate sap could be so blind. I'm a terrible judge of character. My parents ruined me. I've been so determined to have a stable relationship in my life that I invented one. Therapy is exactly where I belong.

Now that I'm looking, I realize the signs were everywhere. He was often too busy to see me. He didn't call when he said he would. He didn't like talking about his friends or family. And he never planned too far ahead.

"I made him cookies," I say.

"Peanut butter and chocolate?" Kali asks. "I loved those."

"He gave you my cookies?" Somehow that hurts more than anything else.

"He said his mom made them," Kali says, gathering her things. "Well, Rick—Eric—is a douche bag and I'm going right over to his house to tell him so." She takes a few steps and turns back. "Where does he live?"

I'd laugh if I could. Instead, I rest my head against Banksy's side and he gives me a sympathetic nudge.

"Making a scene at his house isn't payback," Syd tells Kali.

"Got a better plan?" Kali asks.

"Yeah," Syd says. "I do. I'm going to hit Eric Skinner where it hurts the most. And you two are going to help."

.. ♥ ..

He loves me, he loves me NOT. He loves me NOT. He loves me NOT. He—

"Zahra? What are you doing here?" Saliyah is standing in the doorway of the bedroom looking worried. Obviously the signs of my crying jag are quite visible. I'd planned to do a makeup repair job before everyone got home, but they're early.

After leaving Syd and Kali, I found myself on the bus heading to Anderson Mill, where I knew I could be alone for a while since everyone was supposed to be at the mosque hearing a guest lecturer. All I wanted was to lie on my old bed in my old room, but of course my room now belongs to my grandparents. So instead I'm in Saliyah's room, on the twin bed I use when I'm here, with my laptop open in front of me.

"What happened?" my sister asks. "Is Dad okay?"

"He's fine," I say, motioning for her to close the door. "How come you're home early?"

"Nani got into an argument with some lady she knew from Karachi. I think it was over a recipe, but they were talking so fast I couldn't keep up." She leans over me and stares at the barnyard scene I've created on my laptop. "Why did you stick Rico's head on a worm's body?"

"Actually, it's a snake," I say. Pointing to the Rico-faced animal above it, I add, "And that's a jackass."

Saliyah coils herself onto the other bed. She's shot up a couple of inches since I moved out. She might end up taller than me, and I'm five-foot-eight—taller than my grandparents and Mom. "So you two had a fight," she says.

Closing the laptop, I roll over on the bed and bury my face in the pillow. "I don't want to talk about it."

"I bet he tried making some moves on you," she guesses. "Did you slap him?"

If only it were that simple. "I'd love to slap him," I mumble into the pillow. "Because he cheated on me."

"Oh," she says. "That's bad. Did you catch him with the other girl?"

"I don't want to talk about it," I repeat. Because I can't. I'm barely holding it together as it is. Getting here on two buses without sobbing in public was the hardest thing I've ever done. This was the single worst day of my life—worse even than the day my parents split, I think, because I never wanted to throw up then. Today I had to sit on the bathroom floor for an hour, just in case.

That's where I was when Rico texted me to suggest getting together on Sunday. Eventually, I typed back three words with trembling fingers: "Can't. Too busy." I'm not sure what I'll be busy doing yet, but Syd and Kali and I are meeting on Saturday to develop a payback plan that we'll execute on Sunday. Rico texted back, and I kept my answer short and vague, but friendly enough, as instructed by Syd. "Raise no suspicions," she'd said. It was hard not to say more, to ask how he could do this to me, how he could be so heartless. He called me his "girl." I thought he loved me—that we had a future together. Meanwhile, he was going for the gold in the heartbreaker Olympics.

Saliyah sits in silence for a few minutes before announcing, "Guys suck. Don't they, Dewey?" Dewey is my old gray plush kangaroo. "Big-time," she answers, using her Dewey voice. "Do you agree, Monkey Man?"

"It won't work, Saliyah." My words are muffled by the pillow. I used to put on shows for her featuring Dewey and Monkey Man, my ratty old chimpanzee. When I moved I left my collection of stuffed animals behind. They belong here, with my old life.

"I don't know if ALL guys suck," Saliyah continues as Monkey Man. "Because *we're* guys, right?" She moves from her bed to perch on mine and continues. "I mean, I've always assumed we are, Dewey. Just wait a second while I check. . . . Nope! No nasty bits on me! Or you." She dances a stuffed animal onto my shoulder. "In fact, you don't even have a pouch, Dewey. So I pronounce us . . . Gender Neutral."

I turn my head, and somehow, miraculously, my lips twitch. "Lucky stuffies. No broken hearts for them."

"I hope you dumped that cheating jackass," my sister says, in her own voice.

"Saliyah! Such language!" Nani is standing in the doorway, glowering.

"That door was closed, Nani," I say.

"I heard odd voices coming from your sister's room," she says. "I was concerned."

"It's fine," I say. "Can you please leave us alone?"

"Who cheated?" she asks. "This Vico?" She deliberately gets his name wrong.

"I don't want to talk about it," I say.

Nani steps into the room, takes my sister's arm, and pulls her to her feet. "Go make us some tea. You shouldn't be hearing this."

Saliyah is indignant. "I know all about players, Nani. And Zahra needs me right now."

My protector tries to fight Nani off with Monkey Man, and loses the battle as my grandmother grabs the stuffed animal and throws it onto the other bed. "Tea," Nani says, shoving her out the door. "Downstairs."

Nana arrives as my sister leaves. This is getting better by the second.

"Vico cheated on Zahra," Nani says.

Nana shakes his head. "I warned you, boys are trouble. Especially American boys. You need to start spending time at the mosque."

"How would that help?" I ask.

Nana looks surprised. "In every way. It's time to think of your spiritual growth."

I fall back on the bed. "Forget it."

Bangles jangling, Nani grabs my wrist and pulls me into a sitting position. "You would also meet some fine young men there."

"Americans have no character," Nana says.

I suspect his rant is really about my dad, who—in Nana's mind—deserted his family, but I'm not up to that fight right now. "Nana, Saliyah and I are American, and even Mom's an American citizen now. We have character. Anyway, I don't want to meet any boys. Ever again."

Mom appears in the doorway in a salwar kameez and scarf. Even in my current state, that makes me furious. If she's hitting the mosque in full gear on a Thursday night, my grandparents have won the war. That's why they're moving on to me.

"Vico cheated," Nani tells my mother.

I try to flop back on the bed, but she still has my wrist in a jingling vise.

"Why don't you take out an ad in the paper?" I ask. "There's no privacy in this house."

"If you behaved properly you'd have no cause for secrets," Nana says.

I glare at him. "Are you saying this is *my* fault?"

"I'm saying you have poor judgment, like many young girls. You need guidance."

"Not from you," I say. "You're trying to turn me into something I'm not."

"Yes, a more responsible person," he says.

I turn to my mother and say, "Feel free to jump in anytime."

"Let's all calm down and talk about what happened," she says, pushing back her scarf and smoothing her hair. There's a streak of gray in it that I never noticed before.

"I got taken for a ride, that's what happened. And apparently it was all my fault."

"It's not your fault that guys suck," my sister says, nudging Mom aside with her tray as she enters the room.

There are two mugs on the tray, and Nani reaches for one. "I asked for tea," she says.

"Your tea is downstairs," Saliyah says, herding everyone out. "The hot chocolate is for Zahra." She closes the door behind them and turns back to me. "Because everything is better with a little sugar."

chapter 5

Kali paces the length of the war room, also known as her kitchen, where we've assembled to review our plan to annihilate Eric-Rick-Rico (a four-letter word no matter what it spells). In her arms is an assortment of junk food, which she distributes among the three of us. She deposits two bags of chips in front of me, four bags in front of Syd, and keeps one bag for herself. "The size of the pig-out must equal the severity of the heartbreak, which correlates directly to the amount of time spent together," she says.

"You're just a one-bagger?" I ask, tearing open some BBQ chips. I don't have much of an appetite, but fat and salt may help to revive it. "How long were you together?"

"About a month," Kali says, adding a Symphony bar to her stash. She opens it and shoves a few squares into her mouth. "It was intense while it lasted, but I'm over him now."

"In a day and a half?" I ask, surprised.

She gives me a chocolaty smile. "It helps that I met Owen Gaines last night. Notts County did a benefit for Eco-Nauts. My friend's brother got us backstage, and Owen actually *talked* to me."

"Wow," I say. "Impressive." Owen Gaines is about twenty-two, and his band is starting to get a lot of play. Kali is a cut above the average groupie. "What did he say?"

"Just 'Hey.' But it's a start."

Alternating between handfuls of nachos and corn chips, Syd says, "Is there a point to this story?"

"Just that Owen is *way* cuter than Eric," Kali says.

"So you meet a cute guy, and blam, you're over your cheating boyfriend just like that?" Syd asks, spraying a cloud of cheesy dust in Kali's direction.

"Not just *any* cute guy," Kali says. "A famous musician."

Syd gives Kali a look. "Not that famous."

"Yet," Kali says. But then she drops the carefree front. "Of course I'm not over Rick. I'm so pissed off I want to smash every dish in this kitchen. Since that's not an option, I'm trying to keep my blood pressure stable with distractions. You deal your way, I'll deal mine."

"Fair enough," I say, to bring the temperature down. If we can't keep it civil, Operation Eric will never come off. And I *need* it to come off. We all do.

Kali climbs onto a stool at the marble-topped island and looks at me. "How long were you and Eric together?"

"Nine weeks," I say, opening my second bag of chips. "And I really liked him." That's a major understatement, but there's no need to explain how my insides feel gutted with a sharp knife. No matter how much Kali, Syd, and I apparently have in common, we've only known each other a couple of weeks.

Anyway, it's obvious that we're all miserable. Kali's normally bright face is pale, and her hair's hanging in limp pigtails. Syd has skipped her usual kohl eyeliner because her eyelids are too puffy to hold a straight line. And my face and neck are covered in blotches, like hives.

The only reason any of us got out of bed today was to plot revenge. It's quite a resuscitator.

"At least you two didn't waste over a year of your life on that bastard," Syd says, settling briefly on a stool before getting up again to pace. "All I did was ask Eric for a little space to get over what happened with my dad. Eric knows I need to be alone when I'm dealing with stuff, because he's exactly the same way. When his grandfather died last year, I backed off until he was ready to talk."

"Maybe he thought you'd broken up," I say, feeling hope rise at the possibility that Eric misunderstood, and believed he was a free man.

Syd shakes her head. "We talked, we texted, and I saw him most weekends. But I used to see him nearly every day, before my parents split. I guess he felt my pulling away gave him permission to cheat." She stares at the ceiling and swallows hard. "Either that, or I never really knew him at all."

Morbid curiosity gets the best of me. "Listen, can I ask you guys something? Did Eric ever take you hunting for wild parrots?"

On our first date, Eric told me about the wild parrots that pop up around Austin. More than once, he showed up in Daisy after hearing reports of a sighting, and we went on a parrot safari. Although we never found them, I considered the search "our thing," and I desperately want to keep it that way.

Kali doesn't have to say a word for me to see it wasn't our thing, but Eric's thing—with every girl. It was a ploy to reel us all in. "I'm sorry," she says. "We went looking the day before group started. I thought the parrots were an urban myth."

The knife that gutted me seems to be twisting in Syd too, because she presses a paint-stained hand to her throat for a second. "Quaker parrots," she says. "The little green-and-blue ones. Eric was obsessed with them."

Kali's phone rings, and she squawks, "Oh my God, it's him!" She drops the phone on the counter as if it had burned her hand. "He texted me while I was at the concert last night, too." She looks at Syd. "Don't worry, I stuck to the rule: short, neutral answers."

"Me too," Syd says. "Let's keep it that way until we're finished with him. We have to keep the upper hand."

A horrible thought occurs to me. "You don't think . . . that there might be other girls? I mean, besides the three of us?"

Frowning, Kali reaches for the chocolate again. "It's possible. But I don't see how he'd have the time. He must have been pretty busy, coordinating all of us along with going to school and working."

After a few minutes of intense junk food therapy, I decide we need a break from the relationship postmortem. "Kali, this kitchen is amazing. Every appliance I've ever dreamed about is right here. Is your mom a professional chef?"

"She can barely work the coffeemaker," Kali says. "My latest stepdad designed this kitchen. He was a great cook."

"You don't keep in touch?" I ask.

Kali's smile fades, and she turns to get sodas out of the refrigerator. "I think Mom scares them off. I have no idea where my stepdads are—or my real father, for that matter."

No wonder Kali's a repeat at group. My dad's a workaholic,

but at least he's around occasionally—especially since I'm supposedly grounded because of the fire. Luckily, Dad's more lax than Mom. If I overload him with texts and calls, he feels like he has the situation under control, yet can't quite remember where I said I was.

"Don't worry, I'm used to it," Kali says, showing me how to use the ice dispenser. "My real dad left before I was two. Stepdad One stuck around four years, Stepdad Two hung in for another four, and Greg didn't even last two." She sighs. "I try not to get too attached, but Greg was a great guy."

"Time to stop looking back and start looking forward," Syd announces. "Let's figure out what to do about Eric."

"Who's Eric?" Like Kali, the woman standing in the doorway is tall, slim, and attractive, but her eyes and curls are darker. "And why is a stranger stroking my blender?"

"Actually, it's a limited edition pro series stand mixer with a flour power rating of fourteen cups," I say, offering my hand to the woman. "I'm Zahra, Kali's friend from group."

"I'm Glennis. Kali's mom."

"Notice she didn't give a last name," Kali says. "It changes so often she can't keep track."

"Not funny, Kalista." Glennis sees our soda cans sitting on rubber coasters on the island and swaps them out for fancy wooden ones. "Those coasters are disgusting."

"They're made from recycled car tires," Kali says.

"With recycled roadkill at no extra cost," Glennis says, placing the chips and dip in ceramic bowls. "Honestly, Kali, can't you make things nice for your guests?"

"Why waste water cleaning glasses and bowls we don't need?" Kali asks.

I jump in to lighten the mood. "This is Sydney and her dog, Banksy."

Glennis stoops to rub Banksy's head, and he wags his stump of a tail. "What a handsome boy." Taking a tin of dog biscuits out of the cupboard, Glennis offers one to Banksy, who takes it gently. "One of these days I'll have another dog of my own."

"Your next husband might have one," Kali suggests. "Give it a week."

Glennis shoots her a warning look. "I guess you named him after the English artist?" she says to Syd.

It's the first time I've seen Syd smile since we saw Eric in the parking lot. "Yeah. He's sort of my idol. If I had one." Glennis chats to Syd for a few moments about Banksy's work before asking me about my interest in cooking. I tell her about my dream of hosting my own show one day.

"I miss cooking," I say. "There's no room at Dad's, and it's a hassle at Mom's with my grandparents there, plus Ramadan starts soon."

"You don't fast?" Glennis asks.

I shake my head. "My dad's Scottish and my mom pretty much dropped her culture until my grandparents moved here recently. Now she's a born-again Muslim."

Glennis tactfully changes the subject. "So Kali, this Eric you mentioned. Is he from group too?"

"Top secret, Mom. Like Dieter says, 'What happens in group—'"

"Stays in group," Glennis finishes. "All right, I know when I'm not wanted." She picks up her purse and car keys and heads for the front door. "It was nice meeting you, girls. Zahra, feel free to use our kitchen any time."

When the door closes behind Glennis, I turn to Kali. "Your mom's pretty cool."

"Scratch the surface and you'll find a mess underneath," Kali says. "Hence the rotating husbands." Kali explains that while her mom works in marketing for a hotel chain, she's always wanted to be a photographer. "Maybe she'd settle down if she could follow her dream."

"Now you're psychoanalyzing Mom?" someone asks. "Don't you have enough of your own problems?"

The guy standing in the doorway has Kali's green eyes, Glennis's brown hair, and longer lashes than either of them. It's hard not to notice his muscular build, since he's standing shirtless with one hand on the refrigerator door. His feet are bare, and the waistband of his striped boxers shows above his jeans.

"Brody, we're having a private conversation," Kali says.

"In the kitchen. Where the food is."

He takes chocolate milk out of the fridge and chugs it directly from the carton. Then he offers the carton to me with a smile that could be dazzling if I found dark-haired guys with nice teeth appealing. I don't, anymore. Not even when they're much taller than I am, which used to be a big draw.

"I brushed my teeth," he says.

If he thinks backwash is charming, he's mistaken. "No thanks."

"Okay, you can use a glass," he says. "But I'll have to charge you for the water to wash it. Kali's rules."

"Brody, leave Zahra alone." Kali has that exasperated tone I use on Saliyah.

"It's fine," I say. "I just don't like chocolate milk." Or overconfident guys. Brody reminds me of Rico. If I recover from this enough to fall for someone else, it won't be with a Rico clone, but his polar opposite. Then I'll get character references and hire a private investigator to do a background check. I'll take nothing at face value, and I'll make the guy work like a dog to win me over. Zahra MacDuff is done with being a doormat.

"Everyone likes chocolate milk, Red," he says. "It's a universal truth."

"Don't call me Red." I hate that.

Brody leans against the counter, unfazed. "Did you know that only two percent of the population has red hair?"

"Actually, I did." Lucky me to be a part of such a minority.

"Did you know redheads are a dying breed?"

"Did *you* know redheads don't like hearing about their future extinction?" I ask.

He turns to Kali. "Uh-oh, another one of your friends has a crush on me. Will it never end?" Turning back to me, he adds, "Sorry, Red, I'm taken."

"You are not taken," Kali says, although that's hardly the point. The point is I wouldn't take *him* on a silver platter.

"I am," he says. "As of today. I met a goddess at the drugstore."

"Listen," Syd says, impatience getting the best of her, "I don't mean to be rude, but we've got a project to work on."

"More homework from group?" Brody asks.

We glare at Kali, and she holds up her hands. "*I* didn't tell him where we met."

Brody saws a three-inch slab off the banana loaf on the counter. "She didn't have to. I'm sorry to say it was obvious that you all need some anger management training."

Kali sighs. "Don't you have something better to do, Brody?"

He grins at Syd and me. "Just kidding. I assumed you're from group because the rest of Kali's friends smell like patchouli oil and weed."

Kali snatches a garlic bulb off the counter and hurls it at Brody. He dodges the garlic easily and it rebounds off the wall to hit Syd. Syd gives Brody a look that would burn the skin off someone with a thinner hide.

"At least *my* friends don't walk on their knuckles," Kali says.

"Ah, someone's still burned," he says. "Did she tell you guys about Rick *the dick*?" He wraps the last two words with air quotes.

Syd and I exchange a glance and silently agree to say nothing.

Brody assumes we're out of the loop. "Well, get ready for an earful. She hasn't let up for two days. Like it's my fault the dude was seeing other girls."

"You could have warned me he was taken," Kali says.

Brody's tooth wattage finally dims. "We've been over this, Kal. The guy's a friend of a friend. I didn't know he had a girlfriend. Or two." Tooth wattage amps up again. "Though, with moves like that, I should probably get to know him better."

"You promised you'd never speak to him again," Kali says.

"I said I'd avoid him *for a while*. Guys don't do the 'not speaking' thing. Besides, you only went out with him a few times."

"A few times?" Syd glares at Kali. "You said he was your boyfriend."

"He *was* my boyfriend," Kali says. "We spent weeks flirting at Brody's games, and once we got together, we were inseparable."

"You flirt with everyone, and it mostly doesn't mean

anything," Brody says around a mouthful of banana bread. "And being inseparable for a couple of weekends doesn't mean you're engaged."

Kali takes a deep breath and gives her brother a mellow smile. "I know when a guy's into me. Rick and I spent forty-eight hours together at a music festival, remember? I thought that really meant something."

Kali spent forty-eight hours straight with Rico? That *does* mean something. It means he liked her more than he liked me. I doubt I spent forty-eight hours with him over the entire course of our relationship. And they probably shared a sleeping bag.

"You're easily misled," Brody says. "That's why Mom stuck you back in group."

"And how did *you* manage to escape?" I ask.

"Aw, that's sweet," he says. "Red wants me at the Thursday Crazy Party."

"I know we just met," I say, "but it seems like you could benefit from a dose of Dieter."

"Still sane as far as I know," Brody says. "I'm not the one who ran away when my mom dumped Greg."

"I didn't *run away*." Kali plucks a couple of spoons from the dish rack and starts drumming on the counter with them. Greg's leaving must have been a bigger deal than she likes to let on.

"The basic definition of running away is leaving home without letting anyone know where you're going," Brody says. "And that's what you did."

"I seized an opportunity, that's all." Kali hits a pot hanging on a hook overhead. "I met a band on an open mic night and

I volunteered to be their roadie for a couple of gigs."

"Translation: she was in a bar underage and then climbed into a van with a bunch of stoners," Brody says. "Mom hauled her butt back from San Antonio after the club manager called from the next gig."

"She ruined everything. Do you know how lucky I was to tour with a band at my age?" Kali hits several pots in sequence. "And they weren't stoners."

"You just keep deluding yourself," Brody says, patting her back. "It takes the heat off me. Anyway, I'd love to stay and argue, but Fiesta Mart's shelves don't stock themselves." Grabbing what's left of my BBQ potato chips, he heads back down the hall.

"Hey, Brody," Kali calls after him. "Your friend Eric-Rick-Rico takes off his shoes before getting into his car. How lame is that?"

"You kissed him, not me," Brody calls back.

"Let's move this meeting," Kali says, gesturing to the window. At the end of the driveway, near the back of the house sits a rusty old trailer. "It belonged to Kevin, Stepdad One. Mom kept it because he gambled away half her savings, but she still hasn't sold it. Just one problem—I'm not sure where the keys are."

Syd pulls a Swiss Army knife out of her tote bag. "Keys are never a problem."

·· ♥ ··

"So?" Dad's voice makes me jump, and I quickly refresh my computer screen. "How's it going, honey?"

"Fine," I say. Dad used to stay late at the office nearly every night, but since the fire, he's been coming home early and working here instead. He also picked up a couple of books on helping kids cope with divorce. I found them on his nightstand, so he must want me to know he's studying up.

It won't do him much good, because I'm at the wheel now. I've decided that my parents are a bad influence and I don't need them. But there's no reason to crush them with news of their inadequacy. They've got enough problems. So for the time being, I'll live by my motto that everything is better with a little sugar. "I'm allowed to be on the Internet all weekend, Dad."

I love searching the net for quirky new Web sites, and once Dad and I moved, it turned into a bit of an obsession. Dad said I was becoming "withdrawn" and cut back my Internet time to weekends. A typical overreaction of the type that landed me in group. It's no surprise Dad assumes I'm getting a surfing high now.

"I know," he says. "I'm glad you're staying in touch with your friends."

Actually, I'm doing prep work for Operation Eric, which goes down tomorrow, although I did send happy-happy life-is-great notes to Shanna and Morgan earlier. I can't bring myself to tell them about what happened with Eric just yet.

"Have you made any new friends?" Dad persists, sitting on my bed and thumbing through my latest issue of *Interview* magazine.

I try to be patient. Dad didn't hang around chatting when we were still living with Mom. Back then, he was always too busy with work. Now that he's the only parent in the house, he's introduced these awkward Oprah moments.

"I've met some people." I don't intend to cough up details about group, although now I'm glad he forced me to go.

Otherwise, I'd still be getting played by Rico. Better to be informed and miserable than deluded and happy. I think.

"And how's Rico these days?" Dad glances up from the magazine, and I realize he knows. Mom must have been worried enough over Thursday's impromptu visit to send out a news alert.

"Fine, I guess." It already seems like eons since I found out about Eric. I guess that's because I've spent so much time going over every detail of our relationship: every date, every call, and every text, trying to figure out where I went wrong. I've concluded that I'm boring. The time I wasted scheming to keep my parents together should have been spent trying to become fascinating, like dark, arty-rebel Syd or carefree, sexy Kali. Sticking too close to home has made me as precise and predictable as my recipes.

But that's all going to change. I'm putting myself first from now on. After all, I'll never land my own cooking show if I put an audience to sleep.

Dad says, "I heard you and Rico broke up."

I sigh. "It's okay, Dad. We hadn't gone out that long."

"You're too young to tie yourself to one boy anyway," Dad says. "At this age, they're all trouble."

I give him a sly grin. "Nana says the same thing."

There's no love lost between Nana and Dad, but he blunders on. "Forget about dating for a while. One day, you'll meet the right person and just know."

"Right. Because that strategy worked for you."

He closes the magazine. "I did marry the right person—at the time. But somehow your mother and I—"

"—grew apart. I know."

The breach opened around the time Dad started his own graphic design company. Mom got frustrated that he was never home, and he got frustrated that she didn't see how hard he had to work. I did what I could to try to get them to see things from each others' perspective, and even set up "dates" for them. Last Valentine's Day, for example, I cooked a four-course dinner and took Saliyah to a movie so my parents could be alone. For their twentieth anniversary, in April, I packed a fabulous meal and sent them to see a free outdoor performance of *Love's Labour's Lost*.

I did my part, but they didn't hold up their end of the bargain. They gave up on our family.

I've vowed not to say it, but the words slip out anyway. "You could try again."

"It's not that easy," he says, standing and edging toward the door.

At the very least, this line of attack usually gets him off my back. "Any parenting book will tell you not to shut down conversations just because they make you uncomfortable."

"Log off," he calls over his shoulder. "I brought home take-out."

It's curry again. I can already smell it. Dad used to complain about Mom's cooking, so I figured when he cut out on his own it would be steak and potatoes all the way. Instead all he wants is curry.

It's the sign of a man in denial. But denial means there's hope of a reunion. So I'll push some curry around my plate without complaining. Consider it an investment in my future.

chapter 6

The bus that runs along East 12th Street is empty except for the three of us and a couple of guys with baggy pants and shaggy hair who look like they're heading home after an all-night party. When we stop at a light, I see a handful of seniors in tie-dyed shirts assembling their paints and easels on the corner. Otherwise the sidewalks are deserted. I guess most of Austin is still sleeping off its Saturday night.

"Screwdrivers?" I ask, taking inventory. "Wrenches, pliers, and flashlights?"

Kali rattles a large toolbox. "Check."

"Cameras, superglue, spare batteries, and spray paints?" I continue.

"Check." Syd pats the knapsack sitting on the empty seat beside her. "None of it's biodegradable."

Kali shrugs. "Desperate times call for toxic measures."

"I've got the overalls, gloves, and owner's manual," I say. "Plus the secret ingredient." I tap my foot on the cooler in front of me. "Fish guts—three days old and at their prime."

Banksy's been showing an awful lot of interest in the

cooler, so Syd pulls him around to her other side. Dogs aren't allowed on Metro buses, but Syd nonchalantly flashed the medic alert bracelet she got off the Internet, and the driver didn't bat an eye. "Looks like we're good to go," she says.

"Not quite." Kali takes a comb, blush, and lip gloss out of her bag. "You two have to look extra hot today. Z, you'll need to unleash the hair later."

I put makeup on this morning, but it obviously wasn't enough to conceal the signs of insomnia. At least the hives are fading, although they probably mean I've become allergic to love. Reaching for Kali's makeup and a compact, I apply rose lip gloss and blush. Rico doesn't deserve the effort, but looking nice will give me the psychological advantage.

Syd looks good in faded jeans and a fitted red vintage top that shows off her athletic physique. Her eyelids are still too puffy for liner, but she's made up for it with dramatic shadow and flaming lips. At Kali's prompting, she runs the comb through her sleek hair.

I pull out a container of hand cream and pass it to Kali after using it myself.

"That smells amazing," she says. "Sort of like chai tea."

"My mom makes her own natural beauty products," I say, handing Syd a coriander lime cream instead. "We don't want Eric to notice we smell the same."

When the bus lets us off near the Albany Hotel, a Chihuahua at the end of a rhinestone-studded leash growls at Banksy. The girl holding the leash doesn't look much friendlier than her dog, despite a T-shirt that reads EASY TO PLEASE in sparkly letters. Pulling Banksy away, Syd leads us down the block to our base of command: a parking lot behind a dry cleaner that's closed for the day.

Kali goes over the plan, although we did a thorough dry run yesterday. "At oh-nine-hundred hours, Syd meets Eric at Copelin's Bakery."

That stings a bit. Eric had a shift scheduled at the music store where he works, but he dropped it the second Syd called. As far as I know, Eric never once changed his plans for me.

"At oh-nine-ten," Kali continues, "Syd texts us to confirm the target's in position and she's liberated the car keys. At oh-nine-twenty, Syd meets us at the back door with the keys. At oh-nine-thirty, after the security guard finishes his morning rounds, Zahra and I get to work. At ten thirty, you two switch off and Syd does her stuff. At eleven ten, Syd and Zahra switch back and we regroup here, well before the guard does his noon circuit."

We chose this location for a good reason. As it turns out, Syd's dad owns the Albany and plans to turn it into a boutique hotel in a couple of years. With the hotel and the bakery being in a dodgy area, Syd suggested that Eric leave Miss Daisy behind the hotel and got her dad to clear it with security.

"My dad's stupid real estate scheme is finally good for something," she says.

When Mr. Stark inherited money last year, he quit his job as a landscape worker for the city and poured every cent he had into the Albany. If this venture fails, he'll be bankrupt.

Standing watch at the corner, Kali announces, "Miss Daisy's pulling into the Albany now."

Syd kicks a recycling bin with a steel-toed combat boot that leaves a dent. "I can't do this," she says, running both hands through her hair. "I can't. Zahra, you distract him."

"Calm down," Kali says, coming over. "We're going to stick with the plan. Eric came to see you, Syd. Not Zahra, and not me. You want payback, don't you?"

Syd's breath comes in short panicky bursts. "I thought I could face him, but I can't."

"Sit," I say, gesturing to the curb. "Kali, give me your purse."

Kali hands it over, but tries to snatch it back when she realizes what I'm after.

"A smoke will calm her down," I say, although I'm really just creating a distraction for Syd.

"Gauloises!" Syd says, as I toss her the pack. "Are you kidding me?"

"Give them back," Kali says.

"Picasso smoked Gauloises," Syd says. "Eric's favorite artist."

Kali just shrugs. "So?"

"Where'd you get them? They don't even import Gauloises anymore."

"You can find anything on the Internet," Kali says. "Like your medic alert bracelet."

Syd pulls out a cigarette and runs it under her nose. "Straight out of a museum," she says, offering the cigarette to me. "Stale—with a faint hint of poseur."

"Well, you don't think I'd pollute my lungs for a guy, do you?" Kali says, tossing the pack back into her bag. "Anyway, Zahra's worse. She faked an interest in art and his favorite band."

"Plus spicy food," I offer.

"Poseur times three," Syd says. I notice she looks calmer now. My distraction technique has worked.

"I bet you faked stuff with Eric too," Kali says. "That's why you won't give us details."

"That's not why," Syd says. "And I was one hundred percent honest with him."

"All the more reason to stand tall when you face him," I say, hauling her to her feet, and taking Banksy's leash. "Give him our love."

"Not," Kali calls after her, and Syd manages a faint laugh.

Kali slides the flat head screwdriver all around the windshield, under the weather stripping. "According to my research, we should be able to peel this off now." She tugs gently at the black rubber, and sure enough, it begins to separate from the glass. "With the storm coming in later, this baby'll leak big-time." She reaches over and snaps the clip that holds the windshield wiper in place so that it will fly off after one or two passes. "For good measure."

Pulling the pail of fish guts out of the cooler, I distribute its contents in a few hard-to-reach locations under the hood. Once I stop gagging, I say, "It's a hot day. Miss Daisy is going to smell fantastic."

I worried that when push came to shove I'd feel guilty about trashing Eric's beloved car. Instead, I feel euphoric. It's as if the scales of justice are being rebalanced.

We use a couple of screwdrivers to deflate the tires, and daub glue onto the valve caps before replacing them.

"I'll finish while you freshen up," Kali says, tossing me a container of baby wipes and pointing to something on my cheek with one gloved finger. "You're on in five."

The euphoria fizzles. "Remind me again why you couldn't do this?" I ask, peeling off my latex gloves and dirty overalls. "You're the performer."

"It makes more sense that you'd be checking out a bakery," she says. "And I—"

Her own singing cuts her off. It's her new ringtone:

Eric Rick Rico, one guy with three names
It isn't a shock he'd get caught playing games
Eric Rick Rico, one guy with three girls
He's not going to like how this story unfurls.

"Catchy," I say. "I'm not sure about that 'unfurls' line, though."

"Everyone's a critic," Kali says, reading the text. "It's Syd. All systems go."

·· ♥ ··

My legs feel rubbery as I step inside Copelin's Bakery and see Eric's profile. He's sitting alone in a booth.

Step one of my role is to place my order, turn around, and look surprised when I see him. Shaking my hair back, I walk to the counter and stall over the selection as long as I can before finally turning to the condiment stand with my coffee and a bag of croissants.

Eric is hiding behind an oversized menu. Hiding! The guy who had the guts to juggle three girlfriends has suddenly lost his nerve. He's afraid of what Syd might do if she comes out of the restroom to find me fawning all over him.

What he doesn't know is that Syd's already behind the

Albany applying a fresh coat of paint to Miss Daisy. All I have to do is keep him occupied for the half hour she needs. "Rico!" I call.

He lowers the menu and gives me a forced smile—an Eric smile, not a Rico smile, and the fact that I now know the difference sends a shiver down my spine. My hand twitches to grab his menu and beat him over the head with it.

"Hey, Zahra," he says. "What brings you to this part of town?"

"I wanted to check the place out for ideas. It's gotten some great reviews lately."

After a glance toward the restroom, he half stands and gives me a peck on the cheek. "You look great," he says. "I love that top."

I know he does. That's why I wore it, although it was kind of like choosing what to wear to my own funeral. Our relationship is dead and all that's left is today's memorial service.

Picking up his fork, Eric moves a few bits of lettuce around on his otherwise empty plate. I slide into the booth opposite him without waiting to be asked.

"Where's your friend?" I ask, pointing to Syd's meal, which is sitting in front of me virtually untouched. "Or are you eating for two?"

"Restroom," he says. "Just a buddy from the art gallery. You don't know him."

Actually, I never met any of Eric's friends, a warning sign I managed to ignore.

"He'll be back any second and we have to take off," Eric says. "How about I pick you up later and we go on a safari? I heard some parrots turned up in Pleasant Valley."

No one will be volunteering for a ride in Miss Daisy anytime soon. "I can't today. I've got stuff to do. Let's just hang for a few minutes now."

"Actually, I said I'd pay and wait for my friend at the car," Eric says, sliding to the edge of the booth.

"Okay, I'll walk with you. Just let me get this." I pretend my phone is vibrating and quickly text Syd: *Rat about 2 run. Use 911 plan.*

Eric's phone rings almost instantly. "Oh, hey. Where'd you get to?" I make a show of staring around the shop while he talks. "He is? He must've gotten into some garbage, poor guy. Want me to drive you? Okay, no worries, I'll wait. Call when you're on your way back."

As he puts the phone away, the old Rico smile emerges like the sun from behind the clouds. Sydney's plan worked beautifully. She told him that Banksy was tied up out back, and when she checked on him he wasn't feeling well. So now she's supposedly taking him to her dad's condo a few blocks away.

"We've got a few minutes to catch up while my pal runs an errand," Eric says, getting out of the booth and sliding onto my bench. "There, that's better." He sniffs the back of my neck and murmurs, "I love the way you smell."

I know he does. That's why I used my mom's vanilla sugar shampoo for the last time. I'll never be able to use it again without thinking of today.

I slide away from him until I'm crammed up against the wall. "So, how have you been?"

He slides down to join me. "Great, but I've missed you. I haven't seen you in ages."

"It's only been three days." We've gone longer than that

many times, when his dance card was full.

"Nearly four," he says. "And you've barely answered my texts."

Just enough to keep him from getting suspicious. "Busy time," I say. "Would you mind if I ordered something?"

"Uh, sure." Checking his watch, he summons the waiter and orders for me. "The lady will have the cheese omelet, with cheddar, not jack. And a latte with honey." He looks at me to confirm.

Eric is good. We only had breakfast once, yet he remembers exactly what I ordered. I nod at the waiter. "Perfect. Thanks."

Taking my hand, he leans in even closer. "Is everything okay? You seem on edge."

He's the one who should be on edge, but now he's calm and cool. I guess a professional liar gets used to living that way.

"It's been a bad week," I say.

"I'm sorry to hear that. Anything I can do?"

His blue eyes are so kind, so sincere, that I have a momentary pang. What if this has all been one big misunderstanding? Syd's not a big talker. She might not have spelled out exactly what she wanted. And Kali, well, she was probably just a flirty friend with Eric's taste in music. If he really thought he was single—

I pinch my leg under the table. This is the kind of delusional thinking I used to explain his inconsistent behavior throughout our entire relationship. Answering texts while we were out together, ignoring my phone calls, making and breaking dates at the last minute? I justified it by telling myself he's popular. He's busy. He's important. And that I was lucky to be a part of his life. Ha! What a joke that turned out to be. Even now, when Eric expects Syd to walk back in soon, his arm is snaking around my shoulder. The guy is shameless.

Once I put my mind to it, it's not hard to get him talking, and by the time my breakfast arrives, I'm calm enough to force some food down. Eric eats the fries.

He gets up to pay the bill just as the all clear text arrives from Syd: *Mission accomplished. Clear out so I can return keys.*

"It was so great to see you," he says, walking me out of the diner. "Let's talk soon. There's something I've been wanting to tell you."

"No," I say, too hastily. "You don't have to tell me anything."

Eric looks surprised. "But it's something nice," he says, taking my hand. "*Really* nice."

Another nice, big *lie*. Well, I've heard enough of them.

I tug my hand out of his, but he grabs it again and pulls me toward him, sinking his other hand into my hair. His lips find mine, and my eyes start to close. Then I catch a glimpse of two heads—one blond, one dark—peeking around the dry cleaner's. I put one palm on Eric's chest and push. No matter how tempting it is to rest my head on his shoulder and forget this all happened, I can't. That's not how this story ends.

Eric looks even more surprised. In happier times, I never pulled away first. "Is everything okay?" he asks, as I disentangle his fingers from my hair.

"Fine, but I've got to go. Dad's been crazy uptight since the fire. Bye for now."

Bye forever, I think, as Eric walks back inside the bakery, and I run toward the dry cleaner's.

"What the hell was that?" Syd asks.

"He grabbed me," I say. "I had to play along so he didn't suspect anything."

"We all know the guy has a hot mouth," Kali says. "I would have kissed him once more myself if I'd had the chance."

This pisses Syd off even more. She powers up her camera and zooms in on the last frame. "If I see tongue, you're dead, Zahra."

"You filmed us?" I ask. "What for?"

"Evidence," Syd says. "You do the same."

She heads back to the bakery and stands outside waving until Eric joins her. Kali trains the camera on the door and sees Eric's face brighten at the sight of Syd. "Check out that dopey grin," Kali says, zooming in. "He sure never looked at me like that."

I swallow the lump in my throat. He never looked at me like that either. Not today, not ever. He's listening as if every word dropping from her red lips is a jewel. Obviously, Eric and Syd had something special. He didn't think they were on a break at all. He was just killing time until Syd took him off the back burner.

Eric rests his hands on Syd's shoulders, and I notice she's not pulling away either. Bending forward, he touches his forehead to hers briefly before kissing her. Syd closes her eyes for the merest second. When she opens them again, she says something that makes Eric's jaw drop. Then she shoves him away abruptly.

"Syd, wait, can't we talk about this?" he calls, as she breaks into a run. "Please! I—you!"

The middle word is cut off by the roar of a passing bus.

In the distance, Syd swipes at her face with the back of her hand before disappearing around a corner.

·· ♥ ··

Kali sits across from me at the trailer's fold-down kitchen table, idly strumming her guitar while I work on my laptop. Three feet away, Syd sprawls on a wooden bench strewn with throw cushions, staring at two little fans over the kitchen sink, which are working overtime to push a breeze through the tight space. Her phone buzzes for the fourth time since we left the scene of the crime, and she finally powers it down. Two minutes later, my phone starts to ring. I check the call display and turn my phone off too.

"Well, I guess we know where I stand in the pecking order," Kali says when her phone finally buzzes. She puts her guitar down to shut it off. "He said he loves you, didn't he?" she asks Syd.

For a minute or two, the only sound in the trailer is the tapping of computer keys as I work on a FOR SALE poster featuring a photo of Miss Daisy. On her hood is the sparkly unicorn leaping over a rainbow that Syd painted. We're listing the car at two hundred bucks, a ridiculously low price for a Charger. There are tear-away tags with Eric's cell phone number, which should hopefully trigger an avalanche of calls.

"If he loved me," Syd says at last, "he wouldn't have cheated on me. All I wanted was to take a breather. Turns out while I was doing the breathing, Eric was doing you. And Zahra."

"He wasn't *doing* me," I say.

"Or me," Kali adds, leaning over and taking three sodas out of the trailer's mini fridge. "If it makes you feel any better, he didn't even try—and we shared a tent at that music festival."

Actually, that makes *me* feel better.

Syd sighs. "In some ways, that's worse. He was making you CDs and oven mitts."

"It was a pot holder," I say.

"I don't care if it was a friggin' toilet seat cover," Syd says, popping the top on her soda. "My point is, this wasn't just about sex. He was *into* you. And Kali."

"But you're the only one he was actually in love with," I say. Whatever he wanted to tell me today, it wasn't that. To Eric, I'm purely B team.

Syd rolls onto her side and props herself up with a pillow. "If that's love, I want nothing to do with it. My mom got that kind of love from my dad, and it's messed her up plenty."

I pass around the croissants I bought at Copelin's Bakery this morning. "I'll eat to that."

Syd takes one and shares it with Banksy. "Are you going to finish that poster today or what?"

"Only if you stop distracting me with your girl talk," I say.

Grinning, Syd tosses the last piece of croissant at me. It goes straight into the hole of Kali's guitar.

"Hey!" Kali turns the guitar facedown and shakes the crumbs out of it. "A little respect, please."

The instrument is covered in scratches, the pick guard is chipped, the wood on the side is splintered, and two of the tuning pegs are missing.

"It's a piece of crap," Syd says.

"This piece of crap is all I have left from my real dad," Kali says. "Mom trashed most of his stuff, including this guitar. She says he cared more about his band than his family. That's why he left us."

Poor Kali. It must be horrible to be dumped by your own dad.

"I'm taking guitar lessons and saving up for a new guitar," Kali continues. "A good one."

"Z, I'm begging you. Finish up before she starts serenading us."

"Done," I say, hitting the PRINT button.

Kali takes the first poster out of the printer and laughs. Miss Daisy looks more like a parade float than a muscle car.

"Do you think he cried when he saw it?" Kali asks.

"I've never seen Eric cry, but I suppose if anything could break him, this would," Syd says. "That and the fact that Miz D won't see any action for a very long time."

A surge of adrenaline fills me, and I lift my soda can in the air. "To revenge! Let no man treat us like dirt again."

"To revenge," Kali and Syd repeat in unison as our drinks collide.

I've never been into sports, but this must be what it feels like after winning a play-off game. The strangest thing is that I didn't even know my "team" a few weeks ago.

"Let's celebrate," Kali says. "We can order sushi."

"I'm in," I say. I want to prolong this giddy feeling as long as I can. It won't last forever.

"Sorry," Syd says, punching a number into her phone. "I already have plans tonight. . . . Hey Mom, where are we meeting?" After a pause she turns away from us and lowers her voice. "Spanish lessons? Since when—? Well, what time does it—? Okay, then how about—?" With every fragmented sentence, Syd's sturdy shoulders droop more. "Right, spinning class. You wouldn't want to miss that." Syd's voice has grown eerily controlled. "No problem. Catch you later.

"On the bright side, Mom isn't as needy anymore," Syd says to us, hanging up. "Too bad it's too late to save my relationship." She raises her hand as Kali starts to speak. "I know—it wasn't worth saving."

"At least you can stay and celebrate now," I say.

"I have a better idea," Syd says, hooking up Banksy. "Let's go out."

·· ♥ ··

I catch the silver lighter with my right hand, staring at the tall, blond stranger in the tight pink dress.

"Don't just stand there, sweetie," the drag queen says, offering up a long cigarette holder. "Make yourself useful."

Syd and Kali laugh as they continue to put up Miss Daisy posters outside the gay bar. I'm not the only one coasting on adrenaline.

Sweeping a lock of platinum hair behind his ear with one manicured hand, the drag queen waggles the holder with the other and says, "Ticktock, baby. I go on in ten."

I step forward and flick the lighter, and then drop it into the sequined clutch he holds open for me.

"Your blush isn't doing you any favors," he says, blowing smoke to one side. "Use something peachy to bring out your eyes."

"Thanks, I'll try that," I say.

I've never met a drag queen before. The upside of Eric's downside is that life has gotten more interesting. Luckily, Dad lifted my grounding as soon as he learned Rico was out of the picture. He pretended it was an act of mercy, but it was really about his desperate need to bury himself in work.

"Come back in a few years and see my show," the drag queen says. He checks out a poster and does a double take. "Oh, my. That's quite a paint job."

"There's a Shelby Charger under that unicorn," Kali says. "We're helping a friend post the signs."

Another drag queen comes outside and joins us. He's wearing a red satin minidress and fishnets, with an auburn wig. "Beautiful hair, sugar," he says, taking a flyer from my hand. "What's the catch? Does it run?"

"The owner's desperate for the cash," Syd says. "And he's getting her fixed up as we speak."

"He's good with cars," Kali says. "And so cute." She takes out her phone and shows them a picture of Eric. "You'd like him."

The guys rip Eric's phone number off the posters.

"Why not meet in person?" Syd suggests. "He's got a basketball game in the park down the street at eight tomorrow night."

chapter 7

*W*here *r u? Really need u now!*

The text enrages me to the point where I hurl my cell phone into my locker and slam the door. Yes, it's one of my favorite possessions, but right now it feels like the phone's on Eric's side. But I have to answer him. It's only Tuesday and the paint is still fresh on Miss Daisy. Our plan is to phase him out slowly so he's never quite sure what happened or who to blame for the slam.

I open the locker, grab the phone, and quickly text, *Sorry! Running 2 class now. Ltr.* Then I hurl the phone back into the locker.

"I see the anger management sessions aren't doing much good," someone says. I turn and find Brody leaning against the wall, wearing the red and white uniform of the Travis Rebels basketball team. According to Kali, Brody transferred to Travis when she arrived at Austin High only because Travis has the better sports program.

"It takes more than one session," I say. "Plus, you're supposed to avoid all sources of aggravation. So if you'll excuse me, I'm meeting your sister in the library."

He shoves himself off the wall. "I'll walk with you, Red. It's not safe to set you loose on the student body in this condition."

"I'm fine," I say, scratching my neck where a hive is coming up. "Shouldn't you be warming up in the gym? I heard the Maroons are going to slaughter you today."

"Angry and delusional too," he says, grinning. "Good thing you're getting help."

I walk faster, but Brody keeps pace. "So you really gave it to that phone. Boyfriend trouble?"

"I don't have a boyfriend." I suppose trashing Eric's car makes that official, without the words actually being said.

"Couple more weeks of anger management and you'll be fending them off," he says.

It'll be a lot longer than that before I even think about dating again. Like Saliyah says, guys suck.

A gorgeous cheerleader passes us, blatantly checking Brody out as she heads toward the gym. Without even bothering to say good-bye, he jogs down the hall after her.

In the library, I find Kali chatting with a lanky blond guy while Syd watches them from a table in the corner. Kali's hand is on the guy's arm and she's staring up at him, all smiles. It's astounding how quickly she's getting back in the game. Since Sunday, she's flirted outrageously with everyone from the drag queens to strangers on the bus. Even Stains and Rambo were on the receiving end of some eyelash batting yesterday, although they seemed more puzzled than entranced by it.

Giving Lanky Boy's arm a last squeeze, Kali comes over and joins us.

"Can we at least finish with one jerk before you line up the next?" Syd says.

Kali shushes her and peers around for the librarian. "I was just recruiting the guy for the school's eco-club." Her posture is great and her chin is high. For Kali, flirting seems to have magical healing properties.

I wish it were that simple for me. The adrenaline has drained steadily out of my system since we hammered Miss Daisy, and as it faded, waves of nausea returned, along with a melon-sized lump in my throat. When I'm alone, just one word echoes in my ears: stupid. I was stupid to miss the signs, stupid to trust Eric without asking more questions, stupid to build a whole fantasy about our future. Just stupid.

I expect Syd to look equally depressed, but her topaz eyes are sparkling. Taking her phone out of her backpack, she gestures for us to lean in, and says, "Girls, I bring you tidings of great joy." She cues up her voice mail. "Eric didn't leave us with much, but we'll have this play-by-play forever."

"Syd, it's me—Eric. I just came around the Albany and found Miss Daisy. She's trashed! Trashed! Oh my God, there's a pink horse on the hood! You've got to come back and help me."

"Syd, me again. Where are you? The police are on their way. You should see Daisy . . . it's tragic. Can you at least call me?"

"Hey, me again. I've filed my police report and I'm waiting for a tow truck. Now it's starting to rain! The good news is, Daisy still turns over. So don't worry too much. Call me, okay?"

"Hey, I've tried three garages but no one will take Daisy because she stinks. I took a look under the hood and almost puked. There are sick people out there."

"Good news! I found a mechanic who lost his sense of smell to cancer. He's done triage on Daisy and the damage looks worse than it actually is. She's going to be fine. Where are you? I know you're upset, but this is Daisy. We can work our stuff out later. I need you right now."

"Hey, I left Daisy and took the bus home. Your mom asked me to stop calling your home line, so call me, okay? I need to talk to someone."

"Syd, it's Monday and I still haven't heard from you. I'm worried. Call my home number or e-mail, okay? I've gotta turn off my cell because I'm getting all these crank calls. People think Daisy's for sale. For like, two hundred bucks. As if."

"Me again. I'm out with the guys, tearing down the For Sale signs. There must be hundreds because the calls won't stop. It's some kind of prank. Listen, this is going to sound crazy, but my mom said the paint job looks like the work of a pro. Do you know anyone who might have done it? Someone from the Maternity Ward, maybe? Is anyone that pissed off at me? I know you're upset or you'd have called me back, but you'd never take it out on Daisy, right?"

"Syd, forget I even said that. You know I love you and I know you'd never hurt Daisy. But if you have any clues, my mom wants to press charges."

We're about to hang up when we notice there's a new message.

"Syd, something really weird happened last night. I had a run-in with these . . . ladies. There's a story about it on page six in the *Chronicle*, so you'll probably see it. The guys on the team are calling me Powder Puff, but it'll all blow over. I'd really like to talk to you."

Syd is out of her seat in a flash and digging through the pile of papers the librarian keeps at the counter. She comes back with *The Austin Chronicle*. The daily "Keep Austin Weird" column features a color photo of Eric in his basketball gear standing next to Miss Daisy. Two drag queens perch on the hood, on either side of the unicorn. The story underneath reads:

One Hell of a Ride

Eric Skinner's proudest possession used to be his well-maintained powder-blue Shelby Charger. But everything changed on Sunday when he came out of a café near the old Albany Hotel to find that the car had been vandalized.

It doesn't appear to be a chance hit. Sure, the tires were flat, but how many vandals can paint like that? Factor in the fish guts, and this mystery reeks of revenge.

Lady Luck, a performer at the Cockpit, approached Skinner to make an offer on the car after seeing one of the For Sale signs that were posted all over Austin. "This is a love story gone wrong," says Ms. Luck. "I can feel it in my bones."

Mr. Skinner insists it's a random act of

cruelty. "No one I know would do this," he says. "Everyone understands what this car means to me."

The car is running again, and Mr. Skinner has no intention of parting with "Miss Daisy" anytime soon. But he does hope someone will come forward with information about the crime. "It's going to cost me at least two grand for the paint job and fumigation," he says. "Someone should pay for this."

But don't call the number from the posters. It's no longer in service.

"Two grand for the love of his life? Boo-friggin'-hoo," Syd says.

Kali stares at the article, beaming. "It just doesn't get better than this, does it?"

"I'd frame it if I could," I say. "But do you think we should be worried? Lady Luck saw us putting up the posters."

Syd shakes her head. "She's obviously decided to keep her mouth shut."

I sit up straight in my chair, feeling like a wilted plant that's just been watered. The adrenaline is back, and I feel much smarter. I helped to plan and execute that slam!

Still, it bothers me that Eric left nine voice mails for Syd, and only two for me. Sure, he's texted a lot, but the real measure of a girl's worth is in phone calls.

Kali is clearly making the same calculation. "He's only called me once," she says. "Plus seven texts."

"Two calls for me, and five texts," I say. "I've followed the plan—short, casual, and friendly replies. How long do we have to keep this up?"

"Another week and Kali drops out of sight," Syd says. "Two weeks for you, Zahra, and three weeks for me. I actually left him a voice mail when I knew he was in his guitar lesson and couldn't pick up. Just some basic condolences over poor Daisy. I'll try that again in a few days and slowly wean him off all contact. Hopefully that'll be enough to keep him from stopping by."

The very thought of him dropping in at the store makes my heart drop, but I'll brief René and he'll help me deal.

Kali nods. "If Eric follows his usual pattern, he should be lining up our replacements right now anyway."

·· ♥ ··

Kali and Syd and I meet outside of Bennu Coffee to load up on caffeine before group. Today marks the one week anniversary of our finding out about Eric, and we all look a little worse for wear. It turns out revenge isn't a gift that keeps on giving. I'd hoped to hold on to that feeling for a lot longer than a week.

Syd's wearing a ratty old fedora over unwashed hair, and a wrinkled shirt straight out of the clothes hamper. I'm not much better, with a few stray hives on my chest and my hair in a bulky braid. Kali, on the other hand, is perky, in her trademark green T-shirt and designer army pants. Someone's fresh off a good flirt.

"This is on me," she says, heading into the coffee shop. Syd and I wait outside with Banksy and a cardboard box full of dishes and cutlery that Kali collected to replace the eco-threats she stole from the church kitchen.

"What's taking her so long?" Syd asks, a few minutes later. "Don't tell me she's flirting."

"She is," I say, peering through the window. "Rule number one: never let Kali get the coffee if there's a cute server."

Syd groans. "How can she even think about other guys after what happened? I am never—repeat, never—going out with a guy again."

"That makes two of us," I say.

When Kali finally joins us with the coffee, Syd unties Banksy and marches off.

"What's her problem?" Kali asks. She sets her coffee on the ground and picks up the box, but then she can't carry the coffee. "What'd I do?"

I pick up her coffee and follow Syd, with Kali trailing behind in her high-heeled boots.

"For starters, you didn't put sugar in my coffee," Syd shouts over her shoulder.

"It wasn't organic."

"Plus, you've made us late for group."

"Like you care if you're on time. You're just taking it out on me because you're pissed off about Eric. I was a victim too, you know."

"You have a funny way of showing it," Syd says.

Kali is mystified. "What's she talking about?"

"The flirting," I clarify.

"We already covered this," Kali says. "You sulk, I go for the distraction." She picks up the pace, ceramic mugs clinking in the box. "I'm not going to sit around pining for a cheater. You've got to get right back on the horse."

"Not me," I say, catching up to Syd. "I'm steering clear of

the barn right now. I don't like the smell."

Kali has to jog a little to keep up. When she pulls alongside Syd, I notice there's a paper napkin sticking out of the front pocket of her jeans with a phone number scrawled on it. "I could find nice guys for both of you."

"So now you're a matchmaker?" Syd asks.

"A pretty good one, as a matter of fact. I've set up a lot of people and no one's complained."

Syd snorts into her coffee. "Please. Like you could find a guy for me."

"Hel*lo*," Kali says, rolling her eyes. "I think I know your type."

"She's got you there, Syd," I say. "Eric was her type too. And mine."

Syd shakes her head at the impossibility of it all. "You two have seriously bad taste," she says, cracking a smile at last. "No wonder you're in therapy."

·· ♥ ··

Dieter claps his hands sharply three times as we slink into the room. "This isn't a cocktail party, ladies." He's wearing another black outfit, only this combo is pinstriped. "We do not show up fashionably late for group."

"Sorry, Dieter, it was my fault," Kali says. "I—"

"No excuses," he says. "Just get here on time." He picks up his clipboard and makes a note. "Simon, please continue. For the benefit of our tardy friends, you were discussing your parents' views on your current relationships."

"Yeah," Simon says, tipping his chair back. "My parents have no business commenting on my relationship when they've screwed up their own."

"*You* have a girlfriend?" Kali asks, not bothering to feign surprise.

"Two, actually," Lauren says, pulling a compact mirror and a comb out of a Coach bag that's worth more than the Recipe Box pays me in a month. "The cheater."

"It's not cheating," Simon says, pulling a loose thread from the sleeve of his ancient leather jacket. "It's just an overlap."

"An overlap?" Kali asks. "You're seeing someone new when you already have a girlfriend?"

"Correct." Lauren says. She back combs the crown of her hair, secures it with a rhinestone-encrusted butterfly clip, and holds up the mirror again to admire herself.

"Then he's cheating," Kali confirms.

Simon pushes back the brim of his baseball cap and defends himself. "We're only hanging out. It's not like I'm—"

"—tapping it?" Evan jumps in. "Or are you?"

Dieter deems this a one-clap offense. "Boundaries, boys."

"Look," Simon says, slouching in his chair. "I don't feel the same way about my girl as I used to, but I don't want to hurt her feelings. She's into me."

Lauren drops her mirror back into her purse and shakes an index finger at him. "You've been together a year."

"But I don't feel like we're connecting anymore," Simon says. Feeling the heat from this discussion, he finally removes his jacket, revealing a surprisingly nice polo shirt. I wonder if he bought it on his shopping spree with Lauren.

"How would she know that if you don't tell her?" I ask.

He shrugs. "I'm not around that much. She should figure it out."

The guys share one of those "Duh" looks, and a match

flares in the pit of my stomach. "Excuse me? If she doesn't get it, explain it. Sure, it hurts to get dumped, but it hurts a lot more to get played."

"In other words," Sydney says, "man up and do the right thing."

Simon bristles. "What would you know about—"

Syd cuts him off with a few Dieter-like claps. "I know exactly what it's like to be on the receiving end of the crap you're pulling, and I can tell you that it wrecks people. They start to doubt themselves. They do crazy things."

"Like what?" Simon asks.

"They cheat too, just to prove they can," Syd says. "Or they try to reinvent themselves because they think they need to be different and exciting, although it never works to pretend you're something you're not." The words are tumbling out of her lips. "They get miserable and take it out on other people until—"

Syd stops talking as suddenly as she started. She leans down to pat Banksy, and her hair falls over her face.

"Thank you for sharing, Sydney," Dieter says. "It's good to hear you open up."

Syd's back stiffens. "I wasn't talking about myself."

"It's true for anyone," I say. "When someone you love isn't who he says he was, you doubt yourself and everything else you believed in."

Lauren nods. "The one who got cheated on always pays the price."

"Not always," Kali replies. "Sometimes innocent victims get even. If I were you, Simon, I'd watch my back."

And your car, I add silently.

·· ♥ ··

112

The last thing we expect as we step out of the church is to find Eric at the bottom of the front stairs. Judging by his expression, the last thing *he* expected was to find the three of us together.

He turns, as if to bolt, but Banksy jerks the leash out of Syd's hand and races down the stairs. The dog stands up against Eric's chest, then scrapes his tongue across Eric's four-day-old stubble. If I had any lingering desire to kiss Eric again, that image cured me.

Standing between us, Kali links arms with Syd and me, and we walk halfway down the stairs. "What do you want?" she asks.

Eric pushes Banksy off and holds on to his leash. "Uh, I came to see you, Syd. Your mom said you'd be here."

"She didn't." Syd is outraged.

"Just to get me off her back," Eric says. "Because you wouldn't return my calls. She said you volunteer here on Thursdays."

I notice he keeps his eyes on Syd, as if Kali and I don't even exist. His face is flushed under the stubble.

"Do you have anything to say?" Syd asks.

Eric shakes his head and croaks, "Not now."

"Great," Syd says. "Then screw off."

We march down the rest of the stairs, and Syd holds out her hand for the leash. Eric keeps it, staring at her. You can almost see the last three months flashing before his eyes, every lie, every misplaced kiss. He looks exhausted from the triple-dealing. Finally he says, "For what it's worth, I thought we were over."

"That's a pile of crap," Syd says. "No one said, 'We're over.'

So we were *not* over, and you know it. You cheated and you don't even have the guts to admit it."

Eric swallows hard and makes his next big mistake. "You didn't have to take it out on Daisy."

It's like fire to gunpowder. "Are you kidding me?" Syd pulls her arm out of Kali's and points to us. "Seriously, Eric. Are you kidding?"

Anyone except this arrogant idiot would run for cover at this point. "Look, it was no big deal, Syd. It was nothing."

"Nothing?" Kali says, infuriated. "We are not nothing." She pulls the pack of stale Gauloises out of her purse and hurls it at Eric, followed by a plastic lighter. They hit his shoulder and land on the pavement. "You're a liar and a cheat—and that's less than nothing."

Eric continues to look only at Syd. "I mean *nothing happened.*"

"Look at them," Syd says. "Tell *them* nothing happened."

"We were just hanging out," he says, cutting his eyes in our general direction. "They took it the wrong way."

"You're hopeless," Syd says, grabbing for Banksy's leash. "Don't call, don't write, get out of our lives. You . . . reek."

He holds the leash behind his back. "You trashed my car."

"Give me my dog."

"My mom—"

"Has no proof. Give. Me. My. Dog."

"Not till you—"

A clap cuts him off. "Everything all right out here?" Dieter asks. "Girls?"

"Fine," Syd says, as Eric hands her the leash. "Never better."

·· ♥ ··

We cross the street to a little park and collapse onto a picnic table, Syd on top and Kali and I on the benches. It's a long time before anyone speaks.

"That was brutal," I say, keeping my eyes closed against the late-day sun. "Did we really go out with him? Tell me it never happened."

"We're going to try to forget it ever did," Kali says. "Dieter's got his work cut out for him."

"Well, at least we don't have to worry about phasing him out," I say. "How're you doing, Syd?" I lift my head for a moment. Her heavy breathing has slowed to normal, but she's clutching Banksy's leash for dear life, while the dog lolls in the grass.

"I'm okay." After another silence, her voice drifts down from above. "I guess I'm partly to blame for what happened. When I asked for space, Eric said all the right things, but I could tell he was hurt. I couldn't bring myself to talk about it, and he never brought it up. Instead, he replaced me."

"That makes me the rebound girl," I say. It hurts to know I was never more than that to the guy I believed could be my soul mate.

"Look on the bright side, Syd," Kali says. "Eric must have had it bad if he needed two of us to get over you."

Syd pushes herself up on one elbow and looks down at us. "Listen, I'm sorry for all this."

"No one *made* him cheat," I say.

Syd settles back on the table and grumbles, "I just wish we hadn't gone so easy on his car. I know a guy who does explosives."

"We made our point," I say. "He didn't drive today, and I still smelled fish."

"He probably has an air freshener stuck in his jeans," Kali says.

Someone laughs, and we open our eyes and sit up. Lauren is standing beside the picnic table. "I overheard your fight with that guy. And I'm guessing there's a connection to that article in the *Chronicle* about the unicorn car."

Syd sighs. "Are you going to rat us out?"

"No." Lauren sets her Coach bag on the table, digs out a checkbook, and says, "I want to hire you."

"For what?" I ask.

"To find out what's going on with Trey. I think he's cheating, and if he is, I want you to take him down just like you took down that unicorn car guy."

"But we're not in the revenge business," I say as Lauren fills out the check. "We were settling a personal score."

Lauren rips the check out of the book and slaps it on the table in front of us. "Are you sure?"

Kali leans forward. "Are those *two* zeros?"

"Preceded by a four," Lauren confirms.

The three of us hesitate before coming to our senses.

"We can't," Kali says.

"We can't," Syd says, although it comes out sounding more like a question.

"We can't," I confirm, handing Lauren the check back. "Thanks, but no thanks."

chapter 8

"We were just hanging out," Eric says, grabbing a spoon and dipping it into the simmering soup stock.

Oliver James looks up from the carrots he's dicing. "From what I hear, you were snogging her, mate."

"She threw herself at me," Eric says, turning to the Sweet Tooth audience and shrugging. "All I did was say yes."

There are more than a few embarrassed smiles, including one on Oliver's face.

"I did not throw myself at him," I call to the audience. "He said I was his girl!"

"Only after you cooked me that fancy dinner," Eric says. "What'd you call it, Oliver? The Get Naked menu?"

The audience cackles. I turn to Oliver, who shakes his head. "I told you to keep it casual. You asked for this."

"No," I protest. "You don't understand. He was into me. I know he was."

Oliver faces the audience. "Poor thing's eaten a bad mushroom—she's delusional."

"This is MY show," I say. "You're MY guest. And those are MY fans."

Eric is laughing so hard he has to hold the counter for support.

"Stop it," I shout. "Stop it!"

"Zahra." Dad's voice filters through the laughter. "You asked me to wake you up early. Aren't you meeting your friends at nine?"

I open my eyes and stare at the water stain on the ceiling over my bed. Dad twists open the ugly venetian blinds that came with the apartment, and thousands of dust motes appear in the shafts of sunlight. I'd planned on painting, but so far the only decorating I've managed is to tape up a poster of Yosemite National Park, the last place we went for a family vacation. Doing anything more would feel like admitting that my parents are never getting back together.

"Are you okay?" Dad asks. "It looks like you've been crying."

I touch my cheek and find it damp. "I'm fine. I just had a nightmare."

"I'll make you some toast," Dad says.

As he leaves, I pull the sheets up over my head. It's become my new morning ritual.

Since I found out about Eric, it's a lot harder to face the world.

·· ♥ ··

I beckon to Syd and Kali from behind a display of wooden blinds at Home Depot. "This is a bad idea. I can't believe we let Lauren talk us into it."

"It was her big fat check that did the talking," Syd says, peeking around the blinds in search of our target.

Lauren asked us to think about her offer overnight. After carefully weighing the pros and the cons, we decided to take the job. With our families splitting, we're all on tight budgets, and the extra cash couldn't come at a better time.

In exchange for four hundred dollars, all we have to do is watch Trey's every move over the weekend, starting tonight at his part-time job. I wouldn't have expected a society girl like Lauren to date a working-class guy, but she's hung up on Trey, and lately Trey's disappeared for blocks of time, and has been evasive about what he's been doing.

It seemed like easy money, but now that we're here, I'm nervous. It was hard enough playing secret agent with Eric when I was highly motivated by humiliation. Trey Fuller might be scamming Lauren, but he hasn't done anything to me.

"We're not doing anything illegal," Kali says, reading my mind. "Fancy pastry classes and good guitars don't come cheap."

"Or college," Syd adds, having recently learned that her dad dumped most of her education fund into the Albany Hotel.

"It's not just about money," Kali says. "We're in it to help someone who's at risk of being destroyed by love, like us. You'd feel worse right now if we hadn't shown Eric exactly how we feel."

"Showing is so much better than telling," I agree.

I know I won't get over what happened with Eric quickly, but I believe doing something about it helped. Messing with Miss Daisy, his number one girl, was as close as we could get to breaking *his* heart.

"We're helping someone who's suffering," Kali says. "It's like community service, only with a paycheck."

"Exactly," Syd says. "By supporting someone from group,

we're sort of building on the work Dieter's doing."

"It's like an enrichment class," I add, laughing. "Anyway, it beats sitting around feeling sorry for ourselves."

"Let's get to work," Syd says, pulling some photos of Trey out of the back pocket of her jeans. "We've got to identify this traitor."

"He's innocent until proven guilty," I remind her. At the moment, I believe all guys are jerks and cheaters. But this is a paying job, and we have to keep an open mind.

Syd pinches her nose. "When something smells this bad, there's usually a reason."

The difference between me and Syd is that while neither of us trusts guys anymore, deep down I want to be proven wrong, whereas I think Syd wants to be proven right. Now that she's tasted revenge, she wants another hit. But she'll have to wait because so far we're just investigating.

Kali examines the photos of Trey before raising camouflage binoculars to scan the store.

Syd pushes down the binoculars. "Try using your eyes."

From our position in the Window Coverings section, we have an unobstructed view of Paints and Wallpapers, where Trey works.

"Target at three o'clock," Kali announces. She points to a guy stocking a shelf with paint rollers. "Confirming: Tango, Romeo, Echo, Yankee."

Mocking Kali's use of the military alphabet, Syd says, "Loony Oddball Screwy Eccentric Ridiculous."

"Don't call me a loser," Kali says, not the least bit insulted. She's upbeat and animated again this morning—far from destroyed. "Military precision is what this job requires." She slicks on her favorite lip gloss, fluffs her curls, and adjusts her halter top for maximum cleavage. "Cover me, chiquitas; I'm going in."

She sashays across the store in a short, ruffled skirt that matches her top, and wedge-heeled espadrilles. Her tanned legs seem endless, and several guys turn to admire them as she passes.

Watching her, I feel mousy in my khaki shorts and T-shirt. I could never pull off an outfit like Kali's. I mean, I'd probably look okay in it, but I don't have her confidence.

Syd probably doesn't have Kali's confidence either, despite her funky style. Her clothes seem like her graffiti—a bold statement to the public—while the girl inside remains anonymous.

"Excuse me," Kali calls to Trey. Syd and I take our positions in the next aisle, where we can see and hear the action without being noticed. "I'm thinking about repainting my room, but I'm not sure about what color to go for." She twirls a blond curl around her index finger and gives Lauren's boyfriend the once-over. "You look like you have great taste. Do you think you could help me?"

"Sure," Trey says. He smiles at Kali, keeping his eyes on her face instead of her cleavage. "What kind of mood are you trying to create? Restful or bold?"

Kali giggles. "Something in between, I guess. I want to create a vibe that will inspire my songwriting, the same way people do." She's leaning against the shelf now, casually spinning her web. "So what's your story? What drew you to help people decorate?"

"I needed a job," Trey says. He smiles again and backs down the aisle. "I'll collect some samples for you and be right back."

"Make sure it's nontoxic paint," Kali calls after him. "I'm an environmentalist."

Syd and I collapse in laughter when Trey is out of earshot.

"Dial it back a bit, would you?" Syd says. "You're scaring the guy."

Kali rolls her eyes. "If I can't get this guy to crack, he's either in love with Lauren, or he's gay."

Syd and I exchange a glance. Although I envy Kali's confidence, it can be a bit jarring. I suppose she's just matter-of-fact. Guys are attracted to her, and there's no point in pretending otherwise.

"If you guys wanted subtle," Kali adds, "you picked the wrong girl for the job."

·· ♥ ··

Syd and I are on the bus, heading to the last event in a full weekend of Trey surveillance. Since he passed Kali's experiment with flying colors, we've spent two solid days tracking him. On Saturday night, Lauren pretended to be busy so that we could see how he'd fill "date night." He went to a movie with his pals, which meant Syd, Kali, and I sat through a slasher flick.

This morning, we were up early to make sure Trey really went to church (he did), and now while Kali goes to her guitar lesson, Syd and I are checking out his touch football game. If he shows up without some girl to cheer him on, we'll have to give him the all clear as far as cheating is concerned.

The bus skirts the Albany Hotel, and Syd points to a stack of modern condos built on top of an old library. "That's where I do my time with Dad. He says he has to live in a condo

122

before he designs one. Meanwhile, Mom's renting a basement apartment until she figures out what she wants to do with her life. I miss our old house."

Syd sounds like a wistful kid, and today she looks like one too. She skipped her signature red lipstick and is wearing jeans, a white T-shirt, and a baseball cap. I guess it's her stakeout attire.

If she weren't such a good artist, Syd would have a future as a detective. She's planned every outing carefully, down to the last detail. In fact, both Kali and Syd have given this their best effort, whereas I haven't offered much more than moral support. As usual, with Kali out there at one end of the spectrum and Syd on the other, I'm the gray in the middle.

We get off the bus and circle Trey's school, half an hour before the game. Syd did an advance run yesterday to check out cover options and found dense bushes at the edge of the field. We set up there now, on a fleece blanket Syd pulls out of her backpack. She opens her notepad to record our observations and starts sketching in pencil to kill time. "So tell me," she says. "How serious were you and Eric?"

"I liked him a lot," I say. "Too much. I sort of lost track of what was real and what was in my head. The Rico I made up was perfect."

Her eyes flash up at me for a second, but she doesn't say anything. And after a few more minutes she holds up the pad. It's me, on the best hair day imaginable, which definitely isn't today. The eyes are too intense, but I like the way it makes me look aloof and mysterious.

"I love it," I say. "Can I have it?"

She rips the page out of the notepad and hands it to me. "I

gotta be honest, Z, your hair's a problem."

"You're telling me."

"No, I mean for surveillance," Syd says. "People can ID you. Ever consider dyeing?"

"Every day." I'm not someone who wants to stand out in a crowd. "But this is our last stakeout anyway."

"I guess." She sounds sorrier about that than I am. I've been tense all weekend, but Syd seems energized. Peeking through the bushes, she says, "Showtime."

Eight guys have gathered on the field, and they're moving into position. Trey doesn't seem to be with them.

"Finally," Syd says. "Evidence."

"We only know where he isn't," I point out. "Not where he is."

Syd sticks her hand out for the camera, and I hand it to her. She snaps a few stills of the team. "We know he's lying. He said he'd be here and he isn't. If he'll lie about that, he'll lie about anything."

"You're sure he's not there?" I get on my hands and knees and stick my head into the bushes for a better look. "Wow. Some of those guys are hot!"

"If you think so," a male voice says, "why don't you come out and join us?"

·· ♥ ··

Twigs snag my hair as I withdraw my head from the bushes. Looking up, I see a guy who's over six feet tall—a blond giant with golden fuzz on his legs. I'm close enough to get a good look.

"Oh hi," I say. My voice is squeaky, not undercover-cool at

all. This is exactly what I was worried about. We should have run scenarios. "How's it going?"

He raises an eyebrow. "You're spying on us and that's the best you got?"

Syd pulls down the brim of her cap. "We're bird-watching," she says. "There's a spectacular woodpecker midfield."

The guy snorts. "I'll tell him you said so. Better yet, I'll call Woody over."

"No," I say, desperately trying to come up with a believable excuse for our being here. It shouldn't be that hard. After all, I'm the master of casual banter on *The Sweet Tooth*. Sure, that's all in my head and it's easier when you're handling both ends of the conversation, but ad-libbing lines for two or even three people has to count for something. The question I have to ask myself is, *What would Oliver James do?*

He'd bluff, that's what he'd do.

I smile up at the blond giant and start improvising. "Keri's just protecting me, uh . . . What's your name?"

He answers reluctantly. "Andrew. Protecting you from what?"

"Humiliation." I aim for Oliver's cocky—yet charming—style. "I have a thing for a guy on your team. I thought I could casually run into him after the game."

Andrew rolls his eyes. "What century is this? Just talk to him. I'll bring him over right now and you'll know—badda bing, badda boom." Andrew plucks a twig from my hair.

Easy-peasy. The guy is putty in my hands.

"I bet he'll like you," he continues. "What's your name?"

"Oliver." Oops. "I mean, Olivia. And the guy is Trey Fuller."

"Fuller?" He shakes his head. "Bad news, Olivia: he's taken. The girl's hot, and she's rich too."

"He never mentioned a girlfriend. Maybe they're on the rocks?"

"Doubt it," Andrew says. "He talks about her all the time."

I offer what I hope is a cheeky grin. "You mean he's always faithful?"

Andrew grins back. "Like I'd rat out a friend. Not that I have to cover for Fuller. The guy's a straight arrow, and probably too boring for someone like you. Do you know he actually skipped today's game to volunteer at a retirement home? His granddad roped him into being a dance partner for some of the old girls."

Laughing at the image, Andrew helps me to my feet. Then he grabs Syd's pad and pencil and scrawls a number on it. "You came down here to meet a guy. I'd hate to see you leave disappointed."

·· ♥ ··

Syd wastes no time filling Kali in when we arrive at Kevin's trailer. "Zahra tackled some dude's heart this afternoon. Got his number and everything."

"He was just a flirt," I say, though I can't help smiling as I slide into my place. It was nice to have a guy pay attention to me. After all that's happened, my confidence is in the Dumpster. Well, I have Oliver James to thank for that little pick-me-up. Maybe, just maybe, I will live to love again. But the lucky guy won't be Andrew. He might be cute, but a guy that slick has a roster of girls.

"I can tell you're buzzed," Kali says. "What did I say about getting back on the horse?"

"I'm buzzed about the stakeout," I say. Which is also true.

It topped up my adrenaline tank quite nicely.

Syd helps herself to a soda and stakes her usual claim on the bench. "Zahra BS'd like a pro."

It makes me proud to hear her say that because she's so fearless. So is Kali in a different way. I hope they're rubbing off on me a little.

Taping two paint chips to the wall of the trailer, Kali says, "If we're going to hang out here, the place could use sprucing up. Sonoma Sunset or Swamp Moss?"

"Neither," Syd says. "Our trailer time is over anyway. Lauren's guy may be going dark on her, but we can't prove it's another relationship."

It's not for lack of digging. Even Kali struck out after interviewing a bunch of people, from an old soccer coach to Trey's brother, telling them she was gathering tidbits for a "roast" at work. From all accounts, Trey is kind, loyal, and trustworthy. He must also be a heck of a salesman, judging by the paintbrushes, rollers, trays, and turpentine cluttering the trailer.

I pluck the orange paint chip off the wall to inspect it. "Hey, there's a phone number on this one."

"It's Paolo's," Kali says. "The wallpaper guy at Home Depot. I've already started a song about him."

"Let me guess," Syd says. "Paolo, Paolo, I'm so shallow, I fall for a new guy every day."

Kali strikes back. "Well, at least I'm not stupid enough to think one guy's going to stick around forever."

Going for the jugular, Syd says, "No, you're just stupid enough to think every guy will disappear like your dads."

"Don't take your frustration out on me because you're still hung up on Eric."

"I am not hung up on Eric." Syd's voice is so loud that Banksy whines.

"Even your dog can see you're freaking out."

I step in. "Syd went out with Eric for a long time. She can't get over him in a week."

"Exactly," Syd says, glaring at Kali.

"Similarly, it's not surprising that someone could move on faster if she didn't invest as much in the first place," I say.

"Right," Kali says.

They lower their weapons and settle back into their seats.

"Who needs group when we've got Z?" Syd says.

I have more respect for Dieter now. Refereeing is tough work. Using his technique of redirecting the conversation, I say, "Wouldn't it be great if there were some sort of formula for figuring out if a guy's going to stick around?"

"It helps if you find a good match in the first place," Kali says. "Some of the people I've set up are doing great. My questionnaire about lifestyle and personality seems to be working, so I'm developing a computer program to formalize it."

"A matchmaking program?" Syd scoffs. "Exactly how many people have you set up?"

"Maybe twenty since junior high," Kali says, flipping open her laptop.

"That's a lot for a girl who doesn't believe love can last," Syd says.

"It lasts," Kali says, "Just not forever. That's why I like to focus on start-ups. Nothing beats the thrill of that first spark."

She turns the screen so we can see a flowchart mapping the character traits and personalities of two individuals. I point to the long stretch of purple where a pink line and a blue line intersect. "This looks like a happy match. Who's the lucky couple?"

"Lauren and Trey," Kali says. "I plugged in everything we know about them, and they seem to be perfect together. For now, at least." Smiling, she adds, "And now is what counts."

·· ♥ ··

Lauren bursts into tears when we present our findings.

"What's wrong with you?" Syd asks, with her trademark diplomacy.

We're standing outside St. Joe's after group, and we weren't expecting the drama.

"This is good news," Kali says, handing Lauren some tissue. "Trey isn't cheating."

Lauren collapses onto the steps, sobbing. "If our personalities are so compatible, and Trey hasn't met anyone else, then it can only mean he's not into me anymore."

I look at Syd as I pass Lauren another tissue. It's a possibility we considered, but even Syd, the skeptic, doesn't think that's the case.

"Lauren, you paid us well to give you the truth," I say. "If we thought Trey was opting out, we'd say so."

"Opting out of what?" Simon is standing in the doorway of the church with Evan. He sees Lauren and says, "What the hell did you guys do to her?"

"Girls are vicious," Evan says, sauntering down the stairs. "Especially this one." He stops in front of Syd. "Though, personally, I like vicious." Running his eyes over her peasant top, he adds, "I could get into that whole taming-of-the-shrew thing."

"Don't even think about it," Syd says, making a quick hand signal at Banksy. The big dog stands and bares pointy yellow teeth at Evan.

Evan takes a quick step back.

Another signal and Banksy lets out a series of loud barks that send Evan flying up the stairs and stumbling into Dieter. He might be stoned, but he can move when he has to.

"The dog was attacking me," he says. "Call animal control."

Banksy is now sitting with one paw on Lauren's shoulder, trying to lick away her tears. Lauren is wailing, and Simon takes his baseball cap off for the first time to beg Dieter, "Can't you do something for her?"

Dieter comes down the stairs and pauses beside Lauren. "Do you want to come back inside and talk, Lauren?"

She shakes her head, her hair still perfect despite the hysterics. "No . . . I'm fine."

He lingers a moment, but Kali says, "We got it covered, Dieter. It's a girl thing."

Dieter heads down the walk with Simon on his heels, looking relieved to be off the hook. Evan edges down the far side of the stairs and runs to the sidewalk, afro bobbing. Then he slows to a deliberate amble.

When they're gone, Kali sits beside Lauren and pats her shoulder. "Don't worry, honey. You and Trey just need to spend some time with our mediator."

I look from Kali to Syd. The three of us have never discussed a mediator.

"A mediator is exactly what you need," Syd confirms.

Okay, so two of us have discussed a mediator. I missed the meeting.

Syd and Kali are staring at me like I'm the last burger at a Carnivores Anonymous meeting.

Something tells me I'm about to put the "me" in mediator.

·· ♥ ··

I make a spontaneous Sunday night visit to my mom's, hoping to make a goodwill deposit in the family bank. Although I've demoted Mom to mere custodian, if she doesn't see enough of me she starts asking too many questions. The key to keeping her calm is to volunteer face time. That's especially tough during Ramadan, with the prayer ramp-up, and food and drink off-limits between sunrise and sunset.

The pressure sends me sneaking into the kitchen for a snack, not long after I arrive. It bothers me that Mom's observing Ramadan for the first time in my memory.

Mom catches me in the act, but instead of giving me grief, she opens a box of rice crackers and hands them to me. If seeing me eat is better than not seeing me at all, she can't be that far gone.

"What's with all the takeout?" I ask, doing inventory.

"I got a part-time job at Whole Foods," she says. "I want to support myself now that you and your sister don't need me at home anymore."

I reach for the eggplant purée. "How about selling your beauty products? My friends love them, and you used to talk about making it a business."

"I was dreaming." She dismisses the idea with a wave. "That's just a hobby."

Saliyah descends upon us before I can argue. "Excuse me. We're supposed to be fasting."

I nearly choke on my rice cracker. In addition to my salwar kameez, my sister is wearing an orange-and-gold veil over her nearly waist-length brown hair. "Oh hi, Nani," I say. "I barely recognized you without the facial hair."

My mother shushes us and starts putting the food away, but the damage is done.

"Zahra," Nani says, coming into the kitchen. "You're eating." She checks out my jeans and T-shirt, and purses her lips. They're not modest enough, I suppose. "I have something to discuss with you. Come with me."

"I can't. Saliyah and I are going out."

"We are?" Saliyah says, her dark eyes lighting up as she smiles. "Just give me five." Without any encouragement from me, she runs for the stairs to change, tearing off the veil as she goes.

"Zahra," Mom says.

"You want Saliyah and me to spend time together, and we need to go over our options for her school bake sale. Nani and I can chat next time."

Mom lets me off the hook again. I get away with so much more since taking over my own upbringing. I should have climbed into the driver's seat long ago.

I rush my sister out of the house and up the street to the Taco Shack. The sun still hasn't set when Saliyah, in yoga pants and a sweatshirt, tucks into her chicken burrito. It's a small victory over my grandparents, and I savor it.

"What about Ramadan?" I ask. "Is your soul going to take a beating for this?"

"It's my first fast," she says, wiping guacamole off her chin. "I consider it a practice round."

"Let's hope Allah agrees."

Making a face at me, she changes the subject. "How's Dad?"

"If he isn't working, he's in front of his computer, or listening to jazz and staring into space. I think he's depressed."

"Mom too," Saliyah says. "She always in the basement mixing stuff up."

"Avoiding Nani and Nana, I guess."

"They're not that bad."

"You're getting brainwashed and you don't even know it. Pretty soon they'll have you wrapped up in a sari and on a plane to Karachi. They'll marry you off to the first old guy who offers a decent dowry."

"Zahra! You're like a racist or something."

"It's not racism when you're mocking your own culture."

"Let's hope Allah agrees," she says, smirking.

My phone rings, and I step outside to take it so that Saliyah can't hear Kali and me discuss my upcoming meeting with Lauren and Trey. I've tried to weasel out of it, but Kali and Syd insist I'm the best girl for the job. My so-called mediation skills have never paid off at home, but I'll have to give it my best shot.

Back inside, I find Nani at our table, her fuchsia salwar kameez glowing like a beacon in the dim room. Why can't she just wear regular old lady street clothes? Unless it's a formal occasion, Nana wears pants and a dress shirt.

"Hello again," Nani says cheerfully, as if I didn't blow her off twenty minutes ago. "I was out for a walk and saw your sister sitting alone."

Saliyah's sheepish expression tells me Nani was tipped off. "So what did you want to talk about?" I ask.

Nani takes the burrito and moves it out of Saliyah's reach. "Boys. I didn't want your Nana to hear."

There is no angle on this subject I could possibly want to explore with her. "Nani, don't worry, I've given up on boys. It's not a problem."

"Boys are always a problem until you find the right one," she says. "And even then . . ."

She sounds almost nice, which means I have to be extra vigilant. A master brainwasher tries to get you off your home turf and win you over.

"I want to give you one piece of advice," she says. "It will make all the difference: Marry a man who cherishes you and accepts you for all that you are."

It's hard to argue with something so corny and mundane. "Fine, but I'm not planning on getting married."

"Take your time," she says. "Your mother married too young. Which brings me to my second piece of advice." She opens her bag, pulls out a few sheets of paper, and slides them across the table. "Marry your own kind."

I glare at my sister. These are printouts from Facebook, and Nani doesn't know how to turn on the computer. Saliyah gives me the helpless shrug of the brainwashed.

"Nice handsome boys, all of them," Nani continues. "I know their parents. I know where they come from. I know their values. And I know they'll treat you like a queen. Look at this one."

I slap my hand down on the page and pull it in front of me. To my surprise, the guy is hot. His hazel eyes stand out against mocha skin, and his hair and clothes are cutting-edge cool. The guy has style. Or a stylist.

"Flip it over," Nani says.

On the back, she's noted specifics in her loopy handwriting, in order of *her* priorities.

- Name: Riaz Dar
- Age: 16
- Religion: Sunni Islam
- Pedigree: Mother, father, and grandfather all medical doctors, originally from Karachi
- Education: Straight-A student, aiming for pre-med at Yale
- Future Prospects: Excellent
- Romantic Status: Single (recently broke up with a Shi'ite—no surprise it didn't work out)
- Interests: Soccer, music, volunteering with Big Brothers
- Available: Immediately (but probably not for long)

"What do you think?" she asks.

"I think if it seems too good to be true, it is. He's probably the president of the *Star Trek* fan club and enjoys ant farming."

"No *Star Trek*, no ants," Nani says. "I talked to him for an hour last week when I joined the Eid carnival planning committee. Will you think about it?"

The best way to fight someone as manipulative as my grandmother is to let her believe she's won. "Sure, Nani. I'll think about it. Why not?"

Smiling, she glances out the window and sees the sun has set, meaning the fast is officially broken. She pushes the burrito toward my sister and takes her wallet out of her purse. "Order me one of those, Zahra. Extra jalapeños."

chapter 9

Lauren and I put on our bathing suits and step out of the changing room.

"What are we doing here?" she asks, looking from the Barton Springs Pool to my pale MacDuff skin. "I'm guessing it's not so you can work on your tan."

"Thanks for the reminder." I pull a bottle of sunscreen from my beach bag and spray it on before leading Lauren up the grassy slope that overlooks the water. "There's something I want you to see."

"Can't we see it from the deck?" she asks. "The grass is where the nude bathers hang."

"Trust me," I say, spreading out my towel. "That's all part of the master plan."

The rest of the master plan is a bit sketchy. I downloaded some articles on the basic rules of negotiation and mediation, but you can't become an instant expert. Since I couldn't sleep last night, I spent some time on my fantasy set with Oliver James, working through the angles for my discussion with Trey and Lauren. He was full of good advice.

As Lauren predicted, it doesn't take long for the grass to fill up and bikini tops to come off. I'm amazed how blasé some girls are about skin cancer.

Pulling Kali's camouflage binoculars out of my beach bag, I scan the area. Lauren pushes my hand down. "Zahra, you shouldn't switch teams just because of Eric. Not all guys are jerks."

"I *know*," I say, handing her the binoculars. "There's a nice guy on the diving board now."

Lauren lifts the binoculars and watches as Trey soars into the air, jackknifes, and straightens out to slice the surface of the water. "What's Trey doing here?" she says. "And when did he learn to dive like that?"

"Apparently he's been practicing. A lot."

Lauren lowers the binoculars to look at me. "*That's* why he's never around?"

When I nod, she trains the binoculars on her boyfriend again and watches as he hoists himself out of the water. Girls' heads swivel when he walks back to the diving board, but Trey doesn't give a single bikini a second glance. I'm about to point this out to Lauren when he sneaks a peek in our direction.

"He's not here to dive," Lauren says. "He's here for the skin."

"Lauren, if there are boobs on display, any guy's going to look."

"It's just so— Oops!" she lowers the binoculars. "Busted."

Trey climbs off the board and comes to greet us. With Lauren in view, he pretends the slope isn't littered with half-naked women. I guess that's the best you can expect from a guy. "Hey, baby," Trey says. "What are you doing here?"

Lauren introduces me and pats her beach towel. "It's kind of a long story."

Trey's smile has vanished by the time Lauren finishes. "You hired someone to *spy* on me?"

This isn't how it went in my dress rehearsal. I prepared for confusion, evasion, silence, and remorse. I even worked out a strategy in case Trey dumped Lauren. But I didn't prepare for pissed off. Obviously, Oliver James is too nice. I should have brought in celebrity chef Gordon Ramshead, instead. Anger would have been his default choice.

Then again, I have to be true to my motto. Maybe all Trey needs is a sprinkle of sugar.

"It wasn't spying, exactly," I say. "And everyone we talked to had good things to say about you, Trey. Great things."

"*We?* There's a team out there talking to people about me?"

I try again. "Not a team, per se, just a couple of Lauren's friends trying to solve a mystery together."

Trey looks from me to Lauren, and the anger dilutes with hurt. "We've been together over a year. If you don't trust me now, you never will."

Lauren's eyes fill with tears as Trey gets to his feet.

Worried that this might end in tragedy, I listen hard for the inner voice. *A good chef takes charge in the kitchen,* Oliver says. *When all else fails, go with your gut.*

Counting on Trey's good manners, I say, "Let me ask one simple question: Where was Lauren supposed to be right now?"

"Ballet class," he answers.

"And where will she be tomorrow afternoon?"

"A yearbook committee meeting." He starts down the slope. "Look, ask Lauren about her schedule. I'm done here."

"One last question," I call. "Where will she be Thursday afternoon?"

"She has"—Trey's eye's flick to Lauren then back to me— "an important meeting that's none of your business."

Even when he's this angry at Lauren he won't betray her secrets. Now, that's a guy worth fighting for. "I know she has group, because I do too. But I'm surprised she told *you* about it."

His hands rest on his hips. "Why wouldn't she tell me? I'm her boyfriend."

"Because it meant trusting you with her biggest secret." I breathe a little easier as the conversation starts to resemble what I'd rehearsed.

Trey sees where I'm going, but he's not buying it. "And then she hired spies to trail me."

"Because *you* haven't trusted *her* with your biggest secret, apparently."

"She knows my biggest secrets, and this isn't one of them. It's nothing."

Ha. *This* I anticipated. "Isn't that worse?" I ask. "To shut her out of something as minor as diving?"

"Nothing's worse than spying."

I don't let him throw me off course. "Like you said, it all comes down to trust. And lately you've been unreliable. You barely call, you barely text. You've canceled plans without a good explanation. You're the one who's undermined the trust."

Trey takes a few steps toward us and stops. I've sunk the hook, but it'll take one more good point to reel him in the rest of the way. "Think about what Lauren's gone through this past year. She needs to know she can count on you."

Trey comes back and sits beside Lauren again. "Baby, I was just diving. Sometimes here, but mostly in the diving pool at UT. My swim coach has been pushing me to compete."

"So why all the secrecy?" Lauren asks.

Trey shrugs. "I was afraid I wouldn't make it to Regionals, and I didn't want you to be ashamed of me if I failed."

Lauren throws her arms around him. "Baby, I'm always proud of you."

Trey kisses the top of her head. "Keeping it a secret seems kind of stupid now. I'm sorry."

"Me too," Lauren says. "I should have just talked to you."

"I'll never cheat on you," Trey says. He gives me a last glare. "And you'll never have me tailed again, right?"

"I promise," she says.

"So can we go for a swim?" he asks, pulling her to her feet.

She looks back at me, and I smile.

"Go ahead. My work is done."

I trail after them to the deck, hearing Oliver's voice in my head: *Well done, mate. Absolutely brill.*

After Eric made me believe that happy endings are impossible, it was nice to be part of one today. It's still an adrenaline hit, but milder than the one I got from revenge. I just wish I could keep this feeling going on a regular basis.

My buzz fades instantly as my feet fly off the deck and I hit the water hard—beach bag and all. Someone blindsided me. My back stings from the impact as I kick toward the surface. Sputtering as I take my first gasp of air, I see a familiar strip of blue cloth floating a few feet in front of me. I look down in horror and discover I've lost the top of my bathing suit.

But as I reach out to grab it, a net dips into the water and fishes it out.

On the concrete deck a few feet away, water drips onto ten blue toenails adorned with daisies.

"Oh, is this yours?" Hollis asks, waggling the net just out of reach. She's wearing a tiny bikini that accentuates her angles. Beside her, Fletcher turns away from his buddies to see what's going on, and his eyes light up when he takes in the view. "Well, well. Look who's getting naked all over town now." He pulls the towel from around his neck and dangles it in front of me. "Need some help drying off?"

Hollis whacks him in the arm with the pole, and the impact ejects my bathing suit top from the net. Fletcher tries to grab it, but another hand intercepts and tosses it directly back to me.

Fletcher turns, ready to take on the person who's ruined his game. But when he catches sight of Trey's broad swimmer's shoulders, he lets it go.

I call out my thanks to Trey, and he gives me a guy-nod, to say it's all good now.

·· ♥ ··

Syd and Kali are laughing as we walk up the Congress Avenue Bridge to join the crowd that is already gathering.

"It's not funny," I say. "Fletcher is the last guy on earth I want seeing me topless."

"I know, I'm sorry," Kali says, still smiling from under the brim of her enormous hat. "But that was so nice of Trey."

"What's with the hat?" I ask.

"UV rays aren't sucking the youth out of *my* skin," she says.

Syd snickers. "Forget UV rays. Kali believes the old wives' tale."

"My hair's my best asset—after my legs," Kali says. "I don't intend to lose a single curl because a rat with wings is stuck in it."

We've come to watch the largest urban bat colony in North America leave its daytime roost under the bridge and fly off into the dusk. Syd wants to take photos as inspiration for her new graffiti series—or "street art," as she calls it. Her goal is to commemorate a creature that's barely changed in fifty million years. Apparently she finds their consistency comforting while her own life is in turmoil.

Seeing over a million bats take off at the same time is one of the coolest sights nature has to offer. My family used to come often, until this year. Now my parents avoid anything we did as a family, even eating at our favorite restaurants. No one talks about it, of course. It's the family way.

I finish my update on Lauren's reunion with Trey, and Syd shakes her head. "That was the big secret? Competitive diving?"

"Small secrets can become big problems, I guess," I say. "Anyway, Lauren was so thrilled to hear Trey's still into her that she gave us a fifty dollar bonus."

Kali tips her hat back and beams at me. "You really have a gift, Zahra."

Syd takes off her vintage cat's-eye sunglasses. As usual, she's looking funky, in silver leggings paired with an old T-shirt and a guy's suit vest. "Nice job."

Kali notices a guy rolling past on his skateboard and smiles at him. "You probably bought Lauren and Trey another six months," she says.

"Six months?" I say. "I give them at least until college." Before Eric, I might have said they could go the distance, but that seems the stuff of fairy tales, even with a couple as well matched as Lauren and Trey.

"Like I said before, no one feels the love forever," Kali says. The skater dude is so entranced by her that he wipes out. "But it sure is fun while it lasts."

Syd watches as skater boy dusts himself off with two grazed and bloody hands. "The pain's not worth the gain," she says.

Someone in the crowd shouts, "Here they come!"

Squealing, Kali holds down her hat with both hands and squeezes her eyes shut. Meanwhile, Syd passes me Banksy's leash and raises her camera. The bats emerge in long black columns from beneath the bridge, dimming the rosy evening sky on their way out to hunt.

"That was awesome!" Kali says, opening her eyes in time to see the last line of bats snake over the tops of the buildings and disappear in the distance. She pulls off her hat and fluffs her curls. "Now for some ice cream."

As we head over to Amy's Ice Creams on 6th Street, I fish around in my bag for the envelope Lauren gave me, and divvy up the bonus.

"Making money has never been so much fun," Kali says. "A few more assignments would really build my guitar fund."

"Most people couldn't afford to pay so much," I say.

"True," Kali says. "But I'd have done it for half the price. Maybe we could work out some sort of pay-what-you-can system, depending on the complexity of the job."

"You're talking like this is an ongoing business," I say.

"Maybe it should be," Kali says. "Don't tell me you haven't thought about it."

"I was thinking about it on the bus ride over," I admit. "I bet lots of people need help fixing their relationships."

"Not to mention retribution when they get screwed," Syd adds.

"Imagine the job satisfaction," Kali says. "It felt so great to even the score with Eric, and we'd have been willing to pay for it. I've been thinking about all the people who never get that closure. If Zahra can't help them get a rocky relationship on track, Syd could step in to give them back their pride. Then *I* could help them find love again. Match, patch, and dispatch," Kali starts singing. "Love, Inc. does it all."

Syd ties Banksy up outside of Amy's. "That has a nice ring to it. The name, I mean. Not the song."

While we wait in line for our ice cream, Kali and I discuss how we'd find clients. Since we'd mostly have to fly under the radar, we couldn't exactly advertise.

Syd is quiet until she has her cone in hand and has shaped it into a perfect dome. "I wasn't sure if I should mention this, but there's a photographer at the Maternity Ward who saw the article in the *Chronicle* and recognized my work on the car. Her name is Sinead, and she wants us to set up an Eric Special for her cheating boyfriend. Her mom owns a denim store, and she offered free jeans as payment."

"Sounds like we have our first official client," Kali says, beaming. "I'm in if you are. And the barter system is fine with me."

"Me too," I say. "But let's say we all have to agree that someone deserves to be punished before we slam."

"Fine," Syd says. "But I know the guy, and trust me, he deserves it."

"If he does, Cupid's deputies will bust him," Kali says.

"So we're really going to do this?" I ask, half excited, half

terrified. It's one thing to fumble around in your own relationship, but if you're accepting payment to help other people,
you've got to get it right. I was lucky today, but if we go pro,
I'll have to improve my technique. We'll have standards to
maintain.

On the upside, maybe I'll learn something through this
work that will help me succeed in love the next time—if there
is one.

"Let's do it," Syd says, holding out a fist.

"I hereby declare Love, Inc. open for business," Kali
announces as our knuckles collide. She opens her arms to
embrace us, and Syd steps backward.

"Keep the cones away from the vintage couture."

"Since when does a ripped Bangles T-shirt qualify as vintage couture?" Kali asks. "You want to know my opinion?"

"Not really," Syd replies.

"I think you're hug-phobic."

"And I think you have too many opinions."

Glancing around the empty hallway, I answer my phone.
"Hello, Love, Inc."

"Interesting," a guy says in a low, smooth voice. "This is
Riaz Dar. Your grandmother said you've been expecting my
call."

My back goes up immediately. "She did not." In fact, I was
expecting Sinead, the photographer from the Maternity Ward.

"She did," Riaz continues. "She said you think I'm hot."

I highly doubt Nani used that word, although she shouldn't
have been talking to him about me anyway. "Yeah, right," I

say, heading toward my next class. "Actually, *she* thinks you're hot, Riaz. Lucky you."

There's a pause as he imagines that scenario. "I got the photo you sent, too."

Señora Mendoza rounds the corner and stops at the window overlooking the back of the campus, where students try to sneak in a smoke. To avoid her, I slide into a stairwell and close the door behind me.

"I didn't send you a photo." Nani must be getting more tech savvy, thanks to her twelve-year-old accomplice.

"Well, since we're chatting, what are you doing the first Saturday in October?"

"Not going out with you," I say. If this arrogant jerk is the best my grandmother could do, it's a good thing arranged marriages are a thing of the past in my family.

"Who asked?"

"Sounds like we're on the same page, here, Riaz. I'm hanging up now."

"Wait," he says, laughing. "I'm just messing with you. I'm actually calling because I'm the head of volunteers for the Eid carnival, and your grandmother said you wanted to get involved."

"Like I said, my grandmother lies."

"Okay, but now that you're getting to know me, you might want to help out anyway," Riaz says.

"Now that I'm getting to know you, I want to stay as far away from that carnival as possible. Good-bye, Riaz." I start heading down the stairs. "I hope you and Nani have a great day together."

Riaz laughs. "Are you jealous?"

"Yeah," I say, "I can only hope my love life will be as great as my grandmother's someday."

His laughter is still ringing in my ears as I near the bottom of the stairs, and it takes me a second to realize there's someone else laughing. I back up a few paces to find Hollis leaning against the wall under the last set of stairs. The buttons of her top are mostly undone, and Fletcher has his arm around her waist.

"You want a love life like your *grandmother's?*" Hollis says. "That's sick."

Fletcher grins, and sparkles of gloss on his lips catch the light. "There's no need to settle," he says. "Not when you like to go topless."

"Looks like I've set a trend," I say, looking pointedly at Hollis's shirt. "I hope the admin staff enjoyed the show."

"What do you mean?" Hollis says, starting to button up.

"Don't you read the school paper?" I ask, bluffing. "They installed CCTV at Austin." I look up to the light fixture as I head toward the exit. "They can hide those little cameras anywhere."

"I don't see anything," Fletcher says, spinning slowly.

I smile as I open the door to the lower hall. "Enjoy your detention, superstars."

·· ♥ ··

"Shopping for love at the big box store
Shopping for someone I can adore
I asked you for paint, you said satin or glossy . . ."

Kali muses, "What could come next?"

"'That's when I noticed your teeth were all mossy'?" I

suggest. "'Haven't you heard of dental flossy'?"

"Stick to writing recipes, Z."

Glennis comes into the kitchen and looks around. "Did I sleep through a tornado?"

Dirty bowls, spoons, and spatulas cover every surface in the kitchen, and the island is smeared with batter and frosting. "I took you up on your offer," I say, clearing the way to the coffeemaker.

I made two types of cupcakes for my sister's bake sale: dark chocolate with white chocolate chunks and strawberry icing, and white chocolate cupcakes with strawberries pieces and dark chocolate icing.

After putting the coffee on, Glennis sets her camera up on a tripod and arranges my cupcakes on platters beside the window.

"Every meal's a photo op," Kali says. She points to the three photos of peppers that I've admired since the first day I visited. The angle and the lighting transform a simple vegetable into a modern, sculptural object.

"Maybe you could use these shots in a cookbook one day," Glennis says.

I'm thrilled. No one's ever taken my baking this seriously before. "Thanks, Mrs. Callaghan," I say, choosing her most recent married name.

"Call me Glennis," she says, pouring coffee into a thermal cup and heading for the door with her camera gear. Just as I'm deciding she's the coolest mom on the planet, she adds, "Leave the kitchen like you found it, okay?"

A few minutes later, Syd arrives with Banksy in tow. She was supposed to have breakfast with her mom, but her scowl suggests it didn't work out. I know better than to ask, but Kali isn't as cautious. "What happened with your mom?"

"I'm here to work, Kali," Syd says. "Family problems can wait till group."

Kali blunders on. "Did she make other plans?"

"Did my words come out in Klingon?" Syd asks.

I let them argue while I clean up the kitchen, and they start to lose steam as I put the last dish away. "How's it going with your matchmaker program, Kali?" I ask.

"Almost done," she says. "I think I might road test it on my mom. She's incredibly picky. If I can find a decent match for her, I'll know my formula's a winner."

"Good luck with that." The sentence is garbled because the speaker has his mouth full of cupcake. Brody is standing behind us in rumpled army shorts and an equally rumpled T-shirt. His feet are bare and his hair is sticking up all over. Still, he's cute. Probably better than cute in the big scheme of things. "Morning."

"It's nearly two," Kali says, as he strips the paper off another cupcake and devours it. "Those are Zahra's. You could at least ask first."

"May I?" he asks, reaching for a third cupcake. Banksy stands under him, licking up the crumbs. "These are amazing. Where'd you get them?"

"I made them."

"Get out." He reaches for a fourth, and I notice he's gone for three of the chocolate with strawberry icing. I have my winner.

"Leave some for the bake sale," Kali says.

"There's plenty," I say. For me, there's nothing better than seeing someone enjoy my baking.

"I told you Red likes me," he says, winking at Kali. "Guess you girls heard about what happened to Rick's car?"

I can't help grinning. "We saw the article."

"Don't look so happy about it," Brody says. "It wasn't *you* he played."

"Actually, it was," I say. "And his name is Eric."

"The guy deserved what he got," Syd says.

Brody turns to his sister. "Deserved? This was random, wasn't it?"

Kali shrugs. "Maybe Eric picked the wrong girls to cheat on."

Brody looks at us, lined up with our arms crossed, and puts the pieces together. "You did all that? The paint job, the tires, the slimy crap inside?"

Three of us shrug in unison.

Brody starts backing away. He pitches the uneaten half of his cupcake into the sink, and I watch as my creation slides into a pool of soapy water. "Hey!" I say.

"I just remembered I'm allergic to nuts," he says. "And you guys are crazy."

chapter 10

"**D**oes Kali have a brother?" Mom asks, out of the blue.

I nearly drop the container of cupcakes I'm sliding onto the counter. "Why?"

"You're over at her house a lot lately." Mom's been able to track me because I'm staying with her for a week or so while Dad's away on business. "I thought there might be a cute boy involved."

Since I can't tell her there's a business involved, I go along with her boy theory. "Kali does have a brother, and like most guys, he's a jerk."

"Ah, right," Mom says. "Still mourning Rico?"

I'm not mourning, but you don't get over that kind of thing in a day.

Given how drained she looks, Mom hasn't exactly bounced back from her split with Dad, either. Having my grandparents around and starving through Ramadan can't be helping her recuperation. Still, I can't let her think it's all good between us, so I use her special one-word technique. "Mom."

"Just asking." She hands me a gift-wrapped box. "I put together some lotions for Kali's mom to thank her for letting my messy daughter take over her kitchen."

It occurs to me that this might be just the thing Mom needs to take her mind off both her breakup and what Nana calls "spiritual growth." "Hey, Mom, have you given any more thought to starting your own business?"

Turning her back, she starts unloading the dishwasher. "I wouldn't know where to begin."

It's the first time she hasn't shot me down outright, so I keep going. "You helped Dad launch his company, so you probably learned a lot. And what you don't know, he can teach you."

"I will not ask your father to help me with anything." Her normally soft voice has an edge. "He wouldn't have time anyway. Saliyah said he was barely around when she stayed with you last week."

She's digging for ammo. "He had dinner with us every night." It's technically true, although Saliyah and I had long since finished when Dad joined us in front of the TV with leftovers. "He works a lot because he's depressed. If you let him move back, he'd spend more time at home." I haven't pressured her for a while, but my success with Trey and Lauren has renewed my interest in mediating.

Mom places mugs on hooks in the cupboard. "I didn't evict him, you know. He called the movers himself."

Hitting the same old wall, I go back to my first point. "How about renting a table at the Eid carnival?" I ask. "It's only for a weekend. Saliyah and I will help you set up, and Nani can brainwash everyone into buying twice as much as they need."

"It would be too much work on such short notice," she says, clattering plates on purpose to drown me out.

In other words, this is going to cost me more than a weekend. "I'll help you."

Mom reaches for her bottle of bleach, and pauses. "And you'd spend the whole day with us? From dawn to dusk?"

Dawn to dusk is an eternity when my grandparents are involved. But it's a lot of goodwill in the bank. "Okay."

My sister joins us in the kitchen and squeals with delight when she sees the cupcakes. "Those are awesome! I'll win the iPod Touch for sure."

"Since when are there prizes at school bake sales? All I ever got was ribbons."

Saliyah's eyes widen as she realizes her mistake. "Sometimes the person who brings in the most cash gets a prize. Nothing big. Just video games, DVDs, an iPod."

The last word is almost inaudible—a giveaway. "You won an iPod with *my* baking and didn't tell me?"

From the look on Mom's face, Saliyah didn't tell her either.

"It was just a Shuffle." She turns to bellow, "Nani! Zahra's here. Come look at her cupcakes."

Nani hustles into the kitchen. She's wearing a mustard-colored tunic with bright green trim and matching pants. I guess when you're five-foot-nothing you try to get noticed in other ways. "Zahra! Have you had any interesting calls this week?"

I lean against the counter. "Interesting, no. But what's his name from the festival committee called."

"Riaz? Already! That's a good sign." She's beaming.

"He said that you said he's hot."

"Hot?"

"He thought you wanted to hook up, but you're not really his type, so he asked me to let you down easy," I say.

Nani looks at mom. "What is she saying?"

Mom shakes her head, fighting a smile. "I really can't translate it, Ammi."

"Are you making fun of me?" Nani scowls. "I was only trying to help you find a nice young man."

"I don't need help, Nani. Save your energy for Saliyah's bake sale. She wants to take your *burfi*." My grandmother brags that she makes the best *burfi* in Karachi. That may be true, but Saliyah and I aren't fans of the supersweet, condensed-milk dessert. "It's a definite prizewinner. Plus, it'll give her a chance to show off her culture to her friends."

My sister looks worried. "These cupcakes are really all I need, Zahra. And if I win the iPod Touch, I promise I'll let you borrow it whenever you want."

I look at my mother. "Did she just say that when my cupcakes win, she'd like to borrow *my* iPod Touch whenever *I* say it's okay?"

"That's what I heard," Mom says.

While Saliyah whines, Mom tells Nani about our plans for the Eid carnival. Instead of showing enthusiasm for Mom's business, however, Nani grabs my sleeve. "When you meet Riaz, I want you to tie your hair back and put on some black eyeliner. And don't make any of your jokes."

"So what you're saying is, 'Shut up and look pretty.'"

"Why do you have to twist everything?" Nani says.

Mom rubs her forehead. "Zahra."

It means the usual: "Must you?" And the answer is yes. Because the day I take romance advice from my grandmother is the day I pack it in completely.

.. ♥ ..

I hate running. The only thing I hate more than running is people who say they love running. Searing lungs and aching muscles cannot feel good to anyone. As for the "runner's high" people brag about, it's either a delusion brought on by dehydration, or a ruse to bring suckers into the cult. I've tried it again and again, and I've never felt anything but miserable.

Normally, I'd avoid people like Stacey, who loves running so much she's on a cross-country team. But since she's a Love, Inc. client with a busy training schedule, I had no choice but to lace up my Nikes after group today and join her.

Stacey is our second official client. Lauren was so thrilled to hear she's the inspiration for our business that she immediately referred Stacey for some pre-relationship coaching.

Stacey has no trouble meeting guys, but something always goes wrong before she achieves girlfriend status. Her current crush, Graham, has invited her to a charity event his parents are hosting this weekend, and she wants to get things on track.

Given my history, I'm not in a position to coach, but as Kali reminds me, our own relationships aren't public record. As long as we *act* like we know what we're talking about, we should be fine, especially with the three of us presenting a united front. Our collective history gives us good perspective. Besides, it's easy to see what's going on in someone *else*'s relationship.

I'm surprised Syd agreed to join us, but she was the first to hit St. Joe's ladies' room when group ended, emerging in Lululemon gear she borrowed from her mother. With her hair pinned back, she's transformed into the girl next door.

"Pick it up, Z," she shouts over her shoulder. "A snail just passed you!"

I wouldn't have pegged Syd for a runner, but I guess when your hobby is vandalizing public property, you need to stay fit to outrun the authorities.

Kali's fitness comes as an even bigger surprise. She's bouncing alongside Syd and Stacey without any sign of cardiac arrest. I guess the lungs of a singer outperform the lungs of a baker, which are probably clogged with flour.

Finally, I collapse on a park bench. I'll be no use to Love, Inc. if I'm dead.

Stacey, Kali, Syd, and Banksy travel another twenty yards before they realize the wheezing behind them has ceased. They turn back and Kali claps three times in front of my flushed face. "Up and at it," she says. "In life, we must always move forward." It's a quote from Dieter. "That's what we've been telling Stacey here, who's on the verge of chickening out of her date with Graham."

"What?" I puff. "Why? This is the opportunity you've been waiting for."

Stacey perches on the bench beside me. Her pretty face is barely flushed. "What's the point, when I'm only going to get crushed again?" she says.

Kali gradually draws out the details, and the problem soon becomes clear. Stacey has an extreme case of the Cookie Curse. She goes out of her way to plan her life around her guy's schedule. She sends chocolate on special occasions, and soup when he's sick. Since she has a car, she provides chauffeur services on every errand and date. In fact, she plans every date, just to make it easier on the guy, and picks up the tab, since she has a big allowance.

Syd sums up the situation: "You might as well cut off a

guy's jack-in-the-box and be done with it."

"What are you talking about?" Stacey says. "I treat guys like gold."

Now that my lungs are working, I can translate. "Guys need to feel like they're competing for a prize, Stacey. It sounds like you're doing most of the work."

I know this because I did this. With Eric, I'd drop everything in a second to be available for him. Syd probably never made it easy for Eric, and she's the prize he wanted.

"So you're saying I should become a bitch?" Stacey asks.

Kali hoists a leg onto the bench and stretches, inserting her face between mine and Stacey's. "Just tone things down. Right now you're scaring guys off."

"Scaring them off?" Stacey repeats.

"Guys need breathing room," I say.

"Not too much, though," Syd adds, with a hint of alarm in her voice.

"There's nothing wrong with doing something nice for a guy once you're established," Kali says. "But doing too much in those critical early weeks throws off the natural order."

Syd tries a different approach. "You mentioned having a poodle, Stace. Is she well-trained?"

"Uh, not exactly," Stacey says. "Lulu's sort of spoiled and bratty."

Syd nods. "And I bet she gets lots of treats without doing any work for them?"

"Well, she's so cute, I can't help it," Stacey says. Then the lightbulb goes off. "Oh, I get it. You're saying guys are dogs?"

Kali laughs. "Well, that's a different conversation."

"We're saying training techniques apply to anyone," Syd

157

says. "Rewards have more value when they're earned by good behavior. And consistency is critical: if you give them an inch, they take a mile."

Or two more girlfriends. Syd has put a lot of work into Banksy's training, but she probably thinks she let Eric's slide.

Stacey mulls this over before summing up the lesson. "I spoil guys and they get lazy, like Lulu. And they don't stick around because the rewards have no value."

"You need to be the alpha dog," Syd says.

"If you follow the plan we lay out for you," Kali says, "Graham won't just stick around, he'll be begging you for a treat."

Over the next hour we run through scenarios Stacey could face in the weeks ahead, and put her on a strict diet with regards to phone calls, texts, and Facebook pokes. It's tough going because everything we suggest defies Stacey's normal programming. For every argument there's a counterargument. I understand her resistance. Some people—me, for example— aren't born to be alpha dogs. But if you don't take control, you end up at the back of the pack.

Finally, the three of us wear her down, and by the time she runs off into the distance, she's actually excited about her new, more restrained plan of attack.

Kali bounces on her toes. "I'm totally energized. You guys up for another quarter mile?"

I raise a hand to summon her closer, and when her face is level with mine, I retract my index finger and slowly raise the middle one.

Syd laughs. "Dieter would admire your honesty."

We walk the rest of the gravel path that skirts Town Lake, and Syd fills us in on her investigations for Sinead, the photographer from the Maternity Ward. "The guy's definitely cheating."

"I thought you'd sound happier," I say. "It's a slam waiting to happen."

She sighs. "When I tracked Sinead down in one of the old darkrooms to debrief her, I found her making out with someone—and it wasn't her boyfriend."

"Double duplicity," I say, shaking my head. "I hope this job doesn't make me even more cynical about relationships. Why can't people just be honest with each other?"

"Because it's harder to tell the truth than it is to live a lie," Syd says.

"Does this mean we forfeit the jeans?" Kali asks.

"Nope," Syd says. "Sinead agrees the relationship is over, but she doesn't want things to be awkward. So I convinced her to let Zahra broker their split."

"Syd! I want to help people stay together, not break up." I'm quite sure that helping people break up is not going to bring me the adrenaline buzz I crave. "I want feel-good clients."

"They'll feel good eventually, Z," Syd says. "Right now, Sinead and Leo are prolonging the pain. They know the relationship's over, but they don't know how to get out of it without making it ugly. You just need to mediate the split."

"Mom and Greg had a mediator, and their breakup was pretty civilized," Kali says. She pulls binoculars out of her waist pack as we approach the Texas Rowing Center, and directs them at the water. Then she passes them to me so I can check out four guys rowing in unison.

"The one in front looks familiar," I say. "Isn't he the barista from Bennu's?" I lower the binoculars. "I thought you had your heart set on Paolo, the wallpaper guy."

"That was before Syd told me he plays trombone in a marching band," Kali says. "Obviously I can't go out with someone who wears a hat with a chin strap and a big feather."

"Obviously not," Syd says, holding out her hand. "With a steep company discount, your bill comes to ten bucks."

"What are you talking about?" Kali asks, laughing.

"Z and I get *paid* to stake guys out now."

·· ♥ ··

Kali pours lemonade into three glasses and sets a bowl of water on the floor of the trailer for Banksy. We're here to develop some Love, Inc. "commandments," but as usual, my partners have been sidetracked by an argument.

"I can't believe you actually made me cough up the cash," Kali says.

"That was two days ago," Syd says. "Two weeks in dog years. Get over it already. Anyway, it won't happen again because there's a rule in place. Zahra?"

I look at my laptop and read: "'Thou shalt not use the corporation for personal gain.'"

"Especially when it's all for nothing," Syd says. "We waited an hour for your Bennu boy to come ashore, and then you barely spoke to him."

"I couldn't focus after I saw that ridiculous tattoo," Kali says. "SpongeBob SquarePants in permanent ink? I don't think so."

"He was funny," I say. "You were howling at that story about the customer who wanted to know if the cranberry muffins came without cranberries."

"No one's perfect," Syd says.

"I need perfect at the beginning," Kali says. "Otherwise, what's the point? It's all going to end in heartache eventually."

"You know you've got issues, right?" Syd says.

"We've all got issues," Kali says. "Or Love, Inc. wouldn't need to offer so many services." Kali cranks the Notts County song that's playing on her iPod docking station and lets loose on the air guitar. "I'm telling you guys, Owen Gaines is going to be huge."

"More issues," Syd says. "You're obsessed with a singer you can't have instead of looking at the guys you could have. And from what I can see, you have lots of options."

"I thought you wanted to leave issues for group," Kali says. "Today's meeting is about Love, Inc."

We just finished setting up our pricing structure:

- *Surveillance:* twenty bucks an hour
- *Mediation:* seventy-five per two-hour session
- *Breakup Management:* seventy-five per two-hour session
- *Matchmaking:* thirty bucks a match
- *Relationship Coaching:* fifty bucks per two-hour session

All prices are negotiable, based on client circumstances, and we're willing to accept payment in-kind.

Revenge is in a category unto itself. We've agreed to keep the service on the down-low. No advertising, special request only, and priced on a case-by-case basis.

"All jobs will be acquired through word of mouth," Kali says, adding another commandment. "We need a solid reference to take on a case."

"And we'll meet at least once a week to discuss business," Syd says.

I add these to our growing list of rules. "We'll have to be flexible on the time, though. I do two shifts a week at the Recipe Box."

"If Love, Inc. takes off, you'll be able to quit," Kali says.

Maybe, but I wouldn't. René's more like an uncle than a boss to me, and when the cold front blew in at home, that little store was my haven. I like to be surrounded by cookbooks and foodies. It's soothing.

A loud thump on the side of the trailer makes us all jump.

Kali peeks through the curtains. "It's Brody, and he's got some guy with him." There's another thump, and I join her at the window. The guys are dribbling a basketball in the driveway. Kali flings open the door and flinches as a ball whizzes past and bounces off the side of the trailer again.

Brody glares at Syd and me as we come down the steps, then turns to his sister. "What are you doing in Kevin's trailer?"

"What are you doing home so early?" Kali asks.

"Where'd you find the key?"

"Why do you care?"

The other guy jumps in to break the string of unanswered questions. "The other team didn't show and the game was postponed. I'm Luke, by the way. Sorry about the noise."

Kali introduces us, but when Luke steps forward to shake our hands, Brody intercepts. "Don't get too close. They bite."

Luke, a tall guy with gray eyes and a shock of dark hair, grins. "That's bad because . . . ?"

"They're poisonous," Brody says. "Meet the girls who ruined Eric Skinner's life."

"Exaggerate much?" I ask.

"It's not an exaggeration," Brody says. "A guy's car—if he's

162

lucky enough to have one—*is* his life. Ruin his car, you ruin his life."

"You trashed Miss Daisy?" Luke asks. "Why?"

"Brody's mistaken," Kali says, giving him a warning look.

"Skinner was three-timing them," Brody says. "They were highly motivated."

Kali continues to stare at her brother. "You're giving Luke the wrong idea."

Brody fires the ball a few feet to the left of his sister and catches it as it rebounds, before he relents. "Fine. It wasn't you. But you were pretty happy about it."

"Happy isn't a crime," Kali says.

Brody shoots the ball, which bounces off the wall of the trailer again. Inside, Banksy barks. "In this case, happy equals bitter, and bitterness is a guy repellant."

"I'm not feeling repelled," Luke says, smiling at us.

Kali smiles. "Thank you, Luke. Too bad my brother doesn't have your class."

Brody's phone rings and he steps away. "Hey, Asta. No, you're not interrupting anything. It's good to hear a voice of sanity right now."

Syd and I return to the trailer and try to work out more commandments, but soon the basketball is hitting the trailer again, repeatedly and deliberately. We give up and go back outside.

Kali is still talking to Luke. "Our matchmaking service is just what you need."

"Matchmaking service?" Brody says, indignant all over again. He glares at me. "Is that why you two are always over here? Planting stupid ideas in my sister's head?"

"Give me some credit," Kali says. "It was my idea. We're calling it Love, Inc."

Brody snorts. "I wonder what Mom will think about this business?"

"Ask her," Kali says. "Then we'll find out what she thinks about the party you had while she was away in August—the one where sixty kids turned up and you had to repaint the kitchen wall because of the blueberry daiquiri incident."

"Is it true you had to bribe a neighbor not to call the cops?" Luke asks.

Kali points to a shabby bungalow across the street. "Brody has to mow Mr. Ludlow's lawn for a year. Mom thinks it's sweet. When she hears the truth she'll be so disappointed that she might even withdraw your car privileges. And a car is a guy's life, right?"

Brody stares her down, and they come to a silent sibling understanding.

"I'm glad we sorted that out," Kali says. "And for the record, our business is about enhancing lives. We want to bring people together in happiness until a relationship runs its course, then help them find closure. It's a noble goal."

"Remember to write that down, Z," Syd says. "Sounds like a mission statement."

Brody takes a long swig from his soda before saying, "If you want to take money from losers and give them false hope, what do I care?"

Kali turns to Luke and says, "He didn't mean to call you a loser."

"Tell me you're not getting involved," Brody pleads.

Shrugging, Luke says, "Kali said she could find someone for

me to take to the City Limits Music Festival next weekend."

"You don't need help," Brody says. "Girls love you, and you're offering up a free ticket to the coolest concert in town."

"Yeah, but you know what it's like on a first date: you spend half the night trying to figure out if you've got anything in common, and if you don't, you spend the other half wishing you'd stayed home. Kali could do the weeding out for me."

"I wouldn't trust my sister with your gardening," Brody says.

"I can't really afford to hire you anyway," Luke says. "I blew most of my cash on those tickets."

"Dodge the bullet while you can," Brody says, tossing the ball deep into the backyard. "Come on. I've got time to grab a pizza before my shift at the store."

"Hey, Luke," Kali calls, as her brother drags him away. "We'll do the job for free!"

Luke gives her two thumbs up. "You're on."

"Since when did we agree to freebies?" Syd asks, stooping to kiss Banksy's head as we climb back into the trailer.

"We need a commandment about that," I say. "Plus, I think we need to be a little more careful with how much we talk about the business."

"Agreed," Syd says. "We need clearance levels for information. And we should all have to be on board before we take on a case."

"You're right, but I'm pleading brother immunity," Kali says. "I need to prove to Brody that I can do this."

Syd flops onto the bench and stares at her. "This has more to do with Luke than Brody. The guy was cute."

"He was?" Kali asks innocently. "I make a point of not noticing whether Brody's friends are cute. Anyone who'd want to hang out with my brother couldn't be perfect for me."

"Commandment number five," Syd says. "Thou shalt not covet a Love, Inc. client. Seriously, Kali, it's bad news."

"Why are you assuming I'll be the one to break that rule?"

"Because Z and I don't covet everyone with a Y chromosome."

"Commandment number six," Kali says. "Thou shalt not be a bitch twenty-four–seven."

chapter 11

Syd leads Kali and me up a flight of iron stairs to the kitchen area of the Maternity Ward. It's deserted except for Sinead and Leo, who sip coffee in silence at opposite ends of an old pine table. After making the introductions, Syd leaves to give Kali a tour. Although I'm still mad at them for putting me in this position, I'm relieved that they're close by in case the unhappy couple realizes I'm a fraud and tosses me out on my behind. There's a huge difference between easing a reunion between two people in love and brokering a breakup between two people who've been cheating on each other. Fortunately, I had plenty of time to visit *The Sweet Tooth* set and run scenarios with Oliver James and Gordon Ramshead. Hopefully there won't be any surprises this time, but if there are, I'll go with my gut.

To avoid giving Sinead and Leo a chance to question my credentials, I jump right in. "Syd tells me you've agreed to end your relationship but want to figure out if you can stay friends."

"Or at least polite acquaintances," says Sinead. She's sixteen but looks older, with her wavy dark hair tied in a loose ponytail. "We've pretty much said all there is to say, but it's still awkward when we run into each other here."

"I get that," I say, mentally reviewing the checklist I drafted earlier. First, I have to find common ground. "I can see how it would be hard to create if you're tense and constantly looking over your shoulder."

Leo nods and cracks his knuckles, which are dusty with dried clay. I can tell he'd rather be anywhere else than here right now, letting some sophomore referee his breakup. He probably only agreed to it because he was the first to cheat. Normally, he'd be the one to fade into the background, but he can't face giving up access to their communal property.

"Okay, so the Maternity Ward is important to both of you," I say. "Let's see if we can come up with some guidelines so you can both hang out here. Who likes to work in the morning?"

"Me," Leo says. "The light is better for sculpting."

"And Sinead, you mostly work off-site and use the Ward's laser printer, right?" I ask. "So you could come in later in the day, say after two or three?"

There's a moment where I think she'll argue just for the sake of arguing, but she agrees. "Yeah, mostly I come after school anyway."

"But I can only come after school during the week," Leo argues.

"Okay, so how about Sinead gets Monday, Wednesday, and Friday after school, and weekends after three? Leo gets Tuesday and Thursday after school and weekends before three? Could that work?"

"It's kind of restrictive," Leo says.

"This is just for a while, until you feel more comfortable with the breakup," I say. "What do you think?"

Neither wants to be the first to nod, but finally they do.

"Good," I say, secretly thrilled. "So what else would make things easier?"

Sinead looks at Leo and scowls. "No nude models."

"I'm an artist; that's what I do," he says. "You don't get to be jealous anymore."

"Just because it's a mutual split doesn't mean it won't be hard sometimes," I say. "So, Leo, how about, no *female* models if there's any risk of running into Sinead?"

"I'm supposed to sculpt fruit?" He leans back and crosses his arms. "What does *she* give up?"

"The same thing," I say. "No hot male subject matter. And no hooking up on-site—for either of you."

"But this is where we meet people," Leo says.

I roll my eyes. Leo is gorgeous, with wavy blond hair and a cleft in his chin. "You know you could meet people any-where," I say. "If you've been hooking up here, it's only to piss each other off. Negative attention sometimes feels better than none at all."

They exchange glances that suggest I'm right on target.

Encouraged, I continue. "So we've got two good rules. Let's move on to friends. For the next few months, how about you leave with the friends you came into the relationship with?"

"But our friends overlap now," Sinead says.

"Then let's go through them one by one and decide who gets to 'keep' them for now. Later, when things settle down, you can renegotiate."

And so we progress through their history, dividing their friends, art, music, and DVDs they gave each other or bought together, and the places they like to hang out. It's uncomfortable, especially since they're now looking to me to make the final decisions. Although they seem relieved to have someone in charge, it's scary to have so much responsibility.

"What else could cause tension?" I ask, trying to sound like a professional.

Sinead looks at Leo and says, "What about your mother? Can I still see her?"

This I didn't expect. "His mom? That would be tricky."

"We've been close," Sinead says, and for the first time her voice cracks. "Because my mom is . . ."

"Difficult," Leo says. He reaches for Sinead's hand. "It's okay. Mom's really upset we're breaking up. It would be good for both of you to have coffee now and then."

Sinead brightens. "Really?"

"Great," I say. "But to make that work, Sinead, no discussing Leo with his mom."

"Sounds good," Leo says. "Then I can still play soccer with your brother?"

"Fair enough," she says.

"Shake on it," I suggest. It just seems like a good note to end on.

By the time I head downstairs, I'm stoked. Every time I wear my new designer jeans, I'll remember exactly how I earned them.

·· ♥ ··

The guy sitting beside me in the backseat of the car is venting. "My girlfriend and I are going through a hard time right now," he says. "We've been together for ages but her parents are on the rocks, and she says she wants to take a break." He sticks his hand out the window of the car to catch the breeze as we whiz along the highway.

"Did she say she wants to break up?" I ask.

He shakes his head. "Not in those words. She said she needs space."

"That sounds pretty selfish to me," the driver says, speaking for the first time. "It's like she wants to have her cake and eat it too. Well, she can't expect you to just sit around while she works out her stuff." He rubs the steering wheel with a flannel cloth until it shines. "I've got an idea: why don't you go out with Zahra? She's not girlfriend material, but she's a decent distraction. Easy to please and a good cook too."

I look up at the rearview mirror and find Eric's deep blue eyes looking back at me. They crinkle when they meet mine.

"I'm not easy to please," I say.

Eric shrugs. "That might have changed. I heard you got bitter, and bitter's a guy repellant." He glances at my client. "Go with Kali instead. She's prettier and more fun."

"I'm fun," I say. "Lots of people like me."

"If you say so." Eric looks over his shoulder at my client and mouths, "Run!"

I shoot up in the bed, my hair damp with sweat.

"Another nightmare about Rico?" Saliyah's voice comes out of the darkness.

"Yeah," I whisper, collapsing onto my damp pillow to wait for my heart to stop racing. "It's the first in over a week, though."

At this rate, I'll be in college before my subconscious gets over the humiliation of what happened with Eric.

"Do you want the light on?" Saliyah asks.

I do, but I don't want to admit it to my little sister. "Nah, I'm good."

There's a gentle thud on my bed, followed by another one as Saliyah sends in Dewey and Monkey Man to help. Clutching them, I eventually drift back to sleep.

·· ♥ ··

"Zahra, be careful," Nani calls up to me. She's wearing a hot pink salwar kameez with orange trim, and there's an orange ribbon woven through her long, gray braid. She's even wearing eyeliner for the occasion.

"I'm fine," I say, plugging in the last string of Kali's patio lanterns and looking down at Walnut Creek Park from my perch on the ladder. The sun is just rising on this cool mid-October morning, and all around us people are setting up booths for the Eid carnival. Beyond the carnival rides, I spot my grandfather's plaid cap near the food stalls. These vendors were the first to set up, ready to sell breakfast to the rest of us as we get ready for the fair's official opening at nine.

I climb down the ladder and help Saliyah spread an enormous lime-green-and-aqua cloth over the old plywood tables we're using to display Mom's products.

"You can't use that cloth," Nani says. "Sana, tell them. I shipped that from Pakistan. It will get dirty."

"It's fine," Mom says. "I said they could." Since Mom doesn't have a table that seats thirty, the cloth has never been out of its packaging.

My grandmother crosses her arms and looks up at the huge YASIN VALLEY BODY CARE banner that Syd painted for me. The

Yasin Valley is a beautiful area in northern Pakistan that Mom and her family often visited when she was young. It's lush and green and fed by glacial streams. Since her products bring to mind the fragrances of her youth, the name seemed to fit. She hugged me when she saw the sign, so I guess she agrees. Even Nani smiled, although now she's frowning.

"It's crooked," she says. "Move the left side up."

I scoot back up the ladder to make the adjustment.

"More," Nana chimes in, as he rejoins us, carrying containers full of *halwa puri*, a mixture of curries with chickpeas and potato.

"Did you bring coffee?" I ask, knowing the answer will be no. Coffee is too American for them. My grandparents are tea drinkers. Back on the ground, I take the paper cup of tea Nana offers. In a pinch, caffeine is caffeine.

I open up one of the boxes we stacked near the table and start arranging Mom's products.

"Don't stack those bags of bath salts so high," Nana says, around a mouthful of curry. "They could topple over."

"Zahra, you should eat," Nani says, adding mango-and-onion pickle to her curry. "It's going to be a long day."

For once, my grandmother and I actually agree.

·· ♥ ··

Our booth has been buzzing with steady stream of people for the last three hours. Saliyah and Nana got bored pretty fast, so Nani took them to get a drink at one of the tea booths.

"What's bothering you?" Mom asks, during a lull. Her intuition is going full bore lately, and I bet she's been waiting to strike. "You haven't been yourself lately."

"The usual," I say as she restocks the shampoos. "I hate my teachers, I hate guys. I hate Dad's apartment. I hate that you're split. I hate that Nani and Nana have taken over our life." I consider adding group to the list, but I actually enjoy it now, thanks to Kali and Syd and Lauren. Ganging up on Simon and Evan is becoming a highlight of my week. On the other hand, if I don't mention it, it'll look suspicious. "Plus I hate group. How's that for starters?"

"Anything going right?" she asks, changing tactics.

I pass her the last box of lip balm. "Just this." It's turned out to be a beautiful day, and people are snapping up Mom's products.

I wish I could tell her about my session with Sinead and Leo, and how it left me feeling both elated and sad. They seemed like nice people who truly cared about each other. I don't understand why they had to cheapen it in the end with cheating.

"Did you ever cheat on Dad?" I ask, when I'm sure no one can overhear us.

Mom drops the box of lip balm, and small tubs scatter on the grass. "Zahra!"

"I'm not naïve. I know these things happen." Unfortunately, I know it from personal experience.

"I did not cheat on your father, and he did not cheat on me—at least as far as I know." She stoops to collect the lip balm. "Where's all this coming from?"

"I'm trying to figure things out. You were together twenty years, and nobody cheated, but it didn't work. Is it because Nani and Nana hate dad?"

"If that were true, we'd have split when they found out

about him. Nana flew over here and tried to take me home, you know. He got your aunt Farah to talk her way into my dorm and pack up all my things."

I wait while Mom makes change for a guy buying up the last of her shaving cream. This is the most she's ever said about that time in her life.

"What happened then?" I press, when the customer leaves.

"I refused to go with them. In fact, I locked myself in a bathroom and called the campus police." She frowns, and then laughs. "You should have seen Nana's face when the cops came. He was mortified."

"Did they arrest him?" I ask hopefully.

"Of course not. But they escorted him off college property, and that was humiliating enough. He never came back."

I sell four bottles of conditioner to two girls my age.

"And then he and Nani didn't speak to you for years?"

"They cut me off for a while. Your aunt Farah came around once she got to know your dad. And then Nani cracked when you were born. She sent that garnet set."

At this, we both laugh. Over the years, Nani has sent me several "sets"—a necklace, ring, and earrings—and each has been worse than the last. She must work hard to find jewelry that ugly. I've seen photos of my cousins in Pakistan, who clearly got the nice family heirlooms. I guess she doesn't want the quality gold to be tarnished by my Scottish blood. It's not like I want her stupid relics, but it hurts to be second best.

The booth is quiet for a minute, and I stare down at the last few bags of bath salts as I work up the nerve to ask the question that preys on my mind. I've asked before, but sensed she hasn't given me a straight answer. Maybe she will today. "They're trying to get you to go back to Karachi, aren't they?"

I expect her to lie, but she says, "They'd like that. It's normal to want your family around you as you get older."

"Are you considering it?" I ask, trying not to panic. I may be running my own life now, but it's good to have backup.

A new crowd of customers swarms our booth. While they're busy trying the testers, Mom reaches out and squeezes my hand. "I'm not going anywhere," she says. "I don't think I could live in Karachi anymore. But I do miss my family, my culture. When Aunt Farah moved back there, I gave up my ties to the community here in Austin."

"Maybe you can start making new ones today," I say, getting down on my hands and knees to get the last carton of stock from under the table. "Look around. How does it feel to be the hottest ticket at the carnival?"

"It feels pretty good," a male voice says. "Thanks for asking."

I peer over the table and find Riaz Dar grinning at me. He's wearing dark aviator-style sunglasses, but there's no mistaking the dimple in his chin.

"You might want to lower your voice, though," he adds, "unless you want everyone to know you're into me."

Since Mom is busy serving someone, I say, "Thanks for the tip. To be on the safe side, I'll ignore you instead."

"What kind of customer service is that?" he asks, rolling up the sleeves of a fitted powder-blue–and-white-striped Hollister shirt that tops distressed William Rast jeans. "I'm here to buy some shaving cream."

"We're sold out," I say, tossing him the order book. "Write

down your contact information if you're interested."

Riaz pushes up his sunglasses to reveal his stunning hazel eyes. "Some people will go to any length to get my number," he announces to three junior high school girls who are testing the lip balms.

The girls giggle, and he continues to flirt with them as I make change for a woman who's buying six bars of soap.

"I'm afraid you beautiful ladies will have to excuse me," Riaz says, when a text message interrupts the fun. "Official carnival business."

"I heard the portable potties are overflowing," I tell his fans as he disappears into the crowd.

Undeterred, one of his young fans asks, "Which lip balm do you think Riaz would like better? Citrus Kiss or Papaya Pucker?"

"You know him?" I ask, surprised.

"Sure, everyone at the mosque knows him," she replies.

"Go for the citrus, but be careful: he had a wicked cold sore last week."

When they leave, Mom comes over to tell me that someone is buying up the last of our stock and we've officially run out of merchandise. Still, people continue to use the testers and place orders. I pencil in requests from Kali, Glennis, Syd, and even Dieter.

"I should make you my manager," Mom jokes.

I pull an envelope out of my bag that holds brochures on commerce courses and business start-up loans. "After today, you might finally believe it's time to go pro."

"When did my daughter become such a go-getter?" she asks, putting her arm around me. "Maybe you're the one who should be launching a business."

I just smile. Love, Inc.'s chief commandment: *What happens in the trailer stays in the trailer.*

Saliyah bursts into our booth wearing a new salwar kameez in teal with golden thread.

"It looks good on you," I say. With Mom's promise not to take off for Pakistan, I can afford to scale back my defenses.

"Come on, I'll show you where I got it," Saliyah says, tugging my arm.

"Go ahead," Mom says. "If you see anything you like, it's my treat. It's the least I can do after all your help today."

Saliyah leads me to a booth filled with silk clothing in a rainbow of colors. With the saleswoman's help, I pick out a deep blue tunic and pull it on over my tank top. The saleswoman and Saliyah rave over it as I stand in front of the mirror. The fit is flattering and the color works, but I'm still on the fence about wearing something so traditional.

A sudden movement in the mirror catches my eye. Nani has sensed a cultural window and has swooped in to exploit it.

"*Khoobsurat,*" she says. That means *beautiful* in Urdu. "But it needs a little something." She removes her earrings and hands them to me. "Put these on."

Nani wears these earrings all the time, and unlike the ones she's given me in the past, these are gorgeous. Each has three pearls strung on gold wire, and in between, tiny red-gold beads vibrate and twinkle with the slightest movement.

"I can't, Nani," I say. "I'm afraid I'll lose them."

Ignoring my protests, she threads them through my ears herself. "*My* Nani gave me these on my sixteenth birthday. I was going to wait for yours, but today is a good day." She spins me back toward the mirror, repeating, "*Khoobsurat.*"

Obviously I've been too hard on her. "Thank you, Nani," I say, hugging her.

"You're welcome," she says. "Now, let's see what Riaz thinks of them."

·· ♥ ··

Nani sticks to me and Saliyah like glue as we stroll through the carnival grounds. After accepting the earrings, I can't ditch her as I normally would.

Behind the gaming tents, we find Nana playing dominoes with some of his cronies. To my surprise, I spot a pair of cool aviator glasses in a sea of spectacles.

Nani is excited to see Riaz, so I make it a point to ignore him completely, even after my mother joins us.

Riaz extends a hand and introduces himself. "Ms. Ahmed," he says. "It's a pleasure to finally meet you. Your parents have told me so much about you."

"It's *Mrs.* Ahmed-*MacDuff*," I correct him.

Mom brushes off Riaz's apology and says, "It's fine."

Not to me, it isn't. If Mom's that comfortable using her maiden name, it says she believes there's no going back.

"Hey, Zahra," Riaz says. "Can you give me a hand? I've got something for your grandfather in my truck."

Nani's hand lands on my back and gives me a shove. "She'd love to help."

I trail after Riaz reluctantly. "This had better not be a trick."

"No trick," he says, leading me into the parking lot.

Riaz probably thinks it'll impress me that he has his own set of wheels. It worked with Eric, but Nani's profile said Riaz's parents are doctors. It's not like he bought his own fancy ride.

We pass several nice SUVs before Riaz slaps the fender of a rusted orange pickup truck. As if reading my mind, he says, "My parents are firm believers in earning your own way. I don't make a ton at the theater where I work, but my manager sold me this baby for a song. I think she likes me." He thumps the hood. "It's great for taking my little brother camping."

I try to picture trendy, urban Riaz pitching a tent. "No offense, but you don't exactly seem like the outdoorsy type. Why don't your parents take him?"

Riaz opens the passenger door and hauls out a huge cooler. "He's not their kid," he says. "I volunteer for Big Brothers."

That was on Nani's profile too, but I assumed it was padding. Riaz seems too self-absorbed to be a Big Brother. "For your college applications?"

"I don't need it for that," he says, smiling. "I've volunteered at the mosque for five years. My grades are great, and I'm involved in enough to look perfect on paper."

It's a good thing colleges don't care about humility, because he's running a little short in that area.

Grabbing one side of the cooler, he signals me to take the other. "What's in here?" I ask as we lug it out of the parking lot.

"Ice. I always bring extra bags in case the vendors run low."

I drop my side of the cooler. "You said you had something for my Nana. So it *was* a trick."

"I just wanted to get you alone for a few minutes," he says.

I walk ahead of him out of the parking lot, and he struggles with the cooler on his own. "Then you should have said so," I call back. "I hate guys who play games."

He leaves the cooler behind and trots after me. "You're strung a little tight, aren't you?"

My mouth opens to argue, but the words die as I catch sight of a jewelry booth that's an explosion of color and shimmer. I stare at the booth until my vision blurs, and it becomes a tiny galaxy of fuzzy multicolored stars.

Catching up to me, Riaz flips his sunglasses onto the top of his head and tries again. "I'm actually a pretty great guy when you get to know me."

"Great guys don't act like flirty, arrogant jerks," I say.

"A guy's gotta put up a few defenses when he knows a girl will reject him just because he's granny-approved," Riaz says. "Anyway, your Nani said you have a sense of humor."

"Only when the joke's on her." I head over to the jewelry booth to admire the rows of colored glass bangle bracelets. Riaz trails after me and watches as I take a turquoise blue bangle from the display and slide it onto my wrist.

"You need to wear a bunch of them," he says. "It's all about the noise they make together. At least that's what my cousins say."

I select two bangles in gold and two in pale blue. "Won't they smash if they hit each other?"

"The tighter the fit the less likely they'll break." He selects smaller versions of the bracelets I've chosen, but I can't squeeze them over my hand. "Do you have any of your mom's famous hand cream?"

I give him the small bottle I always keep in my bag. He squirts a dab into his hand, then gently massages it into mine. "The secret," he says, making small circular motions on the palm of my hand with his thumb, "is a smooth, relaxed hand."

It's having the reverse effect, particularly when he's staring at me in close proximity. Holding my hand vertically, Riaz takes a bangle off the counter and coaxes it past my knuckles and down to my wrist. One by one, he slides the remaining four bangles in place. I raise my wrist, smiling at their musical jingle.

He calls over the saleswoman and tries to pay. "To make up for teasing you," he says.

They only cost a few dollars, but I insist on paying myself. I already sold my soul to Nani today for the price of earrings.

Saliyah notices the bracelets as soon as we arrive with the cooler. "You said I couldn't have any, Nani. How come Zahra gets to wear them?"

"You're too young yet, my girl," Nani says. "You're more likely to break them and cut yourself."

Saliyah flushes at being called a child in front of Riaz, and he notices.

"Next year," he says. "When you're fifteen."

It works like a charm, and Saliyah skips off to tell Mom she can pass for fourteen.

Riaz says he has to get back to his rounds. He pulls me along with him for a few yards, before ducking behind a cotton-candy cart.

Before I fully realize what's happening, he leans down and kisses me.

Kali props her elbows on the kitchen island and rests her chin on her hands. "So," she says, "was there tongue?"

I glance up nervously from the bowl of stiff batter I'm stirring. Brody has a habit of appearing out of nowhere. "Could you keep your voice down?"

I've taken over their kitchen again to test some healthy recipes for René's upcoming store promotion. He's paying me to make low-fat snacks to offer people while they shop. I'm glad he has faith in me, but I'm afraid I might let him down. As with Love, Inc., the minute you put a price on your product, you have to up your game. That's not going to be easy when healthy baking usually isn't that tasty.

"No worries," Kali says. "Mom and Brody are out, so don't skip a single detail. Tongue or no tongue?"

I take the first batch of fat- and sugar-free oatmeal spice muffins out of the oven. If they taste half as good as they smell, I could have a winner. "Why does it matter?"

"I can't help you figure out what it means without having all the facts," Kali says.

"Fine. No tongue. That's bad, right?"

"On the contrary. No tongue suggests he wasn't feeling that confident and didn't want to scare you off. He's leaving something for next time—because he's hoping there *will* be a next time."

"Okay, that's good. I guess." Maybe a new guy is what I need to put Eric out of my mind. Despite my current distractions, I still find myself looking back, wondering where I took a wrong turn and lost my self-respect. Next time I want signposts, or better yet, a romantic GPS. "But I can't tell what the guy's really like."

"Don't be so hard on him," Kali says. "Putting on an act at the start is a way to guard against getting hurt. We've both done it. The real question is, how did Riaz measure up against Eric in the kissing department?"

I test a warm muffin and wince. Biting into a haystack

would taste better. "Riaz has promise," I say. "But Eric . . . well, you know."

"Yeah. That was a gift."

Comparing anyone to Eric causes the straw muffin to turn over in my stomach. I'm not ready to be kissing other guys yet.

Kali must see that talking about Eric is bringing me down, because she changes the subject to her matchmaking program. "The test launch is stalled on the pad," she says. "I asked Mom a few basic questions, and she accused me of secretly creating an online dating profile for her. Apparently, when she's ready to find someone new, she intends to 'let the fates provide.' Like that's worked in the past. The problem is that Mom jumps headfirst into relationships before she really knows the guy. She's in love with being in love."

I suspect Kali might suffer from the same affliction, but I'll leave the therapy to Dieter. Friends should not psychoanalyze friends—or criticize their friends' parents, for that matter.

"Maybe your mom doesn't want a new relationship right now," I say. "Why don't you test the matchmaking program on yourself instead?"

"Already in the works," she says, reaching for a muffin.

I block her hand with a spatula. "Don't. Unless you like straw."

Picking up a handful of raisins instead, she continues. "I've started a compatibility profile for me and Owen Gaines. Of course, I don't have enough info on him yet, but the signs are promising. I'd start one for you too," she adds, "but your grandmother seems to have a talent for matchmaking."

"The jury's still out on that one." I scrape the batter into the garbage and put the bowl in the sink. "For all I know, Riaz is an actor she hired to help brainwash me."

Since I'm still staying at Mom's place, Nani has ramped up her efforts to convert me to more traditional ways. She's probably inspired by the results she's had with my sister, who appears to be breaking down faster than a berry in a compost heap. I knew something was up when Saliyah happily handed over the iPod Touch my cupcakes won at her school bake sale. Sure enough, she'd preloaded it with all things Pakistani—from street maps of Karachi, to books in Urdu, to curry recipes, and even Pakistani pop music. It's digital assimilation.

"Listen to this." I take the iPod out of my bag, scroll to Hadiqa Kiani, and press PLAY.

"Hey, this song's kind of cool," Kali says.

She leaps off her stool, grabs my hands, and pulls. Laughing, I give in and start dancing. Tossing a tea towel on my head, I lead her in a mock Bollywood–style dance.

A few minutes later, the sound of clapping stops us cold. Brody has taken a front-row seat at the kitchen island. I shut off the music and return to my mixing bowl.

"Nice moves," he says.

Kali plucks the chicken-print tea towel off my head and flicks Brody with it. "You were supposed to be at practice."

"We finished early," he says. I refuse to look at him, but I can feel that he's still grinning. "Hey, Red, you seemed almost fun there for a minute. Now the frown's back."

Somehow Brody seems to tap into my worst insecurities.

"Brody, she's my guest," Kali says. "Go watch TV or something."

"Don't worry. I'm meeting Jada in an hour. I have to grab a

quick shower." Looking at me he adds, "No peeking."

"I'll try to resist," I say.

On his way out, Brody helps himself to a muffin. I consider stopping him, but decide he deserves it. After a few chews, he makes a face and spits it into the garbage can. "Are you trying to kill people?"

"It's fat- *and* sugar-free," I say.

"You mean flavor-free," he says. "If I were you, I'd add some fruit and maple syrup."

"I do not need your advice on baking," I say.

He picks up a muffin and fires it at me. I duck and it bounces off the wall, intact.

"Yeah, you do," he says. "Unless you have a license to carry a weapon."

chapter 12

The final bell rings and my History teacher flicks on the lights and dismisses the class. Rambo ambles from the back of the room and waits beside my desk while I gather my things. Since our lockers are in the same hall, we've fallen into the habit of walking there together on Thursday afternoons. He's a small, nondescript guy who makes up for his size with silent menace. Behind the front, though, there's a decent guy.

"How cool was that?" he asks, once we're in the hall and it's safe to show some enthusiasm without getting the teacher's hopes up. Rambo is genuinely pumped about the film on ancient civilizations. "Roman war tactics were awesome."

"Definitely," I say. No need to explain that I spent the class on *The Sweet Tooth* set, where Oliver James continues to mock me for my mistakes with Eric. Gordon Ramshead, on the other hand, has become a surprising ally. I'd love to give Eric a dose of Gordon in real life. Gordon shames the shameless without breaking a sweat.

In the next hall, two of Kali's friends are sitting on a wide windowsill, sharing earbuds and singing a Radiohead number. They shout hello as we pass.

My social network here at Austin has expanded because of

Syd and Kali. My favorite group is Kali's fun musical friends, who are always putting on the impromptu performances Syd scorns. Kali's eco-Nazi friends are a little too earnest for me, but they're not as intimidating as Syd's small fringe group of arty friends. Every clique has its own language, and I haven't learned them all yet. Nor have I found any foodies who speak *my* language. But it's nice to have options, and I never have to sit alone at lunch anymore.

After dropping Rambo at his locker, I stop at mine, then head over to Kali's. As usual, she's flirting with a hot guy. Only, this one is really off the charts. He's at least six feet tall, with great bone structure, just the right amount of stubble, and killer arms. Kali introduces him as Miller, and he enters her number into his phone while Syd and I wait.

"That's a step up from SpongeBob," Syd says, when Miller is out of earshot.

"He came to that meeting I organized about getting water-coolers in the caf," Kali says. "He's loves Notts County, *and* he's a junior."

"So he might even last till Halloween," Syd says. "Although that's only a week."

"Why are you always so negative?" Kali asks.

I interrupt the bickering by telling them about the gift I received in the mail yesterday: an *Iron Man* poster signed by Robert Downey, Jr. himself. The poster was the one thing Sinead and Leo both wanted after dividing up the rest of their stuff, so they agreed to give it to me.

"I was thinking that all swag acquired through the business should be enjoyed communally, or sold online with profits divided equally," I say.

Kali and Syd agree we should add that to the growing list of Love, Inc. commandments. Then Syd votes to sell the poster and Kali votes to keep it. Typical, but since I acquired the poster, I get the final word. No sooner have I resolved to hang the poster in the trailer than my partners go to battle again, this time over Kali's pro bono work with Luke. The date she arranged for the City Limits Festival was a bust. Kali was sure they'd click, but when Luke suggested they participate in the Rock and Recycle program, the girl called him a garbage picker and took off.

Kali is determined to try again despite Syd's protests. "I can't walk away now," she says. "Brody will never let me live it down."

"Brody doesn't run Love, Inc.," Syd says.

"Failing will be bad for business," Kali argues. "Especially the way guys gossip."

"Working for free is bad for business," Syd counters.

"It won't take me long to figure out what Luke needs," Kali says. "I'll find him a date for his cousin's wedding and . . ."

A guy's voice drowns out her last words, although it's muffled by a closed classroom door. "I told you not to join that club," he roars.

Beckoning to the others, I peek through the window in the door and whisper, "It's Hollis and Fletcher."

We eavesdrop long enough to learn that Hollis joined the jazz band against Fletcher's orders. Now he's pissed that Bronco Garcia lent Hollis a CD.

Hearing a smash, I peek through the window again. "There goes the CD."

Hollis loses it. "Oh my God, Fletcher! Do you know how

much that cost? We're reworking a classic, and Bronco lent it to me to study. It was a limited edition import, and one of his favorite CDs."

"I think she's crying," Kali says. "Should we interrupt?"

"Nah, she's holding her own," Syd says. "Don't forget she threw Z in the pool."

There's a high-pitched scream inside the room. Syd charges through the door, with Kali and me on her heels. Fletcher is holding Hollis's wrist at an awkward angle.

"Let go of her *now*," Syd tells Fletcher. "Or I'll call for a teacher."

"Chill," Fletcher says, releasing Hollis. "She was about to pick up that broken CD case. I was worried she'd cut herself."

"It didn't sound like she was thanking you," Syd says.

I turn to Hollis. "We were just heading out. Walk with us?"

Hollis wipes her eyes on her sleeve before shaking her head. "And risk being seen with you psychos? I don't think so."

Kali tries again. "Maybe you guys need a bit of space right now."

"Maybe you need to mind your own friggin' business," Hollis says.

We step out of the classroom, and she slams the door behind us.

"That confirms it," Syd says. "Working for free is a bad idea."

$$\cdot\cdot\ \heartsuit\ \cdot\cdot$$

Once we're off school property, Syd announces that we've got our first Love, Inc. revenge client from Austin High. "His name is Drake," she says. "He plays soccer with Leo, who put us in touch."

Drake has just discovered that his girlfriend has been seeing someone else for months. Worse, the girl's only been keeping him around because of the free makeup samples Drake's dad brings home from work. Taking tacky to the extreme, the girl and her new guy are selling the makeup online and making a nice profit.

"I've come up with a plan that's pure genius, if I do say so myself," Syd says, as we take our usual circuitous route to St. Joe's, hoping to avoid being seen by our schoolmates. "We'll have Drake give her one last—mislabeled—product that makes her skin burn. Kind of like a scarlet letter, but for the face."

She waits for our reaction, and is clearly disappointed when Kali, unconsciously touching her own pretty face, says, "I don't know, Syd. That seems cruel."

"It's a perfect punishment," Syd insists. "I'm not going soft just because the target's a girl."

"But it's her face, Syd," I say. "What if it causes scarring or something?"

"Besides," Kali says, "it's our first case with an Austin student."

"She's right," I say. "If the girl ever found out who was behind the slam, our life would be hell."

Syd stares straight ahead, and no matter how hard I work to convince her that we're not ganging up on her, she gives us the silent treatment. "We'll think of a plan together," I say. "Right after group."

"Come on," Syd says at last, turning down a side street.

"But we're going to be late," Kali says.

"You guys owe me," Syd says.

Reluctantly, we follow her to her mom's apartment to pick up Banksy. Somehow, facing Dieter's disapproval is easier than facing Syd's.

·· ♥ ··

Group is already in progress when we arrive, and as expected, Dieter makes a show of jotting down the time in his book. "That's twice," he says. "If you're not careful, I may start to think you girls aren't taking this seriously."

He turns his attention back to Simon, who's pleading with Lauren: "You don't understand. She's like the Marge to my Homer."

"You can't have both," Lauren declares. "Either break it off with Trisha or forget about Marge."

"Are you kidding me?" Kali asks. "You still haven't dumped your girlfriend?"

"I tried to do it last weekend, but I couldn't," Simon says. "She got fired from the dollar store and came home to find out that Watson had croaked."

"Her dog?" Syd says, automatically scratching Banksy's ears.

"Her turtle," Simon says.

Evan laughs hysterically. "Dude, she's playing you," he says. "I'll bet her women's institution warned her you were going to give her the heave, and she made up a sob story to keep you."

"That's women's *intuition*," Dieter says, shriveling Evan with a blast of pale eyes.

"I saw the corpse," Simon says. "And I know how much she loved Watson."

Lauren whacks Simon with her latest fancy purse. "You're

grasping for excuses." She looks to me for support. "I think Simon needs professional help."

"Dude's already in therapy," Evan says. "Let Dieter decide. Should Simon dump girlfriend number one for what's beneath T-shirt number two?"

"I'm not here to fix your love lives," Dieter says. "But I always encourage you to behave like mature adults. And mature adults do the right thing, even when it's the tough thing."

"You've got do it," Kali says. "If you ever loved Trisha, you owe it to her to give her a clean break, so she can move on. Otherwise, you're just punishing her for *your* weakness."

"Make it fast and clean," Syd says. "That's her best hope to bounce back. You owe her that."

"Fast and clean," I agree. "And take the full blame on yourself. Because you're the one who changed, not her."

Simon pulls his baseball cap down and stares at the floor, huddled under the shell of his old leather jacket. Fast and clean aren't in *this* turtle's repertoire.

.. ♥ ..

"Let me get this straight," I say, staring at Lauren and Simon across the table. "You want *me* to dump Trisha?"

"More like broker the breakup," Kali says, proving she's in on the plot.

"And I'll pay for it," Lauren adds. "It's my birthday gift to Simon, and a charitable donation to girlfriends everywhere."

Simon stays quiet, but I notice he hasn't touched his cookie.

"Forget it," I say. "He can do his own dirty work."

"You did it for Sinead and Leo," Syd says. "And look how well that turned out."

"They'd already agreed that the relationship was over," I protest. "Simon's girlfriend thinks they're solid. It'll be a bolt from the blue."

"All the more reason to put an end to the lie," Syd says, glaring at Simon over her coffee cup. "And doing other people's dirty work is one of the reasons we got into this business."

"Besides," says Kali, "It's not for Simon, it's for Trisha. She's stuck in a relationship with a guy who's into someone else. We can't stand by and watch. It's inhumane."

I look around the table at four sets of hopeful eyes, and crumble. "Fine. But I'm charging extra if there are tears."

·· ♥ ··

"Please don't be upset. Do you need another tissue?"

I nod and hold out my hand, afraid to speak in case I start sobbing again.

Trisha passes me the whole box and sits down on the sofa beside me. I came to her house after school because Simon assured me she has the place to herself Friday afternoons. "I'll be fine," she says, although her eyes are glistening, behind funky blue glasses. "It's just been a bad week." She pulls her feet up off the floor and tucks them under her legs. Five feet one and petite, she barely makes a dent in the seat cushions.

"I heard about Watson," I say, dabbing my eyes. "I'm so sorry."

This is ridiculous. There were no tears at my dress rehearsal with Oliver James and Gordon Ramshead. I've never had a pet, and I hate reptiles. The only explanation I can think of for my behavior is that it's like experiencing the breakup I never had with Eric. I deserved closure, and as satisfying as trashing his car was, it wasn't full closure.

Trisha pats my shoulder. "To be honest, I'm more upset about losing my job than losing the turtle. I'll miss the people I worked with. It's like two breakups in one week."

"You'll see your friends," I say, passing the tissues back as she dissolves in tears.

"But not Simon. I really thought we were solid."

So solid, in fact, that she refused to believe it when I first delivered my news, and called Simon for confirmation. "I'm so sorry" is all he managed to croak before she hung up on him, and turned to me for the full story.

"He likes someone else," she says, covering her face with her hands. "How could I be so blind?"

"It's not you, it's him," I say. "And if it's any consolation, Simon couldn't bear to break up with you himself because he still cares about you. He feels awful."

"Not awful enough to resist this other girl," she says, taking off her glasses to wipe her eyes.

"Trust me when I say I know how much it hurts. But you deserve better than someone whose heart isn't fully in it," I say. "Now you can get out there and meet a guy who's crazy about you."

I realize that's easy to say, harder to do. When someone's played you, it doesn't just wreck you once, but over and over, each time you try to trust someone again.

"No one's ever going to love me," Trisha sobs. "I'm a total loser."

"Do you think *I'm* a loser? Because my last boyfriend had not one but *two* girls on the side. And I didn't have a clue."

I tell Trisha all about the Eric fiasco, not sparing a detail.

When I finish, she hugs me. "I'm so sorry. You must feel horrible."

"I still do," I admit. "But you know what I've realized this afternoon? If we let these guys ruin our lives, we're idiots."

Trisha dries her eyes and forces a smile. "You know, for the Grim Reaper, you're really not that bad."

·· ♥ ··

I lie back on the bench in the trailer, having commandeered Syd's favorite spot. She's not the one with the raging headache.

"I still can't believe you cried," Kali says, passing me two aspirin and a glass of water.

I settle a gel mask over my eyes. "Fast and clean it was not."

I'm disappointed that I didn't handle the whole thing better. It was supposed to be about Trisha and ended up being about me. Professionals don't get personally involved. They stay cool and detached. Clinical, like Dieter. I have no idea how he does it.

"A dumping service is a bad idea," I say, glaring at them through the eyeholes in the mask.

"Au contraire," Kali says, digging a bottle of nail polish out of her bag. "Thanks to you, Trisha can move on. And for the record, 'Termination Service' will look better on the Love, Inc. menu."

"She called me the Grim Reaper."

"What you need is more practice," Syd says.

"Not going to happen," I say. "It was too hard."

Kali looks up from the table, where she's applying a coat of orange polish to her nails. "Focus on what you've done for Trisha," she says. "She'd have wasted months, falling more and more in love with Simon until he finally got the guts to tell her it was over. Or worse, she could've run into him with his Marge one day and been really crushed."

"You did a good job, Z," Syd says. "Trisha's already recommended you to a friend. She said you made a horrible experience bearable."

"Really?" My headache starts to recede instantly. "I guess you could say we're not working for cowards, but helping their partners get free of them?"

Kali makes a sweeping check mark with her nail polish brush. "Exactly."

"A hundred bucks a pop, minimum," Syd adds. "Cowards deserve to pay big."

Kali nods. "At that price, only the truly messed up will come to us. And if you're seeing someone that messed up, you need to know about it."

"Remember our mission statement," Syd says. "We bring people together in happiness until a relationship runs its course, and then help them find closure."

"Then we help them find happiness with someone new," Kali says, holding up her hands to admire her nails. "Trisha has hired us to find her a match, and I'm thinking Luke might be a fit."

"I guess the odd termination won't hurt," I say.

"Great," Syd says. "Let's move this meeting along to new business."

"Okay," I say, sitting up. "I got a call from a friend of Trey's today about doing a surveillance case. We have to dangle the bait and see if the client's boyfriend takes it."

"No problem," Kali says. "I'm good to go."

"Sorry, Kal, you're not right for the job."

"What? The guy doesn't like blondes?"

"The guy doesn't like girls." I pull out a photo of two cute guys with their arms wrapped around each other. "Dylan's offering courtside seats to the next Spurs home game. We need to find someone to test his boyfriend's loyalty."

"I've got just the guy," Kali says. Preserving her nails, she uses a pencil to select a name on her phone's contact list. "Hey, Brody, it's me. Someone just offered me a courtside seat to the Spurs game against the Lakers next week. Are you interested?"

Syd and I start to laugh, and Kali holds a finger to her lips.

"There's no catch," Kali continues. "Well, nothing major. All you have to do is flirt with someone while you're there, and let me know if they flirt back." She winks at us while Brody rattles on. "Yes, it's for Love, Inc. We're expanding our services a little. Anyway, I promise, this person is super hot. Forty bucks! Are you kidding me? It's a courtside seat to a sold-out game." She looks to Syd and me, and we nod. "Okay, it's a deal. But if you get a relationship out of this, Brody, we want a refund."

·· ♥ ··

I pull back the curtain and peer out at the neighbor's house. Their porch is decorated for Halloween, with carved pumpkins and strings of skeleton lights. In the twilight, I make out the form of a possum plodding through the fake gravestones on the lawn.

I called Mom an hour ago to say I'd be having dinner at Kali's tonight. She didn't put up a fight because I don't move back to Dad's for another two days. She will have the pleasure of listening to me bicker with Nani all weekend.

There's a scratching noise at the trailer door followed by a low whine. Banksy's nails clatter on the metal steps as he comes inside. Syd follows, carrying a bag of Chinese takeout.

The trailer fills with a wonderful aroma as Syd unpacks the food and sets it on the table. "I got spring rolls for Kali, and fried chicken balls for Zahra."

"How did you guess?" I ask, dipping a chicken ball into a carton of bright orange plum sauce.

"I eat lunch with you nearly every day," Syd says. "I've picked up a few things."

Kali grabs a spring roll and opens her laptop. "Hey! Notts County is doing a free concert at the Plaza in a few weeks."

"Give it up already," Syd says. "Owen Gaines is a professional rocker. He is not going to start hanging with a high school girl."

"I'm willing to wait until I'm a college girl," Kali says. "But it's not too soon to start planning. Besides, it gives me a chance to test my matchmaking program."

As we're finishing up the food, there's a light tap at the door. "Girls? Open up."

Kali lets her mom in and asks, "How'd you know we were here?"

"The electrical cord running from the garage and the lights were a dead giveaway," she says, smiling.

Glennis has just come home from work and is still wearing a sharp suit and heels. Her dark curls are pinned in a neat French twist. "Kalista, we have a nice house. Why would you put your friends up in this heap?"

"We like it here," I say, holding out what's left of the chicken balls.

Glennis blocks the view with her hand. "No, thanks. And you girls shouldn't be eating this junk either. Kali, offer your friends something nutritious."

"I'll make fruit smoothies for dessert," I say. "I've been dying to try your blender."

I follow Glennis across the driveway and into the house. In the kitchen, I pick up a copy of *Interview* magazine off the counter and glance at it while Glennis pulls out soy milk, yogurt, and fresh fruit.

"Should I make some for you and Brody?" I ask, noticing she's put only three glasses on the counter.

"I've eaten, and Brody has a date," she says. "Make yourself at home. I'll be in the den if you need me."

I toss some ingredients into the blender, fire it up, and pour the smoothies into the glasses. I'm about to pick up the tray when a loud blast of Pakistani pop music fills the kitchen. Saliyah's been fooling with my phone again. Scrambling, I pull it out of my pocket, check the incoming number, and say, "No, Mom, I won't stay out too late."

It's actually my sister on the line. "Guess what?" she asks.

"Someone's going to die if she keeps screwing with my phone?" I say. "You know what happens to enemy agents, right?"

"They find the best information," she says. "But if you don't want it, just say so."

"As long as it's free." I perch on a stool at the island and flip through the magazine. "You still owe me."

She can't wait to spill. "I saw Riaz this afternoon. He really likes you."

"And you could tell that *how*?" I ask. "Five days after kissing me, he still hasn't called."

"He kissed you?" Her voice is in the squeak register. "When? Where?"

"Never mind. So you ran into him and he said . . . ?"

"That he lost his phone at the carnival," she says. "So he couldn't call."

"He couldn't find a landline?"

"His cell had all his numbers programmed in."

"Hello, online phone listings."

"Give the guy a break," Saliyah says.

"I barely know him. Why should I give him a break?"

"Because he's totally hot?"

I laugh. "Well, you're right about that. He is totally hot."

"I gave him your number." She lowers her voice and adds wistfully, "I bet he's a great kisser."

"He's a *good* kisser. There's a ways to go before greatness." Unfortunately, Eric set that particular bar quite high.

"Did he French you?"

"Saliyah!"

"I know all about that, you know." She tries to sound all worldly. "Not from you."

"I know where you get all your advice," I say. "And I'm sure Nani won't steer you wrong."

"Ew!"

She's still giggling when I hang up the phone. I close the magazine and look up to find Brody in the doorway, bare-chested and in sweats. All that basketball has paid off. He has great abs. Really great abs.

"Eyes up," he says, pointing at his face. "Five days ago you were kissing some guy and now you're checking out my abs? It *was* the abs, right?"

I jump off the stool and back toward the door. Forget about a comeback. Escape is the only option.

"I guess you learned a trick or two from Eric," he says. "Lining up your next one before the last one's fully out of the picture."

"That's ridiculous."

He grins, enjoying himself hugely. "Just an observation."

"Well, spare me. I thought you had a date tonight."

"Later," he says. "Unless you want me to cancel?"

"Don't flatter yourself," I say, reaching for the doorknob with my free hand.

"I was just being nice because I heard your boyfriend's not calling," he says, grinning as he comes over and takes a glass from my tray. He downs the smoothie in a few gulps.

"He's not my boyfriend."

"Why not? I hear he's a good kisser."

Brody takes a second glass and chugs half of that one, too. "Looking this good takes fuel." Wiping his mouth with the back of his hand, he adds, "Much better than your gut-grenade muffins."

"Those were a work in progress."

"Keep working," he says. "And do you mind if I give you another piece of advice?"

"Actually, I do. Especially when it relates to a conversation you had no business hearing."

"Your crazy music and giggling hurt my brain," he says. "I had to investigate what all the noise was about." He hops up to sit on the counter. "Anyway, here's my take on your situation. That whole 'He'd better drag his butt to a phone or else' philosophy is just harsh. And harsh girls never get the 'totally hot' guy."

"I am not harsh!" If anything, I am too nice with guys. That's how I ended up as a doormat.

"Listen to yourself—voice like a rake on metal."

I take a deep breath to ensure that what comes out next is melodic. "Thank you so much for your advice, Brody." I open the door and step out. "Enjoy your smoothies. The three of us can share this one."

He hops off the counter and follows me to the door. "One last thing . . . if Hot Lips hasn't called in five days, he's not into you."

I consider throwing the last smoothie at him, but decide not to waste it. "Thanks for the insight."

"For you, no charge. Unlike some people, I don't take advantage of the lovesick."

"Thanks again," I say, beating it across the driveway. "Enjoy your date."

He shouts after me. "Maybe your kissing needs improvement. The taste of bitter probably put him off."

It takes a superhuman effort, but I smile. "I'll work on that."

I can still hear him laughing as I slam the trailer door.

Thank God Mom and Dad only produced girls.

chapter 13

It takes two laps of the cafeteria for Kali and me to find a table far enough away from both Fletcher's gang and Hollis's. With more than half the students in Halloween costumes, it's hard to tell who's who. Kali isn't exactly keeping a low profile dressed as Agnetha, the blonde from ABBA, in a stretchy blue jumpsuit, platform shoes, and with a silver headband across her forehead. She tried to talk me into wearing her Ariel costume, because my hair is "perfect for the part," but after the episode at the pool, I couldn't see flopping into Spanish class in a mermaid outfit.

"Willem called again yesterday," Kali says as we settle into our seats. "He upped his offer by fifty bucks."

Willem Orr is one of Lauren's society pals, and he's been trying to hire us to check up on his girlfriend, Addison Mayfield. They've been together since ninth grade, and Willem is madly in love; but lately someone's been sending him anonymous reports of her cheating. Normally we'd be all over this case, but Addison's dad is state governor. That means Willem and Addison hit the society pages a lot, as one of Austin's young "it" couples. We decided unanimously that the job was too risky. Willem says he'll only accept that the rumors are true if we provide evidence on video. But who knows where that kind of evidence could end up? It's one thing to interfere in love, another to interfere in state politics. Plus, we could expose our business too widely in the process. So far we've managed to keep it fairly exclusive by getting client referrals. Messing with public figures could bring unwanted attention from nosy outsiders. An extra fifty bucks—divided by three—ain't worth the risk.

"He's persistent," I say. "But I still say no."

"Agreed," Kali says, peering around for Syd. "I take it Riaz never came through?"

I shake my head. I've been trying to keep an open mind about Riaz, not because I'm that interested, but because I want to prove I'm over Eric. After my speech to Trisha, Simon's ex, I wouldn't mind walking my talk. It would be nice if Riaz played his part, but despite a long conversation on Wednesday, he never suggested getting together. I sent him a breezy e-mail on Friday ending with a "See you soon," and he didn't take the hint. I'm afraid Brody's right—about Riaz not being into me, I mean. He's obviously wrong about everything else.

It's disappointing, but the worst part was having to spend another Saturday night at Mom's. Happily, Dad got home Sunday, and I was on the first bus back to our apartment. He brought me a pretty cool top from New York and took me to my favorite Thai restaurant. Spending two weeks being nagged by my grandparents made me appreciate him a little more, although when I suggested that Mom could use some help with packaging and logo design for her beauty products, he shut me down cold. Mediator Girl is still flunking home repairs.

Syd comes toward us carrying a garbage bag. She looks

very Marlon Brando in a leather biker's cap, but it's not a costume, just her style.

"Hey," I say, "what's in the—"

My question hangs in the air as Syd strides by us to join Stains and Rambo without so much as a "hi."

"Now what?" Kali asks. "She doesn't like ABBA?" She pulls out her sandwich and takes a savage bite. "You know, I am so through with her moods. If she thinks we're going to run over there and beg her to tell us what's wrong, she's got another think coming."

"Let's just give her a minute," I say.

Kali lasts about fifteen seconds before gathering her stuff and charging Syd's table. "What's your problem?" she demands.

Syd tosses the garbage bag at Kali. "You mean besides this?"

Opening the bag gingerly, Kali flinches. "Ew! Is that some kind of sick Halloween joke?"

A putrid odor rises over the usual smell of fried food that permeates the cafeteria. It's almost as bad as the fish guts.

Rambo grins. "It's a message." He's never shown much interest in Love, Inc. before, but this new twist intrigues him.

"It's a raw chicken," Kali tells me. "Complete with head."

"Guess where I found this decomposing bird?" Syd asks. "Duct-taped to my friggin' locker, that's where. With a note attached to its foot."

She gestures to the bag, and I know there's only one way I'm going to get an answer. Holding my breath, I open the bag and peek at the tag: *I want a refund.*

I drop the chicken into the nearest trash can and say, "So we have an unhappy client."

"It's Drake," Syd says. "The guy whose girlfriend was on the take for makeup samples. You wanted me to go soft on her, so I sent one of my mom's prescription antiaging creams. All it did was make the girl's face look a bit flushed, and Drake wanted more of a show."

"Ah," Kali says. "He's saying we chickened out."

Syd helps herself to one of the dozen or so mini chocolate bars that comprise Stains's lunch. "The message is loud and clear."

"Give him his money," I say. "You did the right thing, Syd. We can't go around maiming people."

Kali reaches for one of Stains's chocolate bars, and he flicks her hand away. "Do you think Drake might accept an exchange instead of a refund?" she asks.

·· ♥ ··

Kali is so engrossed in her conversation with Miller that she doesn't notice Syd and me approaching her locker.

"Looks like you were wrong," I whisper to Syd. "This one's lasted an entire week, and she's not sick of him yet."

"Well, she better get sick of him fast," Syd says, waving to get Kali's attention. "The countdown's started."

Kali holds up a couple of fingers to signal she needs more time—time we don't have. We've decided to deliver Drake's "exchange" before the school day ends.

Syd marches the last few feet and grabs Kali's arm. "Sorry, Miller, she's needed in surgery. She'll call you later."

"Oh my God, could you be any ruder?" Kali asks, as Syd hustles us around the corner. "I was in the middle of breaking up with him, and you know that has to be handled with care."

"Breaking up?" Syd asks. "Were you ever going out?"

"We had lunch together three days this week, in case you hadn't noticed I was missing from your table," Kali says.

"What went wrong?" Syd asks. "Were his biceps too perfect?"

Kali ignores the sarcasm and says, "It was truly tragic: he turned out to be a horrible kisser." She gives a little shiver. "We're talking snake tongue."

"When did the saliva swap take place?" Syd asks. "I don't recall your mentioning a date."

Grinning mischievously, Kali sets the stage. "Picture the science lab, two hours ago. He was coming in, I was heading out. He said I look cute in my costume today. I said he looks cute every day, and since the place was empty, we did our own little chemistry experiment. Unfortunately, the results weren't what I'd hoped for."

"Couldn't you look at his arms and pretend?" I ask.

Kali shakes her head. "You know as well as I do that it's either there or it isn't. Nice packaging can't create a spark where it doesn't exist."

Syd is walking so fast we can barely keep up now. "We've only got four minutes before the next period starts," she says. "Give me the glue and let's move."

Nearly running, Kali somehow manages to locate the super-glue she's kept in her bag since our attack on Miss Daisy. "Remember," she says, as we part, "Mr. Dennis keeps a seating plan in his top desk drawer."

Syd and I take up positions around the corner while Kali lets out a piercing wail and collapses with a clatter against the lockers closest to the geography classroom.

Mr. Dennis is out of his room in a shot. "Kalista! Are you all right?"

Kali turns on the drama machine with so much squealing and clutching of stomach that we easily sneak into the classroom. I pull open the top drawer, find the seating plan, then stand guard. Working quickly but carefully, Syd applies a thin line of glue to the edges of the seat where Drake's ex-girlfriend normally sits.

We slip out of the room to find Kali giving an animated account of her abdominal pain. Mr. Dennis looks queasy.

"We'll take her to the nurse's office," I say. "Don't worry."

"Thanks, girls. Even in pain, your friend's a Super Trouper." He chuckles at his lame ABBA joke. "What a delightful young lady."

"I couldn't agree more, sir," Syd says.

Drake meets us at his ex's locker. His zombie lumberjack costume is terrifying. His face is covered in grayish makeup, and there's fake blood caked at his temple. It's not a stretch to believe he'd leave dead chickens in lockers. Or worse.

"Where's my money?" he asks.

"We have it," Kali says. "But first we want to offer you an exchange."

Almost on cue, there's a screech down the hall that makes Kali's seem amateurish. Then we hear a steady thumping noise and a rhythmic scraping that grows ever louder until Drake's ex-girlfriend comes into view, half-walking, half-crawling, and dragging her entire desk with her. The fact that she's dressed like Catwoman only adds to the show.

Drake smiles, and his teeth look yellow against the makeup. "Is she *attached* to that thing?"

Catwoman sees him and bursts into tears. "Drake, thank God. Some A-hole glued my seat and my costume's stuck. Give me your shirt so I can get out of this thing."

"Can't you just use your superpowers?" Drake asks, taking off his plaid jacket.

Catwoman squirms out of her one-piece latex costume, revealing an animal-print bra and G-string.

"ME-OW!" a guy calls.

"Give me the jacket, Drake," Catwoman says. "Now."

Drake puts it back on. "Nah. Get your new boyfriend's jacket."

As more students come out of the classrooms to see what the commotion's about, Drake's ex-girlfriend twists herself into a pretzel, trying to cover up with one hand and open her locker with the other. The Austin High cell phone paparazzi catch a lucky break, because sometime between lunch and her chemistry experiment, Kali found time to glue the lock shut.

Again Mr. Dennis comes to the rescue, this time with his suit jacket. We take that as our cue to fade into the crowd.

Drake tracks us down after the next period. "You're off the hook," he says. "The pictures are already all over Facebook. Look for the video on YouTube later."

"Customer satisfaction guaranteed," Syd says.

·· ♥ ··

My phone rings as I sit down with my Bennu latte. It's become our satellite office, now that SpongeBob has moved up in the world to Starbucks. "She's tried me three times," I say, checking the call display. "We can't ignore this."

Syd flips open her phone to receive an incoming text. "She's trying me too. But group starts in half an hour. Dieter will kill us if we're late again."

Kali's phone is buzzing now. "How can we ignore a client in crisis?"

"Fine," Syd says, texting a reply. "I'm telling her she has exactly ten minutes to get here, and another ten to talk to us. Then we're gone."

The client in question is Stacey, the girl we coached throughout her hookup with Graham. Thanks to our ongoing counseling, she's managed not to spoil or suffocate Graham, and now they're approaching their two-month anniversary. It's an all-time record for Stacey, and she's worried about blowing it.

Breezing into the café just as we're preparing to leave, Stacey flops onto the sofa beside Syd and says, "Can I buy you another round before we start?"

"We need to leave in exactly one minute," Syd says. "You'll have to talk fast."

Stacey lays out her plans for the anniversary: a limo will pick Graham up before dawn and take him to Town Lake, where the caterer she's hired will have set up a table for two on the Pfluger pedestrian bridge. There, they'll have eggs Benedict, followed by cinnamon doughnuts and hot chocolate (Graham's favorites), while they watch the sun rise over the city. After that, they take off in a romantic balloon ride over the canyons and the Enchanted Rock.

Syd sums up her reaction with one word. "Overkill. Scale it all back, Stace. Take a long bike ride in the park, and don't even think about busting out the balloon until you hit the year mark."

Stacey's face falls. I bet she's already bought the tickets. "The balloon's a cool idea," I say. "But it's just too much on top of everything else. Remember, no spoiling that dog."

"On the other hand," Kali says, looking at Syd and me, "she could say her mom won the tickets in charity raffle and doesn't want them herself. That lets Stacey off the hook. What do you think?"

I think floating over Texas in a wicker basket is the opposite of romantic, but then I'm deathly afraid of heights. "Go for it," I say. "But only if you cut all the rest."

Syd gives a nod of approval, and we hastily gather our jackets and head for the door.

"But wait," Stacey calls after us. "Wouldn't the sunrise breakfast be more romantic?"

We are now officially late for group yet again.

"Fine," I say. "Breakfast on the bridge, but you'll have to ride your bikes there and skip the balloon."

Stacey follows us. "Is breakfast too boring?" she asks. "A balloon ride says I'm exciting—a girl who likes to take chances and live life to the fullest."

"Ballooning or breakfast," Kali calls over her shoulder as we start running down the street. "It's your choice, Stacey, but it's one or the other!"

·· ♥ ··

"Relationships are all about balance, aren't they?" I say, after Lauren finishes describing how she resolved a problem with Trey. "You need to do enough to show you're into it, but not so much that the other person gets complacent."

"People would rather be treated like crap than be treated too well," Syd says.

Dieter says, "I don't think that's true of a healthy relationship, Sydney."

"Maybe it's hard to feel like you *deserve* to be treated well," Kali says.

"You all deserve to be treated well," Dieter says. "In fact, you have to demand it. And you prove you deserve it by treating other people well."

"It doesn't always work that way," I say.

"I'll tell you how it works," Evan says, leaning over to pat my knee. "The key is not to aim too high. Zahra, you're a seven-point-five, and you should be shooting for the same." He nods at Kali. "You could go as high as eight-point-five, no problem."

"Evan," Dieter says, frowning. "Do you really think that's helpful?"

Evan nods, alert for once. "I do, because it's realistic. Look at Syd. She keeps turning me down because she's a solid eight and I'm a six."

"On your best day," Syd mutters.

"I'm just saying," Evan continues. "If you date *up*, you end up trying too hard. If you date *down*, you don't try hard enough. Like Zahra says, it's all about balance."

"That is *so* not what I meant," I say.

"Evan's got a point," Simon says. "Although there's more to it than looks. You've got to factor everything into the package. An eight-point-five with issues is just a seven. And a seven who's fun and smart and knows it can clear a nine."

"What do you think about that, Zahra?" Dieter says. He is picking lint off his black pants as an excuse not to look at me. There's going to be hilarity in Father Casey's office later, I know it.

"Simon is probably right about the confidence," I allow. "But there's a lot more to the equation than that."

"Right," Kali says. "Because you can date *up* and be let down. You guys have forgotten to factor in chemistry."

"Syd?" Dieter asks, still fighting a smile.

Syd sighs. "I think it's all too complicated to bother."

·· ♥ ··

Syd, Kali, and I bolt for the exit the second Dieter brings the session to a close. We're halfway down the stone steps in front of the church when three claps bring us to a halt.

"Now we know why he has a room with two exits," Syd says.

"It comes in handy to catch people running away from their responsibilities," Dieter says, strolling toward us.

"Sorry about being late again, Dieter," I say. "We had a . . . friend that needed advice at the last minute. Supporting others helps us work out our problems, too."

"And we were only ten minutes late this time," Kali says.

"Ten minutes today, fifteen last week, ten the week before. That time is mine," Dieter says. "Otherwise, I'm all for your supporting other people." He gives us the avatar stare until we squirm. "Once more, ladies, and I'll be sharing my concerns with your parents."

As Dieter goes back around the church, Simon and Evan come out the front door and join us.

214

"You're in trouble," Evan says. "Even I'm on time for group, and I have the worst attendance record at my school."

He says that like it's something to brag about. "Why do you care?" I ask.

Simon answers. "With three of you missing, Detour has more time to stir up our brains, that's why."

"If you had a brain, you'd remember a certain predicament we got you out of recently," Syd says.

"That's why I want to help you," Simon says, taking off his baseball cap and running his hand through his dark hair. "You've gotta understand how this whole thing works. Look at it from our parents' perspective. They screwed up, and they know it. They feel so guilty about it that they spend their days looking for signs you're about to crack. If you play your cards right, you can use this angst to your advantage. A day off school to chill? Sure. Some extra cash for a movie to cheer you up? No problem. There's just one string attached: *you have to show up for group.* Because if you're there, they think everything's under control. Skip group and alarm bells ring. Bye-bye special privileges; hello surveillance."

"Right, man," Evan says, slinging an arm around Sydney's shoulder. "You just have to show up." He pulls his arm back as Syd's boot jams down on his sneaker. "*Ow!* What the hell?"

"You ran the numbers," Syd says, walking away.

When we catch up with her, she explains that her foul mood has more to do with her dad than Evan. Mr. Stark booked a "special dinner" last night at their favorite restaurant. She hadn't seen him for weeks, and when she arrived, he wasn't alone.

"Her name is Charlotte," Syd says. "She's twenty-two and

she's moving into Dad's condo on Saturday."

"Isn't the condo a bit small for three?" I ask.

"You mean five," Syd says. "Charlotte has the biggest boob implants you've ever seen. Dad was relieved when I said I'd move to Mom's full-time. Even though she wants her space, too."

Syd soon shuts the conversation down by asking me about Riaz.

"Nothing but a short e-mail talking about his trip to Houston," I say. "I don't even need cookies to repel guys anymore."

"He's interested," Kali insists, freshening her lip gloss. "Or he wouldn't bother keeping in touch. I bet he calls tonight. If not, you could shoot him an e-mail, maybe drop a bigger hint."

"I don't want to look desperate. What do you think, Syd?"

Syd shrugs. "I'd hate to see you get burned again."

Kali scowls at her. "Must you always look on the dark side? The guy's probably shy and needs encouragement."

"Riaz is not shy," I tell her. "And if kissing him back wasn't encouragement, I don't know what is."

"You know what might help?" Kali says, glancing at Syd in that way I've come to dread. "A makeover."

·· ♥ ··

"I'm so sorry, Z," Syd says, looking horrified anew when I come into the trailer.

Kali and Syd took me to a salon yesterday after seeing Facebook photos of the slam on Drake's ex-girlfriend. While Syd and Kali aren't exactly generic, my hair stood out in the crowd of laughing bystanders, and I'm the only one of us who got tagged. Not that my presence implicates me in any way, but when it comes to revenge, we agreed it would be better all around if I could blend.

The salon mission didn't go exactly as planned. I should have listened when the stylist explained that red hair strands have an odd shape that makes them resistant to dye. She warned me that she'd have to bleach out all the color, which would damage the texture, before applying a new one. But by this point I was committed, so I let her strip my hair and apply a nice, neutral butterscotch dye. It didn't fully take. What I have now is a frizzy mop in a brassy color unknown to nature. As it turns out, there are worse things than red hair.

Kali shushes her. "It looks fine, Z, really. And the stylist is sure another visit this afternoon will put things right."

"You can show off your new look at the rink tonight," Syd says. "The Wheel Dolls are doing a charity match at the Millennium."

Syd's friend Rambo has a thing for Madison Manson, who skates with a local roller derby league. He's asked us to find out where she hangs out *off* the rink so he can meet her and ask her out. Rambo didn't have much cash, so we agreed to do the job in exchange for a fifty-dollar Gap gift card he got for his birthday.

Barter products account for about a third of our earnings, and since we haven't gotten around to selling them, the trailer is filling up with swag, including movie coupons, an unopened box of perfume, a digital camera, three video games, an empty aquarium, a baseball glove, and an electronic reader.

"I'm in," I say. "I'd like to see the match."

I have zero interest in roller derby, but I'm supposed to

have dinner at Mom's, and I can't face the family's reaction to my hair until I'm sure it's fixed.

"I can't make it," Kali says. "Notts County is doing that freebie at the Plaza."

"Business trumps hormones," Syd says.

"This *is* business," Kali says. "I'm testing my matchmaking program on Owen Gaines and me."

"Nice try," Syd says. "I need you to do your thing on Madison. You know, where you talk so much they'll say anything just to shut you up."

"Zahra can handle this one," Kali says.

"The Plaza's on the way to the Millennium," I say. "And free concerts never last long. So why don't we all go there first, then hit the roller rink as the match ends?"

"Fine, but if I'm making headway with Owen, you guys are on your own," Kali says.

"Fine. And if Notts County sucks, you're picking up after Banksy for a week," Syd says.

Owen Gaines is very cute, but he's seven years older than we are. Kali probably doesn't stand a chance.

After the concert, he and his bandmates set up a table to sell Notts County T-shirts, posters, and CDs. Girls gather like flies to honey.

"How do I look?" Kali asks, giving her hair a toss.

"Like a desperate groupie," Syd answers.

"You look nice," I say, glaring at Syd.

Kali applies a fresh coat of lip gloss. "I'm nervous," she says, sounding surprised. That rarely happens for her where guys are concerned. "I hope Owen remembers me from the all-ages gig. Do you think he will?"

Syd rolls her eyes. "As I recall, all he said was 'Hey.'"

"It was the way he said it," Kali says, grinning.

"He might have noticed you dancing like a freak tonight," Syd says. Some of Kali's friends from school are here, and they banded together in front of the stage, making so much noise, it would be hard *not* to notice.

"Do you think?" Kali asks hopefully.

"Sure," I say. "What's the plan? Are you buying a CD or a poster?"

"I don't know," Kali says. "What do you think? A CD says I love his music, but a poster says he's hot."

"I'd go for the T-shirt," Syd says. "Keeping him close to your boobs says it all."

Kali's brow furrows as she notices Owen talking to a pixie-ish girl with brown hair and a pretty face. "Who's she?"

"Not his sister, judging by the steamy eye contact," Syd says.

"You're not afraid of a little competition," I remind Kali.

"Right," she says, throwing back her shoulders. "I can take that pixie."

Syd and I stand a few feet back, watching as Kali moves in for the kill. In her black skinny jeans and lace-up boots, she's all legs tonight. Walking straight up to Owen, she says, "Hey. Great gig."

Owen barely glances at her as he says, "Thanks."

Syd elbows me in the ribs. "Stee-rike one!"

"We met in September at your all-ages show," Kali says, twisting a ringlet of hair around her finger.

"Oh yeah?" Owen's eyes are still on the pixie.

"I'm Kali."

"Hi, Kerry." It's obvious he doesn't remember meeting her.

"Stee-rike two!" Syd says.

But Kali isn't out yet. "I liked your new version of *Star Sleeper* today," she says. "The transition to F minor in the last refrain gave the piece such a haunting quality."

Owen's eyes finally meet Kali's. "That's what I was going for. You're a musician?"

Kali shrugs. "I dabble. I've been playing guitar and writing songs for years, but there are so many riffs I haven't mastered."

"You'll get there," Owen says, giving her his full attention. "You're way ahead of where I was at your age. I didn't pick up an instrument until eleventh grade."

"I'm almost in college," Kali says, smiling up at Owen.

Syd's snort is loud enough for Owen to hear, and it's my turn to elbow her in the ribs. "Shut up and let the maestro work."

Playing with the chain around her neck, Kali says, "So when did you switch from piano to guitar?"

Owen puts his hands in the back pockets of his jeans and smiles. "Did I say that the instrument was a piano?"

Busted, Kali pretends to examine a CD. "I think I read that somewhere."

"Well, you read right." Owen lets her off the hook and continues to talk to her for a good ten minutes. Finally, Syd claps her hands three times to remind Kali we have other plans.

She rejoins us carrying a CD, a T-shirt, and a poster. "As predicted by my matchmaking program, Owen and I are destined for greatness. I got enough information in just ten minutes to confirm the key aspects of our compatibility."

Syd laughs. "Now all you have to do is convince him."

"I will," Kali says. "Just give me time." She hands me the CD before squirming into the T-shirt. "Listen and love it," she says.

"That poster is not going into the trailer," Syd warns.

"You're right," Kali says with a huge smile. "It's going directly over my bed."

.. ♥ ..

The referee blows the whistle to signal the start of the final "jam." A pack of eight girls takes off around the rink. The four from the Wheel Dolls are wearing short, puffy pink skirts with poodles appliquéd on them—the kind you might see in a movie like *Grease*, only way shorter. The cap sleeves on their tight black shirts reveal a variety of colorful tattoos on bare arms. Fingerless gloves and bright pink neck scarves complete the outfit, along with knee and elbow pads and helmets.

The four girls from the Diner Dames are dressed like goth waitresses. Their formfitting powder-blue smocks are trimmed with white piping and lacy handkerchiefs, and blue garters hold up their seamed stockings. In contrast, their lips and nails are painted black, and there are black semicircles under their eyes.

This is a lot more interesting than I expected. It's theater on wheels.

After twenty seconds, the ref blows the whistle again, and Madison Manson takes off, alongside a girl from the Dames. Running a few steps on the stoppers of their old-school roller skates, the two "jammers" glide down the rink toward the rest of the pack. Each girl has two stars on her helmet.

"Rambo says that's so you can keep track of them," Syd says.

The reason for the title and the stars quickly becomes obvious. When the two girls reach the rest of the pack there's a sudden blur of blue and pink. Madison tries to battle her way past the Dames' blockers, who simultaneously try to stop her while helping their own jammer force her way through the Dolls. It's a mass of thrashing limbs. Just when it seems that Madison will be the first to emerge from the battle, a Dame bodychecks her and sends Madison careening to the side of the rink.

Syd jumps to her feet and bellows, "Go, Madison!" She's as excited as Kali was during the Notts County concert.

Madison fights her way back into the scrum, but the Dames' jammer is almost out of the pack. One of the Dolls checks the teammate in front of her, causing the girl to fall hard onto the rink and block the Dames' jammer for a couple of seconds. That's just enough time for Madison to squeeze past the last blocker and break free of the pack. Once clear, she drops her hands to her hips several times to signal the end of the bout.

After the ref blows the whistle, the tackled Dame struggles to her feet with the help of her teammates.

"That was brutal," Kali says.

"That was nasty," I say.

"That was awesome," Syd says, grinning as she hops down the bleachers and heads toward the locker room.

"She forgot Banksy," Kali says.

But a second later, Syd whistles and Banksy trots off after her.

By the time Kali and I make our way to the Dolls' locker room, Syd is already chatting to Madison. Up close, Madison seems to be quite pretty, although she's sort of a cross between

Marilyn Monroe and Marilyn Manson. Her platinum hair, false eyelashes, and pink lipstick are offset by a row of eyebrow piercings and a Celtic cross tattooed on her neck.

"That's blood," Kali whispers, noticing the dried trickle under a gash on Madison's right cheek.

"It must be a badge of honor," I say. Most of the other girls in the room are bruised and bloodied, too.

We wait for Syd to call us over, but it never happens. She's so engrossed in her conversation with Madison that she forgets all about us—and her purpose in coming.

Finally, we introduce ourselves, and Kali quickly steers the conversation in a more personal direction to get the information we need for Rambo.

"So much for business trumping hormones," she says, as we drag Syd out of the Millennium. "Syd's discovered love after Eric—roller derby."

chapter 14

Mom drags the black kohl liner along her eyelid before sweeping gold shadow above it. She stares at me in the mirror, trying to make me spill my guts by arching a perfectly shaped brow.

I sit on the edge of the tub, watching her get ready to go out, as I have so many times before. Only this time my seat's getting pretty hot. "What?"

"You know what," Mom says. "You look ridiculous."

Mom is about as pissed off as she gets—or at least *shows*— and she didn't even see my hair at its worst. Another dose of light brown and some blond highlights have made it quite passable.

"Dad didn't think so," I say. All he said was that he preferred my hair its natural color, which used to be *his* natural color before the gray crept in. "My life's changed a lot lately, and I didn't have any choice about most of it. This is a change *I* wanted to make. Anyway, my friends like it."

Mom pauses between coats of mascara. "I assume they pushed you to do it."

That's actually quite insulting. It suggests I don't have a mind of my own. But picking a fight with Mom won't get me anywhere. *Everything is better with a little sugar.*

"You know I've never liked my hair," I say. "This was my decision."

Granted, I probably wouldn't have made it without Syd and Kali pushing me. They've pushed me into a lot of things, and I've been better off for it every time. They push, but I make the final decision. Sometimes you need that to move ahead with your life—especially if you're not a natural risk taker. I think I've always played it too safe. While it's great to consult with fantasy cooks on my fantasy set, I've learned now that it's better to get out there and gain practical skills that will help me down the road.

Even René has noticed a change in me lately. After seeing my hair, he brought up the idea of my signing up for a course at a local pastry school again. He must think I have more confidence, which I'll need if I take the course. Most of the students are experienced chefs, and it would take guts to match whisks with the big guys. I've saved enough money for it, but I don't know where I'd find the time.

"I'm not sure what to think these days, Zahra," Mom says. "You've changed since you started hanging out with this Syd and Kali."

I prickle at her tone. "A month ago, you were happy I was making new friends."

She remains silent and leans into the mirror to apply another coat of mascara, opening her eyes unnaturally wide.

I try not to ask, but the words come out anyway. "What changes are you talking about?"

"The way you speak to your mother, for one," she says, sweeping blush across her cheeks. "And the way you change your plans on a dime. You used to be a homebody, and now you're out all the time." She turns around and eyes my clothes. "Since when did you care about designer jeans?"

Since when does Mom know what designer jeans are?

"I'm working more," I say, to explain both the time out and extra cash flow.

"There's more to it than that," Mom says.

"True. You're forgetting a key piece of the story," I say. "*Group.* If I've changed since you set Dieter loose on me, can you really complain?"

She looks slightly taken aback. "Well, you can't blame a mother for worrying, especially when you've given up all your old friends. Syd and Kali aren't exactly what I expected." She sweeps blush across her cheeks. "Kali seems very . . . assertive. And Syd's so . . . I don't know, goth?"

"You met them for five minutes when you picked me up from Kali's one night," I say. "Syd isn't goth and Kali isn't pushy, which is what you really meant. Since when did you get all judgey?" I pause for effect. "Oh, right. When Nani and Nana moved in."

The sugar deficit causes Mom to head into the bedroom without answering. I trail after her and belly flop onto her bed as she disappears into the closet. All remnants of my dad have been cleared off his bedside table. There's a photo of Nana and Nani where Dad and Mom's wedding photo used to be. I shove it under the bed.

"Look, Mom, if they're different from my old friends, it's because *I'm* different. We all come from broken homes."

Mom comes out of the closet wearing dress pants and a pink silk tunic. "That guilt card you keep playing might work on your father, but it's getting old with me. I'm willing to give you a bit more rope, Zahra. If you hang yourself with it, you can use that twin bed in your sister's room on a permanent basis."

Okay, so I pushed it too far. I may be raising myself, but by law she's still the boss, and twenty-four/seven surveillance would kill my involvement in Love, Inc.

"Relax, Mom. I'm doing exactly what you wanted. I go to group, I made new friends, and I've kept my grades up. Frankly, I don't see a problem. If you check out Dad's books on raising a teenager, you'll see that it's totally normal for me to want to be more independent."

At the mention of Dad's manuals, Mom sighs. She passes me a gold chain to latch around her neck, and perches beside me. "Don't make me regret trusting you."

"Mom, it's fine. Syd and Kali are good people."

She reaches out and twists a strand of my hair through her fingers, examining the color. Pushing it behind my shoulders, she shakes her head. But then she walks over to the mirror and runs a brush over her own hair. For now, the subject is closed.

Since we've reached a cease-fire, I can afford to sprinkle more sugar around. "You look nice," I say. Too nice to be heading out for dinner with her girlfriends. Alarm bells ring. "Oh my God, are you going on a *date*? You're married!"

"I'm legally separated," she says, selecting a wrap from the dozen heaped over a chair. "And I'm not going on a date. I'm having dinner with Xavier, my business school instructor, to get some advice on my products."

The woman who bought so much of Mom's stock at the Eid carnival recently offered to carry the Yasin Valley line in her spa if Mom can produce and professionally package enough of her products.

The doorbell rings, and Mom checks her watch. Now I regret encouraging her to start a business.

"I have news for you, Mom: unless the rest of the class is going, it's a date."

"I realize I've been off the market for a while, but I still think I'd recognize a date if I saw one," she says.

"You only ever dated Dad."

She smiles. "That's what he thinks. Anyway, Xavier's doing me a favor."

Xavier's a vulture. Our home may be wrecked, but he doesn't need to swoop in and pick over the remains.

"Favors that involve dinner and wine probably have strings attached," I say. "Anyway you don't need this guy's help. Dad was excited to hear about your business, and you know he'd come up with the best logo ever."

She stands and puts a few things into a clutch. "I'm sure your father would love to believe I can't do this without him, but I intend to prove I can."

What is wrong with my parents? I go out of my way to pass along nice comments they made about each other, and all they hear is insults. For two people who have five college degrees between them, they're hopelessly stupid.

The doorbell rings again, and Saliyah thunders through the house to answer. "That will be Xavier," Mom says, heading into the hall. "I'd better not leave him alone with your sister. You never know what she might say."

There are footsteps on the stairs and my sister appears, grinning from ear to ear.

I glare at her. "How can you look so happy that Mom's dating again?"

Saliyah laughs. "I'm happy *you're* dating again. Riaz is here!"

·· ♥ ··

Nani is literally quivering with excitement as she helps me put on my coat and pushes me out the front door behind Riaz. Thank God he turned down her repeated invitations to stay for dinner, because I don't think I could have survived it.

"So where are we going?" I ask. Judging by the way Riaz is dressed: a black wool jacket over a chunky gray sweater and dark blue jeans, we could be doing anything from dinner to the movies, or maybe even a play. That would be cool.

Riaz isn't giving me any clues. "It's a surprise."

I stare at Riaz's profile as he steers his old pickup onto Lamar Boulevard. I don't get this guy at all. First, he comes on like a jerk. Then he reveals a sweet side and kisses me like he means it. After that he practically goes AWOL, and just as I'm about to give up, he materializes on the doorstep without warning. Since Eric also liked to show up without warning, this does not bode well.

"You're looking at me like I'm a stranger," Riaz says. "I'm the one who should be looking at *you* that way."

I put my hand to my hair but resist the urge to ask if he likes it. If I want to be more independent, I need to stop worrying about what other people think.

"It's the ambushing thing," I tell him. "It's weird."

"I thought girls liked spontaneity."

"Some might, but I like to know what to expect from a guy. I've had too many surprises."

Riaz smiles. "But you're here, aren't you?"

When I don't answer, he takes my hand. The warmth of his palm against mine reminds me of how he massaged lotion into my hand at the carnival.

I realize I'm holding my breath, and release it slowly. I can't let this go to my head. People on the rebound need to proceed with extreme caution. Like Kali says, things should be perfect in the beginning. You have to keep your standards high and take nothing at face value. You have to demand more, not less. That's what we've started to tell our Love, Inc. clients.

"I'm here," I say, "because it gets me out of dinner with my grandparents." It would have been a very tense dinner. Nana hasn't spoken a word to me since he saw my hair, and Nani hasn't *stopped* talking. She seems to think I'm just one short skirt shy of a sex scandal.

I try to pull my hand away from Riaz, but he grips harder.

"It's too bad we couldn't stay," he says. "I hear your Nani's a mean cook."

"Mean is the word, all right. She knows I hate curry, but she keeps serving it up. I guess she figures one day I'll wake up a fan."

"You will," he says. "And once you develop a taste for it, everything else seems flat in comparison."

"Well, at least flat's reliable. You never know what to expect with curry."

"It's good to spice things up," he says. "Stick with me and I'll show you."

Releasing my hand, Riaz gears down and steers the truck onto a side street in a semi-industrial neighborhood. "Almost there," he says. "I can't wait for you to meet my friends."

·· ♥ ··

"It's freezing in here," I say, pulling my jacket tight around me as Riaz leads me into a warehouse that seems too well lit for a party.

As we move through the room, I see flats of boxes piled high to the ceiling. Dozens of people are wrapping more boxes in plastic and sorting them into piles. There are five stainless-steel tables, each surrounded by people wearing clear plastic gloves. As I watch, someone plucks a handful of something pink out of a large vat, places it into a plastic bag, and weighs it. Someone else seals the bag and stores it in a box. When we get closer, I see the boxes are labeled goat, lamb, or beef. All are stamped HALAL.

I stare at Riaz in confusion.

"It's a meat drive," he says.

That explains nothing except for the fact that this is not a party. I'm beginning to suspect it's not a date either.

Several people wave to Riaz, including a few pretty girls in head scarves and salwar kameez. He greets everyone warmly.

He introduces me first to Nikki, a blond woman in her late twenties, and her son, Sam, who is Riaz's "little brother." Sam immediately drags Riaz away to show off the pile of boxes he's been working on.

Nikki tells me that Sam was so shy he'd barely speak when he joined Big Brothers. "Riaz has been a godsend," she says.

"He's just so good with people that he's pulled Sam right out of his shell."

Watching Riaz and Sam goof around, I can't help but wonder if I'm Riaz's next project. I push the thought away. I don't know what this event is about, but it isn't about me. And since I'm relying on Riaz for a ride home, I might as well make the best of a bad situation. "So, what exactly is a meat drive?" I ask.

"Do you know about the feast of sacrifice?" she asks.

I nod. Eid al-Adha is the feast that marks the end of the pilgrimage to Mecca, when Muslims sacrifice a domestic animal and divide the meat into thirds for themselves, their friends, and the poor. "Don't people usually donate money now?"

"Yeah," Riaz says, joining us again. "We used those donations to buy meat that we'll distribute to about fifteen hundred people in Austin. It's community outreach."

On behalf of his mosque, I assume. If I were on the receiving end, I'd rather reach out for cash than meat, but there's no bargaining with ritual.

Riaz takes me over to a table to meet his friends, all of whom are girls.

One named Fatimah snaps latex gloves onto my hands and slides a box of cubed lamb in front of me. "You don't have to weigh every bag," she says, adjusting her dupatta with the back of her hand to avoid getting blood on it. "You can ballpark it once you've got a general sense."

She smiles encouragingly as I slip my gloved hand into the box of lamb. The cubes are cold and squishy, but I try not to cringe as I scoop up a handful and toss it into a bag. If she can do it, I can do it. After all, I cook with meat, just never in such vast quantities.

Pasting on a smile, I weigh my first bag.

"Good," Fatimah says. She points down the row to a group of girls. "They're new this year, too. Riaz recruited them at the carnival."

The new girls are giggling, and I follow their gaze to a forklift that's headed our way. Riaz is standing on an empty pallet on the front, wearing a white apron tied around his neck like a cape, pretending to fly. He smiles and waves as he buzzes past, and every girl at the table raises a bloody hand to wave back.

I shudder as I realize that instead of being swept away on a date, I've been recruited as the Meat Drive Superhero's new slave.

On Riaz's second pass, however, he blows a kiss that is either intended for Fatimah or me. I look at her in confusion, and she smiles. "He's met my boyfriend," she says.

All right, so this *is* a date. Riaz can't help it if he's a popular guy. He's smart, he's charming, he's confident, and he's cute. It's no surprise that he has a lot of fans, and I'm flattered that he's making time to fit me into his busy life.

As I turn to watch him go, Riaz and his plywood chariot suddenly morph into Eric and Miss Daisy. The chill that runs down my spine is even colder than the meat locker. I give my head a shake to dispel the image.

If one of our Love, Inc. clients were in this situation, I know exactly what I'd say: "Not good enough. If he likes you, he'll make spending time with you a priority. Demand more, not less."

It's good advice, and it's time I took it myself. Zahra MacDuff is done with harems.

"Excuse me," I say, turning to leave.

In the parking lot, I strip off the latex gloves and toss them into a garbage bin. That's when I realize I've left my purse inside.

I kick the metal bin, and curse. The noise startles a rat, which scurries away around the side of the building.

"Forget something?" Riaz is coming toward me carrying my purse. The apron "cape" is still tied around his neck.

I snatch my purse from his hands and stomp toward the street.

"What happened?" he says. "Did I do something wrong?"

"No." What am I supposed to say? He was just being himself, after all. He leads a busy social life, and he probably thought I'd enjoy this evening together. There are plenty of girls who would think that's enough. I ought to know. I used to be one of them.

"Zahra, wait. Let me drive you home."

"No thanks. I'll catch the next forklift—I mean, bus."

"Does this mean you're breaking up with me?" he calls.

Breaking up with him! I peer at him over my shoulder, but he's standing in the shadows and I can't see his expression.

"It means I'm not joining your cult," I yell back.

"Since when is a fund-raiser a cult?" he asks. "You really can't spare a few hours to help people?"

"Sure I can. But I prefer to be asked, not ambushed." At the corner, I turn back and bellow, "And for your information, I just became a vegetarian."

·· ♥ ··

"If it makes you feel any better, it's over with the guy from my guitar class, too," Kali says.

"I didn't know there *was* a guy from your guitar class," I say.

"Didn't I mention him?" she asks, reapplying her lip gloss. "Well, he didn't last long."

"No kidding. Miller only just bit the dust," Syd says. "Anyway, you can't compete. Zahra fell headfirst into a cultural divide."

"So did I," Kali says. "My guy openly admitted his favorite band is the Pussycat Dolls. That's not even a band, it's pop porn."

"I thought you were holding out for Owen Gaines anyway," I say.

"That one could take a while," Kali says. "And I don't want to get rusty in the meantime. Relationships are like sports. If you want to compete, you have to keep in shape."

Someone knocks at the door, and I don't even sit up. Kali nudges me with her boot. "It's your client."

I close my eyes and groan. I made an appointment to help a girl figure out whether her ice-dancing partner is interested in her. I even promised to join her at the rink to check him out in person. "How can I help her when it takes me so long to see the signs myself?" I say. "I'm a fraud."

The girl knocks a second time.

"Save your money," I call. "I have no idea if he's interested, but I'm pretty sure he'll break your heart either way."

Syd slaps a paint-stained hand over my mouth. "Are you crazy? You might not care about this business, but I have to. Dad drained the last of my college fund for Charlotte's new boobs."

Opening the door, she greets our client with a rare smile. "Zahra's just kidding. But I'm afraid she's not feeling that well, so I'll be coming to the rink with you instead."

She leans back in to give me a malevolent glare before disappearing.

"Oh man, you're in trouble," Kali says.

Even I have to smile at the thought of Syd dispensing relationship advice at the ice rink. "You know, when push comes to shove, she's a true professional."

"I know," Kali says. "She's always thinking about how we can improve the business. Before you got here today she suggested we create a business e-mail account and buy a cheap, pay-as-you-go cell phone for initial contact with potential clients. That way, we won't all be going over cell phone minutes every month."

"Good idea," I say, coming over to the table, where Kali is working on her laptop. We probably should have done that from the beginning, but who knew the business would take off like this?

She looks up at me. "I worry about Syd sometimes. She buries herself in Love, Inc. to avoid the real thing. I don't think she's checked out another guy since Eric."

"Well, someone wise once said that the severity of the heartbreak correlates directly to the amount of time spent together. She's not ready to move on, and there's no use pushing her. You and I spent less time with Eric, and we still have trust issues."

"I guess," she says. "But I wish there was a way we could help her." Brightening, she brings her matchmaking questionnaire up on the screen. "Maybe I could just—"

"Don't even think about it. Syd's a private person."

"But my matchmaking questionnaire is working like a

charm," she says. "I've road-tested it on three of our clients, and two are thrilled with the results."

The third is Luke Barnett. Kali's narrowed the field to two candidates, including Simon's ex-girlfriend, Trisha.

"Why don't you fill out my questionnaire?" Kali asks. "I guarantee I'll find you a guy to take your mind off Riaz."

"Forget it. Guys are too much work."

"Don't get all Syd on me," Kali says. "You're being too hard on yourself." She opens her laptop. "Name: Zahra MacDuff."

"Ahmed-MacDuff," I correct her.

"What, you saw the light at the meat drive?"

"I just figure I can't expect my mom to keep both names if I don't."

"Hobbies," Kali says. "Baking, reading, Web surfing."

"I'm not doing your questionnaire."

"Favorite Web sites?"

It's a trap, because Kali knows I can't resist showing off my latest Web discoveries. Soon we're surfing and laughing, and by the time Syd gets back, we've even set up a Gmail account in the name of Group Daisy, the two things that brought us together. The password is Banksy.

It's not enough to cheer Syd up. "That was horrible," she says.

"Why? What happened?" Now I feel guilty about abandoning my client. "You think her friend isn't interested?"

"He didn't show," Syd says. "So I spent forty minutes delivering a pep talk about taking chances, about true love being hard to find, about it all being worthwhile in the end. Blah, blah, bleh." She crashes onto her bench. "Total hypocrisy."

"In short, you pimped yourself out for college," Kali says.

"Exactly. Because if I can't get into a good school, I'll never escape my parents."

I promise I'll take care of the client myself on Saturday and offer to take Kali and Syd for dinner afterward, but Syd already has plans. The Maternity Ward is curating a photo exhibit of the real Banksy's work. Syd's been invited to the opening, and she's taking her mom.

We wrap up our weekly meeting with two new rituals. First, we list our latest barter swag on eBay, and package up the sold items for shipping. Next, we divide up the contents of our cash box four ways: a quarter for each of us, and a quarter for the company, which goes into an old cookie tin to cover Love, Inc. expenses.

There's a knock at the trailer door, and Kali barely has time to hide the tin before Brody bursts in on our meeting. I sink in my seat as he enters, remembering our last discussion.

"You guys set me up." His deep voice bounces off the trailer walls and makes it feel even smaller. "That guy at the Spurs game was all over me." He tries to pace, but there's only room for one stride.

"Oh no, poor Dylan," Kali says.

"Poor Dylan? How about poor Brody?" he says, rolling up the sleeves of his Fiesta Mart shirt. "The JumboTron caught me fighting off the octopus. Now I'll never get another date unless it's with the concession guy. He saw us on screen and slipped me his number with my french fries."

"Maybe you should consider it," Kali says. "It's been at least a week since you had a date."

"Did you get the photo?" Syd asks.

"Oh, I got the photo. Whoa." He stops pacing to stare at

me. "Lookin' hot, Red. Love the hair."

"Think of a new nickname," I say, to cover my embarrassment. "Red doesn't fit anymore."

Brody flips open his phone and displays our client's boyfriend, Raphael, kissing Brody on the cheek.

"Excellent work," Kali says.

Brody snaps his phone shut. "Well worth fifty bucks."

"We agreed on forty."

"That's when you implied the prospect was female. Given the damage to my rep, fifty's a bargain."

"He earned it," I say. "He got the job done even though we tricked him."

"I hope you're not going soft because the guy paid you a compliment," Kali says.

"Brody's never paid *me* a compliment, and I agree with Z," Syd says.

Kali shrugs. "The majority has spoken."

"It's been a pleasure doing business with you ladies," Brody says. He slides into my side of the banquette, purposely crushing me against the window. "Hey," he says, pointing to Kali's laptop. "AwkwardFamilyPhotos. I love that site. Since when did you get so cool, Kal?"

"It's Zahra's latest find," Kali says.

"Glad you're trying to lighten up, Red," he says. "And I'm still calling you Red, because this"—he points to my hair—"is just surface. You can't change what's inside, so it's highly unlikely that you'll have more fun as a blonde."

"That's not why I did it!" Brody has a gift for pressing my buttons. "And I have plenty of fun. Not that it's any of your business."

He shakes his head. "There's that tone again. I'm concerned, Red. How can you fix other people's love trouble if you're all bitter and harsh yourself?"

Kali leans across the table and punches her brother, but as usual, there's an element of truth to what he says. I am feeling bitter about guys.

"Sweet sells," he says. "Sugar-free didn't work for Red's baking, and it won't work for your business either."

"A month ago you were dissing our business, and now you're telling us how to run it?" Kali asks.

"That was before I knew how lucrative it could be. Besides, apart from getting pimped out to a guy, it was fun. So if you need stud services again, just ask."

"Actually," Kali says, "we could use a male opinion about a hypothetical client. What would you say about a guy who initially seems into a girl, but when he finally takes her out, it's to do some volunteer work for a charity he supports?"

I must have flinched, because Brody turns to watch me with eyes that are as green as Kali's but so much sharper. "I assume we're talking about the totally hot, mediocre kisser here?"

Did he memorize every single detail of that conversation? What normal guy takes so much interest in relationships? "I never said mediocre."

Kali tilts her head curiously. "You told Brody about Riaz?"

"Not voluntarily! He eavesdropped while I was on the phone with my sister." I push open the little window beside me. I'm feeling flushed all of sudden. Brody seems to be radiating heat.

"She was in my kitchen at the time," Brody says. "It was fair game."

I squirm as much as I can, being crushed into the wall and all. "Can we not discuss this?" I say.

"Kali asked for my opinion on the hypothetical client, and I'm going to give it," he says. "I'm on the Love Stinks Auxiliary Squad now."

"What do you know about romance?" Syd asks.

"More than you guys," he says. "I didn't get three-timed. And I'm not getting my chain yanked by some do-gooder."

"No, you'd rather go out with a ton of girls and never get serious about any of them," Kali says, seemingly oblivious to the fact she's describing her own approach to dating.

"Playing it safe makes you a coward, not an expert," I say.

Brody turns to his sister. "Did she just call me a coward?"

Syd's voice drifts up from her bench. "Would you two like us to leave?"

"Of course not," I say. "I'm done."

"Finally," Brody says. "Because in addition to being bitter, you talk too much."

"Brody, stop," Kali says. "This is a business. We don't trash our hypothetical clients."

"Fine," he says. "But without all the details, it's guesswork here. Either buddy is trying to impress this chick by looking like he's some kind of humanitarian—"

Kali interrupts. "The guy does a *ton* of volunteer work for his community."

"Okay. Then it's probably important to him that a girl shares an interest in his causes."

That's one scenario I never considered.

"So, he might like this girl after all," Kali says.

"Possibly," Brody says. "But if I had it bad for a girl, I'd take her someplace *she'd* enjoy, not put her to work."

I turn and release a sigh out the window. That makes sense. Even if it does crush what's left of my pride.

"If this girl's not the humanitarian type, buddy's just wasting her time anyway," Brody says.

"Maybe she could be," I say. "She's not shallow or anything."

Brody slides out of the seat. "It's not shallow to hold out for a great kisser. It's common sense."

I shiver as he takes the heat with him. Standing at the door, he takes off his jacket and tosses it to me.

"If you want my advice, cut the guy loose," he says. "The do-gooder's not good enough."

chapter 15

Kali is leaning on the counter talking to René when I come out of the back room after my shift. Normally he's in a big hurry to cash out on a Saturday, but today he can't escape Kali's endless chatter.

"Night, René," I say, herding Kali toward the door. "Have fun at the dog show."

"Dog show?" Kali whispers, looking over her shoulder. "Z, he likes dogs and he just said he's into photography. He'd be perfect for—"

"Your mom doesn't want to be set up, Kali, and this is too close to home anyway. You know you can't mix business with pleasure."

She sighs. "It can get messy. I hate my guitar class now because I have to see that loser every week."

We catch the bus to the community center to meet my ice-dancing client. I'm still suffering from a Riaz-induced crisis of confidence, so Kali offered to share her expertise in reading the signs of interest. Since she sees interest *everywhere*, I have my doubts.

Lily is still in sneakers when we arrive. She leads us to the locker room and introduces us to Jason, her dancing partner, and tells him we want to watch their practice. Jason, as tall and muscular as Lily is petite and lithe, welcomes us warmly. A nice guy. A good start.

"Let us begin," Kali whispers in my ear. "Step one: Make sure he's on the right team."

Unzipping her jacket to reveal a low-cut sweater, Kali sits beside Jason on the bench and leans over to admire his figure skates. After a few minutes of small talk about their make and model, she saunters back.

"All clear," she says, zipping up. "No straight man can resist a free peek. Now we can move on to step two: Observation."

We stand a few yards away as Lily and Jason lace their skates and plan their workout. Jason leans over and checks Lily's laces and tightens them for her.

"Attentive," Kali whispers. "Check."

They walk to the door together and Jason stands back to allow Lily to pass, his hand grazing her lower back.

"Gratuitous contact," Kali says, continuing the play-by-play. "Nice."

Lily cracks a joke about something, and Jason laughs and jokes back.

"Anxious to please her," Kali says. "Sweet."

We follow a few yards behind as they bounce toward the ice on their skate guards. Jason "accidentally" nudges Lily into the boards and rights her. She punches his arm and he feigns pain.

"Roughhousing," Kali says. "School-yard flirtation, basic."

As they glide onto the ice, Jason lifts Lily up and spins her as if she were a doll. Lily squeals, and he spins faster.

"School-yard flirtation, advanced," Kali says.

Putting Lily in a headlock, Jason calls back to us. "I hope this one can stay on her skates today. Sometimes she spends half the practice on her butt."

"Good, the faux dis," Kali tells me.

I shake my head. "How do you know this isn't just an act he's putting on for us?"

"I'll show you." Raising her voice, she calls, "Yeah, I heard Lily's a bit of a klutz."

Jason releases Lily and turns to stare at Kali. "I was just kidding," he says. "Lily's a great dancer—totally elegant."

"Spontaneous chivalrous defense," Kali whispers. Raising her voice again, she calls, "Well, looking good is half the battle, right? And Dan says she's smokin'."

Jason's hand drops off Lily's shoulder. "Who's Dan?"

"Don't worry," Kali says. "He's just a friend."

Laughing, Lily skates out to center ice and Jason follows. They take up positions opposite each other, the music starts, and suddenly it's all business.

"Step three: Conclusions," Kali says. "Simple. All signs point to interest."

Sitting on the sidelines, it was totally obvious that Jason's into Lily. "But why isn't he doing something about it?"

Shrugging, Kali says, "It's probably what you said earlier, about mixing business and pleasure. Maybe he's afraid of ruining their chemistry *on* the ice with chemistry *off* the ice."

We watch as they twirl and swirl around the rink, mostly touching, yet still apart.

"It's beautiful," Kali says. "Foreplay on skates."

"They should just leave it for now," I decide. "They can't afford to mess it up before state finals."

"I don't know," Kali muses. "When there's this kind of tension, something's gotta give. If one of them gets frustrated and starts seeing someone else, it'll mess them up anyway. Meanwhile, they could be dating each other and steaming up the arena."

I'm still not convinced. "They're a team. What if dating throws everything off balance?"

"They'll bounce back. It's like I keep saying: if you sit in the stands, life passes you by. You gotta get out there and skate for glory."

"Okay, you win," I say. "Let's see if I can spin them in the right direction."

When the music stops, I wave Jason and Lily over and ask if they're busy after practice. When two heads shake, I pull movie premiere passes out of my pocket and hand one to each. "My dad got these from a client, and we can't use them."

Kali has come up behind me and she's not leaving any room for error. "In case either of you is wondering, this *is* a date."

Jason looks at Lily and smiles. "Sounds good to me."

Lily does a pirouette and skates off. "Gotta catch me first."

"And that," Kali says, watching them career around the ice, "is how you mix business with pleasure."

The Maternity Ward has basically turned into a nightclub for the Banksy photo exhibit. A DJ is spinning tunes, and waiters in long white aprons are weaving through the fashionable crowd, offering appetizers and glasses of wine on silver trays.

I'm so glad we crashed it. I've never been to anything so slick and sophisticated in my life.

Luckily, I wore the coolest dress I own. It's a short, silky black shift with a bold, geometric pattern in a soft green and yellow. I'm wearing it with a wide black belt, black leggings, and green flats. I bought the dress on a whim last summer, and afterward it felt too hip and edgy for me, so I never wore it. Tonight, though, it feels just right. If I can crash a party in this dress, I must be gaining some confidence.

Kali gazes around, looking as dazzled as I feel. "Sure beats the movies," she says, biting into a quesadilla. "There are lots of hot guys here, so if Syd's mom bails, the food and scenery will help." Kali is catching a lot of looks tonight in a gray miniskirt, black boots, and sleeveless silk turtleneck in her trademark green.

Syd's mom doesn't make good on many of her promises, and she's gotten worse since Charlotte came on the scene. Online dating is Mrs. Stark's main priority now, but Syd still thinks tonight's a sure thing, because her mom knows that Banksy (the artist, not the dog) outranks God in Syd's universe.

Kali and I have seen Syd let down so many times that we decided to show up for moral support, just in case. As we scan the crowd for a glimpse of Syd, Kali plucks a wineglass from a passing tray. Before she can raise the glass to her lips, however, a guy with the face of a movie star and the physique of a body builder arrives to take it from her. "ID first," he says.

Kali stands up straight in her heels to look him in the eye while she opens her purse. "If you insist."

"Just understand that I'm trained to recognize a forgery when I see it," he says.

Kali closes her purse again. "Are you a bouncer or something?"

"An art historian. Steven Quo," he says, holding out his hand. "The curator of this event."

I shake his hand next and say, "Sorry for crashing, Steve. We're just here to support our friend Sydney. She's a huge Banksy fan."

"Ah, Syd," he says. "She's a fine artist in her own right."

Since Syd's street art is anonymous, I'm not sure how to respond.

He winks at me. "It's okay; I'm in on the secret. Syd's so talented that I've offered her space in my gallery if she ever decides to work on canvas."

Steve turns to another guest. It's the videographer we saw on our first visit here. She's in the same kimono, only it's been cut off at the thighs and paired with dark green tights and high black boots. Pirate meets Geisha.

"Wow," a voice behind me exclaims. I turn and see Sinead grinning at me. "You are looking good!"

To my surprise, Leo is standing beside her. "Have you ever considered modeling for the arts?" he asks, grinning.

"What are you guys doing here?" I ask. "*Together?*"

Sinead laughs. "Don't worry, your good work hasn't been undone." She waves to a pretty girl who's approaching with three drinks. "Leo's here with his new girlfriend. I just came over to say hi."

Kali and I wish them well and move off through the crowd in search of Syd. Finally we spot her leaning against a bar, drinking something pink from a martini glass. She looks great, in smoky blue leggings, gold flats, a short black skirt, and a halter top she made out of an old Pearl Jam concert T-shirt. At her feet, Banksy looks dashing in a white T-shirt and black bow tie.

"Who's she talking to?" Kali asks, eyeing the tall guy whose back is to us. "He's got a nice butt."

He's got a nice face too, because it's Eric Skinner. His wavy hair may be buzzed short, but I'd know that ass anywhere.

"Crap!" Kali says, clueing in. "What's *he* doing here?"

"And why is Syd talking to him?" I ask. "Oh my God, she's laughing."

Syd is indeed chuckling over something Eric is saying. My disbelief turns to fury. After all we've been through together over Eric, how can she be having fun with him? Emotions bubble up in me so fast that for a moment, I can't speak. I'm angry and hurt and maybe even a little jealous. If Eric still has the power to make me jealous, I haven't made as much progress as I thought.

"Let's go," I tell Kali. "Four's a crowd."

"Wait," Kali says. "She owes us an explanation."

"What's to explain?" I ask. "She's obviously still seeing Eric and lying to us about it."

Kali shakes her head. "They can't be back together."

But when Eric puts his hand on Sydney's shoulder, she doesn't bite it off at the wrist. Anything less than a bleeding stump is an outright betrayal of our friendship.

I'm glad to see the buzzed-off hair doesn't suit Eric at all. His head looks misshapen. Dented. I wish I'd known what was under that hair before. It would have made getting over him a lot easier. His jeans don't fit as well as they used to, either. I haven't seen him in ages, because I walk the long way to the bus stop to avoid passing his music store. Once, when I saw Miss Daisy in the distance, I ducked behind a Dumpster.

Luckily, I am over him now. So over him. Two hundred percent over him.

But what I am feeling is not indifference. My fingers are twitching to heave my quesadilla at his dented skull. And there's a distinctly bitter taste in my mouth.

Revenge obviously wasn't enough. Seeing him again makes me realize I'm still seriously pissed off. That guy was my boyfriend before he used me to get over someone else.

And there's that someone else chatting away, all twinkly topaz eyes and animated paint-stained hands. Every so often, Banksy—the dog, not the artist—rests his head against Eric's knee. Traitors!

Once my bubbling emotions separate into layers, I realize that I'm more upset about Syd's betrayal than I am angry at Eric. "I thought we were friends," I say. "I guess I was wrong."

I turn to walk away, but Kali grabs my arm and says, "Wait, she just slapped him!"

Together we rush to Syd's side. I only have a moment to savor the look on Eric's face before he fades into the crowd.

Syd is flustered. "What are you doing here?"

"We thought your mom might not show, and we wanted to keep you company," I say. "That was before we knew you had a date lined up."

"A date?" Syd says. "You mean Eric? I didn't even know he was coming."

"Please," I say. "Give us some credit."

Before Syd can argue, a tall, handsome guy walks up to

us. His clothes are conservative yet hip, and probably expensive—the kind you'd expect to see on Prince Harry or some other hot royal. "Just the girls I've been looking for," he says, smiling. There's something oddly familiar about his face.

"Do we know you?" Kali asks. I've never known her to speak so tersely when meeting a cute guy before. She's obviously as upset about Syd's betrayal as I am.

"Only through e-mail," he says. "And voice mail and texts."

"Willem," I say. He looks familiar because his picture is in the paper so often.

"Lauren told me I might find you here tonight. I wanted to introduce myself and try to talk you into taking my case."

"Sorry, Willem, we can't," Kali says. "You can afford a private investigator."

"That would be . . . tacky," he says. It makes me smile to think we're classier than a PI. "I don't want anyone else to know. Addie's not cheating, I'm sure of it. But if she were"—he pauses and swallows a couple of times—"it wouldn't just hurt me, it could affect her dad's career."

"That's why it's too risky, Willem," I say.

"But I was planning on proposing to her soon," he says, flushing.

"You want to get *married*?" I ask, glancing at Syd and Kali.

"After we graduate," he says. "I already know I want to be with Addie for the rest of my life. Why wait?"

It's crazy to consider marrying someone you don't fully trust, but at Love, Inc., we try not to judge.

He turns up the pressure. "I'll pay you well. On top of the five hundred I've already offered, I'll throw in one free service a month for a year at the spa in my grandfather's hotel. Each."

"*Any* service?" Kali asks.

Willem nods. "Nothing's too good for the ladies of Love, Inc."

"Forget it, preppy," says Eric, who's clearly been lurking nearby. "These girls are not for sale."

"Is that chivalry?" Kali says. "Coming from the knight in tarnished armor?"

"Screw off, Eric," I say. "It's none of your business."

Syd has been silent through the discussion, but now she laughs. "Eric thinks he's driven us to prostitution."

"I was only telling this perv he's barking up the wrong tree," Eric says. "Love, Inc. sounds like some kind of escort service."

"Escort service?" a woman asks. She looks like an older, pumped-up version of Syd. "What are you kids talking about?"

"Nothing, Mom," Syd says, as the woman wraps a veiny, muscular arm around her shoulders.

Mrs. Stark pulls a man forward with her free hand. "Thiziz Dwayne," she says. Over-tanned and dressed for a trail ride, Dwayne looks out of place. "He's a gen-u-ine cowboy." Mrs. Stark lurches forward to hug Eric. "Ohmygod! I almost didn't recognize you bald. Are you and Syddie back together?"

"No," Syd says, with convincing force. "Have you been drinking, Mom?"

Mrs. Stark nods a little too hard. "Dwayne and I were having a cocktail when I told him how bad I felt over missing my little girl's art show thingy. He insisted we come. Right, Dwayne?" Dwayne isn't listening. He's entranced by Kimono Girl, who's dancing alone in front of the DJ.

Turning to Kali and me, Mrs. Stark says, "I'm Violet. Are you friends of Syd's?"

"Violet?" Syd looks mortified. "That's your middle name."

Violet lowers her voice so Dwayne can't hear. "There are a million Jennifers on Lavalife."

"I'm Zahra," I say. "And this is Kali. And our friend, Willem."

"You look awfully familiar," Violet says to Willem as he shakes her hand. "Have we met before?"

"We'd better go," Kali says, turning so hastily that she collides with a waitress, knocking a silver tray out of her hands.

Dozens of tiny meatballs shoot up into the air and rain down on the elegantly dressed crowd. In the commotion, Banksy breaks free to get in on the action. There's a screech as his enormous head disappears beneath the hem of a woman's long dress, followed by Steve's voice shouting Syd's name.

·· ♥ ··

The three of us walk down the street in silence, stopping and starting while Banksy sniffs at every vertical object.

Finally Syd speaks. "If jumping to conclusions were a sport, you two would be champions."

"It wasn't a leap," I say. "Because we observed first. He was talking, you were laughing, there was gratuitous contact. Kali?"

"Conclusion: All signs point to interest."

"Not on my side," Syd says. "You guys may be burned because you think I hooked up with Eric behind your backs, but I'm just as burned that you'd think I'd do such a thing. There's a Love, Inc. commandment about acting on circumstantial evidence, yet that's exactly what you're doing here."

"You're right," I say, relenting. "You deserve your day in court. Tell us what happened."

"Until tonight, I hadn't seen Eric since that day at the church, I swear. But we like a lot of the same artists, and he knows people from the Maternity Ward through me. I assumed he'd steer clear of it after all that's happened."

"He came because he wants you back, Syd," Kali says. "He still loves you. We were only distractions."

"That's not true," Syd says.

"It is, and it's okay," I say. I am still angry—at myself. I'm disgusted I was so easily duped, and disgusted that I can't fully put it behind me. "Hey, you can't change the facts," I say, repeating my favorite new mantra. "Only the way you react to them."

"Well, there is no way in hell we will ever get back together," Syd says.

"Why'd you slap him?" Kali asks.

"He blindsided me," Syd says. "He showed up tonight wearing my favorite shirt, and my favorite cologne, and told our old jokes. When he pulled out this picture, I snapped." The photo in her hand shows her sitting on the front steps of a cabin, smiling as I've never seen her smile. "We were at his parents' place in the country. They thought a big group was going, but it was just the three of us." She pats Banksy's head. "And my parents weren't paying attention anyway—it was right before they broke up. I wanted to escape all that, so we went on a long hike and watched the sunset over Canyon Lake. Eric burned the steaks at dinner, but nothing ever tasted better. We ate on the porch, under a million stars. It was a beautiful night." Her voice trails off to a whisper. "Everything you'd want your first time to be." She crumples the photo and tosses it at a rusty fence. "Now it's all ruined."

I always figured Syd had slept with Eric, but hearing her say so puts my situation in perspective. Eric and I had barely gotten off the ground, and while he wounded me, he devastated Syd.

Leaning over, I pick up the photo, smooth it out, and hand it back to her. "The moment itself wasn't ruined. The memory's just stained. And that's not your fault."

"He was seeing you a month after that picture was taken," Syd says. "And spending the night at a festival with Kali."

"Like I'd ever give it up in a place with Porta-Potties," Kali says. "My first time is going to be in Paris."

Syd manages a smile while she tears the photo up into tiny pieces and lets it fall from her fingers like snowflakes.

Kali waits a beat and says, "I feel a song coming on."

Syd and I plead for mercy.

"Seriously, I can't just let that image go," Kali says, staring down at the fragments.

"You're going to have to," Syd says. "Because I am."

She loops her arm through one of Kali's, and I loop mine through the other, and we drag her down the street. Kali's singing about tattered fragments of love when we reach an old auto body shop. Syd offers to show us something if Kali will shut up.

Behind the shop, there's a stack of oil drums. We circle the drums to find Banksy's face painted on the end of each one. Ten doggy faces, with ten different expressions. He's adorable.

"It's the first public work I ever did," Syd says.

While Kali whips out her phone to snap a picture, I check

out Syd's tag: a heart with a silver arrow through it. "Where's the ax?" I ask.

"A lot's changed since then," she says.

We ask Syd to show us more, and it turns into an hour-long tour of the neighborhood. She points out her handiwork on a garbage can, a construction container, an abandoned car, and several vacant, run-down buildings. It's fascinating. We can chart Syd's progress as an artist and see how her life has affected her work.

We turn down an alley, and Syd picks up the pace as we pass a row of old garages. A motion light triggers as we clear the last one, and I catch a glimpse of something bright green on the wall inside. "Did you tag that garage?" I ask, backing up.

"Can't remember," Syd says, walking on. "There's something I want to show you up ahead."

I turn back to the garage. The light goes on again, and I see Syd's piece on the rear wall: it's a row of bright green-and-buff Quaker parrots perched on a telephone wire. The image must have been here for a while, because the paint has flaked away in places.

"Eric and his friggin' parrot safaris," I say.

Kali wanders back to join us. "Ugh."

"I did it as a birthday gift for him," Syd says, sheepishly. "Because as hard as he tried, he could never catch up with those birds."

"I hope he never does," I say.

"Syd, why don't you take Steve up on his offer to show your work at his gallery?" Kali asks.

"That'd be like asking you to switch from rock to classical

guitar," Syd says. "I can't express myself like that." We walk on, and after a few minutes, Syd adds, "I wish you'd met my mom before she lost it."

"It's your basic postdivorce identity crisis," says, Kali, the voice of experience. "Regular programming will resume eventually. In the meantime, a nice aromatherapy massage would take your mind off everything."

Syd laughs. "A risky case with spa benefits is still a risky case."

"Riskier than ever," I say. "I feel sorry for Willem, but if that evidence went public . . . Eric is already curious about what Willem wants from us. If he figures out he's not our only slam, we'd be in trouble."

"He's still furious about Miss Daisy," Syd says. "I wouldn't put it past him to get even with us someday."

"We'd be handing him our heads on silver platters," I say. "And silver platters have gotten us into enough trouble tonight."

·· ♥ ··

Saliyah is lying in wait for me when I get back to Dad's—a leopard in green spotted pajamas.

"You were supposed to be home at ten thirty," she says, pouncing.

"And you were supposed to be in bed at nine thirty. So technically you shouldn't be awake to know I'm late."

She trails after me into the bedroom. "You're lucky Dad isn't here to catch you. Especially in that dress." She smiles. "You look really pretty, though."

"He'd have called if he was worried," I say. Basically, I was counting on Dad going back to the office, which he does most nights now—even on the weekends Saliyah stays with us. She hardly ever gets to see him. "Were you alone long?"

"Couple hours," she says, climbing into her twin bed. "Mostly I surfed."

I stop with my dress halfway over my head. "Surfed? On my computer?"

"Dad said I could."

I pull off the dress and hang it in the closet. "You better not have been reading my e-mails."

"How could I?" she says, pulling up the covers. "You've got a password."

I make a mental note to change it to something more obscure. Saliyah is quite capable of spending hours trying to figure it out, and I still have messages about the business that predate our Love, Inc. account. Hopefully Saliyah doesn't know me as well as she thinks she does.

"So, what's Love, Inc.?" Saliyah asks, giving me a sly smile.

Okay, she knows me. "That was a total invasion of my privacy, Saliyah. Mom will not be impressed."

"Just tell me what it is and I'll forget what I read."

"It's a . . . *club* Kali and Syd and I formed."

"To help you get over the three-timing slug?"

"Sort of."

"But why are people paying you for slams? And what is a slam anyway?"

If I can't silence her, I may have to kill her. "I don't know what you're talking about."

She rolls over onto her side and closes her eyes. "Maybe Mom will."

"I'm not playing your game, Saliyah." The green leopard plays dead, holding out. "Okay, what'll it take?"

Sitting up, she pretends to mull it over. "I like that new pink sweater."

"I like it too," I say. "Pick something else."

"No, I really like that one." She gets out of bed to try it on over her pajamas. "It must have been expensive. Is business that good?"

"I got it on sale. And now it's all yours."

She slips it into her suitcase before I can change my mind. I see that my black Abercrombie cardigan is already in there. Obviously she knows she's on to something good. On the bright side, it's nice that she's interested in regular clothes again.

"So I was thinking," she says. "I'd really like to borrow your pearl earrings sometime. Like for my school play next week."

I glance at my dresser and see my jewelry box is open. "Not the earrings. Nani gave them to me." I sit on the edge of my bed. "You're pushing your luck."

"Let's see what Mom thinks."

"Let's," I say, calling her bluff. Saliyah's knowledge of Love, Inc. will be pretty sketchy. Our charter and commandments are on Kali's laptop, and we do most of our planning by phone or text. "I may get grounded, but you'll lose the sweaters and whatever else you've socked away in that suitcase. And don't forget, if I'm grounded, I won't be available to help you with bake sales or homework."

"Fine," Saliyah says. "Mom's probably too busy with Xavier to care about what you're up to, anyway. They're out again tonight."

"What? Why didn't you tell me?"

"It's not a date. He's just helping her with the Yasin Valley stuff."

"But Dad should be helping her. He's the designer."

"Xavier's really pushy, and Mom doesn't seem to mind." Saliyah gets back into bed, and suddenly the extortionist is replaced by my little sister. "What if she really likes him, Zahra?"

Sighing, I sit down on the side of her bed. "Hopefully Dad will get it together and win her back before then."

"But Xavier's an MOT. I met him."

"He is?" I ask, wondering why it didn't cross my mind to ask Mom before. "Did you tell Dad that?"

She shakes her head. "He was in one of his moods. After dinner, he put on the music really loud."

"Jazz?" She shakes her head so I go into the living room to check Dad's ancient turntable. The Smiths. They're his go-to band when things are tough. When Mom kicked him out, he kept dropping the needle on "Heaven Knows I'm Miserable Now."

"When did Dad get so grumpy?" Saliyah asks.

I climb into my bed and turn out the lights. I hope that seeing Eric tonight won't reactivate my nightmares. It's been weeks since the last one. "He always had his moments. He just has a lot more of them now. But Mom used to blame Dad for stuff that wasn't his fault." Thanks to my mediation work, I'm getting better at seeing both sides of the story.

Her voice comes out of the darkness. "Do you think he's really at work right now? Maybe he's seeing someone else, too."

I want to tell her she's crazy, but if Mom's dating, it's possible

Dad's also putting himself back into circulation. Maybe he even has a girlfriend at work. That top he brought back from his last business trip was cooler than anything he's picked out for me before. What if there's a female behind the fashion?

"It's all going to be fine," I say. My voice sounds uncertain even to me.

"But what if it's not?" Saliyah says.

"Then at least you have my pink sweater. And my black one."

"Plus your blue hoodie," she says, giggling. "I'm tired of scarves."

"That," I say, "is the best news I've heard all day."

chapter 16

The first thing that hits me is the smell. It's like a hundred pairs of dirty socks rotting in a laundry hamper during the hottest week of the summer.

I expected Joe's Sports Center to be like the gyms on TV—bright, clean, and spacious, with high-end machines lined up in front of gleaming mirrors or windows. Joe's is exactly the opposite. The windows are covered with a dark blue film, leaving overhead fluorescent lights to cast a sickly green glow over a collection of ancient weight machines and mats. Chipped mirrors mounted along one wall reflect a row of cracked leather punching bags hanging from the ceiling.

Two guys are sparring in a boxing ring that sits in the center of the room, while a dozen others work at the bags or weight machines. There are no signs of female life, but the guys seem too focused on their workouts to pay any attention to me, as I stand watch for Angel Garcia, the object of our newest client's affection.

Patrice contacted us at the urging of Stacey, Love, Inc.'s biggest fan. Stacey took our advice and kept her two-month anniversary celebration (relatively) simple, with a bike ride and a sunrise breakfast, and Graham said the magic words: "I love you." Stacey was so thrilled that she gave us the ballooning tickets as a bonus.

After noticing Angel in her neighborhood, Patrice is thinking about inviting him to a formal dinner-dance at her private girls' school. The only problem is that they haven't exchanged more than a few glances on the street. Patrice has never made the first move with a guy before and wants to know if it's worth the risk. She hired us to find out if Angel is single, and whether they have anything in common.

A guy matching Angel's photo comes out of the locker room. I take a deep breath to settle my nerves. This is a bit different from my usual Love, Inc. cases. Kali wanted to do it, but Syd and I worried that Angel would hit on her, which would ruin everything for Patrice. I'm only slightly bummed that I'm considered the safe bet. I remind myself that it's just business. We exploit Kali's natural gift for some cases and put a lid on it for others. I have my own skills. Kali bubbles over with options, so if she were in charge of mediation, no one would stay together long. She's a "grass is always greener" type; I'm a "look how green this grass is" type; and Syd's a "torch the lawn" type. The balance works for us.

Through my various mediations, I've become nearly as good as Kali at drawing information out of people. I no longer stay up all night before one of these assignments, trying to hash out every angle with Oliver and Gordon, but I still wake up nervous.

Taking a deep breath, I join Angel at the free weights, introduce myself, and make my pitch: "I'm doing a story for community television on combat sports, and I wondered if we could talk about boxing."

Angel shrugs and sits down on a bench. "Sure. As long as I can do my workout at the same time."

I turn on Syd's video camera and zoom in on his impressive biceps. "That's a great tattoo. What does it symbolize?"

He slides under a set of barbells and positions his hands. "It's Chinese for 'invincible.' It inspires me to work harder."

I bluff my way through a few superficial questions about his training regimen and fight strategies before shifting to his personal life. As I follow him around the circuit, he tells me that he recently moved here from Chicago, loves screamo music, reads graphic novels, watches war movies, is failing English, acing math, eats mostly chicken, and is allergic to shellfish. His best friend is a competitive swimmer back in Chicago, he has one younger brother and a pet iguana named Neville. He refuses to wear designer labels or watch reality TV. He can't decide who's hotter, Megan Fox or Scarlett Johannson— but he spends an entire set of bicep curls considering the question. He's traveled to Mexico and Canada and is working part-time at this very gym to save for a trip to Asia after high school. When his fighting career ends, he'd like to be a sports commentator.

I'm not sure where Patrice's interests lie, but by the time Angel is finished pumping iron, I've pumped him for enough information to give her a sense of what makes this guy tick.

Only one key piece of the puzzle is missing.

"So, does your girlfriend look more like Megan or Scarlett?" I ask, tagging along to a punching bag.

"My ex had a bit of Scarlett in her, I guess," he says, holding out his hands so a gym staffer can put on boxing gloves. "But I don't go for a particular type."

Once the staffer leaves, he adds, "I like a pretty face and a hot body as much as the next guy, but I also like what's in here." He taps a big glove against my head. "And here." He taps the other glove against my chest and I know he's referring to my soul, not my bra size. "My ex was a contender."

"So why'd you break up?"

"Because Chicago's a long drive." He takes his first jab at the bag. "I didn't want to spend my last year of high school staying true to a girl I'll hardly ever see."

"Then I guess you weren't that into her in the first place."

He drills the bag with a series of quick punches. "I was crazy about her, but life's too short to spend it waiting. There are other contenders around."

"That's not very romantic." Not after what he said about loving what's inside. It doesn't say much for love's staying power.

"It's honest," he puffs. "And who knows; maybe we'll get back together later."

With the camera as a shield, I feel bold enough to ask the question that's always on my mind. "Did you cheat on her?"

He stops punching and catches the bag. Looking straight into the camera he says, "Nope. That's not respect. I told her the truth and now we're friends."

"So exes can be friends? A lot of people have trouble with that concept."

"I think it's possible as long as you fight fair."

I guess that's true. After all, I helped Sinead and Leo fight fair, and now they're friends.

Using the back of a glove to brush away a strand of hair from his sweaty forehead, he says, "You're asking a lot of personal questions. Is this story about boxing or dating?"

Oops. "Boxing. But I want viewers to know the man behind all that muscle."

He smiles. "And what if I wanted to know the girl behind that camera?"

Double oops.

·· ♥ ··

"I'm not wearing it, and you can't make me." I know I sound like a brat, but I've been totally blindsided by Nani and Mom. There wasn't time to develop an elegant resistance strategy.

They have some nerve. It's Thanksgiving weekend and I volunteered to come to Mom's. For the first time ever, my family is spending Thanksgiving apart. Saliyah is at Dad's, and they're going to Uncle Paul's for the big dinner. Uncle Paul isn't really our uncle, just Dad's best friend since forever, and unlike Dad, he knows what to do with a turkey.

I could have gone too, but it didn't feel right to leave Mom alone at Thanksgiving—at least, alone without a kid. I could tell from her expression when I arrived that I'd made the right call. She'd even made a batch of my favorite lemon-and-basil shampoo.

Turns out she was just warming me up for the news that we've been invited to a *mehndi*—basically a pre-wedding event, featuring a lot of curry and henna. To me, it sounds just as boring as a bridal shower. At first I outright refused to go, but Mom got that look again—the "I only have one kid home at Thanksgiving" look—and I folded. Would it kill me to spend a couple of hours of my life making Mom happy? No, it would not.

Then Nani stepped in and insisted I wear a salwar kameez.

The bride is the granddaughter of one of Nani's oldest friends, Naheed, who's come from Karachi for the monthlong lead-up to the wedding. Nani wants me to make a good impression. Well, I've got news for her: she can dress me up, but I'm never going to pass for an MOT.

"This is a big day for your grandmother," Mom whispers. "You wear that tunic you got at the carnival all the time anyway. What's the big deal?"

The big deal is that I wear it on *my* terms. If I wear a tunic out for dinner with Dad, it's cool. If I wear it into a crowd of MOTs, I'm a fraud. That should be obvious to Mom, but apparently it isn't, because she's practically forcing my arms into the sleeves.

Nani bustles into the bedroom carrying the matching pants. She must have picked them up at the carnival when I wasn't looking.

"No way," I say. "Nani, for girls my age, mehndis are casual."

She tilts her head. "Oh? How many mehndis have you attended?"

That would be zero, a record I'd hoped to maintain.

I put the pants on. Otherwise, there would be two pairs of hands helping me into them.

Mom pulls the car up beside the bride's house and lets Nani out before parking down the street. "Zahra," she says, looking at me in the rearview mirror.

"What?" I can feel my lower lip jutting just like Nani's does when she's sulking.

"Don't embarrass me, please. It's only two hours."

I undo my seat belt and get out of the car. "You said an hour and a half."

The least she could do is acknowledge that I'm walking into alien territory. Nani's friends are going to ooze disapproval at my hair, pale skin, and freckles, and she'll make sure they know I'm a disappointment to her in every way. Either that, or they'll try to assimilate me. I'm heading into battle.

On the stairs, where Nani is waiting for us, I pause to collect myself. I can do this. I walk into tougher situations with Love, Inc. all the time, and while I stumble now and then, I come out feeling stronger for the experience. Today's MOT chick party will not defeat me. I will show them Zahra Ahmed-MacDuff isn't ashamed to be hyphenated.

An old woman only an inch taller than Nani squeals and throws her arms around my grandmother as we come through the door. "Abira!"

This must be Naheed. Although her granddaughter was born and raised in Texas, like me, she's marrying an MOT and having a traditional wedding with about three hundred guests. Fifty or more women and girls will come and go this afternoon as the bride and her wedding party get tattooed with henna.

Nani's friend embraces my mom. "Sana, you're more beautiful than ever. And this must be Zahra." She releases my mother and reaches out with a tattooed hand to run her fingers lightly over my braid. *"Khoobsurat."* Turning to Nani, she rattles off a stream of Urdu.

Nani's smile fades. "Naheed loves your hair," Mom translates. No wonder Nani is upset. With my roots starting to show, there's no hiding that I'm a redhead in denial.

Grabbing my chin, Naheed shakes me so hard that the little gold beads on my heirloom earrings vibrate. "Nice to meet you," she says.

"Khush aamdeed," I reply, offering one of the few Urdu expressions I know as I squirm out of the finger vise. "Welcome" might not be quite the right greeting in someone else's home, but it's the best I've got.

Naheed leads us through the house to the family room. The decor is quite modern, with traditional tapestries hung on white walls, making them appear more like art than stuffy antiques. Among the tapestries is a huge canvas, adorned with watercolor squiggles.

"Quite pretty, isn't it?" Mom says, catching me admiring the painting. "It means 'Allah.' A lot of Muslims have similar paintings in their homes."

The smell of curry blends with perfume as we step into a family room buzzing with the chatter of nearly thirty women, who are sitting on furniture, rugs, and throw cushions. As I suspected, several girls my age are wearing jeans. I catch Nani's eye and gesture to the jeans, but she pretends not to understand.

The family room opens up onto the kitchen, where a granite island is stacked with enough food to feed an army.

Naheed takes us over to meet the bride, a beautiful girl in her mid-twenties. After greeting us in a Texan drawl, the bride says, "Y'all have fun, now."

Mom gets sidetracked by an acquaintance, leaving me to be paraded around to the old ladies by Nani. They're not shy about pinching and prodding me, and scanning me head to foot.

"Abira, how pretty she is," one old lady says. "She has your eyes." Giving me a wink, she adds, "We must introduce her to my grandson one day. He's going to be a dentist."

Finally I escape to the kitchen, where Mom is loading a plate. "They knew everything about me," I complain. "From my grades to my birth date. Two ladies asked about Riaz."

"It's a tight community," Mom says. "Nani and her friends like to share."

"Well, I don't need strangers knowing my business."

Mom passes me an empty plate. "How *is* Riaz?"

"History, that's how he is." I select a couple of beef kebabs with a yogurt dip and some salad.

Mom drops a samosa on top of my pile. "They're lentil," she says. "Not spicy."

We head back into the family room to find a seat beside Nani and a woman of about Mom's age. "Your grandmother tells me you're a wonderful cook," the woman says.

"Oh, yes," Nani says. "Her little cakes won first place in a baking competition a few weeks ago."

"Just at my sister's school bake sale," I add.

"But there were fifty entries," Nani says.

Nani is bragging about me. Me! I've never witnessed that before. I guess it takes the right company to bring it out.

Smirking at my expression, Mom whispers, "It was only forty entries."

"Of course, I am quite a cook, myself," Nani says, taking credit for my talent. "Many have said I make the best burfi in all of Karachi."

"My daughter, Liza, loves burfi," the woman says, summoning a girl about my age.

Liza is wearing a cool purple tunic over faded skinny jeans. "I've seen you at Austin," she says. "So tell me, what are Stains and Rambo really like?"

Mom's smirk has vanished. "Stains and Rambo?"

"Those are nicknames they got in Boggle club," I say.

Liza laughs. "Do you want to get your hands painted?"

I follow Liza to the small circle of teens sitting on a rug with the henna artists. Some are having designs painted onto their hands or feet, or even their shoulders. Liza's friend, Tara, another MOT who goes to Austin, is getting the finishing touches on a delicate vine that winds up her arm and bursts into a display of leaves and flowers.

I decide on a simple pattern of swirling lines and dots that circles my upper arm in an inch-wide band. It looks great, but smells of fermenting grass and mud.

A loud noise makes me jump. Behind us, a woman is sitting with a *dhol*—a double-sided barrel drum—strung around her neck. She's beating on one end with a spoon, and a girl joins her, beating the other end with both hands. The rhythm slowly picks up until Tara and Liza get up to dance. Soon the bridal party joins them, spinning until their colorful silks blur.

Tara beckons for me, but I stay where I am, watching as Naheed tries to pull Nani to her feet. Nani resists, until a few other women start chanting, "Abira, Abira." Finally, Nani stands, and someone puts another dhol around her neck. It looks big enough to topple her, but she stands up straight.

Nani starts beating the end of a drum with her hands, settling into a rhythm that becomes faster and more complicated. I watch in fascination as my grandmother's ancient fingers fly nimbly around the rim of the drum, coaxing combinations of sounds from the hide.

"I told you she played the drums back home," Mom says,

standing over me. "You didn't know the old bird had it in her, did you?"

Laughing, she pulls me to my feet and starts to dance. I haven't seen Mom look so happy in a long time.

An hour later, Nani signals that she's ready to go. I'm still hanging with Liza and Tara and their friends, who are teaching me traditional wedding songs and dances. No one seems shocked that I didn't know them already.

While Nani says her good-byes, Mom and I head out to collect the car.

"I have a lot to be thankful for," she says, slinging an arm around me. "Including my gracious daughter, who made me very proud today."

"Thanks," I say. I don't need the credit, though. My trip to an alien land turned out to be fun.

Her grip on my shoulder tightens. "Now, let's talk about Stains and Rambo."

·· ♥ ··

"Oh my God, I love this place," Kali says, flitting from rack to rack in Blue Velvet, a funky vintage clothing store where the sales staff knows Syd by name.

I suggested we check it out together, mostly to cheer Syd up. She's still mad at me for using my so-called "wiles" on Angel, even though Patrice understood. The interview proved they had nothing in common, and she's asked Kali to find her a more appropriate date.

"I can't believe you've never been here, Z," Syd says. Then she takes stock of my outfit and adds, "Or maybe I can."

"Gee, thanks," I say, although it's not like I don't know I

play it safe in the fashion department. If you've seen it in the Gap, chances are you've seen it on me.

"I just mean you could afford to spice it up a little," Syd says. "Where's that fashionista who showed up at the Maternity Ward party?"

"It would be nice to see her more often," Kali says, holding up a teal satin top that ties over one shoulder. "This would look great on you."

"Try it on," Syd says. "Maybe with a little bling." She passes me a black choker adorned with a gold-and-green butterfly.

By the time we make it to the fitting room, they've loaded me down with stuff and picked up a few choice items for themselves.

Since one of the fitting rooms is occupied, we all cram into the other. It's small, but we manage to squirm into clothes, jewelry, shoes, and wigs, giggling the whole time.

Eventually we hear the curtain slide open in the next room, and a girl calls, "Bunny?" The bell over the door jingles and she calls again, "Bunny? Where are you?"

A gruff voice answers. "Don't call me that."

Inside our changing room, we all stop talking, and Kali mouths, "Fletcher."

We take turns peeking through the crack between the curtain and the wall.

Hollis is standing in front of the mirror in a long, low-cut sapphire blue dress accessorized by white elbow-length gloves and a chunky blue rhinestone bracelet. The look is vintage and elegant, but the ugly still shines through.

"So, what do you think?" Hollis asks.

"You look amazing," a guy says. The voice isn't Fletcher's.

"She wasn't asking you, skidmark." *That* was Fletcher.

"I'm not hitting on your girl," the stranger says. "It's a nice dress, that's all."

The bell jingles again, and Kali, whose eye is to the crack, says, "Smart guy. He left."

"The gloves are stupid," Fletcher says.

"But I want to look old-school jazz for the gig," Hollis says.

Fletcher laughs. "Gig? Your gay little band is doing one song and you call it a gig? That is *sad*."

"It is sad," Kali whispers. She's disgruntled and I don't blame her. Kali's studied music for years, whereas Hollis seems to have become a jazz singer overnight.

"It's two songs," Hollis says. "I know it isn't the Bass Concert Hall, but sometimes music promoters check out events like this."

"Who says? Bronco?" Fletcher scoffs. "You need talent to get noticed. Or at least you need to be hot."

"That's just mean," I whisper. Even if she's deluding herself, he should be supporting her dream. He's her boyfriend.

"He's jealous because that guy told her she looked great," Kali says, stepping aside so I can look.

Hollis seems to have shrunk in her dress. "You used to think I was hot."

"Hot for high school isn't the same as hot in the real world," Fletcher says. "Like Rihanna or something."

"You don't think I look good in this dress?" she presses.

Fletcher sighs. "If you want the truth, you look like a skank in that dress."

Syd, Kali, and I glance at each other, and without a word passing between us, decide this has gone far enough.

Kali pulls back the curtain with a flourish, and we tumble out of the tiny room.

"Buy the dress," I tell Hollis. "It looks amazing on you."

"She's right," Kali says. "It's a knockout."

Hollis's expression seems to morph from gratitude to embarrassment to hatred, all in a matter of seconds.

"Wow, Hollis," Fletcher says. "The lesbians think you look hot. Wonder what they were up to in there."

Hollis smiles, and I know Fletcher has won again. "I have seen that one"—she points at Syd—"checking me out in the locker room at school."

"True," Syd says. "I was looking for horns and a tail."

Twice we have extended an olive branch to Hollis; twice she's fed it through the wood chipper. We turn back to the fitting room.

"Can you believe that guy?" Kali whispers, closing the curtain. "Hollis is a bitch, but I wish she'd hire us for a slam."

"We could do it for free," I say. "Under the category of public service."

To my surprise, it's Syd who dismisses the idea. "We're better off using our energy on paying clients. We can't save Hollis until she saves herself."

"I guess you're right," I say. "If we ran around slamming every goof who insulted us, we'd be exhausted and broke."

We're still changing when the curtain is yanked open. Already in my jeans, I clutch my T-shirt to my chest. Syd is wearing only an old bowling shirt with the name "Stanley" embroidered on the front, while Kali sports a hot pink petticoat and a bra.

Syd grabs a pair of white go-go boots off the floor and fires them at Fletcher. He dodges the first, but the heel of the second hits him so hard in the temple that a human would pass out. Fletcher just laughs.

"Nice way to treat someone who's offering to help you out," he says.

"Help us how?" I ask, peering around and finding Hollis combing the racks for something Fletcher will approve of.

He stares at Kali's chest. "A 34C, right?"

Kali tries to close the curtain, and Fletcher holds it open.

"Hollis says you three are going through a rough time at home with your dads all taking off," Fletcher says. "I want you to know I'm available."

"To what, mow the lawn?" Kali says.

"To keep the cougar population under control." He leers at Kali's chest again. "I bet your moms are pretty hot."

Kali's hand slips off the curtain and she turns to me. "Did he really just say that?"

Hollis comes back and sees us in various stages of undress. "Oh my God, you guys are pathetic. How many times do I have to tell you Fletcher is taken?"

I pull the curtain, and Syd turns to kick the wall with her bare foot. "That jerk is going down."

chapter 17

"**I** keep having these dreams," Evan says. "I'm living in my old tree fort, in our backyard. Then one day, I try to go back into the house and the door's locked. My key doesn't work either, so I ring the doorbell, and when the door opens, Darth Vader's standing there saying he's moved in and my parents have moved out, leaving no forwarding address."

Dieter slides to the edge of his seat, eager to analyze, but he lets us take a first crack at it. "Does anyone have ideas about what Evan's dream might mean?"

Kali gives it a shot. "You're worried about your parents moving on with their lives. Last week, you said your dad is moving to San Antonio and your mom has a new boyfriend."

Evan nods. "So you're saying Mom's new guy is Darth?" He cups a hand to his mouth and breathes like Darth Vader. "Shhhhh . . . Evan. Shhhh. I am your step*father*."

We all laugh, and Dieter lets us get it out of our system before saying, "Anyone have anything to add?"

I raise my hand. "Maybe these dreams are telling you that you're afraid of being left behind by your parents— abandoned."

"But what does Darth Vader mean?" Evan asks.

"That you're obsessed with *Star Wars?*" Syd says.

Dieter gives her the avatar stare before weighing in. "At our first session I said you'd need to focus on moving on with your lives. Evan, let's talk about what steps you've been taking to do that."

Evan stares at his hands and twists a leather bracelet around his wrist. "I'm not, I guess. I'm in a rut."

"It's natural to want to cling to the familiar," Dieter says.

"And it sucks when our parents are the ones changing," Kali says, taking her lip gloss out of her pocket to slick on a fresh coat. "They should have it all figured out by now."

"Parents are only human," Dieter says.

"Maybe, but this is supposed to be *our* time," Syd says.

Lauren taps Evan on the knee to get his attention. "You need to do your own thing and forget about your parents for a while. Try something new."

"Do something completely outside your comfort zone," I suggest. "Trust me, it will make you feel great—like you're ready to take on the world."

"Like what?" Evan says.

"Like get a dirt tattoo," Simon says, pointing to my arm where the faded henna can still be seen at the edge of my T-shirt. "*That's* living on the edge."

"I bet I've pushed more boundaries than you have," I tell Simon.

"This isn't a competition," Dieter says. "But you're absolutely right. Getting out of your comfort zones is a great idea. That's why I recently started to run a team-building ropes course. It's mostly for my Family Therapy group, but I'd like all of you to take it next session."

"Ropes?" I say. "If it involves hanging from them, forget it. I don't do heights."

"It's completely safe," Dieter says. "And the more nervous you are, the more you get out of it."

"I don't know," Lauren says, getting out her compact. "It sounds messy."

"It can be," Dieter says, packing up his briefcase and heading for the door. "Still, rain or shine, attendance is mandatory."

"Wait," Simon calls after him. "Can I tell you about my recurring dream? It involves two cheerleaders."

"No," Dieter says, without slowing down.

"You didn't get a chance to mention your nightmares about Eric," Kali says.

"I think they're done," I say. "The last one was right after the Maternity Ward party, and it featured Eric getting pecked to death by a flock of wild parrots."

"That's not a nightmare," Syd says. "That's a beautiful dream."

We walk out of the church together and find Trey waiting for Lauren at the bottom of the steps. Unfortunately, he's not alone. The blond giant at his side looks up at me and says, "Olivia?"

It's Andrew, the guy Syd and I scammed at Trey's touch football team. This is definitely going to be awkward.

"Don't you remember me from the football game?" he says. "You—"

"Hey, babe," Lauren interrupts, pushing past us and racing down the stairs to clutch Trey's arm.

Andrew's face is a study in confusion as he processes the incoming information. "But you were— Do you already *know* Lauren?"

Trey explains to his friend that Syd and I were doing Lauren a favor by trailing him for a weekend. Better yet, he gallantly takes the blame by admitting he hadn't been honest with Lauren about his diving. "You know how girls look out for each other," he says. "So, Andrew, meet Zahra and Syd."

We join them on the path and introduce Kali.

"Sorry I couldn't be honest with you," I say.

"It's okay," Andrew says. "I like a girl who can BS a little— as long as it's for a good cause."

Lauren kisses Trey's cheek and says, "A *very* good cause."

Andrew smiles at me and says, "Then how about using the phone number I gave you?"

·· ♥ ··

Syd opens our meeting in the trailer by bringing up the one case that doesn't pay. "Word in the weight room is that Fletch likes to play dirty. Really dirty."

Stains is surprisingly well-connected, and to thank him for his undercover work, we've given him free movie passes and DVDs from our stash.

"It's not just that Fletcher's brutal with the opposition," Syd continues. "There are rumors that he's taking out the competition within his own team."

Apparently, the Maroons' previous noseguards dropped like flies until Fletcher landed the position. The first guy got kicked off the team because Coach found steroids in his locker. Same thing with the next guy, only this time it was booze. Then Fletcher's immediate predecessor missed three games because of an illness that mysteriously struck on game days. In fact, the only three guys who've been kicked off the team in the past year have all been noseguards. Now that Fletcher's in place, the turnover has ceased.

"That can't be a coincidence," Kali says, handing me the packing tape so I can finish wrapping up a DVD player, which is ready to be shipped to the highest eBay bidder. "But how can we prove anything?"

"We can't," Syd says. "All we can do is watch and wait."

College scouts are scheduled to attend some upcoming Maroons games, and Stains predicts Fletcher will strike again. Although the scouts focus on the seniors, they also check out the up-and-comers, and Fletcher will want as much field time as possible.

"The Maroons have a couple of strong defense players," Syd says. "It's entirely possible that Fletch will sideline one or two of them before the big games."

"All we have to do is catch him in the act," Kali says, as if it's the simplest thing in the world.

"And once we have evidence he's been screwing over his teammates, they'll slam him for us," Syd says.

"Score!" Kali says. "I love it when a plan comes together."

I think I just missed the actual plan, but I'm sure my genius partners will put more meat on the bones soon.

In the meantime, I have more pressing concerns. "Snack time," I say, pulling a container out of my bag.

"Have mercy," Syd moans.

I've continued to test recipes for René's healthy eating promo, which he's decided to run during Christmas season. Despite the extra time to prepare, my results have been dismal. It's like I lost my baking mojo, and I blame Love, Inc. for that. Baking is such a precise craft. If you don't add exactly the right amount of each ingredient, you ruin the result. It's black and white. But the more jobs I do for Love, Inc., the more I learn that life isn't black and white. It's more like Syd's graffiti—a canvas of wild colors. That idea seems to have spilled over into the kitchen. I used to stick to the essential rules of baking, but lately, I've traded in my measuring cups for a more organic approach. If I add something sweet, I offset it with spice. If I add something wet, I balance it with something dry. No measuring. No rules. And while that approach works in our business, it's wreaked havoc on my baking. In the end, I had to take it back to basics.

"Come on," I say. "These are different: apple-maple crunch squares."

"Let Fletcher use them in his campaign of death," Syd says, waving them away.

Even Kali protests as I serve her a square. "Do I have to, Z? To be honest, low-fat isn't your calling."

"I've cracked it this time, I promise," I say. "If you taste these, I'll bake caramel brownies for our next meeting."

Kali takes a tiny bite, chews slowly, and swallows. Finally, the verdict: "By George, I think she's done it."

"You'd better not be bluffing," Syd says, taking an even tinier bite of a square. After a moment, she polishes off the rest of it. "Okay, these are keepers."

It's a relief to hear. I've been worried because Love, Inc.'s growing popularity hasn't left me with much downtime to experiment. Even with our referral policy, it's getting harder to keep up with the demand for our services. We all know we should turn down some requests, but we can never agree on which ones. The cases that look quick and dirty often take more time than we expected, and that means the lines are becoming blurred on who does what.

One thing we do agree on is that we like the money. Kali has enough for a decent guitar and private lessons. Syd is starting to fill the hole her dad made in her college fund. And my Sweet Tooth start-up account is growing nicely. Money makes us all feel like we have control over our lives. The more we have, the less we'll need our parents.

But money isn't the whole story. I know I'm not the only one who feels the buzz that comes from working together to help people. Plus, it's the first time I've excelled at something outside the kitchen.

The only downside is the pressure not to disappoint a single client. It's a lot of responsibility, when I still have to work, keep my grades up, and visit Mom's regularly. I can't risk setting off any alarms.

Kali and Syd are spread equally thin. This week something had to give and we decided it was Dieter's ropes course.

"He won't call our parents," Kali says. "Dieter's all talk. He's always lecturing us to take responsibility and move on with our lives. That's exactly what we're doing, even without his stupid exercises."

"It isn't even a regular session," Syd says. "And I've got to admit I'm glad I won't have to talk about how my mom broke her wrist falling off Dwayne's horse."

Kali and I try not to laugh, but Syd's grin is permission.

"Then she dumped Dwayne because he didn't sit holding her good hand for six hours in Emergency," she says. "And guess who had to pick up the slack? If that's not taking responsibility, I don't know what is."

"My mom's still dating that Xavier guy," I say. "And Dad's out more than ever. We think he's seeing someone at work."

"D-I-V-O-R-C-E," Kali sings, and picks up her guitar. "May-king parents cra-a-zy."

Syd bends over to pat Banksy. "Come on, boy, that's our cue to leave." Banksy barely stirs, and Syd's brow creases with worry. "He's a little under the weather. Maybe he ate something nasty in the park this morning."

"Why don't you leave him to rest while you meet your client?" I ask. "I'm going to do my homework here before meeting mine in a couple of hours."

Syd hesitates. She rarely goes anywhere without Banksy. "Well, okay. But call me if he barfs or anything."

"Definitely." I'm glad she trusts me enough to look after him.

Syd plants a kiss on Banksy's head and sets off.

Once Syd clears the trailer, Kali tells me about her newest crush, a guy she met at a Clean Water rally. "He's way cuter than the goof from my guitar class, and we obviously share the same values. He was hanging with some people I know, so I should be able to get his number. And unlike *some* people, I won't be afraid to use it."

It's a dig at me for not calling Andrew yet. I'll admit, I've been thinking about it, but before I get involved with anyone new, I want to know he's seriously interested. Andrew is flirty, which proves nothing. If he's into me, let him track me down.

Kali's phone starts to ring. "It's Luke," she says, checking call display. "He's reporting in on the wedding." Trish ended up the final winner, once Kali discovered that she's a vegan and a leader in school recycling. "Hey, Luke, how fabulous was it?"

Kali's grin fades fast as she listens to Luke talk . . . and talk . . . and talk. Sinking back on the bench, she stares straight ahead.

"But Luke, I don't understand," she says. "You and Trisha passed every test and you liked her when you met for coffee. Everything should have been perfect." He complains some more. "I know you're upset, but please don't call my match-making program a piece of crap. No questionnaire can predict that someone will get drunk at a wedding. Or flirt with the groom."

I cringe, and Kali mouths, "It gets worse."

"She called the groom 'Simon' and made a toast to his *hot ass*?" Kali asks. "I'm so sorry, Luke. Simon's her ex. She seemed ready to date again, but I guess the bubbly brought up old memories. But no real harm done, right? Why don't I send some flowers to the happy couple and sign your name? Stop by the trailer next week and I can look through my roster for someone new—"

She stares at her phone incredulously. "He hung up! No wonder he can't get a girlfriend. He's a frickin' drama queen. His parents are mad that his date got tipsy, and he acts like I poured the champagne down her throat. Poor thing probably didn't have anything to eat, either. There aren't many vegan options at a traditional Italian wedding."

"Well, you can't win 'em all," I say.

"I still say Trisha's a good match for Luke," she says, reaching into the cupboard. She pulls out a big white envelope that holds their questionnaires. "This came down to booze and bad timing. The worst of it is that Brody will rub my nose in it unless I can match Luke up again fast."

"Kali, maybe you'd better let this one go."

She shakes her head stubbornly. "My reputation is at stake."

Sighing, I reach for my ringing phone. "It's Riaz," I say, checking the display before letting the call go straight to voice mail.

"I thought Riaz was out of the picture," Kali says, tossing the envelope onto the table and giving me her full attention.

He was, until Saliyah dragged me to a Bollywood action movie last night and we ran into him at the theater. It probably wasn't a coincidence, either. There was a definite whiff of Nani about it. Riaz's apology sounded scripted.

"Maybe you're being a little—"

"Do not say 'harsh,'" I interrupt. I've heard that word enough from her brother. "I might have been more receptive if Riaz had called right after the meat drive. Instead, he waited till we ran into each other."

I check my voice mail to find Riaz suggesting we hang out over the weekend. As if a half-assed apology fixes everything. "We're done," I say. Thanks to all that I've learned from Eric and Love, Inc., I have much higher standards now.

"Just as well," Kali replies, strumming. "Nothing rhymes with Riaz."

A few minutes later, Kali packs her guitar in its case and gathers her things. She has another lesson in half an hour.

Banksy raises his head as Kali puts on her coat. "Do you think he has to go out?" she asks.

Thumping his tail, he clambers to his feet.

"Syd wants him to rest," I say.

"Don't worry," Kali says, hooking Banksy up to his leash. "We used to have a dog, and a walk always seemed to perk her up. I'll take him with me to my lesson. My teacher won't mind, because she has a dog, too."

My phone rings again, and Kali slips out with Banksy while I answer it. It's my six o'clock appointment canceling. That leaves me free to head over to Mom's to work on my Social Studies assignment. We have to write about an event in the life of one of our grandparents. Nani offered to help, but I've been stalling because I know she'll use this opportunity to push some propaganda about culture, community, and religion, not to mention the benefits of marrying within the tribe.

I'm texting Syd and Kali about my change of plans when the trailer door swings open. It's Brody, and he's inside before he notices me.

"What are you doing here?" he says, frowning. "You guys have Crazy Class."

There's a giggle behind him, and someone repeats, "Crazy Class?"

Brody steps aside to let the girl enter the trailer. She's almost as tall as he is, with long limbs and fine features. Her strawberry blond hair is cropped into a boyish cut that frames bright blue eyes. In her skinny jeans and bulky brown sweater, she looks like she popped out of an *Interview* magazine spread.

"Hi, I'm Juliette," she says, holding out her hand. "As in Romeo-and."

As opposed to Einstein-and, I suppose. I notice her other hand has landed on Brody's hip, and he acts like that's exactly where it should be. Obviously he's been using our office to make out with girls. It's just so . . . tacky.

"I'm Zahra," I say.

Juliette slides a limp hand into mine, and it's gone before I can clasp it. "Cool name," she says as I squeeze a fistful of air.

"Thanks," I say. "Cool sweater."

"Enough bonding," Brody says, throwing his schoolbooks on the table. "Take a seat, Juliette. Zahra was just leaving."

He can't kick me out of this trailer even if I *was* just leaving. His mom might own it, but it's also his sister's place of business—a business that's put dollars in his pocket to spend on this Juliette.

"I'm in no hurry," I say, ignoring Brody's glare and sitting across from Juliette.

"Hey, I've heard of Love, Inc.," Juliette says, picking up one of Kali's questionnaires, which has our company logo in the top right corner. I designed it on the computer using Syd's graffiti tag for inspiration. It's a tiny heart pierced with a lightning bolt on one side and rays of sun on the other.

Reaching for the questionnaire, I tell her that I'm just a client. Although our business is growing, we don't advertise, and we still try hard to keep the revenge service under wraps.

"Well, you're going to love them," she says. "My sister's ex-best-friend's cousin hired Love, Inc. to help her figure out if her ice-dancing partner is gay. Turns out he isn't, and now they're totally in love."

Even though the details aren't quite right, it's nice to hear about a satisfied customer. Especially in front of Brody.

"I've heard mixed reviews about this Love, Inc.," Brody says. "For every minor success there's a massive screwup. They really burned one of my best friends."

"What happened?" Juliette asks, staring at him with eyes the color of my Eid festival tunic. Her hair is pretty, too, if you like red, which I don't. I suppose I can see why Brody would sacrifice substance for surface. It's a shame he's not more like Angel.

Brody takes my coat off the hook by the door and tosses it at me. "It's a long story. I'll tell you all about it when Zahra leaves."

"Save your breath," I say. "Love, Inc. doesn't need your negativity."

Sitting down beside Juliette, Brody gives me the back of his head. "So here's what I heard . . . Some crazy girls started this so-called business after getting burned by a guy, and now it's all they have. None of them can even get a boyfriend. They just sit around telling other people how to solve their problems without taking their own advice. All in all, they're kind of pathetic."

I yank my notebooks out from under the pile of stuff Brody's strewn across the table, and grab the envelope of questionnaires. Giving Juliette another air handshake, I say, "I wouldn't write off Love, Inc. based on Brody's opinion. They've got a great track record."

I make a point of closing the trailer door gently, because I know Brody is hoping for a slam. In the end, though, he's the victor because his words are echoing in my head as I walk to the bus stop.

I am not crazy or pathetic, and Eric Skinner is not the end of my story. Maybe I've been sitting on the sidelines sulking for a bit, but I'm as capable of a normal relationship as Brody Esposito is. More capable. I can do better than Juliette. I will find substance *and* surface. In a city as big as Austin, there must be a cute, honorable guy who shares enough of my interests. I will see if Kali can help me find him. That would be the best victory of all against a hater like Brody.

By the time the bus arrives, I've decided not to tackle my Social Studies project with Nani. For that, I need to be on my toes. Instead, I'll go to Dad's, where I can think about the compatibility profile Kali will have to put together for me. To get a head start, I pull out the envelope with Trish and Luke's questionnaires.

Instead, I find a stack of photos in the envelope. The first is of a football player spiking the ball past the goal line. His teammates are rushing into the picture from the right edge of the frame, forever frozen in this moment of triumph. The next shot is of a basketball player mid-leap, followed by several photos of soccer players chasing the ball.

I'm not a sports fan, but these images are vivid and captivating. It's strange that Syd's never mentioned an interest in photography, especially when art is one subject she's actually willing to talk about until your ears bleed.

Unless, of course, these aren't Syd's pictures.

chapter 18

Kali and I are having lunch with Liza and Tara when I notice Syd walking through the cafeteria toward our table.

"Don't you have Spanish?" I ask as she joins us.

"Mendoza thinks I'm in the can," she explains. "Anyway, I'm only jumping the bell by ten minutes. There's something I need you guys to see."

Kali and I excuse ourselves and follow Syd back through the halls to one of the girls' restrooms. Inside, someone is locked in a stall, apparently sobbing and smoking at the same time.

"It's Hollis," Syd whispers, as the person inside sputters and chokes on the cigarette. "She was bawling at the sink when I came in earlier."

"Go away," Hollis says now. "I already told you I didn't want to talk."

"Yeah, and then you told me that your pinhead boyfriend broke up with you and dumped your bag in the hall," Syd says. "Tampons and all."

Hollis hiccups. "People were just walking all over my stuff, and he didn't care."

"Hollis, there's no nice way to say this," Kali begins. "Fletcher is a bully."

"A bully who cheats on you," Syd says. "You know that."

"You can't put up with this anymore," I say. "Time to cut him loose."

A few more puffs of smoke drift from the stall before we hear the toilet flush. Hollis steps out. Her makeup is running, and her eyes are red and puffy.

"We break up all the time," she says, looking at us through the mirror as she washes her hands. "And we always get back together. I've been with him nearly two years—one-eighth of my life. I don't think I can live without him."

"You're stronger than you think, Hollis," I say. "Who else could have survived two years with Fletcher?"

Hollis actually laughs. "No one."

"So make this break stick," I say. "Just do it."

She mops at her face with the wet wipes and sighs. "I guess if you can stand being single, I can too."

Kali rolls her eyes and says, "I'm sure you won't be single long. Remember that guy at Blue Velvet? The one who liked the dress?"

"He said I looked amazing," Hollis says, brightening.

"Moving on?" I say.

"Moving on," she says, dusting her face with powder.

Kali, Syd, and I exchange glances, knowing it's futile to expect a thanks. But one day, after Hollis has shaken off Fletcher's influence, we might find there's a decent human being beneath the barbed wire.

The door bursts open and Señora Mendoza appears. "Aha!" she says. "I thought I smelled smoke."

There's no way she smelled smoke from her classroom in the next hallway. She's just doing a routine spot check.

Hollis continues to stare at the mirror as she slicks on lip gloss. "I tried to tell them, Señora. Smoking is never going to make these losers cool."

·· ♥ ··

Kali is chatting up a sales clerk from Hollister's when I meet her at the mall. With less than three weeks to go before Christmas, the place is packed. I have Love, Inc. money to burn on gifts this year, but my list isn't that long—Kali and Syd, Morgan and Shanna, Dad and Saliyah. Mom only celebrated the holiday for Dad, so I know there won't be a Christmas tree in her house this year.

"So what are you shopping for, other than boys?" I ask, leading Kali away.

"Perfume," she says. "Destination: Sephora. I'm hoping an exotic scent might attract more interesting guys. Things have been kind of dull lately."

"What happened to the guy from the water rally?" I ask.

She snorts. "He wants to become an organic farmer. I can't be with someone who's tied to the land. My guy needs to carry my suitcases when I go on tour."

She peers over her shoulder and waves at the Hollister guy. "That one wasn't for me. I'm just trying to build my Love, Inc. roster."

"He's not my type either," I say, in case I'm the target in mind.

At Sephora, she picks up a bottle of the new Burberry scent and sniffs at the nozzle. "Before we get down to business, Z, I have to tell you I'm honored you've agreed to let me help you in this pivotal, life-changing moment."

"It's just a preliminary discussion, Kal. Don't get carried away."

"Don't downplay it, Z. This is huge." She grabs my right wrist and spritzes it with Eternity. "You are saying *yes* to love."

I roll my eyes. "I'm saying *maybe* to a date, if you can find someone normal who isn't a client."

"My database is full of non-client possibilities, don't you worry." Kali grabs my other hand and sprays on Viva la Juicy. "That's why I'm always on the lookout. Even if people aren't in the market now, a lot of them are glad to hear from me when I call with a prospect later." She shows me a price tag with the Hollister sales clerk's name and number on it. "He could be perfect for someone in January."

"Do you seriously just call people out of the blue and say, 'Have I got a girl for you'?"

"Not out of the blue. I keep in touch to nurture my contacts. You know, a text here, a Facebook message there. And then when I've got a prospect, I let them know. If people are single they can't resist hearing more."

"So what do you do then?" I ask, watching as she sprays her own wrist with Stellanude.

She lets the perfume dry for a second before taking a deep sniff. "I send over the specs and we chat."

"Specs? You are not sending anyone my 'specs.'"

"I hate to break it to you, Z, but no one you'd want to date would go out with a girl sight unseen," Kali says. "Men are visual creatures. They need a photo. Why are you worried, anyway? You're gorgeous. Better than that, you're unique. No one else has your coloring."

That, unfortunately, is quite true.

"Plus, you have this way of studying someone as if they're the most interesting person on the planet," Kali continues. "Guys love that. It confirms their own opinion of themselves."

I laugh. "You're just saying that."

She eyes the Sarah Jessica Parker testers and blasts her other wrist with Covet. "As your *friend*, I might just say that. But now that you're my client, I have to be honest. And you have to be honest too, or this won't work."

There's no money changing hands, but I've agreed to cater two dates of her choice in exchange for her services. "Okay, let's get this over with before I change my mind."

"I was hoping for some enthusiasm," she says.

That's asking too much. I'm only doing this because of what Brody said. As usual, his delivery sucked, but he had a point. A mediator who can't make a relationship work for herself isn't setting much of an example to her clients. It's fine for Syd to stay single when her specialty is revenge. And it's fine for Kali to flit from guy to guy when her focus is on the match. But for me, being alone suggests I don't walk my talk. So, no matter how nervous I feel about it, I need to get serious about the game.

"It'll be fun," I say. "Like a migraine. Or cramps."

Rolling her eyes, Kali grabs my wrists and sniffs. Then she sniffs her own. Finally she decides on the Juicy and takes it to the register, along with a tube of her favorite lip gloss.

Afterward, we head back through the mall to the Apple Store, where Kali snags one of their test computers. "Are you sure you're ready for this?" she asks. "Are you completely over what happened with Eric?"

"Probably not. But Love, Inc. has shown me that not all guys are cheaters, and at some point I'm going to have to try again, right? Otherwise, Eric wins."

"You have to go in with an open mind, Z."

"I'll do my best; that's all I can promise."

Satisfied, she reaches over and squeezes my hand. "This is so great. It's taking us to a whole new level of friendship. It means a lot that you trust me like this."

"I've always trusted you. You've had my back from the beginning."

"This is different," she says. "It's personal."

I guess it is. She understands better than anyone except possibly Syd how difficult it will be for me to take this leap. I don't trust myself to make the right choice, but I do trust Kali. I know she has my best interests at heart. In fact, Kali and Syd are my friends *and* my family now—*framily*. We're bound together by loyalty, trust, and responsibility, not to mention trade secrets.

"You're safe in my hands," Kali says, putting a memory stick into a port. "I already filled in your survey, but I want to ask a few more questions. First, what's really important to you, besides the obvious—hot, nice, and trustworthy?"

I struggle to come up with an answer. "Brains? Sense of humor?"

"How about values?"

"Yeah, I'm all for them. I especially like it when guys know that cheating is wrong."

"And?"

"I don't know, the normal things. Decent. Honest. Kind."

"Okay, so with everything I know about you, I've narrowed the choice to three preliminary prospects. I even have photos, but since you're above all that, I'll just *describe* them to you."

I jab her mouse hand. "Get clicking."

She's prepared a PowerPoint presentation, with my picture occupying the top of the first slide. It's a photo Syd took on Congress Avenue after we watched the bats fly away, and I look excited and happy. Below the photo, my "specs," or interests, appear one by one: baking, pop culture, reading, movies, business, and art.

"Business and art? That's stretching it."

"You're helping your mom with her business and you seem to like it. Plus you're good at graphic design."

She clicks her mouse and my specs disappear. Under my picture, another box slides into place. "Since I couldn't use real clients, my information is still a bit sketchy on the first two guys. If you like them, I'll call and go through the survey. According to my program, Option One is sixty-eight percent compatible, Option Two is seventy-seven percent, and Option Three is ninety-two percent. Since no one's a perfect match, the last guy's obviously a very lucky find."

"Can't we proceed directly to Mr. Ninety-two?"

"Nope," she says, grinning. "I'm taking you through my entire process."

It's nice to see Kali from a client's perspective. She's a positive force, a zealot for love—or at least for the initial hookup.

Option One's photo slides into view. He's attractive, with dark hair and eyes and cocoa skin that suggests we might have more in common than his love of pop-culture blogging.

"Is he an MOT?" I ask Kali.

"A half-and-halfer, like you. I figured he'd relate to the pressure you've been under from your grandparents."

I'm becoming cautiously optimistic about this process. "Okay, who's next?"

Kali advances to Option Two, and a familiar blond giant comes into view: Andrew.

"I've done some digging," Kali explains. "You two like a lot of the same bands and movies and the same subjects at school. And you already know he's adorable."

I point to the screen. "It says here he has an interest in extreme sports. What if he wants to go hang gliding on our first date? Have I mentioned my fear of heights?" I shake my head. "No. Show me what's behind door number three."

She hesitates for a moment. "You're keeping an open mind, right?"

Uh-oh. "He's part chimpanzee or something, isn't he?"

"Z, they all are. Accepting that will help you move on."

She clicks, and the photo slides into view. It's Brody. *Brody!*

"This is a joke, right?"

"Ninety-two per cent compatible," she says.

"That's impossible. We have *nothing* in common. Except you."

She counts off our mutual interests on her fingers. "You read the same magazines, like the same Web sites, watch the same movies—over and over, I might add. Believe it or not, he even likes to cook."

"Kal, you told me to be honest, so I have to say that your brother is a jerk. Feel free to dis any of my family members in return. You've got plenty of ammo."

She just laughs. "You and Brody got off on the wrong foot. Actually, if you think back to the first time you met, he was flirting with you."

"Flirting! He made fun of my hair."

"Like I said, flirting. You'd know that if your hormones hadn't been knocked off-line by Eric."

"Brody is rude to me ninety-two percent of the time."

"He was thrown by our slam on Eric, that's all. I know my brother's a pain in the butt, Z, but he's also a really good guy. We've been through a lot together and he's always been there for me." She stares at the screen as an excuse not to look at me. "Remember what he said about my running away with the band? That wasn't the first time I took off, but it's the only time Mom knows about because Brody always came after me. I mean it when I say he's put up with a lot. Because he went through everything I did with Mom, and had to help me, too."

Her eyes well up, and this time I take her hand and ask, "Things are better now, right?"

Nodding, she pulls a napkin out of her bag and wipes her eyes, blurring the name of another of her prospects. "Partly because of you and Syd, and Love, Inc."

I try out my new term. "We're framily now—friends *and* family."

"Yeah," she says, smiling. "I like that. But Brody deserves a nice girl like you. And in case you haven't noticed, he's funny, smart, and cute."

That may be so, but he doesn't seem like the cherishing type, and he certainly doesn't accept me for who I am. Nani's advice might be corny but at least it's a starting point. "I don't know, Kali. Isn't he seeing someone?"

"Brody dates a lot, but it's never serious," she says. "He had a girlfriend in ninth grade, but she moved away and that was really hard on him. He's played the field ever since."

"What makes you think he's ready to get serious now?"

"I know my brother," she says. "Ultimately, he's the settling-down type. And did I mention a ninety-two percent probability of success? How can you settle for less?"

"Easy. Seventy-seven is my lucky number."

She sighs, but the smile is back almost instantly. "Well, the customer's always right. And Andrew is going to be very happy."

"Hey, Kali? Thanks."

She shrugs. "We're framily. I'd do anything for you. In fact, I've already got your first date planned."

She slaps two tickets in front of me for a balloon ride—the ones Stacey gave us as a bonus.

"No way," I say. "I am not going airborne for any guy."

"Gee, who was just bragging about pushing boundaries in group?" Kali says, pretending to think. "Right. That would be you."

I slide the tickets back to her and cross my arms. Walking my talk can still mean keeping my feet on the ground.

·· ♥ ··

The pilot pulls on the handle. There's a sudden *whoosh!* as the two burners ignite, filling the enormous purple-and-yellow balloon with enough hot air to send our little basket up, up, up, to cruising altitude, four thousand feet over Austin.

I scream. A few times. They sort of run together in a continuous shriek. Luckily, one of the other passengers—an eighteen-year-old Canadian girl—shrieks even louder. Well, that's not so lucky for Andrew or the pilot, or even the girl's best friend. But it makes me feel better.

With five people, a fire extinguisher, and four fuel tanks, the four-by-five foot basket is a bit cramped.

The pilot cuts the gas, and all is quiet aboard our little craft.

"Zahra," Andrew says gently, "you should try facing out. The view is fantastic. I can already see the Enchanted Rock."

From the moment the ground crew released our drop line, I've faced Andrew's chest. Since he's so tall, it's been quite an effective barrier between me and my fear of looking down. But I've committed to pushing myself out of my safety zone today, and that means turning—slowly and cautiously—until I'm staring out at the horizon.

"Wow." To my right, Austin is spread out below, its buildings bathed in a soft golden light against the evening sky. "There's the Capitol dome! And the UT tower!"

Lake Austin looks beautiful, shimmering in shades of blue and pink. The traffic over the bridges is congested, and I think about Dad driving home.

"I told you the view was worth it," Andrew says, pulling my fuzzy blue hat snugly down on my head and wrapping his arms around me. The brochure wasn't kidding when it said it was a lot cooler up here than it is on the ground.

I lean back against Andrew's puffy down jacket and smile. It's such a strange, wonderful feeling to be soaring above the earth in a little basket. This is an oasis of tranquility over a bustling city.

We lose a little altitude, and once again the pilot fills the balloon. As we drift northwest, away from the city, I catch a glimpse of Lake Travis and the small sprawl of houses that makes up Anderson Mill, just to the right.

Tracking along the Pedernales River, we pass ranches and reserves, and in no time we reach Fredericksburg and the Enchanted Rock park. The pilot brings the balloon down so we can admire the enormous rock face, nestled among the trees and glowing deep red like a hot coal in the last of the day's sunlight.

I lean over and pull the video camera I borrowed from Syd out of my backpack. Staring at the screen, I zoom in on the rock, where a few hikers have stopped to wave at us. I wave back and pan the camera to catch a flock of grackles silhouetted against the rosy sky. The flock turns and flies toward us, and I track them with the camera.

"Aren't those birds getting a little too close?" I ask, lowering the camera.

The pilot is already trying to change course, but the birds are coming fast and steady. Cursing as he ignites the burners, he explains that we're going to have to climb. "Hang on, everybody," he says. "It's gonna get a little windy."

The Canadian girl lets out a scream as the first current hits us and the basket pitches and sways. Andrew puts one gloved hand on the edge and keeps the other firmly wrapped around me. I try hard not to panic when the basket pitches again and tips a little toward the ground.

The Canadian girl is losing it. "I want out!" she shouts, lunging to the other side, making the basket wobble even more.

"Keep her calm!" the pilot snaps, as he works to steady the craft.

Instinctively, I yank on the girl's hand and pull her to the floor of the basket with me, where she can't see the horizon. Since there's only room for two people to be down here, Andrew stands, resting a hand on my shoulder.

"This will be over before you know it," I tell the girl. "It's going to be okay."

The basket wobbles again, and she screams. "We're going to die!"

"We're not going to die," I say, glancing up at Andrew with a silent, *"Are we?"*

"Not today," he says. His blue eyes are an ocean of calm, as if he's stared death in the face before and knows this isn't it. That calm must come from experience with even more extreme sports.

"Get her to focus on her breathing," he says. "In . . . out . . ."

I do as he says, breathing in through my nose for two counts, and out through my mouth, encouraging the girl to do the same.

"You're doing great," I tell the girl, already feeling much calmer myself.

A few minutes later, Andrew tells me that we're clear of the grackles and coming down for a landing. The pilot radioed his ground crew, and they're going to pick us up near Fredericksburg.

The landing is surprisingly gentle. The girl has stopped crying, but it takes her friend and the pilot to get her out of the basket. My legs have turned to rubber too, but Andrew helps me upright and half carries me into the field, where we're surrounded by curious cattle. The minute he lets go of me, I sit down in the grass. It still feels like the world is shifting under me.

We're quiet for a moment, then Andrew says, "You have to admit, it was fun up to a point."

"And then it wasn't," I say. I won't be ballooning again any-time soon, but I'm still glad I went. It feels good to know I faced one of my biggest fears and survived.

Andrew looks down at me and laughs. "You're keeping your feet firmly on the ground from now on, aren't you?"

A cow bellows behind us, and I start laughing too.

"Yup," I say. "Till the cows come home."

chapter 19

Kali arrives at the Recipe Box just after it opens, to help me set up for the healthy living promotion, and I fill her in on my date with Andrew.

"Oh my God, Z!" she says, when I finish the story about the balloon. "Who needs Dieter's stupid ropes course? That's for amateurs. You guys must have been feeling pretty pumped after that."

Actually, the rest of the night was quite a contrast to the beginning. If you break it down, it was a perfect date from the moment we arrived at my favorite Italian restaurant to the moment Andrew walked me to Dad's door. Like Kali said, we have a lot in common. He laughed at my jokes, I laughed at his, and we never ran out of things to say. He's cute—really cute—but when he kissed me good night, I didn't feel any spark, which surprised me after all we'd been through earlier. Kali must be right about my hormones being off-line. Eric may have wrecked me permanently. "I liked him," I sum up as I start putting apple-maple crunch squares on the serving platters René provided. "And he's even higher than seventy-seven on the compatibility scale. If he asks me out again, I'll go."

"But . . . ?"

"But nothing." There's nothing negative to say.

Kali sighs. "There was no magic."

"Not really," I admit. "At least, not yet. I'm sorry, Kali."

"Don't be." She arranges her own platter of squares. "Your numbers were solid, but there's no accounting for chemistry. You'll give him another try, though, right? Maybe you need to kiss him again to shock your hormones back to life."

Someone behind us says, "I'm glad to hear you two discussing such serious matters."

Kali gives a little shriek. Dieter is standing at the register wearing dark jeans, a fitted turtleneck sweater, and a black leather jacket.

"Dieter," Kali says. "Hi. What a nice surprise to see you. On a Saturday."

"Because Thursday's our day, isn't it?" He lifts a motorcycle helmet off the counter and retrieves three envelopes from beneath it. "Here are your letters of warning. I'll let you deliver Sydney's for me."

"Our what?" Kali asks.

"You're officially out of rope, ladies—no pun intended. Full attendance from now on, or I'll start making house calls. Understood?"

"It's not like we skipped a *real* session," Kali says.

"A session is a session no matter where it takes place," Dieter says.

He waits till we nod before tucking the helmet under his arm and heading for the door. "Thanks for this, René," he calls, waving a book I recognize: *Romantic Meals for Lovers.*

Outside, Dieter packs his book in a black box mounted on the rear of a gleaming motorcycle. Climbing aboard, he guns the engine a few times, then takes off.

"How do you know Dieter, René?" I ask.

"We went to college together," he says.

"I bet he was all work and no play," Kali says.

René laughs. "Quite the opposite. He got suspended for pulling a prank on the dean."

"A prank? Dieter?" I say.

"All I remember is it involved the college mascot, a wheel-barrow, and a lot of fake blood on the dean's new carpet," René says. "It was a short suspension, but for some reason, Dieter didn't come back until after I'd graduated. I heard he turned into a model student, but never saw him again until today. I was surprised to find him waiting when I got here."

Taking one of my squares, René changes the subject. "You've hit the bull's-eye this time, Zahra. And I'll bet whatever you have in mind for next week's Christmas baking promo is every bit as good. I had your recipe professionally printed, and we'll display the cards in some old recipe boxes. I'll get them from the back room, since I have to check on Sherman anyway."

"Sherman?" I ask.

Smiling mysteriously, he heads into the back, reappearing a few minutes later carrying a tiny puppy with fur the color of straw, and big, worried-looking eyes. "Meet Sherman," René says.

Kali beats me to the puppy. "My mother would love him," she says. Then she looks at me. "My mother would *love* him."

She's not talking about the dog anymore. "We've discussed this," I say, after René takes Sherman outside. "René's off-limits."

We're still arguing about it when Syd arrives a few minutes later. Banksy picks up Sherman's scent immediately and starts sniffing around excitedly.

"Is he feeling better?" I ask, stooping for my face lick. What once seemed disgusting has become a ritual.

"I think so," she says. "But I left him at home last night when I went out with Rambo. We hit Madison Manson's favorite café, and there she was, with her brother and some friends. I got Rambo and Madison talking, and faded out of the picture."

"Another match for Love, Inc.," Kali says.

"I trolled by your dad's office after that, Z," Syd says. "I've been doing some work in the area."

By work, she means tagging. Since Dad's office is a storefront, you can see most of it from the sidewalk. "And . . . ?"

"As far as I can tell, he's working alone," she says. "At around nine, he went over to Mama Fu's and sat by himself with a double order of egg rolls. For what it's worth, he looked like a guy who misses his wife."

"Mama Fu's egg rolls are Mom's favorite," I say. "Thanks for checking."

Kali passes Syd her envelope. "Dieter stopped by, and it wasn't a social visit."

"Crap," Syd says, after opening it.

Coming back into the store, René lets Banksy take a good sniff at Sherman before putting the puppy on the floor. The big dog bows in an invitation to play, and then they're off, tearing around the displays, with Syd in pursuit.

The next person through the door is Brody. He's wearing khakis and a nice shirt. "Mom sent me to pick you up, Kal," he says. "We've got a reservation at Chez Zee in twenty minutes."

"Try the gingerbread pancakes," René suggests. "Perfection."

"That's my mom's favorite, too," Kali says, shooting me a

look. I'm quickly losing the battle to save René from Kali. She tails him around the store, peppering him with questions.

"Gee, no rush, Kal," Brody says, leaning against the counter and helping himself to one of my squares. He chews and swallows without the usual facial contortions. "Much better than your gut grenades."

"So you're talking to me now?" I ask. "The last time I saw you, you booted me out of the trailer."

"You were leaving anyway, drama queen." He leans against the counter, all mocking white teeth and evil green eyes.

"There are tread marks on my butt."

"Really? Let me see."

He cranes for a better view, and I feel an odd stirring sensation inside. It's as if someone replaced the batteries in my stalled hormones. I don't like it. I don't like it at all. Kali should never have planted her stupid idea in my head.

"Rude," I say, to cover my confusion.

"Again with the harsh tone," Brody says. "Nice way to talk to the person who saved your rep as a baker. Because of *my* good advice, none of your customers will require hospitalization today."

"Like you know anything about baking."

"Excuse me, I suggested adding fruit and maple syrup, and look"—he makes a show of examining a recipe card—"there they are."

"Good call," one of our regular customers tells Brody.

"I would have—"

Kali's scream cuts me off. "Banksy!"

.. ♥ ..

Brody lifts the big dog out of Glennis's car and carries him through the automatic doors of the veterinary hospital. A receptionist ushers him and Syd directly into an examination room.

We sit in the waiting area until Brody comes back out. "They're running some tests," he says. "The vet says it could be some form of heart disease, or it could be something toxic he ate."

I pat Kali's knee, knowing she's worried. "He was already under the weather when Syd brought him over yesterday. It wasn't anything he ate on your watch."

"Maybe he stole one of Zahra's gut grenades," Brody says.

Kali glares at him. "This isn't funny, Brody. You should head over to the restaurant. We're sticking around here."

"I'll wait," he says, picking up a copy of *Sports Illustrated* from the table. "You'll need a ride home anyway."

We sit in silence until the sliding doors open again and Glennis appears with René.

"Mom!" Kali hits her forehead with the heel of her hand. "I forgot to call you."

"You did," Glennis says. "I waited at Chez Zee for half an hour, and when neither of you answered your phones, I went to the Recipe Box because Brody said he was picking you up there. René was kind enough to drive me over. Is Banksy okay?"

"We're still waiting to hear," Kali explains.

Glennis walks René to the door, where they stand chatting about dogs and photography as if they have all the time in the world. It's not like René to leave the store in the hands of part-timers, especially during peak season.

Finally, Syd comes out of the examination room—without Banksy. "You're still here," she says.

"Of course," I say. "How is he?"

"Conscious." She sinks into the seat beside mine. "The vet thinks it's a congenital heart problem. Noticing Glennis and René, Syd asks, "What are they doing here?"

"We forgot to call Mom," Brody says.

"Sorry to wreck your brunch," Syd says. "You guys should go. It'll take hours to get the blood results."

"We're staying," Kali says. "No matter how long it takes."

Glennis turns to Brody. "You hang on to the car and make sure everyone gets home safely," she says. "I'll take a cab."

"You certainly will not," René says, smiling at her. "I'll run you home." She opens her mouth to protest, and he says, "I insist."

I've never seen René look at any of our female customers the way he's looking at Kali's mom right now.

Never one to pass up such an opportunity, Kali says, "You can still eat at Chez Zee, Mom. Take René for lunch to thank him for the ride."

Glennis blushes. "Kalista!"

René winks at Kali as he guides Glennis to the door. "The answer is yes, but lunch is on me."

When they're gone, Brody pulls out his phone. "Thin crust work for everyone?"

Kali smiles at him. "Double cheese."

"Mushrooms," Syd says, before returning to the back room.

"Hot peppers," I add. Pizza is the only food I like fiery, and I make sure my grandparents don't know about it. It would give them false hope.

"So few girls like hot peppers," Brody says. "Must be the hair."

Kali gets up to hold the door for a tall, slim guy about Brody's age, with closely cropped brown hair. He's carrying a cage in one hand. The other hand is bandaged.

"I'm Caleb," he tells the receptionist. "Hannibal's here for his shots."

"Hannibal's a funny name for a cat," Kali says, smiling, as Caleb takes the seat beside her. Cute guys are to Kali what a double espresso is to the rest of the world—an instant pick-me-up.

He smiles back. "But it's a great name for a killer rabbit."

"And . . . she's off," Brody whispers to me. "Give her nine minutes and she'll find three things wrong with him. Her average is only slightly lower than my mom's."

Even though Syd and I tease Kali about the same thing, I have to defend her. "When she meets the right guy she'll stop looking for faults."

"Please. She doesn't want to find the right guy. She just thinks she does." I glance at him curiously. "Don't look so surprised," he says. "There's more to me than great abs and a pretty face."

"Your inner beauty is so well hidden."

"I grow on people," he says. "Like mold on a gut grenade."

Rolling my eyes, I reach into my bag and pull out the envelope I found yesterday. "Does this belong to you, by any chance?"

His smug smile fades. "What were you doing snooping through my stuff?"

"Hello? You mixed it up with *my* stuff in the trailer."

"Well, you better not have looked through it." He pushes

up the sleeves of his black shirt, then pushes them back down again. It's the first time I've seen Brody nervous.

"Of course I looked through it. I needed a distraction after you called me crazy in front of a stranger."

"Why are you always so sensitive?"

"Look who's talking, Mister Don't Look at My Art."

"It's not *art*." He sounds mortified. "It's photojournalism."

"Call it what you like, they're great pictures. And I don't even like sports."

He gives me a sideways look. "Really? Which one did you like best?"

I glance up at Kali and find her engrossed in conversation with Caleb. "The one where the football player just scored a touchdown," I say. "It's a perfect moment in time."

"That's what I was aiming for. The hardest part is being patient long enough to let those moments happen. You can't force it."

I nod. My mediation work is like that. You have to get everything into position and then let things unfold. Trying to rush the process always derails it. "Are you going to study journalism?"

"Who knows? Right now it's fun. If I make it official, it becomes work."

"When you love something enough, it probably never becomes work. That's how I feel about baking, anyway."

"So you're going to make the world a better place one cupcake at a time?"

"Why not?"

"Everyone loves a baker," he says. "At least, I do."

He smiles, and I feel it again. Something is definitely stirring for Brody that did not stir for Andrew.

The receptionist calls for Hannibal, and Caleb takes a pair of thick oven mitts out of his backpack before picking up the crate. Kali opens the door to the examination room for him.

"Doesn't Caleb remind you of Owen Gaines?" she asks. "You know, his build and the way he walks? I wonder if he can sing."

The pizzas arrive a few minutes later. Brody offers some to the staff and sends a couple of pieces back for Syd and Caleb.

"Brody makes a wicked goat cheese pizza," Kali says. "He even makes his own dough." She ignores my warning look and forges on. "You should make it for Zahra sometime, Brody."

Brody shakes his head. "There is no way I will ever cook my signature dish for Zahra."

I knew it. Kali just gave him an opening to skewer me again.

Then Brody amends his statement. "At least, not until she publicly admits she used my ideas for her squares without sharing credit."

Kali laughs. "Just give it up, Z. He'll never let this go if you don't."

"Fine," I say, biting into my pizza. "I guess you inspired me to experiment in a new direction. I'll footnote the recipe card."

"Do it and the pizza is yours," he says. "All you can eat."

His eyes lock on mine, and my stomach does an odd rolling dance. Hot peppers are always so risky.

I can feel Kali watching us, upgrading our compatibility quotient. But then Brody's phone rings and breaks the spell. It's on the coffee table in front of us, and I can see the call display: Juliette.

Tossing a half-eaten slice of pizza back into the box, he grabs the phone and steps outside. "Hey," he says, as the door closes. "Still on for tonight?"

My hormones may be running again, but they're obviously misfiring horribly.

I barely have time to beat myself up, though, before Syd reappears. She sits down across from me and drops her face into her hands.

And if there is anything sadder than a pissed-off-at-the-world rebel crying as if her heart would break, I hope I never live to see it.

chapter 20

Three things I never thought I'd need to know:

- A pacemaker built for humans also works for dogs.
- A used pacemaker is free—but someone has to donate it, and that means dying first, which may not happen on the dog's schedule.
- A brand-new pacemaker costs about five grand.

Obviously, Banksy is worth every penny for a new pacemaker, but Syd can barely afford the cost of the surgery. Mrs. Stark picked up the huge bill for the emergency clinic, but the rest of her savings are tied up in a nonrefundable down payment for a face-lift. Mr. Stark is tapped out because of Charlotte's implants. Neither of Syd's parents sees the sense in borrowing money for a five-year-old dog that has a life expectancy of ten years.

It's a crime. Apart from Kali and me, that dog is Syd's family. The reason she depends on him is because she can't depend on them.

Syd would probably resort to desperate measures to get the money if she could, but the vet told her to stay close and keep the dog calm and quiet. For the moment, she's in a holding pattern, calling the vet constantly and rushing home at lunch and after school every day.

Kali and I are trying to raise the money ourselves, although we decided not to tell Syd in case we fall short. Half a pacemaker isn't going to cut it. We're off to a strong start, though, with over four hundred dollars already.

As usual, inspiration came to me first in the kitchen. I baked hundreds of gourmet dog biscuits, and Kali packaged them with bows. We've been hawking them in the dog parks and at the Recipe Box. Unfortunately, we can't sell the biscuits at school. It would be too much of a blow to Syd's pride, given her cherished outsider status.

Meanwhile, we've also been holding down the fort on Love, Inc. Luckily, our only current revenge case is strictly voluntary. Even if Hollis has dumped Fletcher for good, someone still has to teach that guy some manners. Since we can't stake out the Maroons' equipment room every night, we bought a couple of tiny wireless cameras and a monitor off the Internet.

Kali interviewed two of the team's former noseguards who suspect Fletcher is behind their fall from glory. One of them was only too happy to lend Kali a key to the equipment room. The other did a little legwork to find out the best time for our visit.

"A bunch of college scouts are coming to the game tomorrow," Kali says as we flip the laundry cart in the equipment room and clamber on top of it. "If Fletcher's going to make a move, it could be tonight."

Our theory is that Fletcher will try to take out at least one of the Maroons' two star defense players so that he'll get a higher profile in the game. We have no idea how he might strike, though. Fletcher may be vile, but he isn't stupid. He knows that using the same approach repeatedly will eventually get him busted. We're hoping that this time he'll decide to tamper with a teammate's equipment. If so, we'll catch the whole thing on camera.

Kali holds the flashlight as I tuck the first camera into a nook overhead. "So, was I right about René and my mom, or was I right?" she asks.

I shush her. There is no way we can explain our presence here if the coaches get out of their meeting early and hear us. But Kali is stoked that her little nudge in pushing René and her mom together worked out. Their lunch went so well that they went out the next day, and again yesterday.

"It all starts with one shared interest," Kali says.

I'm hoping it takes more than that. Mom and Xavier share an interest in business, and it's blinded her to the quality of the design and logo he developed for the Yasin Valley line. I know Mom wanted blues and greens to conjure up images of the real valley, but Xavier says the orange-and-brown image he's chosen will test better in consumer surveys. He says it's earthy. I say it's depressing. Mom claims to like Xavier's design, which can only mean she likes *him*.

Kali and I mount two more cameras to capture every angle of the room before making a discreet exit. Next door, in the girls' locker room, we hide the receiver that picks up the transmission through the walls and records the information onto a downloadable file. We'll have to screen hours of footage, but Kali claims to be looking forward to it.

We're giggling with relief as we make our way through the

mostly empty halls toward the main exit.

"I can't wait to tell Syd we pulled this off," Kali says.

"I really hope Fletcher comes through with some black magic," I say. "Slamming him is probably the only thing that could cheer Syd up right now."

Brimming with energy, Kali tells me that she's had two dates with Caleb—a personal record since Eric.

"Just don't ask me to babysit Hannibal while you're touring someday," I say, recalling the oven mitts Caleb needed to handle the killer rabbit.

She turns the tables. "How about you and Andrew?"

"We talked for half an hour last night, and we're getting together this week."

"Get out," Kali says. "Is your cold heart thawing?"

"Maybe," I say. "I'm giving it my best shot—for my matchmaker."

As we make our way down the steps and across the lawn, a guy with spiky black hair and a dusting of stubble on his cheek calls Kali's name. He's wearing a brown jacket over a red T-shirt, skinny black jeans, and pointy brown shoes. The overall effect is punk-meets-rockabilly.

"Max!" Kali says, sounding surprised. "I am so sorry. I forgot to cancel our meeting. She introduces me and adds, "Max is Madison Manson's brother."

Max grins. "Madison *Simpson* when she's not on the rink."

Now I know what's going on. After history class last week, Rambo told me that Madison's brother had been asking about Syd. They met briefly when she went to the diner with Rambo to track down Madison. Now Max has asked Rambo to find out if Syd will go out with him, and Rambo is reluctant to bring up the subject with the lady herself, when she has sworn off guys forever.

Kali was only too pleased to take over. She gave Max a call to find out a bit more about him. He goes to an arts school, when he's not keeping score for his sister's roller derby team. That information, combined with his quirky good looks and friendliness, were all she needed to decide that she would help Max catch Syd's attention. A direct setup is highly unlikely to work on Syd, so Kali must have arranged for a casual run-in today. Then Banksy got sick.

"Syd's dog collapsed on the weekend," Kali explains to Max now. "We'll have to postpone."

Max jams his hands into the pockets of his jeans. "Is there anything I can do?"

"You could make a donation if you want," Kali suggests, describing the Banksy fund.

Max counts out four five-dollar bills before heading off.

"How nice was that?" I say. "I know he has a crush, but twenty bucks is—"

"Syd!" Kali sounds a lot guiltier than she needs to, given the circumstances.

Syd has appeared seemingly out of nowhere, looking anxious and exhausted.

"What are you doing here?" I ask.

"I go to school here," she says.

"Usually you're at home with Banksy by now."

"I came back to ask my Science teacher if I can postpone my exam until Banksy is better. Which he isn't, thanks for asking."

"We haven't had a chance to ask," I say. Syd is clearly so

miserable, she wants the rest of the world to suffer too.

"I can see you're distracted," she says. "That guy is Madison's brother and I saw him give you money. Are you doing a job without me? Keeping me out of the loop on purpose because you think I'm such a mess over my dog that I'm going to screw up?"

"Syd, we're trying to give you some downtime," I say. "You've got enough on your mind without worrying about work."

"Don't take this the wrong way," Kali says, always dangerous words, "but you're being irrational."

I jump in to preempt Syd's strike. "She's probably not sleeping much."

Syd opens her mouth, but before anything caustic escapes, a little head on a big bike streaks toward us across the lawn. Braking at the last minute, the biker spins out his back wheel and sprays a perfect arc of turf all over us.

"If it isn't the three raging lesbians," Fletcher says. "Setting out to convert unwilling girls to their cause."

Kali herds us off school property, and Fletcher follows. "What do you want?" she asks.

"I want you to mind your own business," he says, cutting in front of us and blocking the sidewalk.

There is no way he could know what Kali and I have just done, so she gives him a fake smile. "What are you talking about?"

"For starters, stay away from Hollis. You're filling her head with ideas."

"Consider it done," I say.

We fan out and walk around him, but he circles us again and blocks our path. "I know you've been talking about me.

Did you really think you could ask questions and I wouldn't hear about it?"

"It was for a term paper on bullying," I say. "We were researching the master."

We start walking, but Fletcher continues to circle us, cutting ever closer. "Well, I've been asking about you too. I've heard some interesting stories."

"Whatever," Kali says.

"No, I mean it, matchmaker. If half the stuff I hear is true, it's amazing you guys have time for school."

We stop in our tracks.

"I thought that might get your attention," Fletcher says. "I don't know what you're up to right now, but I want you to think long and hard before you ever play one of your stupid tricks on me. Because it'll be the last thing you do."

"Oooh, scary," Kali says. She probably is scared. I sure am. Fletcher is as mean as they come, and we know he likes to play dirty.

He stops in front of Syd. "I hear your doggie isn't doing too well these days. It would be a shame if anything happened to him."

What little color there was in Syd's face drains. "Stay away from my dog."

"Then stay out of my business," he says. "Even a sick pooch can't resist a poisoned wiener. Catch my drift?"

He doesn't wait for an answer, but pedals back toward the school.

"Call off our slam," Syd says.

"But—" Kali starts.

"Fine," I interrupt. "We can't put Banksy at risk."

A silver Audi is idling by the curb. As we approach, the driver's window rolls down. "You guys wanna lift?" Willem asks.

Syd walks around the car and gets into the passenger seat, so Kali and I jump into the rear.

Willem gets straight to the point. In addition to the spa offer, he'll pay us seven hundred dollars to get the answer he needs, with a bonus of a hundred each if we can pull it off before Valentine's Day.

"Addison is starring in a big musical revue for one of her dad's charities that day," he explains. "Afterward, the governor is throwing a coming-out party for her. Everyone we know will be there. It's the perfect time to propose."

"If you really have doubts about Addison, maybe you should hold off on proposing," Kali suggests.

He shakes his head stubbornly. "We're meant to be together. I want to know if you can help me or not. I'm leaving with my family for the holidays next week."

"Consider it done," Syd says, from the front seat.

"What she means," Kali says, "is that we'll need to discuss this privately. The majority rules."

"What I mean is that I need the money," Syd says. "And I'll do it myself if I have to. This is my area of expertise anyway."

The car pulls to a stop for a light, and Syd hops out. "I'll be in touch, Willem. I've got your number."

·· ♥ ··

I sit down with my hot chocolate and try calling Syd. The call goes straight to voice mail as it has each time I've called her over the past four days. Three friends are chattering happily at the table next to mine, and it gives me a pang of regret over our recent trouble with Syd. She's been dodging us at school, she hasn't been returning our calls or texts, and today isn't any different. I understand why she'd want to take on Willem's case, but with Fletcher's network of evil keeping an eye on us, we have to be extra careful.

That didn't stop Kali and me from collecting our equipment from the locker rooms, but unfortunately we can't use the evidence we found. I know the Maroons' coach would be interested in seeing the footage of a hooded intruder creeping into the football equipment room and messing around in two specific cubbyholes just hours before the big game. At one, he made adjustments to a helmet and smeared something on the mouth guard. At the other, he fiddled with a pair of cleats and sprinkled some powder under the cup in a jockstrap. For a while it looked like we wouldn't get a good look at the intruder's face, but finally he pushed back his hood to reveal a pinhead and swampy eyes.

Fletcher's threats to Banksy meant our hands were tied. Luckily, neither Maroon defenseman was seriously hurt, although both were benched early, giving Fletcher a chance to shine for the college scouts. It makes me sick to think he got away with it, but there's nothing we can do right now. Kali and I didn't even mention it to Syd. We don't want to add to the tension.

That doesn't mean I can't keep calling Syd, though. Framily doesn't give up on framily.

I'm just finishing another voice mail when my next client comes in—a cute guy with auburn hair and freckles. "Zahra?" he asks, taking a seat on the sofa opposite me. "I'm Ben."

Ben and I have spoken several times but never met in person. He's booked a session with me because he's worried that his girlfriend is slipping away. She's been distant lately, but whenever he's tried to discuss what's bothering her, she insists everything is fine. Hopefully a frank conversation with an impartial third party will clear the air.

We're still waiting for Ben's girlfriend to show when a tall strawberry blonde straight out of the pages of *Interview* magazine steps into the café and looks around: Juliette. I sink into my seat, hoping she won't notice me. The last thing I need is her hanging around while I'm trying to work.

"Over here, babe," Ben calls. Juliette turns and smiles.

Correction: the last thing I need is to waste my mediation skills on the girl who's two-timing Ben with Brody.

"Hi," Juliette says, joining us. I'm still trying to figure out how to play this when she takes the reins. "Nice to meet you. I'm Juliette."

"Zahra," I say, extending a hand for the air shake.

"Benny," she says, slipping into the chair beside mine. "Could you grab me an herbal tea before we get started?"

He leans over to kiss her cheek before walking to the counter.

"So you're not just a Love, Inc. client," Juliette says, proving she's a bit sharper than she came across originally.

"No," I say. "But we try to keep a low profile."

"Client confidentiality guaranteed?" she asks.

I take a sip of my hot chocolate and force a smile. "We do our best."

"Then please don't tell Ben we've met," Juliette says. "If he finds out about Brody, he'll flip."

"I won't," I say. "Does Brody know about Ben?"

"Yeah, but don't discuss this with him either, okay?"

I have no intention of discussing this—or anything else—with Brody. He might be free to go out with whomever he wants, but seeing a girl you know is taken is another form of cheating, as far as I'm concerned. I'm ashamed my hormones came out of hibernation for that guy.

Ben comes back with Juliette's tea, and I get down to business. It *is* business, I remind myself. I don't have to agree with everything a client wants. The Love, Inc. charter says we have to deliver what's asked unless it's illegal or dangerous. Ben wants his girlfriend back, and it's my job to help him get her—even if she is a lying, ditzy, air-hand-shaker. I am not here to judge. I am here to ease communication.

I fire off my usual warm-up questions about how they met, how long they've been going out, and how they spend their time together. I do this partly to get a sense of how a couple feels about each other. If the love is still there, it shows.

Today, as Ben describes the moment he first saw Juliette, she chimes in, correcting small details, filling in blanks. They talk about it like it only happened a few days ago, even though they've been together a year. I can tell their story is not over yet. All I have to do is find the roadblock and guide them around it.

"I thought she was the most beautiful girl I'd ever seen," Ben says, squeezing Juliette's hand.

Juliette takes her hand away. "You changed your mind about *that* pretty fast."

Ah. The roadblock.

"What do you mean?" Ben asks. "You're gorgeous."

"If that were true, you would have been more supportive when that modeling scout approached me at the mall."

"But that was a scam," he says. "Dude was trying to pick you up."

"You don't think I'm pretty enough to make it as a model."

Ben runs a hand through his auburn hair, leaving it crushed down the middle. "I never said that."

But he's not saying she *is* pretty enough, which tells me there's more going on here than meets the eye.

"My dad checked out the agency," Juliette says. "It's totally legit."

Ben snorts. "A legit agency doesn't need to find models at Abercrombie & Fitch."

"Actually, I've read that agencies *do* scout for models in malls," I say. I hate to help Juliette's cause, but the truth is the truth.

"See?" Juliette says. "You're more uptight than my dad."

"Excuse me for wanting to protect you. I saw an exposé on how fly-by-night agencies get girls to blow a lot of cash on a portfolio, then skip town."

I make a suggestion. "What if Juliette approached a well-known agency and they were interested? How would you feel about that?"

Ben squirms in his seat. "I don't see why she has to put herself out there like that. You do okay in school, Juliette. You'll get into college."

"Modeling could help me pay for college," she points out. "I don't understand why you're so negative about this."

I put my shoulder to the roadblock and push. "Ben, if Juliette started modeling, how do you think it would affect your relationship?"

Ben stares at the floor. He probably wouldn't have hired

me if he thought it would get this awkward, but he rises to the challenge. He must really love Juliette. "I'd never see her. She'd travel all the time. Hang out with cool people."

"So," I say, shining a light on the problem, "you're worried that you'll lose her."

"I guess." He flashes a quick look at Juliette. "That makes me sound like a jerk."

Juliette doesn't think so. She gets out of her chair and sits on Ben's lap. "You'll never lose me, sweetie. I promise."

They quickly become a mass of groping, intertwined bodies on the sofa. I get up to leave and they don't even notice.

It's a bit much for a café, but on the bright side, two redheads going at it like that could bring our kind back from the brink of extinction.

chapter 21

"You're stirring too much. Just leave it." This, from the woman who was singing my culinary praises a few weeks ago.

"If I just leave it, it'll scald. The thermometer says—"

"Forget the thermometer; use your eyes."

I knew cooking with Nani was a bad idea. Even with the apron, she's a tyrant in a tunic. But when she suggested teaching me how to make her burfi while I interviewed her for my Social Studies assignment, I couldn't say no. I knew Mr. Kahn, my teacher, would love it, especially if I include samples. Despite my best intentions, my grades have started to slip, and I need all the help I can get.

As an added bonus, if this recipe turns out well, I'm going to put a seasonal stamp on a couple of batches and let René give them away to customers on Christmas Eve later this week. I was supposed to bake cookies, but time is running short and René's a sucker for a twist on tradition.

"I'll just stir a little," I say. "You can start telling me about life in Karachi when you were my age."

Her hand hovers, ready to snatch the spoon at the first opportunity. "Well, I was quite a scholar. I wanted to go to England to study medicine like my brother, but Abba wouldn't hear of it, even though my grades were better than Mohammed's."

"That wasn't fair." She makes a play for the spoon, and I block her with an elbow.

"No, not when I worked so hard. But for girls, marriage was the only option. And by the time I turned fifteen, my parents had already begun looking for a suitable man. There were plenty to choose from because I was very beautiful then."

Very might be overstating it, but I suppose Nani is attractive for her age, and she passed on some good genes. Lately she's started taking credit for my eyes as well as my cooking skills.

"So my parents could afford to be picky," she continues. "It took two years to find someone with the right pedigree and prospects. And by the time they finally found your Nana, I was already in love with someone else."

I'm so shocked I drop the spoon and she snatches it. "Someone else?"

"An American," she says. "He was studying in Karachi. Abba was a scholar, so Thomas was often at our home. He was handsome and charming and brilliant. I wanted to marry *him*, not a stranger my parents picked out."

"What happened?" I ask, forgetting the burfi.

"I spent an hour with your Nana, and he seemed so . . . boring."

I laugh. "Nana's not boring." I mean, considering. He doesn't get a chance to say very much.

She laughs, too. "I suppose he was shy, and naturally we were chaperoned. For me, no one could compete with Thomas anyway. I panicked. They were going to force me to marry this boring man I didn't even know. So I arranged to

330

go for a walk and meet Thomas to tell him about my parents' plan. I hoped he would propose."

Now she has full control of the spoon while I lean against the stove, watching her. "Did he?"

"Well, he kissed me. In my world, that came *after* a proposal. So I thought our fate was sealed."

"But . . . ?"

"But all of Karachi has eyes, and a friend of my father's saw us. Thomas took me home, and Abba . . . he was so angry, so ashamed." Fifty years later, her voice still quavers at the memory. "People gossiped. My reputation was ruined."

"By one kiss?"

"By one kiss in public with the wrong man. An American. It really couldn't be worse." She turns to look at me so that I'll understand what follows. "At that time, in some circles, girls simply disappeared for less. Abba was very modern for his day, but in the eyes of the community, I was ruined. No man would ever want me. Nana's parents withdrew their offer."

"But what about Thomas? Did he know? Did he fight for you?"

"He knew," she says, sighing. "Because my father, uncles, and brothers arrived at his door."

"To kill him?" I whisper.

"To talk to him," she says, smiling. "Although, my uncles did want to whip him and ship him home. They told Thomas he'd ruined my prospects and that Abba wanted him to take me to America so that the shame I'd caused could die down. There were my younger sisters to consider. They would be tainted, too."

Nani has stopped stirring, her mind far away in another time.

"And Thomas said . . . ?"

"That he couldn't marry me. That his family would never accept me." She takes a deep breath. "And that he was already engaged to an American girl."

"Oh, Nani!" I throw my arms around her. For the first time, it occurs to me that she was once a girl like me, with the same feelings about boys. My eyes fill with tears, and when I pull away, hers have, too. "I'm so sorry. Thomas played you."

"Yes. He played me." She wipes her eyes on her apron. "But it wasn't a game. It was very serious. The men gathered to decide what to do with me. My mother wouldn't speak to me, or allow my sisters to speak to me. I cried all day in my room, thinking they would send me away, disown me. But then your Nana came to the house and told Abba he still wanted to marry me and on the same terms. He insisted on speaking to me first to see if I was willing. And when I saw what a wonderful, kind man he was, I realized he was not boring at all."

I laugh again. "The gossip didn't bother Nana?"

"No, because his own sister had been judged unfairly once." She takes the pot off the stove and turns to me. "It helped that I was the most beautiful girl in Karachi."

"She was," Nana says, coming into the kitchen with my sister. "She still is. The Ahmed women deserve to be cherished."

Nani turns to me with a wink. "What did I tell you? Marry a man who accepts you for all that you are."

"Don't try to tell me you cherish her burfi," I say, showing Nana the lumpy and burned mass.

"Just how I like it," Nana says.

I usher my grandmother to the table and push her into a

seat. "I learned all I needed to. Let me try it for myself."

By the time my mom comes home, I've made four more batches in different flavors, including two batches of cherry chocolate for the store. Nana tests them all and pronounces each better than the last—but none quite as good as Nani's.

If that's brainwashing, I sure hope I inherited Nani's talent, along with her beautiful eyes.

·· ♥ ··

I find Mom in the basement laundry room pouring shower gel from a large pitcher into hotel-size vials. The room is filled with the scent of nutmeg and cardamom.

"How's Sydney's dog?" she asks without looking up.

"Still sick, I guess."

"You guess?"

"She's not speaking to me and Kali."

Mom sets the pitcher on the washing machine and turns to me. "How can she not be speaking to you when you've worked so hard to raise money for her dog's surgery?" Even Mom helped out, suggesting I hit up her colleagues at Whole Foods. "What's wrong with that girl?" Mom asks.

"She's going through a hard time, and she doesn't have any brothers or sisters. Banksy's all she's got," I say. "She'll come around when she hears how much we've raised."

Mom picks up her pitcher again. She's heard enough about my problems. We're back to hers. "I don't know how I'm going to fill all my orders," she says. "And then there's the packaging . . ." She shakes her head. "I'm sure Xavier knows what he's doing. He's been in business a long time."

"Just admit you hate the packaging. Let me try to design it."

"You?" She peers over her shoulder and spills the fragrant gel over the washer.

"I know how to use a computer, you know. Some people think I'm good at graphic design."

"Well," she says, backpedaling, "you *do* design beautiful cakes."

I start screwing lids on the vials. "So I'll come up with something better, and you can tell Xavier that you can't hurt my feelings. Daughter trumps boyfriend."

"He's not my boyfriend."

"Whatever. Just give me a week to see what I can come up with. After all, I've been helping from the start."

"All right," she says. "But this had better not be a ploy to get your father involved."

"He's too busy anyway."

Mom changes the subject. "What did you and Nani talk about for your assignment?"

"The American dude who broke her heart."

"Thomas," she says, and I'm surprised that she knows. "That's why she's more progressive than a lot of parents from her generation—at least in my culture. She's the one who made sure I could study whatever and wherever I wanted."

"And that's why Nana was so upset about your hooking up with Dad. He thought all American men were players."

"He'd say 'dishonorable.'"

"Nani liked 'player.'"

Mom laughs. "I told you she was progressive."

"Not progressive enough to accept Dad," I point out.

"They were afraid I'd give up my culture and religion. And I did."

I set the vials into a box and add it to the pile in the hall. "Dad didn't want you to do that, did he?"

"I don't know," she says. "Sometimes things happen so gradually you don't even realize it at the time. Then one day you look around and realize you've lost a whole piece of yourself, and it seems like there's no going back. Look at *your* reaction when I tried to reintroduce my culture into my life."

"It was more like a hostile takeover, with Nani and Nana driving the tank."

"You can't keep blaming your grandparents for everything," Mom says. "I was questioning my choices long before they got here." She drains the last of the shower gel and sighs. "Still, I could have handled the whole thing better."

"No kidding. But Dieter says parents are only human."

"Well, thank him for that."

"He also says everything depends on communication. Frankly, Mom, you suck at that. In two languages. And before you say it, Dad sucks too."

She proves my point by remaining silent as I help her move the products.

"I bet you never even told Dad you were having a crisis of faith, or whatever you'd call it. And when someone just starts changing like that, it's scary. You wonder where you fit into the new picture."

"If he wondered, he could have asked," she says.

I shake my head in disgust. "You two are hopeless. I'm inviting Dieter over for an intervention."

She drops the box onto the pile with a deliberate thud. "I should have married a man who accepts me for who I am," she says. "The Ahmed women deserve to be cherished."

．． ♥ ．．

Andrew holds the door open for me as we walk into the Paramount Theatre. "For the record," he says, "not every girl could talk me into seeing *The Sound of Music*."

"Well, I appreciate the sacrifice," I say, as he places his hand lightly on my back to guide me through the crowd to the ticket booth. "It's a bit of a holiday tradition for my family, but I'm the only one who wanted to go this year." I turn to the cashier. "Two, please."

"Oh no, you don't," Andrew says, pushing away my hand as I try to pay. "This is my treat."

I race him to the concession stand, and we have another tussle over paying for the popcorn. This time, he lets me win.

"I hope there are at least a few good car chases," Andrew says as we settle into our seats. His legs are so long they jam into the seat ahead, and anyone stupid enough to take the seat behind him will have a seriously obstructed view.

"I've got some bad news for you."

He pretends to pout. "As long as there are a few fight scenes."

"You're in luck, there," I say. "I believe there's a pillow fight."

"Excellent! And I assume something blows up?"

"Oh, it's explosive, all right," I say.

Andrew smiles as the lights dim. "Promise you'll hold my hand through the scary parts?"

．． ♥ ．．

Kali catches up with me outside the church as I hang up the phone with Ben. He said things couldn't be better between him and Juliette now. Well, I hope for his sake that she's not still seeing Brody on the side.

"Do you ever wonder if you're doing the right thing for some of our clients?" I ask, sitting down on the front steps.

"Sure," she says. "But people pay us to make their dreams come true, not shoot them down."

"I guess." I put Juliette out of my mind and focus on the challenge at hand. "Where are we with the Banksy Fund?"

"I sold a ton at the solar power symposium," she says. "Who knew there were so many dog-loving activists in this town? Plus, René delivered cash from selling dog treats at the Recipe Box. That puts us at seventeen hundred."

It's weird for me to be hearing about René through Kali, but he and Glennis are seeing each other regularly now.

"And Mom managed to raise another three hundred through her coworkers," I say.

"Which still leaves us short by three grand," Kali says. "We're going to have to kick this up a notch because time's running out for Banksy. I was thinking—"

"Count me in."

"You don't even know what I was going to say."

I smile. "I was going to say the same thing: We'll throw in our Love, Inc. savings, too."

A quick calculation shows that even with our combined savings and the money from Willem's job, we're short by six hundred dollars. We don't have time to wait for Willem's payment.

She pulls me to my feet. "Don't worry, Z, we'll come up with it. It's a noble mission, like Love, Inc. And noble missions don't fail."

·· ♥ ··

Dieter claps the session to a start at four thirty on the dot. "Who wants to speak first? Zahra?"

"I'm sorry, was my hand in the air?"

Dieter ignores the snickering. "Since you skipped the last session, I'm sure you'll have plenty to say." He gives me an evil smile. "How's it going at home?"

"Well, my dad's refusing to celebrate Christmas this year, and my mom's dating her business instructor. Only she refuses to tell him that his ideas for packaging her products suck. I guess her broken marriage didn't teach her anything about communication."

"Can they learn at their age?" Lauren asks. "I think neurons stop firing after you're thirty or something."

"There's no age limit on learning, Lauren," Dieter says. "But people have to *want* to change. And that applies whether you're fifteen or fifty."

"I hope my mom wants to," Kali says. "She just met the greatest guy, and if she makes the same mistakes again, I'm giving up on her."

"They're supposed to be role models," Lauren says.

"My dad's a great role model," Evan says. "I've visited him in San Antonio three times, and there's always a new lady sitting at the kitchen table when I get up on Sunday morning."

"That's gross," Kali says.

"I keep telling you, parents are just human," Dieter says. "And when they're in crisis, you need to cut them some slack, just as you would your friends."

"Cutting them slack only gives them more room to obsess about their own lives and ignore our family," I say.

Dieter's eyebrows shoot up. "That's harsh."

Now even Dieter's using the H-word. "You're the one who keeps telling us to focus on changing the things we can control and getting over the things we can't."

He studies me for a long moment. "Zahra, you've gained a lot of confidence in the past two months, but you could work on becoming more tolerant, especially with your parents."

"And others," a raspy voice says. While we were talking, Syd slipped into the room and took the chair closest to the door. I was sure she'd skip group today, but here she is, hands clasping and unclasping, leashless. "Dieter, do you think it's possible that some people are so unlikeable, *everyone* gives up on them?" She looks from me to Kali.

"No one's given up on you," Kali says.

"Please," Syd says. "I'm not stupid. I can see what's going on. Everything in my life sucks right now. *Everything*."

Dieter raises his hand to stop me from speaking. "Syd, obviously something's happened this week. Could you be more specific?"

Syd struggles to find the words, and eventually they come out in a rush. "My dog is dying. My parents are mostly AWOL. And my friends disappeared. I'm alone. Is that specific enough for you?"

Before he can answer—before any of us can answer—she gets up and leaves.

.. ♥ ..

Even in heels, Kali manages to catch up with Syd first. She grabs Syd's jacket and hauls on it. Syd fights to get away, and they're still struggling when I get there.

"Stop it," I say. We're still in view of the church, and Dieter will probably come after us. "Just tell us what's going on, Syd."

"There's nothing to say," Syd says, yanking her jacket out of Kali's fingers and walking away. "You guys have written me off."

"Written you off? What are you talking about?" I say, following her. "You're the one who won't return our messages."

"The minute I ran into trouble, you started leaving me out of everything. I've seen you together at the Recipe Box and the dog park at Auditorium Shores. You're working for Max Simpson behind my back." She takes a deep breath. "You want me out of Love, Inc., don't you?"

"Of course not," I say. "That's not what—"

"You're sneaking around," Syd says. "And you blew off our meeting this week. I showed up at the trailer and no one was there. No note. Nothing."

Kali and I look at each other. We were so busy selling dog biscuits that we completely forgot about the meeting.

"I know a meaningful look when I see one," Syd says, walking away. "You want me out and you don't even have the guts to admit it. So I'll save you the trouble: I quit. I don't need Love, Inc., and I don't need you. Have a great Christmas and a great life."

"Syd, please," I say, jogging after her as Kali falls behind. "Listen to us."

"Save your breath, Zahra. There's no mediating a friendship that never existed."

Her boots are pounding the pavement now, and I have to slow down. Her final statement drifts over her shoulder: "The only friend I have in the world is lying at home with a sick heart. I'm not wasting another second of the time he has left on you two."

·· ♥ ··

René restocks the plate of cherry chocolate burfi that sits on the counter, then hands me an envelope. "A Christmas bonus," he says. "Consider it a thank you for today's treats and all your work on the healthy snack promotion."

"But you already paid me extra for both of those things."

"Now that I've done the math, I can tell that your healthy snack promo brought in more sales than anything else I've ever tried. When the other part-timers stood outside with a tray of your treats, we had a ton of new customers. And the same thing is happening today." He points to the door, where half a dozen customers are filing inside to take a look around while munching on burfi. "I want to share the spoils."

I lift the back flap of the envelope and pull out a gift certificate to the pastry course I want to take. The one professional chefs take.

"Zahra, you *are* a professional," he says, when I protest. "I paid you to bake for me. So stop hiding behind that inventory gun and sign up."

Smiling, I slide the envelope into the front pocket of my apron. "Thanks, René. I know that course costs a bomb." A bomb that I'd saved up myself before Love, Inc. even started, but I threw it into the Banksy fund with the rest of my savings.

"You can make me a coconut cream pie when you graduate," he says. "It's my favorite. And did I mention it's Glennis's favorite too?"

"You did." I try to inject some enthusiasm into my voice, but

I've already heard about how he's found his ideal woman three times. I'm happy for René, happy for Glennis, and especially happy for Kali. But I'm also a little sorry for myself. How come I can't pull off a happy ending for my own parents? Kali's obviously a much better matchmaker than I am a mediator.

René follows me. "I can't believe how much we have in common," he rattles on. "I mean, what are the chances of meeting someone like that? And so beautiful, too. A woman like that—"

"Deserves to be cherished," I suggest, although this discussion is making me a little queasy. René is Dad's age. He's supposed to be past gushing. *I'm* past gushing. The gushing part of my life ended the day I found out about Eric, and I don't expect it to come back. The way I feel about Andrew, for example, is more serious and mature. After two dates, I can see we're a good match. It's completely rational, so there's no need for gushing.

"Exactly," René says. "We saw each other two days ago—is it too soon to ask her out again? I don't want to scare her off."

"René, you're starting to scare *me* off. What time is my boss coming back?"

The door of the store opens, and Riaz comes in carrying a bunch of pink lilies. I'm not thrilled to see him or his lilies, but at least it's an opportunity to dodge René's love-struck ramblings. I excuse myself and say hello.

Riaz presents the bouquet. "I want to apologize for not being more up front about the meat drive. And I should have warned you about meeting my ex-girlfriends."

I didn't realize I had, but it doesn't matter. "Plural?"

"Uh, well, that's all in the past anyway," Riaz says quickly. "Can we please start over? Don't write me off just because your grandmother likes me. Be glad she has great taste."

I laugh. Riaz may be arrogant, but he does have a certain charm.

He takes my hand, which is still holding the lilies, and examines my wrist. "I remember when we picked out these bangles."

I try to pull my wrist back. "Riaz, I—"

"Need a hand?" someone asks. "You seem to be missing one."

Brody is standing a few feet away from us, and despite the joke, he isn't smiling. I don't know what he's got to be sullen about. Maybe Juliette broke the bad news that she's rediscovered monogamy.

I yank my wrist out of Riaz's grip and make the introductions. Riaz is polite, even friendly, but Brody barely grunts a greeting. It's an awkward moment, and I grasp for any topic that might ease the tension. "Brody's on the basketball team," I tell Riaz, who's mentioned liking sports.

"You play?" Brody asks, sounding bored.

"I can't, unfortunately," Riaz says. "I'm planning a career in medicine." He holds up his hands like a surgeon entering the operating room. "These are going to save lives one day. I can't risk injuring them."

And I can't risk glancing at Brody's reaction to that comment.

Riaz claps Brody's shoulder lightly. "It was good to meet you, man. I've got to get going—another fund-raiser. Put one in the basket for me, okay?" He leans over and kisses my cheek. "*You* I'll call later."

Pulling his shades down, Riaz struts out of the store. Two girls who must be college age stop flipping though cooking magazines to watch him go.

"So," I say, turning back to Brody, "what brings you to the Recipe Box? Another great idea for low-fat treats?"

He just glares at me as if I've done something wrong. I don't get it. When I saw him at the vet's office last week, we got along fine. Maybe Juliette told him I know about their tawdry affair, and he's mad at me for wrecking it by getting her back together with her boyfriend. Well, if he is, too bad.

At any rate, I can't ask. Ben's a client, so it's all confidential.

"I just wanted to give you this," he says, handing me an envelope. "Kali told me that you were running short on the Banksy fund, even after kicking in all your savings."

I peek into the envelope and see a thick stack of bills. "Oh my God! Is it yours?"

"Half of it," he says. "The other half's from an anonymous donor."

"But it must be—"

"Six hundred dollars," he says. "I think that brings you to five grand."

I tuck the envelope into the pocket of my apron. "Wow! Was it Glennis?"

"Can't say. Just someone who likes charitable work. Like Dr. Do-Good." He smirks. "No wonder he's a mediocre kisser—his lips are jammed halfway up his own butt."

I'm not into Riaz, but Brody's in no position to be so critical. "I guess a little arrogance helps when you're an aspiring surgeon."

"So you like his bedside manner?" he asks.

I shrug. "Probably not as much as you like Juliette's."

"Juliette?" He looks puzzled. "What's she got to do with anything?"

To hell with confidentiality. Brody could snoop through our files whenever he's in the trailer anyway. "You know she has a boyfriend and you're hooking up with her anyway. That's cheating, in my book."

"You don't know what you're talking about," Brody says.

I turn to walk away. "I know when something stinks. Luckily, I have these beautiful lilies."

"Zahra." Brody takes my hand to stop me. I pull it away, and my wrist connects with the metal bookshelf, shattering one of my glass bangles.

"Nice work," I say, nudging the bits of blue and gold glass with my sneaker. Taking the envelope out of my apron, I kneel and start scraping the floor with it.

"It was an accident," Brody says, crouching to help me. "Did you get cut?"

I check my wrist, displaying a tiny nick and a droplet of blood. "Yes. Thanks a lot."

"Use a dustpan and broom," calls René, who's obviously been watching.

"Just go," I tell Brody, embarrassed to be causing a scene at work. Especially when René is busy "cherishing" Brody's mom.

Brody stands, towering over me. "I'm sorry."

"It doesn't matter." I can't believe I'm getting so upset over this. I have Andrew now—perfectly lovely, hopefully faithful Andrew. If Brody's happy being Juliette's piece on the side, it's not my problem.

"I shouldn't have come here," he says, backing away. "You're determined to hate me."

"Well, harsh is what I do best, remember?" I say, keeping my eyes on the broken glass. I don't hate Brody, but I do hate that I'm jealous of Juliette. Hopefully, a little more time with Andrew will cure me of that.

He backs away. "Get the brilliant Dr. Ri-Ass to hook you up with a new bracelet. Just tell Kali how much, and I'll pay for it."

"Whatever," I say. I keep scraping at the glass until I hear the door close. Then I collapse on the floor, completely drained.

René appears above me holding a broom. "Double dating with you two is going to be hell."

chapter 22

Kali steps through the torn fence at the Albany Hotel and looks back at me. "So in other words, you're saying my brother's got it bad for you."

"What?! Where'd you come up with that interpretation?"

"He brought the money to you, at your store, when he sees me at home every day. Conclusion: he wanted to impress you."

"By being totally rude to Riaz and mean to me?"

"I guess they could have fought a duel with spatulas or something. Guys have no flair for the dramatic these days." She grins over her shoulder at me, nose a little red from the chill.

I pull my hat over my ears and glare at her. "They weren't fighting over me."

"All I can say is, it's a good thing Andrew wasn't there. René would have had to close the store."

"Actually, I haven't heard from Andrew since we went to the movie last week." I count off on my fingers. "Five days." I haven't thought about him that often, either, which is a bad sign. Still, with the other guys I know behaving like idiots, I'd better try to keep the stable one around.

"Why don't you call him now?" Kali suggests.

"Uh, because it's Christmas Day? Normal people are busy with their families."

"Right," Kali says, leading the way across the parking lot. She had brunch with Glennis and Brody but decided not to join her mom for dinner at a friend of René's.

Meanwhile, I've basically had no Christmas at all. Dad followed through on his boycott of all things festive, so Saliyah went to Mom's to not-celebrate there. I thought Dad might pull through his funk, but when he rolled out of bed at eleven, all he did was hand me an envelope of cash before crashing on the couch to watch a *Godfather* marathon.

It's pathetic, but at least it left Kali and me free to try to ambush Syd. After striking out at her mom's apartment and her dad's condo, we took our search to the streets. If we don't find her soon, we'll have to drop off the money we collected at the animal hospital. Banksy can't wait for Syd to get over her snit and return our calls.

"How'd Brody come up with that kind of money anyway?" I ask, getting back to the point.

"Beats me," she says. "I guess he hit up his teammates. Anyway, I hope Syd wasn't serious about quitting the business. She's not thinking straight right now."

Syd doesn't look stressed at the moment. She's on the scaffold, sweeping her spray can in wide arcs. In the boarded-up window to her right is an image of Banksy. His paws are hooked over the sill as he looks out at the world with sad, brown eyes. The word BROKEN is painted on his collar.

The window she's working on now shows three familiar-looking girls inside a hotel room. They're all smiling, as if sharing an inside joke. But the joke's on us because Syd's begun to cover the lower left-hand side of the painting with black paint.

"Stop!" Kali shouts. "My legs are my best feature."

Syd turns and directs the spray can at us like a gun. "Give me one reason not to," she says.

"Here are five thousand of them," I say, tossing a fat envelope onto the scaffold.

Syd bends to retrieve it and stares into the package, stunned.

"It's enough for a new pacemaker," Kali says.

She sinks to the floor of the scaffold and dissolves into tears. "But . . . how?"

"Love, Inc., a mysterious donor, and a whole lot of home-made dog biscuits," I say.

"That's what you were doing in the dog park?" Syd wipes her eyes with the back of a paint-stained hand.

"And at the store," Kali says. Tears are streaming down her face, too, now. "And that's also why we missed our Love, Inc. meeting, and collected money from Max. We didn't want to say anything in case we couldn't pull it off."

"How is Banksy?" I ask. "Did we make it in time?"

"I think so," she says, pulling out her phone. "I've got the vet's cell number." Her feet dangle over the side of the scaffolding. One boot falls off and nearly hits me in the head, but Syd doesn't even notice.

A short conversation later, Syd is standing between us as she delivers the good news. There are more tears all around, apologies, and a group hug.

"This is the best Christmas gift ever," Syd says, staring into the envelope again. "But you must have drained your savings. What about the guitar? And the Sweet Tooth fund?"

"We couldn't enjoy them if Banksy didn't pull through," I tell her. "He's part of our framily."

"Besides," Kali says, "since you took on Willem's case, we'll have more money in no time." She digs around in her bag for a compact and tries to mop up the damage. Then she hands Syd a few tissues. "You look like hell."

Syd's hair is limp and dull, and her jeans hang off her hips. "Thanks," she says, dabbing at mascara rings. "I missed you too."

I glance up at the happy girls in the window. "We look great up there, though. Evan is wrong: I'm at least an eight."

"And I'm closing in on ten, in my humble opinion," Kali says, grinning as she shoves her hands into the pockets of her dark gray pea coat—her Christmas gift from Glennis.

Laughing, Syd promises not to paint it over. She slips her boot back on and climbs the scaffolding to gather her things. "I'll catch the bus back with you so we can talk business. With the Banksy situation under control, I want to focus on Love, Inc. again so I can start paying you back."

"No," Kali says, and I chime in. "You're not repaying us. Let's just focus on Willem's job, and then we'll worry about taking on more clients."

"So where do we start?" I ask. "How do we find this guy that Addison is cheating with?" I think about adding, "if there is one," but I don't. Lately it seems like there's always some-one on the side. Maybe monogamy's only possible for people like my grandparents.

"By sticking to what each of us does best," Syd says, her

old spark already returning. "Zahra, prepare to get someone to spill her guts. And you"—she points to Kali—"warm up your guitar. We've got an audition right after New Year's."

·· ♥ ··

As I slide into the booth across from Andrew, I can tell it was a mistake to call him. His eyes, usually so warm, are icy today.

"How are you?" I ask, keeping my jacket on against the chill. I get the feeling I won't be here long.

"Fine," he says. "How's Love, Inc.? Business slow over the holidays?"

Uh oh. I could try to BS, but he'll be expecting it. Besides, it seems wrong after two really nice dates. So I keep it simple. "What are you talking about?"

"Trey Fuller got into a keg of truth serum at a Christmas party. When I said you were the kind of girl I could get serious with, he told me to ask you about your business. He said relationships need to be built on honesty." Andrew lets out a bitter laugh. "Apparently he learned that from you."

"Andrew, I'm sorry I didn't tell you about my mediation work."

"It's not the mediation that bothers me," he says. "Another guy at the party told me about what you guys did to Eric Skinner. You're like black widow spiders, biting the head off your boyfriend and leaving him for dead."

"That's the praying mantis," I say.

Andrew is incredulous. "You seriously want to argue about bugs right now?"

I don't want to argue about anything. I just want to leave before this gets any worse. It turns out we haven't contained

Love, Inc. as well as we'd hoped, and now it's biting me in the butt. Helping other people with their relationships is ruining my own.

Well, there's nothing I can do about it now. I signed up for this ride and I'm not about to abandon ship.

Nothing I can say will make a difference to Andrew anyway. He's made up his mind that I'm trouble, and seventy-seven percent compatibility doesn't outweigh that. This mediator has learned when to cut her losses.

"I guess I'm lucky to get out while I can," Andrew says. "You're obviously crazy."

There's that word again. But I've been called crazy before and survived. "I've gotta go."

He watches me zip up my jacket and asks, "You don't even want to defend yourself?"

"There's nothing to defend. You've already made up your mind." Pushing myself out of the booth, I paste on a fake smile. "Take care, Andy."

It's a parting shot, because Andrew hates being called Andy.

The cold wind freezes tears on my cheeks as I walk up the street, but I don't cry for long. Andrew said some hurtful things, and I worry I'll never find someone who can accept me for who I am. But he's in no position to judge me. If he doesn't want to know the real me, it would never have worked anyway.

The Ahmed women deserve to be cherished. Even the renegades.

·· ♥ ··

Mom comes up from the basement, looking pretty rough. With all the Christmas orders that came rolling in, she's been mixing her products day and night for weeks, and she's still going strong with New Year's approaching. The house smells of so many different fruits, herbs, and spices that it's nauseating. How can I tell if my shortbread is working? A baker needs her nose.

Watching as I pound my dough into a disk, Mom asks, "Is something wrong?"

"No, nothing's wrong." What could be wrong? Christmas was a complete bust, and Saliyah is upset. Dad's barely moved off the couch for days. The one nice guy I met this year thinks I'm a man-murdering insect. And Syd's freaking out because Banksy's surgery is tomorrow. Life is perfect.

Instead of working behind me to clean up, Mom sits at the kitchen table and watches as I start to measure and mix my next batch. "Does this have anything to do with Riaz? Nani said you two went out last night."

The community grapevine is better than a newswire.

"It was a huge mistake," I say, throwing cutlery into the sink.

I only agreed to it because I was feeling down over what happened with Andrew. I wanted another guy to pay attention to me, but the only person Riaz really pays attention to is him-self. He blathered on about his great future, then lectured me about how I should start embracing my heritage. I was wearing the tunic I got at the Eid carnival, and Nani's earrings, so Riaz accused me of accepting only the frivolous aspect of my culture instead of the spiritual one. He actually called me a hypocrite. On a date! I told him I considered myself one hundred percent American—and that's enough of a definition for me. Then we sat in silence for about five minutes until I couldn't stand it any-more and got him talking about himself again.

It was horrible—mostly because he's right: I am a hypocrite. Or at least a dilettante.

Mom laughs when I describe the argument. "It's none of his business how much of your culture you embrace."

That sounds like my old mom, the one who cared about my life. I perch on the chair beside hers for a moment. "But am I a hypocrite?"

"You're fifteen," she says. "No one has it figured out at your age, and deciding how to blend two cultures is never easy. Obviously your dad and I didn't do a very good job of it." She rests a hand on mine. "I'm proud of my Scotistani Texan daughter, and the only thing I care about is that she's happy."

I go back to my cookies, suddenly inspired to flavor my shortbread with chai spices.

"Christmas cookies!" Saliyah says, coming into the room. "But it's New Year's Eve."

"Not for us," I say. "We didn't really have Christmas, and I demand a do-over." I hand her a reindeer cookie cutter. "Let's make our own rules this year."

Saliyah plugs my iPod into the docking station, and together we sing along with the Christmas playlist I put together for the occasion. When we draw a blank for the last verse of "Oh Come All Ye Faithful," we just go back to the beginning, singing at the top of our lungs. Mom joins in, and the three of us are joyful and triumphant when my grandparents step into the kitchen.

Nana scowls in a way I've never seen before. "No daughter of mine celebrates Christmas," he says.

"Abba—*Dad*—I've lived in the United States for twenty-five years," Mom says. "It's impossible not to know Christmas songs. Alec introduced the girls to his family traditions."

"Yet you've barely introduced them to yours," Nana says.

Saliyah drops her cookie cutter and comes to Mom's defense. "That's not true. Mom told us the story of Layla and Majnun and gives us candy for Eid. We fly kites at Basant, and we even know some Pakistani songs." She sings "*Hawa hawa eh hawa*," the old 80's pop song Mom always used to sing around the house.

Nana's frown deepens. "That's the best you can do, Sana?" He shakes his head. "I've said this before: these girls would benefit from going to mosque. They need more guidance."

He points to the order book on the table. "You spend too much time on this business of yours when you should be focusing on your family. Zahra needs to live under this roof so we can keep an eye on her."

"I'm not moving back without Dad," I say.

His usually calm voice rises. "It's not your choice."

Nani finally pipes up. "Sana, do you know how many boys' names are programmed into your daughter's cell phone? Eighteen."

Eighteen! That sounds like a lot, even to me. Of course, many of them are Love, Inc. clients. "You can't touch my things, Nani. That's a total invasion of privacy."

"You left your phone on the coffee table," she says. "I happened to see the list."

Saliyah has proven you can teach an old dog new tricks. First Facebook, now cell phones. Thank God I never left my iPod Touch unattended. If Nani saw the footage of guys in gyms and locker rooms, moving back home would be the least of my worries.

Nana raises his hand and makes a pronouncement. "No more arguments. The girls need structure, and if you can't give it to them with Alec out of the picture, Sana, then you'd better let me."

Saliyah bursts into tears and runs out of the room. "Dad is NOT out of the picture!" There's the thump of her footsteps on the stairs, and finally her bedroom door slams so hard it rocks the house.

"That's Zahra's doing," Nani says. "Saliyah never slammed doors before."

"She can slam doors if she wants," I say. "This is Dad's house."

"Your father left," Nana says. "No man should do that to his wife and children. I always said he lacked character."

I throw the measuring cup I'm holding onto the counter. It tips a cookie tray and sends it crashing to the floor with a clatter. "Stop trashing my dad! You don't get to walk in here after twenty years and be the head of this family."

Mom gets up from the table. "Zahra, enough."

But I can't hold it back. It feels like my head is going to explode. "You didn't want Mom to marry Dad, and you didn't want anything to do with Saliyah and me because we're not full-fledged Members of the Tribe."

"That is not true," Nani says. "We tried and tried."

I ignore her. "We were doing fine until you two showed up."

Mom reaches out and grabs my shoulder. "Don't say things you'll regret later. But Abba, for the record, Alec didn't leave by choice. I basically forced him out. He said it was mutual, for the girls' sake."

Saliyah has reappeared in the doorway. She's staring at

Mom wide-eyed. "I hate you," she whispers. "I'm moving in with Dad."

.. ♥ ..

As soon as we get off the elevator, I know we're in trouble. The Smiths are blaring loud enough to hear down the hall. No wonder Dad didn't pick up the phone when I called from the cab.

He doesn't hear me when I open the door, either. We walk into the living room and find him lying on the couch, snoring. Half a dozen empty beer cans litter the coffee table beside him.

"Girls," he says, rousing himself. "You aren't supposed to be here."

He's slurring, and his eyes are bloodshot and swollen, as if he's been crying. I've only seen that once before, when his father died. It was scary then and it's scary now. I expect Dad to leave the crying to us.

"Daddy?" Saliyah sounds scared too.

Instinctively, I wrap an arm around her. "It's okay. Right, Dad?"

"This is the worst New Year's Eve ever," is all he says, before collapsing onto the couch again. He's asleep almost instantly.

This is a Dad I don't even know—or want to know. "Come on," I say, spinning my sister around. "Dad will feel better in the morning."

Noticing his laptop sitting open on the dining room table, I tell Saliyah to go brush her teeth. After checking to make sure he's snoring, I give the mouse a gentle nudge. Maybe there's a clue here as to what's caused Dad's meltdown. The screen lights up and I see half a dozen e-mails from Uncle Paul. At the bottom of the string, I find the bad news: Uncle Paul saw Mom kissing another man in a restaurant.

"This is all your fault," Saliyah whispers, reading over my shoulder. "If you hadn't pushed Mom to start her own business, she'd never have met Xavier."

Dad stirs on the sofa. "Xavier? You know about this guy?" Pushing himself up, he staggers toward us. "You keep your mother's secrets, but you have no problem invading my privacy," he says, slamming the laptop closed.

"Dad, I'm sorry," I say. "I shouldn't have done that, but I wanted to know what's wrong with you."

"What's wrong with me?" It sounds like he's directing the question to himself instead of me. "I'm going to bed."

After he staggers down the hall, Saliyah leans over the coffee table and nudges the beer cans aside to read the pages underneath. "Divorce papers," she says.

"Saliyah."

"Don't talk to me."

I follow her down the hall until she slams my own bedroom door in my face.

chapter 23

S yd hangs up the phone and hugs Kali and me voluntarily. It can only mean good news about Banksy. "The vet says he can come home on Saturday," she says. "This is going to be a great year!"

"That's fantastic," I say as we file into a pew. "When's he coming home?"

Syd and Kali look at me strangely.

"What?" I stifle a yawn. Kali let me crash in the trailer last night to escape the tension at home. Both Dad and Saliyah are still mad at me, and I can't say I blame them. I pushed Mom into starting her business and taking the course with Xavier. I thought it would be good for her and ultimately good for Dad. But if she was making out in a restaurant, all hope of a reunion is lost.

"Never mind," Syd says. "You've got a lot on your mind."

A woman turns from the pew ahead and shushes us. The Clarksville Players are holding auditions at St. Joe's for the Have a Heart Valentine's Day Broadway Revue. The governor took over as chair of the event last year, and the revue raised a ton of money for charity, largely due to the vocal stylings of one Addison Mayfield.

We're trying to get into the chorus to gain access to Addison. It's a great idea, but I can barely carry a tune, and judging by our rehearsal in the trailer, Syd's even worse.

I look around and see the pews filling fast. It figures the auditions would be held in the same place we meet for group, but St. Joe's is in constant use by community groups.

The director welcomes everyone, and introduces his two stars, a chubby man in his thirties named Bobby Rae, and Addison Mayfield. Addison is even prettier in person than she is in the newspaper. She's about five-feet-ten, with soft brown eyes, high cheekbones, full lips, and a wide smile. Her shiny dark hair swings in a ponytail over her pink cashmere cardigan and gray wool pants.

"She looks like a deb," Syd says dismissively.

"But apparently she's not behaving like one," Kali says.

The auditions progress in alphabetical order. When they get to the L's, I slide down in my seat. "Oh, no," I whisper. "Client in the house."

Dylan Langley has risen from the front pew to pass sheet music to the pianist. He's trim and stylish in dark jeans, an expensive-looking sweater, and a bright striped scarf. "Remember the guy whose boyfriend fell into the trap we baited with Brody?"

"He'd better suck," Syd says. "We don't need clients buzzing around when we're working on Addison."

It seems like the world is shrinking as our Love, Inc. client roster grows. Now the business isn't just biting our butts socially, it's biting us all over.

Dylan launches into something from *Phantom of the Opera*, and Kali whispers, "He so doesn't suck. And he's cute, too.

Why would his ex choose Brody?"

In the end, he didn't; Raphael groveled and Dylan forgave him. That happens a lot in our line of work. Hollis is another classic case. Despite her resolution in the restroom that day, we've seen her talking to Fletcher in the halls again.

When Dylan finishes, Bobby Rae leaps to his feet and yells, "Bravo!" Addison echoes his shout, and the director announces, "You're in."

"Crap," I say, holding sheet music over my face as Dylan returns, grinning, to his seat.

"MacDuff?" the director calls. "Zahra Ahmed-MacDuff?"

Dylan turns and waves. Since we're busted anyway, I wave back at Dylan, and we file to the front of the church.

"Break a leg," he says as we pass. "I need to talk to you later."

Kali gets her guitar out of its case, and we perform "Do-Re-Mi" from *The Sound of Music*, with Syd and I tackling the kids' parts. Kali sings to win, and does her best to drown us out with vigorous strumming.

When we're done, Bobby Rae doesn't look impressed, but Addison claps hard. Her vote clearly carries more clout, because the director welcomes us into the chorus.

Dylan joins us when we return to our pews, and launches into a long complaint about Raphael, who cheated on him again. On New Year's Eve, when Raphael was supposed to be out of town, Dylan ran into him at a party with another guy. It turns out Raphael and the new guy work together at a bistro attached to the bar where we put up posters of Miss Daisy.

"I suspected something was going on for weeks," Dylan

continues, despite glares from the people around us. "Why did he have to lie and sneak around?"

"Well, I'm sorry things didn't work out," I say, as the auditions wind down. "But it sounds like you're better off without him."

"I know," he says, sighing. "But I want that bastard to pay." He clutches my arm as I try to follow Syd and Kali toward Addison, who's already been surrounded by admirers. "And I hear you guys have a revenge service."

How is he hearing this? Somewhere, Love, Inc. has sprung a mighty big leak.

"Dylan, please," I say. "We don't talk about business in public."

"Can I call you, then?" he asks.

"Only if you're looking for a new match," I say. "Then maybe we can help."

By the time I break free of Dylan, Addison has disappeared. The director hands us the sheet music for fifteen Broadway numbers. "Learn them all before first practice," he says. "We meet next Thursday, from four thirty to six."

Fabulous. That's exactly when group reconvenes.

·· ♥ ··

"Zahra!" Lauren's voice practically launches all three of us into the air. "I heard about what happened with Andrew. Trey feels horrible about shooting off his mouth."

I pull Lauren into the clump of cedars beside me and keep my voice low. "Trey called me to apologize, but it's fine. Andrew and I weren't meant to be anyway."

"Why are we hanging out in the bushes?" Lauren asks,

pulling a twig out of her perfect hair.

"Just keeping an eye out for Dieter," Kali says.

"Tell me you're not skipping," Lauren says. "Without you, it's just me against the guys."

"We're not skipping," Syd says. "But we do have a bit of a conflict."

The light dawns on Lauren. "Oh, you're on a mission. Who is it this time?"

"Privacy guaranteed," Kali says. "You know that."

"Come on, I got you started," she says.

"And you continue to be a great source of business," I say. "We appreciate it."

Lauren peers through the bushes. "Hey, that's Addison Mayfield. So Willem finally convinced you guys to take the case."

I neither confirm nor deny. "So how well do you know Addison?"

"I've known her since grade school," Lauren says. "Let me say, there's a side of Addie that her daddy wouldn't like."

I nod, exchanging a look with Syd and Kali. "Thanks, Lauren," I say. "We've got a lot on our plates today. If you could help us keep Dieter distracted, we'd cut you in."

The three of us need to trade off between group and the revue rehearsal, and we want to keep the discussion so lively that Dieter doesn't fuss about our shaving off a little time from each end. It's not much of a plan, but it's all we've got.

"I can't take a cent after what you did for Trey and me," Lauren says. "Plus, I believe in your cause." She points to Dieter pulling into a parking spot. "It'll be fun."

.. ♥ ..

Dieter has barely clapped off a round when Lauren is out of the blocks. "So, Evan," she says, "how's your love life?"

Evan eyes her suspiciously. "Why?"

"Well, the rest of us are always spilling our guts about that stuff, and you hardly ever share," Lauren says.

"Maybe I don't have anything to say," he says, flipping up the hood of his sweatshirt. "Some things are off-limits."

I take the baton from Lauren. "Off-limits?" I say. "Nothing's off-limits here. You already know that my family is a complete wreck. Plus, I've just had two dating disasters. Now it's your turn."

"I'll share," Simon says.

"Simon, it's sweet of you to jump in to save Evan like that," Lauren says. "I notice you two have become really close since you broke up with Trisha and her replacement."

Her insinuation is lost on Evan, but Simon gets it. "I'm not into guys, if that's what you're implying."

"Come on, Simon," Lauren urges. "This is the place to open up. No one will judge you here."

Dieter claps once. "Enough, Lauren. If Simon isn't comfortable with this discussion—"

"I am not gay," Simon says.

"Closets can't exist in this room, Simon," I say. "Come out. You're among friends."

"Yeah man," Evan says. "It's a free country."

"I AM NOT GAY," Simon says.

"It's normal to be confused at this stage," I say. "Especially when there are problems at home."

Dieter's hands are frozen mid-clap, as if he's not quite sure what the offense is.

"I wish I were into girls," Lauren says. "At least I understand how they think. God knows I never understand men."

"I'm especially good with girls being together," Evan says.

"It's a common male fantasy," I say. "Right, Dieter?"

Dieter's hands are still raised, the clap unclapped, when Kali and Syd slip in, apologizing for being late.

I toss the baton to them. "Hey guys, we're talking about homophobia. Sorry to miss the rest of the discussion, but I've got a doctor's appointment."

$$\cdot\cdot\ \heartsuit\ \cdot\cdot$$

Dylan, our revenge-seeking former client, clings to me like a magnet on metal from the moment I slip into the pew. "Have you changed your mind?" he asks. "Will you take my case?"

I shake my head. "Please, Dylan. I'm here to sing."

Luckily, he sings well enough to drown me out through five Broadway hits. When the break comes, however, he starts up again. "Raphael and his new boyfriend are saying terrible things about me, and it's a tight community, you know."

"Your best revenge is to move on, Dylan," I say, trying to push past him.

"What I need is closure," he says, scratching absentmindedly at a hive on his neck. It reminds me of how I felt after Eric cheated on me.

"If I say we'll think about it, will you leave me alone today?" I ask.

He clutches my arm and says, "Thank you. Thank you."

"That wasn't a yes," I say, slipping away. But hopefully it was enough to buy me some time to meet Addison and get her talking.

The crowd around Addison is tough to penetrate. Most of her fans are guys, because even in a demure dress and zero makeup, Addison is stunning.

"It's so nice to meet you," I say, when I finally get close enough. "I see your picture in the paper all the time. You and Willem make such a great couple. Does he sing too?"

"Oh, no," Addison says, smiling. "He's not into music. But he always comes to watch when I'm performing."

"That kind of support keeps couples together," I say. "My boyfriend's a saint too."

"Lucky us," she says.

I shrug. "Yeah, but between you and me, it's a burden sometimes. I don't even like to swear in front of him."

Addison laughs. "Come downstairs and you can swear all you like. We're having tea and sandwiches in the kitchen."

"Oh, I can't," I say. I really can't. I'd have to pass Dieter's room to get there.

"You should get to know everyone," Addison presses. "It's hard to sing in harmony when you're all strangers."

Reluctantly, I shadow her downstairs. Rushing past Dieter's room, I catch a glimpse of Kali, Syd, and Lauren. They've pulled their chairs into a tight circle, and judging by Dieter's raised eyebrows, there's a lot of sharing going on.

I grab a cup of tea and a cookie. "Your Dad seems so nice on TV," I say. "And he's a great governor."

Her smile tightens ever so slightly. "Yeah, he's all about the governing."

"Strict?" I ask.

"You have no idea." Now her smile disappears, and her long

elegant fingers fiddle with the gold chain that hangs around her neck.

"Well, I know all about family pressure," I say. "My family hates me." It's about the only true thing I've said so far.

"They don't hate you," she says.

Somehow, infuriatingly, my eyes water up. "They do."

"Well, that's just today," she says, offering me more tea. "At least you have your perfect boyfriend."

"Yeah, he's pretty amazing, but—"

"You have a boyfriend?" Dylan asks. He's popped up beside me, with a cookie in one hand and his sheet music in the other. "Then you must get how I feel about Raph."

I turn nervously to Addison, but another chorus member has grabbed her arm.

"You promised not to talk about this," I hiss, pulling Dylan a few paces away.

"But I can't think about anything else," he says. "I can't eat, I can't sleep. It's only when I'm singing that I forget for a while." His blue eyes swim for a moment. "Raphael needs to pay, Zahra. Help me get my self-respect back."

I can tell that Addison's conversation with the other choir member is coming to a close. If I don't make a move, I'll lose my chance.

"We'll do it," I say. Dylan comes forward to hug me, and I block him. "Under two conditions: You can't come anywhere near me in this church again, and you can't say a word about this to anyone. *Anyone.* Understood?"

Dylan disappears like the Cheshire cat, leaving only his huge smile behind.

"Sorry about that," I say, rejoining Addison. "Poor guy's

going through a rough patch with his boyfriend. Relationships can be tricky."

"They can," Addison agrees. "But yours is solid, isn't it?"

I hesitate for just a nanosecond. "Oh, sure. Though I'm not sure I deserve my guy. He's so sweet, you know. But sometimes I start wondering what it would be like to be with someone else. I guess that makes me a bad person."

"I don't know," she says. "Sticking it out with someone is tough, no matter how sweet they are."

"You and your boyfriend have been together a while, right?"

"Two years. And everyone thinks we're this perfect couple—especially my parents. I feel like I'm too young to be perfect. It's a lot of pressure."

"You *are* too young for all that pressure," I say. "How do you cope?"

Glancing around, she whispers, "When I need to blow off a little steam, I have Viper."

"Viper? Sounds dangerous."

"He is," Addison says.

I take a bite of my cookie and chew. "How would a nice choir girl like me ever meet a guy like that?"

Addison smiles. "You just need to know where to look."

chapter 24

Syd returns from the church with fresh pails of warm soapy water. "I still can't believe it," she says, putting one pail in front of me and another beside Kali in the St. Joe's parking lot. Dipping her brush into the water, she gets straight to work scrubbing a tarp. "Addison Mayfield, Austin's sweetheart and queen of her daddy's upcoming debutante ball, is screwing around on Willem with a guy named *Viper?*"

"Apparently," I say, putting the last of the wet harnesses to one side and rubbing my hands together to get the circulation going before starting in on the carabiners.

It's our punishment from Dieter for missing half a session last week. Apparently he wasn't so riveted by our animated discussions that he forgot to make another note in his black book. He's agreed to "let us off the hook," however, if we clean the equipment from a particularly muddy ropes course.

Willem was crushed when I told him what I learned from Addison, although he's still clinging to the hope that "Viper" is a fast car, or a fun-park ride. That means we have to forge ahead and collect the video evidence he needs before Valentine's Day and Addison's coming out party.

"So where do you find a poisonous snake in Austin?" Syd

says, stretching out a clean tarp to dry.

"That's the hitch," I say. "Vipers are most easily found in Hill Country—at all-night dance parties."

"Sound like fun," Syd says, cheering up immediately.

"But not as much fun as our slam on Raphael," Kali says, gaily waving a brush at Dieter, who's come out of the church to check on us. "Don't you love our business?"

.. ♥ ..

As we march down the sidewalk, I turn to Kali and continue my quiz. "One more time. Raphael's birthday is . . . ?"

"April ninth," she says. "He'll be eighteen."

"Favorite food?" I ask.

"Hamburgers. With mozzarella."

"Allergies?"

"Cats and tree bark."

"Family?"

"Single mom, two sisters, dad's a deadbeat, last seen in Iowa," Kali rattles off. "Z, relax. I've got it. Every shred of information we pulled from Dylan is all up here." She taps her temple. "He's hoping to study musical theater at NYU, rubs his nose when he's nervous, and his mom still calls him 'Nuddiepie.'"

"I think she's ready," I tell Syd, pulling the photos out of my bag and handing them to Kali. "Remember, keep this short and sweet. Don't get carried away."

"I've done a little acting before, Z," Kali says, putting away the photos and pulling out her brush and lip gloss. "I think I know what I'm doing."

"Kali, Raphael's gay," Syd says. "You don't have to reel him in."

"I still like to look good when I hit the stage," she says. In fact, she has played down her style today, with nerdy jeans, sneakers, and Brody's old checkered flannel jacket. But her hair is still fabulous.

When we reach the bistro, Kali and Syd hold back while I peer inside. "Target's serving a table at the back." I recognize Raphael's dark, chiseled looks in an instant. He takes an order from a couple of men about Dad's age, who are holding hands over the table. As Raphael turns, a tall, well-built blond waiter emerges from the kitchen and winks at him. "And there's Raphael's new guy, Loverboy."

"Let's do it," Kali says. Throwing back her head, she squeezes eyedrops into each eye. Then she flings open the door and makes her entrance. Syd and I follow, a few paces behind.

Marching straight up to Raphael, Kali demands, "How could you?" The fake tears stream down her face.

"Excuse me?" Raphael says. "Did I get your order wrong?"

"Are you trying to pretend you don't know me, Raphael Augustus Moneiro?" Kali says.

A few customers turn and stare.

Raphael looks around nervously and says, "I *don't* know you."

Kali unravels her scarf and throws it dramatically onto an empty table. "I should have known you'd try this." Rifling through her bag, she grabs the photographs I've been tinkering with all week in Photoshop. Up close, Syd's little cousin bears a pretty strong resemblance to Raphael. "Does this help jog your memory?" She waves a baby photo under his nose. "Or this?"

Loverboy steps in to get a look at the images.

Kali makes it easy for him. One by one, she slaps the photos down on the table beside her scarf. A shot of Raphael and Kali with the baby in the park. A shot of them in someone's living room. A shot of them in a nursery, with Raphael standing over a crib. "You bastard," she says, flopping into a chair.

One of Raphael's customers reaches over to pat her back reassuringly. "What happened, sweetie?"

Kali turns, thrilled at the opening. "This . . . this *deadbeat* left me all alone with a baby. I'm only seventeen and I'm trying to be a good mom, but it's so hard."

Loverboy is going through the pictures now. "What's going on?" he asks Raphael. "You never mentioned being with women—let alone having a kid."

"I've never seen this girl before in my life!" Raphael says, rubbing his nose.

"Oh, come on," I say, moving into position beside Kali. "She's the mother of your child. You can change teams, but you can't change *that*."

"I don't know you either," Raphael says, rubbing his nose harder. His eyes are wild and confused.

"Lucinda loves you," I say. "You can still come home and be a good father." I hold out another picture. "Little Raffie looks just like you."

"He *does* look like you," Loverboy says, looking from the picture to Raphael and back.

Kali wipes her eyes. "That one was taken on Raphael's birthday—April ninth. We had hamburgers with mozzarella, and we took the baby out to Mount Bonnell to watch the sunset." She smiles at the memory. "No matter what happens, that will always be our special spot."

Loverboy turns on Raphael. "You said that was *our* special spot."

"Then we put our little Nuddiepie to bed," Kali continues, "and watched *A Few Good Men*." She's on a roll now, spitting intimate details about Raphael's life. Loverboy continues to stare at Raphael as Kali goes in for the kill. "What I love most is just snuggling on the couch." She gives the sympathetic customer a sad smile. "Raphael has the cutest birthmark on his chest, in the shape of Italy."

"That's it." Loverboy rips off his apron and turns to leave. "We're done."

"Done?" Raphael says. "We can't be done. I've never met this girl, I swear."

"You've got *guilty* written all over you," Loverboy says, pointing to Raphael's nose. "If you rub that thing any harder, it's going to fall off."

Loverboy walks out of the bistro, and Raphael runs after him. "Please! You've got to believe me. That is not my kid."

With our mission accomplished, Kali, Syd, and I quickly gather our props.

"What's all the commotion?" a deep voice asks. "We're trying to rehearse."

It's Lady Luck, the drag queen we met outside while we were putting up posters of Miss Daisy. He's stepped through a thick red velvet curtain that separates the bistro from the nightclub behind.

"You," Lady Luck says, pointing at us with an empty cigarette holder. "You girls gave me a bum steer on that Charger. It absolutely reeked." He approaches the table. "I covered your butts once, but I am done with the charity work. What are you selling now?"

"Nothing," Kali says, stuffing the photos back into her purse. To the guys at the table she adds, "I tried to sell Raphael's car out from under him. I know it was wrong, but I was desperate."

One of the guys reaches out and takes her hand. "It's okay, sweetie."

Kali squeezes his hand. "It was for the baby. A mom does what she has to do."

The guy reaches for his wallet and takes out twenty bucks. "Here."

"No, I couldn't," Kali says, backing away. "Thank you so much, though."

The customer insists, and Kali takes the money just to make a break for it.

"Arnie," Lady Luck bellows. "We've got panhandlers in here again."

Six-feet-six in platform heels, Arnie charges out of the back room, his wig askew.

That's when we run like we've never run before.

Since it's the warmest January that Austin has seen in ten years, we hold our last meeting of the month at Café Mozart, sitting outside at the picnic tables.

"Dylan's going to be so disappointed we're missing the rehearsal this week," I say, tilting my face toward the sun.

He could not have been more thrilled with our slam on Raphael. The cheater actually had the nerve to go running back to Dylan after Loverboy dumped him. This time, however, Dylan stood firm. If only Hollis would be as strong.

"I'll miss it too," Kali says. "I would have liked to do the show."

If all goes as planned, we won't need to attend more rehearsals. This week we'll be going to group, on time and in full force.

"Speaking of happy customers, did you guys see the paper? Lily and Jason won their skating competition," I say, spooning the whipped cream from my hot chocolate into my mouth. "That kiss in the photo sure didn't look professional."

"I knew they were a good match," Kali says, booting up her laptop. "Stacey and Graham are still together too. And Trisha has had her second date with one of my match recruits from the mall, and a third is in the works. I still haven't found anyone for Luke, but I'm thinking Z's old friend Morgan might be a possibility."

Syd bites into her almond croissant and says, "Madison and Rambo have hit it off, too."

"Speaking of Madison," Kali says, "there's been something I've wanted to run past you." She clicks her mouse a few times and turns her laptop toward Syd.

"Compatibility file," Syd reads, "for Max Simpson and . . . Oh, no you don't." She pushes the computer back to Kali. "You want to set me up with Madison's brother?"

"Actually, *Max* wants me to set you up with him," Kali says. "I'm just the go-between."

Syd shakes her head. "I'm done with guys. In case you missed it, I got burned this year. I might be out of intensive care, but I'm still in recovery."

"According to early projections," Kali continues as if Syd hasn't spoken, "you and Max are sitting at eighty-four percent compatibility." She spins the laptop toward Syd again. "Look how cute he is. Plus, he's a dog lover and he wears vintage and he loves roller derby. What could be—" Kali has to raise her voice above the noise the birds are making in the trees. "I'm sorry, did you hear that?"

Above the familiar squawk of grackles, there's a screechy chatter.

Kali is the first one out of her seat, and we follow her across the deck.

"There!" Syd points to a clump of twigs at the bottom of a telephone pole just beyond the noisy tree.

I stare at the clump and see a flash of bright green. Another flash follows, and two Quaker parrots hop out of a hole and onto the telephone wire.

"There's more!" Kali points to three birds hopping around a second nest, on the next telephone pole. They fly over to join the first three on the wire.

"We found the wild parrots," Kali says, her eyes sparkling with wonder.

"Actually, they found us," I say, taking a picture with my phone.

"It's a sign," Kali says.

Syd hooks one arm over Kali's shoulder and the other over mine. "It's closure," she says, smiling. "Hand me the discharge papers."

chapter 25

"**A**re you *sure* he didn't hear us?" I ask Syd and Kali, who are sitting on either side of me in the backseat of the car. "It looked like he might have been loitering."

After group this afternoon, we hung back in the basement until the rehearsal ended so we wouldn't risk bumping into Addison. We ended up talking through some of the details of our plan for tonight's dance-party slam. When I got up to go to the bathroom, Dieter was at the end of the hall.

"Eavesdropping isn't Dieter's style," Kali says. "Confrontation is. And I haven't had any text messages. My mom would be on me so fast if he'd called."

"But we can't get reception out here," I say, peering out the window into the darkness of the hill country.

"If Dieter had heard us, we'd be swabbing dirty tarps right now," Syd says.

"I guess. I just have a bad feeling about this," I say.

A voice from the front seat says, "Quit your whining or my fee doubles."

It's Brody, riding shotgun beside Luke.

Kali whacks her brother in the back of the head with a map. "We're paying you to keep quiet."

Actually, we're paying for a ride. Glennis's car is in the shop, so Brody enlisted Luke to take us to the party. Having male backup makes me feel better about heading into a remote field in the middle of the night—even if I can't get along with one of the guys, and Kali can't get along with the other.

"There!" The headlamps illuminate the road in front of us, and Syd points out an orange rag tied to a tree. "The last marker."

Luke steers the car off Ranch Street onto a bumpy dirt road that winds around the back of Enchanted Rock State Park. "I can't believe I let you talk me into this. If I wreck the suspension on the car, my dad will kill me."

Kali grabs Luke's shoulder belt and jerks hard. "You agreed to take this job."

"I'm merely expressing concern for my dad's property. Thanks to you setting me up with that loose cannon I took to my cousin's wedding, I'm in enough trouble with my family already."

Kali flops back in her seat and snorts. "Brody, could you change the CD? This one is stuck."

·· ♥ ··

By the time we find a place to park and follow the noise to a clearing, a crowd has already gathered. On the far side of the open space is a huge pickup truck with a long, low platform hitched to it. Behind this makeshift stage, two white cube trucks are parked lengthwise. Random images project onto the side of the trucks like movie screens as the screamo band onstage whips the crowd into a frenzy.

Inside the last cube, a DJ dances among his turntables and

computers, pausing every once in a while to feed some new images through the projector that's hooked up to a laptop. Outside of his truck, a tangle of cables run into the woods beyond, where I assume they connect to generators. There are torches and twinkle lights, but the full moon overhead is bright enough to light the clearing all on its own.

"This is so cool," Kali says, twirling to take it all in. "There must be at least five hundred people here."

"We'll have to divide and conquer," Syd says, taking charge. She hands a walkie-talkie to Kali and another to me. "Brody, you stick with Zahra, and Luke you're with Kali. I'll be fine on my own."

Kali and I glare at her, but neither of us wants to give the guys the satisfaction of complaining. This is business. We can get along for a couple of hours.

Tuning in to channel three, I hear Syd's voice come over my radio. "Test, test."

Syd is the model of efficiency as she outlines the rest of the plan. Brody and I are to cover the stage and DJ area, while Kali and Luke cover the dance floor. Syd will scope out the perimeter, ready to rush in with the video camera when someone locates Addison.

We split up, and Brody leads the way to the stage. "How come Ri-ass couldn't come along to serve and protect tonight?" he asks. "Did he need to rest his delicate pre-pre-med hands?"

"Riaz got traded," I say, peering around for Addison. "Not that it's any of your business."

Brody raises his eyebrows. "I didn't realize there was a new player in town. What's his name?"

"Doesn't matter," I say. "He's history too."

The smug smile is back. "Don't tell me perfect Zahra got caught double-dipping?"

"No," I say. "Unlike you and your model friend, Juliette, I don't need the thrill of deception." It still bugs me that Brody would fool around with a girl he knows is taken. He should be better than that; he's Kali's brother.

"You really think you've got me pegged, don't you?" Brody's green eyes flash with anger.

"Whatever." I have to shout the word because we're close to the stage now and the music is deafening. The lead singer is screeching into the microphone.

Brody circles around in front of me so that I can't ignore him. "All I did was take Juliette's picture for her portfolio. She hit me up at a football game when I was photographing her boyfriend. I had Mom's camera, so she thought I was a pro."

"She hit *on* you too. I saw you in the trailer, remember?"

"Yeah, and you just assumed I'd go for it, because you're expecting the worst from me."

The news that Brody isn't with Juliette ignites fireworks inside. I realize now that he's a good guy that came into my life at a bad time, right after I found out about Eric. From the moment Brody offered me that carton of chocolate milk, all cute and cocky, I transferred my anger about guys onto him and haven't been able to let it go. It was stupid. Hating him has wasted a lot of energy.

I send out a peace offering. "Ben's glad to have her back anyway."

Brody accepts it. "He's a control freak. They'll never make it."

"They'll make it," I shout. "I know more about relationships than you do."

"Ya think?"

"I've studied enough of them," I say, smiling. "I'm practically an expert."

"In *theory.*"

"For now," I say. "One of these days I'll be applying everything I know."

"Lord help the guy," Brody says. But he takes my hand and leads me through the crowd to the front of the stage, where I finally spot Addison dancing with some girlfriends. She's barely recognizable in a short suede skirt, fishnet stockings, and a sequined halter top under a fake-fur bomber jacket.

Seeing me, Addison breaks away from her friends and comes over. Her hair is flowing around her shoulders, and when she gets close enough, I notice she's wearing fake lashes and heavy eyeliner. Leaning over, she yells into my ear: "Is this your boyfriend?"

I shake my head and grin. "We just met."

"You work fast." Checking Brody out, she says, "Nice."

"Thanks. So where's Viper?"

Addison points to the lead singer, who's licking the microphone with his pierced tongue. Despite the chill in the air, he's in a short-sleeved T-shirt that reveals two large snake tattoos that wind around each arm. His dirty blond hair is swept forward from the crown in an emo-type shag.

Addison waves at Viper, and I notice a pretty ring on the fourth finger of her left hand. When I comment on it, she takes it off and slips it into her pocket.

"That's my promise ring from Willem," she says. "I think

he's going to replace it with his grandmother's diamond on Valentine's Day."

"You're going to marry Willem?" I ask, fighting to strip the judgment out of my voice.

"Sure, eventually," she says, shrugging. "Our families expect it. With our combined connections, we'll practically rule the state."

"But you love him, right?"

"Willem's a great guy, we look good together, and he treats me like a princess," she says. "There's no spark, but that doesn't really matter." She sighs, and then grins. "Because Vipers aren't that hard to find."

If I had doubts about bringing this girl down, I don't anymore.

After inviting us to hang with Viper and her in the parking area after the set, Addison goes back to dancing with her friends.

Brody and I circle behind the stage, where it's a little quieter, and I walkie the others to let them know we've found Addison. Syd joins us almost immediately, followed a few minutes later by Kali and Luke, both of whom are carrying bulging plastic garbage bags. "Recycling," Kali explains. "You wouldn't believe the number of people who put water bottles in the trash."

"We're going to talk to the organizers about providing water stations for the next event," Luke says.

"By the way, we bumped into Max," Kali says to Syd, while Brody helps Luke take the recycling to the car. "Madison's brother."

I glare at Kali. I can't believe she's cramming in a

little matchmaking on the night of our biggest gig. "What a coincidence," I say.

Kali's smile is all innocence. "Isn't it?" Syd is scowling at her, but Kali waves Max over anyway. "Well, it would be rude not to say hello."

Max looks super cool tonight. His hair is all spiked up, and he's wearing a long vintage police coat. "Hey," he says, smiling at Syd.

"Hey," Syd says. She fights to hold on to her scowl, but it fades quickly.

Kali pulls me aside to give them a little privacy. "Guess what?" she says. "Caleb and I have gone out three times, and I still like him. It's a miracle, right?"

"Not really," I say. "He's built like Owen Gaines."

The real miracle is taking place beside us, where Syd is actually giggling. She enters her number into Max's phone, before he heads back into the crowd.

"What?" she says, joining us. "I agreed to help Max keep score at Madison's Valentine's Day exhibition match. It's no big deal. Understood?"

"Understood," I say.

"Syd's got a boyfriend!" Kali shouts to Brody when he comes back from the car with Luke.

When the band launches into the last song of their set, we get back to business. Syd double-checks the battery power on her video camera, plugs an earpiece into her walkie-talkie, and repeats the plan. I'm to put my walkie in my coat pocket and keep it turned on. When Addison's in position with Viper, all I have to do is hit the talk button a couple of times. The static will alert Syd to come with the camera. Kali and Luke need to be ready to create a diversion while Syd records.

Syd delivers a last warning. "Don't forget to turn off your walkie after you signal us, Z. Otherwise, Addison will hear voices coming out of your pocket if Kali and I need to communicate, and we're dead. The code word for trouble is *coyote*."

"Press several times for static. Turn it off. *Coyote* means trouble," I say. "Got it."

As we're about to split up again, someone calls my name. I turn to see Angel, the boxer. "Hey, Angel," I say, trying to be friendly, although we're in the middle of our biggest sting ever.

"You look great," he says, hugging me.

"Thanks." I break the hug as soon as I can without being rude. Angel looks amazing in a fitted sweater that shows off his hard-earned physique. I glance around and see that the only one *not* checking him out is Luke.

"You never said you were into Jack Spit," Angel says.

That must be Viper's band. "Recent convert."

"Lucky for me," he replies. "I didn't think I'd see you again."

Brody touches my arm. "We'd better get going."

Angel catches the gruff tone. "Hey, dude, I'm sorry. Zahra didn't mention a boyfriend."

"I'm not her boyfriend," Brody says, too quickly and forcefully for someone who was holding my hand ten minutes ago.

Waving to Angel, I say, "We're all meeting some friends. It was nice to see you, though."

Brody and I break away from the others as Jack Spit finishes its set and the DJ takes the stage to introduce the next band.

"Can you slow down?" I ask, as we head into the field that serves as a parking lot. "What's wrong with you?"

"For a girl who hates guys, you seem to lead a lot of them on."

"I do not hate guys," I say. "And I don't lead them on."

"Right. Unless you have to for a case."

His comment takes me aback. I'd never really thought about it that way before. "Then it's business," I say, worried now that Brody might see me as a man-eating insect, like Andrew did. "That's different."

"Yeah, well, how does someone know where the acting ends and the real Zahra begins?"

"I guess someone would have to ask," I say. "In Crazy Class we call it *communication*."

Brody ignores this, but he slows down as we weave our way through the cars and trucks until we spot Addison. She's sitting with Viper on the tailgate of a truck.

Before we reach them, I haul on Brody's sleeve until he finally turns. "Whatever's bugging you, save it until we're done," I say. "Right now, *you're* getting paid to act too."

Brody slides an arm around my shoulder. "You'll get your money's worth."

We join the group, and Addison introduces us to Viper and the rest of the band.

Viper bends over a cooler and hands us a couple of beers.

I crack open the can and take a sip. It's just as bitter and horrible as I expected, but I smile. "A cold beer on a beautiful night—what more could you want?"

"Just a beautiful girl," Brody says, pulling me closer.

"Hear, hear," Viper says. He taps his can against Brody's and wraps an arm around Addison. One of his rings is like armor, covering his finger from base to tip.

Reaching out with her beer can, Addison touches mine and whispers, "To blowing off steam."

Brody compliments Viper on the band's set, and Viper shares his plan to drop out of school and tour Czechoslovakia, where Jack Spit has a big Internet following.

"Poor Addison," I say. "You'll be left all alone." With just one boyfriend, the devoted Willem.

"I know," she says, kissing Viper on the cheek. "Poor me."

Viper leans over and nuzzles her neck.

Deciding the time is right, I reach into my pocket and press the button on the walkie-talkie a few times.

Brody whispers, "Let's show them how it's done."

Leaning over, he kisses me, letting his hand slide down my back to pull me closer. It feels so good that I take my hand out of my pocket and put it on the back of his neck. He kisses me again, and the soles of my sneakers seem to fuse with the rocky soil. I open my eyes and see the stars and the moon overhead and forget where I am for a moment. This is the best kiss ever. It makes all the kisses I've had before seem ordinary. Mediocre. This is what Brody was talking about before. No one should settle for less than this.

It could be two minutes or ten before Brody finally stops for breath. "Wow," he says.

"Yeah," I say. "Not acting. In case you were wondering."

"Thanks for communicating," he says.

We grin at each other for another few seconds before I suddenly remember our mission, and glance over his shoulder. Viper has pulled Addison right onto his lap and they're going at it hard. Off to our right, I see Syd's head between the parked trucks. She has the camera trained on Addison and Viper. When they finally come up for air, Syd gives me the thumbs-up and slips out of sight.

"Thanks for the beer," I say to Addison and Viper. "I think we're going to find somewhere a little more private."

We rendezvous with the others and watch over Syd's shoulder while she replays the footage. "Phase one complete," Syd says, handing me her phone. "Call Willem and fill him in. I managed to get a cell signal near the Porta-Potties."

Despite the noise and distractions, I try to break the bad news tactfully, but Willem is beside himself. After a string of curses, he takes a deep breath. "You have the evidence?"

"It's all on video."

He's silent for so long that I worry the call has dropped. Finally, in a steely voice, he asks me if there's any video playing at the party. I tell him about the film clips they're showing against the trucks behind the stage.

"Put up the footage of Addison," he says.

"What? No, Willem, you don't really want to do that. This is personal."

"Do it," Willem says, "and I will double your bonus."

That's a total of two hundred dollars each, on top of the seven he's already owes us. I'm not sure Syd and Kali would appreciate it, but I argue anyway. "Her father—"

Willem cuts me off. "—is hosting a party next week to debut fifty of Austin's purest. Do you really think their role model should be Addison? Just put up the video, Zahra." His voice cracks. "I mean it."

I return to tell my friends what happened.

Kali nods. "He wants to lash out because he feels so helpless."

"What the hell," Syd says. "We've come this far. If that's what the guy wants, we should give it to him. We don't owe Addison any favors. But Kali, you're going to have to do some more acting to get us onto that DJ's truck."

Kali doesn't respond. Her eyes are glued to the stage, where a familiar, angular figure is standing at a microphone in front of the Austin High jazz band. "This is the gig Hollis was talking about at Blue Velvet," she says.

The band launches into a loungey trip-hop cover of an old jazz standard, and Hollis sways to the beat. She's wearing a long silver dress with a higher neckline than the one we liked. The gloves are gone, but the rhinestone bracelet made the cut. As Hollis starts to sing, a backlight comes up and shines through the thin material of her dress, outlining her legs. It's a sexy effect, and the crowd cheers.

To our surprise, Hollis is actually pretty good. Behind her, images from old black-and-white movies flicker across the cube trucks. A few people start waving cell phones and lighters.

"I don't see Fletcher, so Hollis must have chewed through her leash tonight," Syd says. "I'd love to stay and watch, but we have work to do."

Outside the DJ trailer, Kali takes off her pea coat and turns on her charm to lure the DJ away from his post. Once they're deep in a conversation about music, Syd and I sneak past them to figure out how to project the images of Addison with Viper.

The program to run the projection is open on the laptop, so it only takes a few seconds to download the footage from Syd's memory card. I'm about to hit ENTER when a horrible wailing rises over Hollis and the jazz band.

We peer out of the truck and see Fletcher staggering around on the stage behind Hollis, wearing long white gloves and a tiara. Drunk, he starts gyrating behind his girlfriend. She tries hard to finish her piece, but Fletcher keeps leaning into the mike to mimic her.

Half the Austin High football team has gathered in front of the stage, and they cheer Fletch on. It's all the encouragement he needs to pull off his shirt and twirl it over his head. Laughter ripples through the crowd as he begins to stomp around Hollis in an over-the-top striptease. Layer after layer of clothing falls at Hollis's feet as the audience chants, "Go Fletch! Go Fletch." Finally, Hollis gives up and stands frozen and silent at the microphone, a humiliated prop for a drunk guy in boxer shorts.

"I'm seriously sorry we didn't take his ass down," Syd says.

Watching Hollis wipe tears away, I say, "We still have the chance." I pull my iTouch out of my bag and remind Syd what's on it.

"Let's do it," she says.

I wave the iTouch at Kali, and she simply nods.

Syd pulls the memory card out of the laptop and jams it back into the camera while I connect my iTouch and download the video of Fletcher tampering with the other players' equipment.

"I think I can play both clips in a loop," I whisper to Syd.

I manage to bring up the Fletcher video into a preview screen. I'm working to try to attach the downloaded clip of Addison and Viper, when someone yells, "Coyote!" It's Luke's voice and it's coming from my pocket.

The DJ turns and sees me messing with his equipment. "Hey! What are you doing?"

"Sorry, just admiring your setup." I give up on trying to attach the footage of Addison and quickly initialize Fletcher's clip before we push past the DJ and leave the truck. As I climb off, I see the DJ examining his laptop to figure out what I've done.

Outside the truck, Luke gestures toward Brody, who's distracting Addison and Viper as the band gathers for its second set. We're trying to get Brody's attention when the DJ sticks his head out the back.

"Viper!" he shouts. "They downloaded video of you and your girl on my laptop."

Meanwhile, the crowd jeers and then boos as people recognize Fletcher in a more sinister role. Since the show's going on behind him, it might take the drunken star himself a little longer to clue in.

Addison sprints past us and into the DJ's truck to see what's cued up on the computer. "They set us up," she says. "Do *not* play that video." Then she turns to Viper. "Get that camera!"

Instantly, the band members surround us, and the drummer snatches the camera right out of Syd's hands. Brody sneaks up behind him, grabs the camera, and tosses it to me.

"Run!" Luke yells.

We all take off with Viper and his band hot on our heels. Fortunately, their tight leather clothing slows them down, and we manage to put a little distance between them and us. We're almost at the parking lot when I see Fletcher running toward us in his boxer shorts. He appears to have sobered up quickly, and his eyebrows shoot up when he sees us. In that second,

I know he's figured out who's behind the film loop. But there isn't a lot he can do about it with the football team in pursuit.

Luke manages to pull the keys out of his pocket while he runs, and unlocks the car remotely. For a moment I think we're going to make it, but then the drummer kicks the camera out of my hand. An army boot lands on it with a mighty crunch.

Meanwhile, a big pickup truck rolls in front of Luke's car, blocking our exit completely. We don't stand much of a chance against this mob.

Parking lot partiers gather to gawk. "Fight!" someone says, and the word echoes through the crowd. Nearby, a motorcycle engine revs and a single headlight is coming straight at us. Other vehicles appear out of nowhere, blinding us with their high beams. All around me, people scatter.

"It's the cops!" someone yells, and the word carries. "Cops! Cops!"

Suddenly the crowd is moving. One minute I'm holding Brody's hand, and the next I'm swept away in a mass of people fleeing into the dance area. Running hard, I search for a familiar face, but I can only see silhouettes in the glare. As I try to work my way sideways to the edge of the crowd, I'm hit hard from behind.

It seems as if I'm falling in slow motion, arms flailing, but when I hit the ground, it's in real time, and it hurts. For a second, I lie on my back staring up at the stars. Then a dark shape blocks the moon as someone leaps over me. There's a sharp pain in my side as someone else kicks me. I catch a fleeting glimpse of boxer shorts in retreat as I roll onto my side.

Then I curl up and moan.

chapter 26

Standing on the steps of the trailer, Syd trains her binoculars on Kali's kitchen window. "I never thought I'd see my parents in the same room again," she says.

"Except for at your wedding to Max," Kali suggests, hovering behind her.

Syd casts a withering look at me over her shoulder. "Or my funeral."

"No one died," I say.

Kali and Syd ignore me, just as they ignored everything I said on the way back from Hill Country in the paddy wagon, a.k.a. Dad's van. Admittedly, I couldn't say much, lest it be used against me in the Court of Parents. But even now that we're alone in the trailer, awaiting the outcome of our trial, they're freezing me out.

"I can't believe you took off when our parents came," Syd says, lowering her binoculars.

"I got *carried off* by the crowd." I yank up my T-shirt and show them the massive bruise forming on my side where I got kicked. "It wasn't a choice."

"Ouch," Kali says.

"It's Fletcher's shoe size," I say. "I'm lucky Angel found me and helped me back."

Syd steps inside to collect a couple cans of cold soda, and I hold them against my shirt. "It's late and I guess we're all overreacting," she says, by way of an apology as she returns to her surveillance post on the steps.

"They're all talking at once," she reports. "Wait. Now Dieter's clapping—one-two-three. He's firing off three more because they won't shut up. Okay, they're settling down. Except for my mom. She's yelling at Charlotte. . . . Ha! Charlotte's starting to cry." Syd smiles, but it only lasts a second. "Oh God, Dad's hugging the crybaby. . . . Now Glennis is pouring Mom another glass of wine . . . and Zahra's dad has taken the floor."

"Well, he'll keep it short," I say. "Dad isn't much of a talker."

Syd lowers the binoculars and steps inside again. "Can you believe it? My parents can't spare a minute for me, but call a midnight meeting and they're both available. Dad even brought a date."

"At least he didn't bring your boss," I say. René was having dinner with Glennis when the all-points bulletin went out, and got pulled into the action because he has wheels. My bad feeling about Dieter was justified. He was eavesdropping on us in the hall, and he ratted us out, starting with Glennis. When she couldn't reach Kali, she tried my dad, since Kali had told her she was spending the night with me. Meanwhile, I'd told Dad I was spending the night at Kali's. So then Glennis called Syd's mom and got the same story. That's when she raided the trailer and found directions to the party.

Another round of calls brought the rescue posse together. Dieter led the charge on his motorbike, with three minivans full of irate parents in the rear. Their sudden convergence on the parking lot sparked the panic, although it must have been another ten minutes before the cops really did arrive. We passed them on the highway.

Now we're being held without questioning. Brody rode back with Luke and hasn't been heard from since. The only good news is that Addison and Viper disappeared with their bodyguards before our parents could talk to them, and we're pretty sure Addison will keep her mouth shut because of her dad's reputation, if not her own. Fletcher probably won't say anything either, after his teammates are done with him. He won't want to admit three girls are responsible for his downfall. But that won't stop him from plotting his revenge.

We're in pretty deep with our parents. They won't have any trouble piecing together a long list of rules we've broken, and clearly no one is willing to let us make a case for all the good work we've done—the relationships we've saved, the lives we've improved.

I pick up the binoculars and watch Dad pacing around Glennis's marble-topped island. For once he's in a mood to talk. "It's not fair," I say.

"It doesn't matter," Syd says. "We lost the evidence to our highest profile case. That totally undermines our credibility anyway."

Syd throws herself down on the bench, gathering pillows in her arms. "Willem will never pay us now. So how am I going to pay for Dad's video camera? It cost about a grand, and he doesn't even know I've been borrowing it."

"I'll pay for it," I say. "I'm the one who forgot to turn off my walkie, which tipped off the DJ."

"Making out with Brody wiped your memory clean," Kali says, grinning.

"It was just acting," I say. "Addison and Viper were mostly just talking, so Brody decided to plant the idea. It worked, too."

"It didn't look like acting to me," Syd says.

Okay, it wasn't acting for me. But if it meant anything to Brody, where is he now? Surely he isn't mad about Angel, who just happened to be in the right place at the right time to rescue me. Brody let me get carried off in the crowd and booted by strangers. I guess we didn't pay him enough to take the hits for us.

"I'm not into Brody." Maybe saying it out loud will make it true. I am not getting involved with a guy who doesn't stand by me when the chips are down.

"Sure you are," Kali says, picking up the binoculars to see what's going on in the house. "You just don't know what it feels like anymore. Oops." She quickly lowers the binoculars again and stuffs them into an overhead cupboard. "Looks like showtime. Remember, our only hope now is damage control, so we've got to pull together. If the jury senses we're rattled, we'll be grounded till college."

"That's right," I say. "We need to show some remorse, while subtly reminding them that it's their fault for screwing us up in the first place. Would we even be here if it weren't for them?"

"No, we would not," Syd says, sitting up. "So forget subtlety."

"Here they come," I say, sliding into the banquette beside Kali.

Glennis is the first to enter the little trailer, followed by my parents, and then Syd's. Charlotte insists on crowding in behind them but can't get past the doorway. René and Dieter have the decency to stay behind in the house.

My dad has obviously been elected jury foreman, because he's the first to speak. "Zahra, I don't know where to start. The sneaking around, the lying, the drinking . . . You've put yourself in so many dangerous situations."

I choose the one area I can refute. "Dad, I only had a few sips of beer and I hated it. I don't know how you drink so much of the stuff."

Dad's face turns an ugly mottled shade. Mom almost smirks, but recovers enough to say, "Zahra."

Glennis can't wait for her turn. "Kali, I am so disappointed in you. I thought you'd matured a lot these past few months, and now I find your judgment is dubious at best."

"*My* daughter never had any," Syd's dad says. I don't know what I was expecting, but not this handsome, silver-haired man with a chiseled jaw and a mean streak.

I wait for Syd to fight back, but she doesn't. Fortunately, Violet steps in. "Brad, she hasn't had much of a role model."

He scowls at her. "That's for sure."

Violet turns the scowl on Charlotte. "And it's going downhill from here."

"Stop," Syd finally whispers. "You're embarrassing me."

"Embarrassing *you?*" Brad says. "How do you think this makes me look in front of Charlotte? Why would she want to marry into this family?"

"Marry?" Violet gasps. "I don't recall signing any divorce papers."

Charlotte reaches from the doorway to Brad. "Oh, honey, you know I can't wait to marry you. I don't care how crazy y'all are." She crushes Glennis and my mom into the walls and leans over to hug what she can grab of Syd, which isn't much. "Don't be too hard on your little girl. I was even wilder at her age."

"And look how *that* turned out," Violet says.

If I didn't feel so bad for Syd, I'd be laughing at my parents' stunned expressions. I'm tempted to let it get worse, but then I see Syd's hand reach under the table for Banksy, who's still at the vet. I have to move things along.

"We've been through a tough time lately," I remind them.

Dad shakes his head to get himself back on track, but decides to skip the rest of his lecture. "You girls are lucky we've decided to be lenient. Your business is officially closed and you're all grounded for a month."

"That's lenient?" I ask. "What are we supposed to tell all the people who need our help?"

"That's your problem," Dad says. "You've got half an hour to sort everything out here. René's offered to drive you home."

Verdict delivered, my parents slip out the door. Glennis follows, and I hear her ordering bath products from Mom. At least someone's profiting from this.

Syd notices Charlotte's hand, and says, "Is that an engagement ring?"

Holding it out, Charlotte beams. "Isn't is gorgeous? Two full carats."

Syd's eyes are swimming when she looks up at her father. "You drain my college fund, you couldn't spare a dime for Banksy, but you could afford two carats for Charlotte?"

He brushes this off. "We're engaged, Sydney. It's a symbol."

She throws the only thing she can at him—a pillow. "My

friends raised five thousand dollars for me. *That's* a symbol."

Brad grabs Charlotte's left hand and leads her out the door. "One day you'll understand, Sydney. People come before pets."

Violet pats Syd's shoulder. "Don't worry about him, sweetie. It's a midlife crisis and it will pass. I hope." Stepping to the door, she says, "Can you catch a ride with Zahra? I'm going to run home."

"Run? It's the middle of the night, Mom."

"I know, but I've got to get in shape. If I can't get your father back, I'll make him regret losing me."

"You don't want him back," Syd says.

But Violet is already gone, jogging off into the night.

Kali offers up her own brand of comfort. "I bet if I found someone great for your mom she'd turn back into Jennifer again."

Syd shakes her head. "I'm stuck with Violet until she gets her head on straight. No one else can do that for her."

"Besides, Love, Inc.'s out of business, remember?" I say.

"The way I see it is that it's only a *business* if money changes hands," Kali says. "It doesn't mean I can't bring a few people together on the side."

I can't help smiling. Kali loves her work so much she'll do it for free. I plan to put my efforts into the Sweet Tooth instead. I'll start by signing up for that pastry course and take it from there. "We're still going to be friends, right?"

"Friends?" Syd says. "We're framily." Kali comes at her with outstretched arms, and Syd raises her hands. "That doesn't give you hugging rights."

·· ♥ ··

I'm surprised to see Mom sitting on the couch when I get to Dad's apartment. They're drinking tea and talking, something I haven't witnessed in months.

Unfortunately, they're talking about me. I try to sneak past, but Mom stops me with a "Zahra." This one means, "We aren't done with you yet."

"What?"

"We sent you for counseling so that you could learn coping skills from a licensed therapist. How did that translate into opening up your own therapy business?"

"Entrepreneurship runs in the family," I say. "Besides, I've helped a lot of people with their problems. The whole business grew from satisfied customers recommending us to others."

"We'd make you return every penny if you hadn't donated all of your profits to Sydney's dog," Dad says.

I flop into a chair. "See? Love, Inc. made me a nicer person."

"Don't push it," Dad says. "Four hours ago, we picked you up from an illegal all-night party in the middle of nowhere, with boys we don't know. Some of those thugs scared *me*."

"You've gotta get out more, Dad. You used to love concerts."

"Zahra," Mom says, "this is no time for jokes."

For a couple that can't live together, they sure remember how to sing the old duets.

Mom continues. "What really hurts is that you've been lying to us about where you've been spending your time and what you've been doing."

"I didn't lie," I say. At least not often. "I told you I was with Syd and Kali. Maybe I left out the details, but you didn't care enough to ask." My voice wobbles, and I fight hard to steady it.

"You think you're the only ones going through a tough time."

My parents look at each other, and I can see I've struck a chord.

"Zahra," Dad says, "maybe we have been caught up in our own concerns, but that doesn't let you off the hook. You girls were getting paid to take revenge on people you'd never even met."

Mom nods. "Did you think about the example you're setting for your sister?"

For the first time, I feel slightly ashamed. I know how my sister copies me. "We only took the job if people deserved it."

"You're not in a position to make that judgment," Dad says.

"If it makes you feel any better," I say, "*my* role was mostly to help people to get along better."

"And what qualifies you to do that?" Mom asks.

"Lots of practice." I'm too tired now to be tactful. "I tried running interference between you guys for years before you split."

Dad looks surprised. "If that were true, you'd know that it takes more than a quick chat to get people back on track."

"Talking usually works. You'd know that if you'd gotten counseling yourselves, instead of sending *me* into therapy. I tell my clients to listen to each other instead of tuning out." Realizing that I'm on the verge of shouting, I take a deep breath, and glare at Mom. "Plus, I tell them not to jump right into another relationship."

"I haven't," Mom says. "Your uncle saw me kissing Xavier good-bye. I was thanking him for his work. But I wasn't ready for the relationship he wanted."

Dad gives me a sheepish look over his teacup. "I'm sorry

for taking out my frustrations on you, Zahra—and I should have apologized a lot sooner."

He picks up a folder from the table and presents it to Mom. "This is a joint effort."

I lean over her shoulder and see that my rough work for the Yasin Valley line that I "accidentally" left open on the kitchen table has evolved into a gorgeous, professional design. Watery ripples of turquoise and aqua spread out from the center of the page as if a single drop of water had just hit the surface and the paper were liquid. The words YASIN VALLEY appear at the bottom of the page in a simple blue font. The effect is contemporary, clean, and calming.

"Perfect," she whispers. "How did you know?"

Dad smiles at her. "I know *you*." He reaches out to take her hand, and Mom doesn't pull away.

Within seconds they're so engrossed in a discussion of cardboard weights and recycled paper that I can slip out unnoticed. It's not exactly romantic, but it's the first time in ages they've had a pleasant conversation.

So maybe Mediator Girl isn't a total waste of space after all.

·· ♥ ··

Our meeting room in the church basement has never looked better. Kali asked Dieter if we could turn our last session into a graduation party, since our grounding means we have to miss the event of the season. It's Hollis's annual Valentine's Day bash on Saturday, and much to our surprise, we all found invitations in our lockers. Fletcher, apparently, did not. Another blow after being kicked off the Maroons—permanently.

With Lauren's help, Kali brought in fresh flowers, balloons, and an iPod docking station. Syd made the HAPPY GRADUATION banner that stretches across one wall. Beneath it is a long table covered in food everyone brought. The only reminder of our therapy sessions is the pile of folding chairs in the corner.

Dieter opens his final sessions to friends and family to prove that we have a support system—or should. It's a bold move with our group, but for the moment, everyone appears to be behaving themselves.

Despite the fact that her dad brought Charlotte, Syd is smiling. That's because Banksy's leash is back in her hand, where it belongs. Other than a couple of shaved patches and the bulge on the side of his neck where the pulse generator for the pacemaker sits, Banksy's his old self. "I almost didn't recognize you, Z," Syd says. "That's some outfit."

I spin to let my friends appreciate the splendor of my royal blue silk sari. The material wraps around my waist several times, is gathered at the front, and then swoops up and over my left shoulder. "It's a gift from Nani," I say. "Check out the embroidery."

Kali and Syd lean in to examine the tiny gold thistles, a nod to my Scottish roots.

Across the room, Nani gives me a little smile before returning to her conversation with Syd's dad, who's working his way through a large serving of her curry. Nana is doing his part by keeping Violet entertained.

"I thought you and your grandparents were still at war," Syd says.

"Mom mediated a settlement," I say. "She showed Nani my Social Studies paper. I got an A+ on it, and I guess it got Nani thinking about our situation, and how she doesn't want to be as judgmental as her father was. So she had a talk with Nana and then they apologized, and I apologized, and here I am, wrapped up in a sari." I look over at my sister, who's wearing a regular salwar kameez. "Saliyah's so jealous."

"So all's well that ends well," Kali says.

"I haven't told you the best part yet," I reply. "Nani and Nana are moving back to Pakistan! But they're going to visit regularly, so it's the best of both worlds. Nana and Dad had a man-to-man chat, and I guess they sorted things out. Plus, Dad says he's fully open to whatever my mom wants to do about getting back to her roots."

It's too early to say whether Dad and I will be moving back home, but it looks promising. My parents have spoken every day since Love, Inc. got busted, and not just about Saliyah and me. Dad's been helping Mom get her products on the shelves in time for spring promotions. They even had dinner at Mama Fu's to discuss marketing strategies. An early dinner—they don't trust me on my own for long yet.

"With any luck they'll soon be embarrassing you as much as Glennis and René are embarrassing me right now," Kali says, tilting her head toward the buffet table, where René is feeding Glennis a spoonful of his classic chocolate mousse.

"They do make a great couple," I say.

"Speaking of great couples," Kali says, "I'm having Caleb over for dinner, which you'll be catering, Z. You owe me for matching you up with Brody."

"It's not a match if we aren't together," I say. "But I'll make your dinner anyway."

Violet joins us, wearing a long, formfitting skirt with platform shoes and a low-cut blouse. "Excuse me, girls, do you know that gentleman?" The man she points to bears a resemblance to Simon.

"I think he's single," Kali says. "Do you want me to see what I can do?"

Violet declines. "You're out of business, sweetie. I'll handle this one myself."

"I can't watch," Syd says, turning away.

I pull Kali and Syd into a corner. "I have something for you." I pull two envelopes out of my purse. "Keep a straight face."

They gape anyway as they peek inside. "How much is in here?" Kali asks.

"A lot," I tell her. "Syd's is double because I put in my share. It's my first deposit toward replacing your dad's video camera."

"Did you rob a bank?" Kali asks.

"I gave Willem the footage of Addison and Viper, and he paid in full. Bonus and all."

"But how?" Kali asks. "The camera was totaled."

"*After* I pulled out the memory card," I say. "I ejected it while we were running to the car, but I didn't want to say so in case it got wrecked when I fell. It broke Willem's heart, but now he can save his grandmother's ring for someone who deserves it."

Kali hugs me. "Z, you're a genius!"

"Impressive save," Syd agrees. "But why did he pay the bonus when we didn't come through with showing the video?"

"A lucky break," I say. Minutes after telling me to air the clip, Willem started to regret it. Although he was hurt and furious with Addison, he decided he didn't want to go that route.

Unfortunately, he couldn't reach any of us by phone. When I told him what happened, he was relieved.

"My only worry is that the DJ could use that footage," Syd says, "since it did get downloaded onto his laptop."

"It's all good," I say. "Addison told Willem that she deleted it."

"You shouldn't have to pay for Dad's camera," Syd says. "Equipment destroyed on a Love, Inc. mission is a company responsibility."

"We'll settle up later when there aren't so many eyes on us," Kali says.

I take another envelope out of my bag. "Here's the money we owe Luke and Brody."

Kali puts her hands behind her back. "Deliver it yourself. Now's as good a time as any. He hasn't taken his eyes off you since he got here."

Brody catches us staring, but continues his conversation with Saliyah. As usual, she's managed to corner the cutest guy in the room. In a couple of years she's going to be a handful, if she doesn't find a better role model than me.

Three sharp claps draw our eyes to the front of the room. "As I tell my participants," Dieter begins, "group therapy is a journey of hard work and self-discovery. But leading that journey is a learning experience for me too. This group has been particularly enlightening. I discovered that a lot of support was taking place outside this room. Certain participants probably helped each other more than I could help them."

Kali, Syd, and I look at each other nervously. What is he up to?

"Friendship and support are essential for change," Dieter

continues. "Twenty years ago, my life was coming off the rails. If it hadn't been for Father Casey's kindness, I'm not sure where I'd be today."

Father Casey waves away his thanks. "He's repaid me a hundred times."

"So I had an idea for improving my program," Dieter says. "From now on, all my sessions will use the pay-it-forward model. Kali, Zahra, and Sydney have graciously agreed to be the first volunteers to help me with my next session. Please give them a big round of applause."

"What just happened?" Syd asks, over the applause.

I catch my mom's evil smile. "We just got slammed," I say. "Our parents are in on it."

Dieter joins us to gloat. "Oh, lighten up, girls. This will look good on your college applications."

Syd starts to protest, but Dieter claps in her face. "Sydney, you owe me." He points at Banksy. "That slobbery thing is ticking partly because of me."

Ah, the anonymous donor. Dieter must have gotten money to Brody through René.

Dieter is so startled when Syd hugs him that he instantly fades into the crowd. Kali and Syd are still laughing when they go to greet Caleb, who's come into the room with a freshly bandaged hand, another gift from his rabbit, Hannibal. Banksy's story might have more than one happy ending, if Kali is still seeing the guy she met at the vet's.

I head into the kitchen to get a pitcher of punch, and Brody follows me.

"Hey, MacDuff," he says, taking in my sari. "Your Ahmed is showing."

"Yeah, I'm fully integrated now," I say.

"Good," he says. "Because I have something for you."

He takes a box out of his pocket and hands it to me. Inside, I find two blue and gold glass bangles even prettier than the one that broke.

I smile. "Technically, you only owe me one."

"The other is a one-week anniversary gift." He glances around to see if anyone is looking, then leans over to kiss me.

It's what I've been waiting for, and relief and joy wash over me in a wave. "Has it been a week already?" I say. "It doesn't feel like we've been together at all."

"Funny," he says. "Maybe that's because I got grounded for aiding and abetting. Mom even took away my car and e-privileges. I'm older, so apparently I'm supposed to know better."

He wraps his arms around me, and the kiss that follows is so hot, it makes me wonder if silk is flammable.

"So, tell me something," he says, a few minutes later. "You used to be pretty down on relationships. Any chance of turning that around?"

"The odds are excellent," I say. If anyone could change my mind about love, it's Brody. After all, the guy knows *exactly* what he's getting, and he still likes me. To be on the safe side, however, I don't plan on creating a cookie in his name anytime soon.

Brody begins to examine my sari. "This thing is pinned in a billion places. How do you get it off?"

"You don't," someone says. "Ever."

It's Nana, and the fire in his eyes sends both of Brody's hands deep into the pockets of his jeans.

"Sorry, sir," Brody says. "I wouldn't try, sir."

Nana circles Brody, inspecting him. "What are you planning to study, young man?"

"Photojournalism," Brody says. "I'd like to work in the East Asian bureau."

Nana nearly smiles. He knows Brody's sucking up, and he's gratified.

Nani appears in the doorway, taking in the whole situation at a glance. "It's a good thing we've decided to buy a condo in Mr. Stark's development."

"You have?" I ask.

"It will give us someplace to stay when we visit," Nani says.

Glennis and my parents join us, and I take the opportunity to slip away to fill Kali and Syd in on the latest news.

"Hey, Red," Brody calls after me. "Did you try my pizza today?"

"Yeah." I toss my newly restored auburn hair and grin at him. "I'd add some olives."

Lauren descends on us as Kali, Syd, and I regroup in the hallway. "Hey guys," she says. "I've got another client for you."

Kali shushes her. "Haven't you heard? Our parents shut us down."

"You can't stop. People need you," Lauren says. She points to Evan, who's sulking in the corner of the room. "The least you can do is get the guy a date. Simon's back with his new girlfriend, and Evan's feeling left out."

"We'll look into it," Kali says.

Lauren heads over to tell Evan the good news, and I turn to Kali. "We will?"

"Maybe we could just let things slide for a while," Kali says.

"Be on our best behavior. And once our parents are caught up in their own dramas, we start up again—only smarter. Willem is going to need a match, too."

Syd smiles. "I like the way you think."

I grin at my framily.

"Love, Inc. is dead," I say. "Long live Love, Inc."